Pra

Jessica Reisman's *Substrate Phantoms* strikes me as a parsec-pioneering SF novel of the highest pedigree . . . an out-and-out breakthrough, with mystical and sociological roots trailing back to Arthur C. Clarke's *Childhood's End* and Ursula K. Le Guin's *The Left Hand of Darkness*. Indeed, true aficionados of humane hard SF will applaud Ms. Reisman for bequeathing them this beautiful tale of a heretofore uncreated tomorrow.

—Michael Bishop, author of *A Funeral for the Eyes of Fire*

Jessica Reisman has accomplished a rare feat, melding a mind-stretching interplanetary adventure with an intimate tale of flawed human beings struggling against both tragedy and treachery. Readers who crave full-immersion science fiction will want to jump headlong into the gravity well of *Substrate Phantoms*—and trust it to whisk them to a world surreal yet solid, cerebral yet heartfelt . . . and terrifying yet beautiful.

—Bradley Denton, author of *Buddy Holly is Alive and Well on Ganymede*

A brainy beautiful space adventure that conjures wonder from the quotidian detail of everyday life, real longing for authentic community, and language as freshly vivid as the beautiful planets you once imagined—a book that lets you see nets of coruscating light in the darkness.

—Christopher Brow, author of *Tropic of Kansas*

Substrate Phantoms evokes the stories and characters of CJ Cherryh and the social complexity of Maureen F. McHugh, ringing insightful twenty-first-century changes on classic sf tropes and questions. It's a sharp, fun read.

—L. Timmel Duchamp, author of *The Waterdancer's World*

Substrate Phantoms

Jessica Reisman

Arche Press

This is A006 and it has an ISBN of 978-1-63023-033-3.

Library of Congress Control Number: 2017936815

This book was printed in the United States of America, and it is published by Arche Press, an imprint of Resurrection House (Sumner, WA).

All signals off line . . .

Edited by Mark Teppo
Book Design by Mark Teppo
Copy Edit by Shannon Page

First trade paperback Arche Press edition: May 2017.

Arche Press
www.archepress.com

For my sister Cindy, who knows where I'm coming from.

Substrate Phantoms

Termagenti Space Station

Esker dreamed of space-floating, the cold smear of distant stars on his faceplate, his own breath in his ears, weightless in the endless of space. The deep-suit chafed slightly at his knees.

He woke when station link chimed with a summons. The blanket was pulled about his knees and trapped in the twist of Darshun's limbs beside him. All he could see of her was a head of wooly hair.

"Through," he said, giving voice permission for station mind to play the message.

"Esker. We're getting strange readings from a Zebulon tube—Zeb 12," the tube team supervisor's voice came through link, brief, dry. "Need a team in there soonest. Team four was next on rotation, but Song Joli's gone sick and I don't want to send them in without their cyber-relay."

"Received." Esker coughed, his voice rough.

There were groans from all around quarters.

"Sorrow take it." Beside him, Darshun spoke muffle-voiced into her pillow.

Esker and his team were one of five tube teams on Termagenti Station. Esker's team was all House Kiyr, though of diverse family association: Kiyr Esker James, Kiyr Darshun Park, Kiyr Tomas Oolambai, Kiyr Sara Mehet, and their ward, Kiyr Jhinsei—no family association. They were sometimes referred to as the Doom Crew. The name stuck after a stunt in a Yang tube. They'd simultaneously saved support on two decks while fragging three other tube systems and putting all of Echoria deck on life systems flicker for three full cycles.

The current groaning was because they'd all drunk heavily and late into the previous cycle in celebration of their ward's nineteenth birthday. Esker vaguely remembered Jhinsei, said ward, taking on all of Tube Team One in a dare fest, Tomas dancing on the rec center bar, Sara dicing with another tube team, winning, then losing.

Darshun had whispered stories to him, esoteric lore out of humanity's long ago. Her breath had been warm and tasted of vaact, an expensive liquor imported from outsystem, when her lips met his. They'd all been hella luced.

Esker listened to them grousing now, knowing what each one was doing and picturing it as he lay with his back to the room: Across quarters, Tomas stretched, dark limbs graceful even in post-revel stiffness. Sara, their cyber-relay, sat on the edge of her bunk, pinching between her eyes with finger and thumb, eyes closed over a headache, while her cybered brain connected to station mind to suss the specs on the job. Jhinsei was up and at the heatleaf making coffee.

The bitter-warm smell of the speciated beans grown down on the planet Ash confirmed this, and finally made Esker open his eyes. He rubbed at them blearily and sat up. His crew were scattered about the large, airy quarters rated by tube teams in much the disposition he'd imagined. Tomas was folded in half in a position that made Esker's back ache to see, Sara sat pale and pinched and not pleased, and Jhinsei's hair was stuck up in a ruffled thatch, though otherwise he seemed mostly recovered from last night's debauch as he puttered, warming coffee on the heatleaf's thin, filament-veined disk, while yawning and rubbing a hand over his chest.

"Jhinsei, sweet angel," Esker said.

Kiyr Jhinsei—the almost-orphan, Sara had dubbed him—grinned at his team leader, turned back to the heatleaf and asked of quarters at large, "Isn't Zeb 12 near the bay where House Tiyo stashed the derelict they found?"

"Hoping for a sighting of the alien ghost ship, Jhinsei?" Tomas asked, stretching out into human shape, then diving back to his toes.

Sara came out of info-fugue and massaged her fingers around her eyes, where shadows smudged her pale skin. She looked hagged. "Tiyo has thoroughly debugged, dissected, and filed the derelict—"

"Much to the petite chagrin of House Toveshi's SciTech," Tomas said from between his feet.

"—as a hunk of space debris," Sara finished. "Though at least House Kiyr's SciTech got in on the action."

Esker grunted. "It's the use of Khat makes House Tiyo kind to House Kiyr." Khat was Kiyr House Authority, station's security force, which had been under House Kiyr's control since station's founding by the original Kiyr, Song, Tiyo, and Toveshi.

Sara grunted in agreement, and then leveled a severe look at Jhinsei. "That thing is of unknown origin, Jhinsei. Okay? Unknown. I don't want to hear any prattling about alien hauntings. You spend too much time listening to tales on Revelation deck. As of this morning, dear almost-orphan, you are a full standard year past majority."

Jhinsei made a face as Sara snagged her jump and headed for the showers. She ruffled a hand through his hair along the way and Esker watched a blush climb Jhinsei's cheeks, just light-skinned enough to show it. Two years and he still blushed. Esker figured it was growing up in House Kiyr nursery made him shy. No blood association meant no sibs or cousins or teasing uncles and affectionate aunts to rub the raw off of one's physical shyness from early on in life. But the unassociated kid who'd bounced around ops like a not-quite adopted puppy had attached to Esker and his team, fitting with them in work and off-time. Like the magic element they'd needed to become fully themselves.

Esker took the bulb of coffee Jhinsei handed him, savoring the warm sting against his palm. Jhinsei's glance slid after Sara, and then he said, "The problem in Zeb 12 could be related to the derelict, though, yeah? I mean, that ship's not of human origin, they think, so how do we know?" He grinned again, happy in the possibility, and Esker laughed. Tomas, overhearing, gave a laugh, too, then followed Sara to the showers.

Esker sipped his coffee. "Anything's possible."

Satisfied with that, Jhinsei went to start equipment checks.

Esker tugged on a tight, wooly coil of Darshun's hair. He leaned over to whisper in her ear. "Wake up, Sister Drift. Work to do."

"Don't call me that," she muttered into her pillow, then sat up. Her hair stuck up in all directions and her face wore creases from the bed clothes. Even in disarray, she bore remarkable resemblance to the figure of the Drift Witch—also known as Sister Drift—depicted in the mural of the legend that ran the length of the main causeway on Semiramnis deck.

She looked Esker up and down, reached out a pale-palmed, dark hand to touch his cheek and said sweetly, "You look like the wrong side of some heavy gee. No more debauches for you, jefe mio."

A short time later they assembled themselves into their tube diving gear. Suit hoods undone, the faceplates dangled on their chests, lozenges of hard light. They tramped out of quarters and took the lift to Zebulon deck. Everyone went quiet on the lift, each in their own heads. Esker yawned repeatedly, and then caught Darshun watching him, an amused expression curving her lips.

The lift opened on Zebulon deck. Metal surfaces reflected unfiltered collector light up the long curve of corridor. Their breath puffed in the chill. The deep hum of station was louder on systems-access decks, Zebulon loudest of all, the tramp of their boots muffled under it. Smaller access passages snaked left off the main corridor, maintenance bays, with ship docks strictly for the use of station-owned vessels, caverned off to the right.

They passed the bay where House Tiyo's derelict sat, the entry guarded by two Khat officers who stood straight from bored slouches as Esker and his team came into view. Then the shorter of the two grinned sheepishly at Esker. A cousin, she was, Kiyr Cecile Kolie-James.

"Hey Esker." She tugged on her Khat uniform tunic. Her companion nodded, unsmiling, one hand resting on his sidearm, the usual Khat-issue stinger. Cecile's smile was uncustomary and very non-regulation, grim humorlessness being a Khat merit course. She glanced at her fellow officer and shook her head just slightly, then gave them all the once-over. "Going diving?" Then she laughed at her own question. "'Course you are. Hey Darshun."

"Hey Cecile. Good seeing you, kiddo."

Esker surveyed his cousin. "Being Khat agrees with you, little seal. Still think it was a hella choice."

"Mine to make," Cecile chirped, refusing to take offence. She nodded to the rest of them and grinned at Jhinsei, who was craning past Esker's shoulder for a better look at the derelict.

"Want to see it?"

The other Khat officer frowned, hand still on his holstered stinger. "Cecile—"

"Brinden, it won't hurt for them to get a visual. SciTech from Kiyr and Tiyo have been taking samples of it, lots and lots of samples and testing. And then there was an accident—something happened with one of the laser cutters; no one's been down in a few cycles since."

Jhinsei peered between the Khat officers into the dark bay. "I heard it was like some of the other hauntings—weird reports of visions and unaccountable phenomena."

Cecile shrugged with a sideways glance at Brinden. "I can't comment on that; but do you guys want to see it?"

Brinden's eyes narrowed, his gaze on Jhinsei. "I don't think—"

"Love to," Esker said, "at least Jhinsei would, clearly—but we have to get to the tube and earn our keep."

"Maybe after?" Jhinsei said hopefully, not looking at Brinden.

Sara snorted.

"Maybe."

"I'd like to see it, too," Darshun said and Sara snorted again. "Got something up your nose, Sara?"

"See you after, then," Cecile called as they moved on. Then she said, "Brinden, take a pill why don't you? And stop fondling your stinger."

"Void's sake, Cecile, that brat is unassociated. Have sense."

Their voices faded. Sara grabbed Jhinsei's arm and shook him slightly, bringing his head up. "Paying attention to idiots won't get you anything worth having, eh?"

"Yeah," Jhinsei muttered and ducked his head, "I know."

Further along the curve they came to Zebulon tube 12. Iris entry controls were in a recessed globe at the side, keyed to tube team leaders and seconds—meaning Esker and Darshun in their case. Someone getting in the tubes could cause serious havoc with any number of station's systems, not least life support and rotation. Esker sealed his face lozenge into place while the rest of the team did likewise. Tubes had atmos, but with a very low oxygen mix, air too thin for sustained activity.

"Link check, everyone live?"

They chorused back in sequence, Darshun, Sara, Tomas, Jhinsei, voices separated from bodies.

Esker pulled off his glove and pressed his sequence into the globe; station mind had to have the sequence plus his particular chemical signature. The globe pressed back, sizzling little gold and blue trails. The lock irised open with a hiss and they tramped in.

As the tube lock rotated shut behind them and the entry went gravless, Esker assisted his drift with a toe push and bounced lightly. The others followed. The suits were light, just line clamps and life systems. The myriad glowing readouts of station systems ranked down the tube reflected in bent arcs and trails on their faceplates.

"Darshun, specs?" The tinny flattened sound of his own voice through suit link echoed in Esker's ears.

Darshun's voice came back, her faceplate flashing at him briefly as she turned her head from examining the main readouts. "Three anomalous readings, out of sync. One in the collector feedbacks, two in life support. They scaled right off the monitors, like energy surges."

"No such failures have been reported," Sara supplied. "Nothing in station mind about the surges either."

"Localized monitor failure, then?" Darshun sounded dubious.

"That's mind's first analysis, unlikely as it seems," Sara said.

"Okay, Tomas, power down the relays. Darshun, dive the hole and do recon. Jhinsei, Sara, and I'll take individual board checks. Tomas, after you cut power to the relays, sit on the main board and monitor it. If there's some kind of localized surge problem, we can't trust that the relays are doing their job."

He fanned his legs and arms and swam. The suit smelled of its last cleaning. His muscles felt stringy, eyes aching, and a tepid sweat made him feel grimy, despite the shower. Getting too old to get luced and be in the tubes so soon after.

Latching his clamp to a hitch in the curved panels, he slid a reader out of a side suit pocket, and threaded its link until it made connection on the first set of relays.

"Tomas?"

"Powered down."

"Okay, Jhinsei, Sara, get to it." He activated the hand reader and studied the link-ups on each individual board. His awareness focused down to the reader and the whereabouts of his team. Sweat rolled down his face, dripped over his eyes as he did the tedious work.

"Darshun, you in the hole?"

"Yup. Everything looks okay. I'm going to start a scan for energy leaks."

"Okay." The first board checked out. He started on the next. Sara worked from the other end toward him, while Jhinsei, across tube, checked the secondary system boards.

For a time there was silence and the sound of everyone's breathing, then Jhinsei said, "There's a frag on the third filter system board. Cap's burned out, melted to slag."

"Mother hell." Sara's voice cut him off. "Esker, you'd better come see this. Caps all down the rotation sequence are fragging over as I watch."

Esker registered both Jhinsei's and Sara's words as he watched his own reader stutter to a halt: all the readouts blazed, then began to fade, then blazed again. He switched the reader off and tried to disconnect it, but the power kept coursing through it. It wouldn't budge. The reader fused to the boards—but the heat didn't radiate past the fusion, the reader still at body temp in his hand.

"Hella fucking void, what is that?" Tomas' voice brought Esker's head up. He looked around.

A shimmer of light played through the darkness of the tube, then disappeared down the hole. Readout lights, power lights, sequence keys—all began flickering on and off in a slow wave pattern, all around them. A shiver crept up from Esker's gut.

"Leviathan's bloody craw," he whispered.

"What was that?" Darshun's voice, startled. "Esker, did you just curse?"

"Darshun, up and out of there, fast as you can. Terminate all system engagement. We're out of here as of now. Sara, contact station mind, initiate emergency isolation and containment of all Zebulon tube interfaces and inter-station functions. There's some kind of—something—loose in here."

"Esker, what the hell does—Mother Void! What the drift? Esker, can you—"

The link suddenly bit off in static. “Darshun?” His voice bounced against the faceplate, his own breath loud in his ears. With a push off the side, Esker sailed back toward Tomas. Jhinsei swam from the other side. The play of lights reflected off their face lozenges, obscuring expressions. Esker waved them both toward the lock and changed direction to go for the hole, for Darshun. Jhinsei drifted past him and Esker caught a brief glimpse of his face, perplexed and scared. He gestured once, get out, hurry, and then grabbed the rim of the hole’s access to swing himself in and down the chute—

—and blinked, resisting the urge to try and rub his eyes through the faceplate.

Shimmer filled the hole: a swarm of motes coalescing and fading in waves. Darshun hung at the center of the hole, head down, arms and legs starfishing. Her hook line, detached, drifted in a loose, snaking coil around her. The shimmer rolled over her and she spasmed, fell still, then spasmed again. The shimmer was moving, in its waves, up the hole toward him, a tide coming in.

Esker watched the shimmer roll, fade, surge again, gauging seconds between surges. He held to one of the guide rungs, clipped his hook line to it, braced booted feet against the panels. As a surge peaked below him, he dove toward Darshun, just behind the receding edge. Inches from his faceplate the shimmer was a scintillant buzz.

With one practiced hand he slowed his motion as he reached Darshun, grabbed one of her arms, then hit the take-up for the hook line on his belt. They were hauled up, a sharp tug at his back. He kept one eye on the shimmer as it faded, re-coalesced, began another surge. Darshun flopped limp in his arms.

The line reeled them to the hatch. He pushed Darshun through it, fumbled at his hook, unclipped, pulled himself through after her, and slammed a hand down on the entry key.

The hatch didn’t move.

A surging, shimmering wave rose to within inches of the access rim. He pushed off the hatchway, dragging Darshun with him. The tube system lights still stuttered chaotically, as if systems throughout had become confused, addled. His team clustered by the tube entry, bent over the unit that controlled the lock. One of them glanced up, faceplate flashing, Tomas, by the suit markings. Tomas touched

Sara's shoulder where she bent over the lock controls, then pushed off and came toward Esker.

Maneuvering was difficult with Darshun in his arms. He drifted awkwardly, relieved when Tomas reached him and took up her other arm. Tomas pivoted neatly, the most graceful of them in zerogee; his momentum carried them the rest of the way.

At the lock unit, Esker bent over Sara's shoulder. She was working with a tiny relay pin, trying to bypass the unit and access the override. But the system was fragged, fused.

They couldn't get out.

A glittering reflection on Jhinsei's faceplate brought Esker swinging around. Shimmer surged up out of the hole and flowed toward them. Sara kept working. Esker pushed Darshun into Tomas' arms and gestured them, with Jhinsei, to the entry overhang. He turned back to help Sara at the controls.

It was as if all the links had been fused at a molecular level, rendering the unit a hunk of useless alloy. Sara gave up and pounded at it.

The wave surged over them, lapping halfway up their suits.

It felt like warm water at first, gentle, enveloping heat. Then all at once it felt like millions, billions of tiny electrostatic charges, microscopic lightnings moving over his body, lapping over his thighs, thrilling through his groin—immediate erection—up his ribcage, arms, into his chest and heart, up into his throat, a thick, fizzy air filling his mouth with a tang of ozone.

A rushing sound filled Esker's ears. Distantly, he noted the shimmer receding, resurging, but the charge it had worked through him stayed, tingling throughout his body. He floated, caught in its lightning flicker against his skin, within him, licking through his brain.

Out of the incandescence came voices. The voices tasted familiar.

What is it? That was Tomas.

Esker, Sara, do you feel it? That was Darshun—voice, sense, mind, and presence.

Darshun? His own sense echoed. By the feel of the echo, he understood that he was hearing himself as he felt and sounded to the others.

What's happening? Jhinsei.

The energy, said Sara, *whatever it is, it linked us, and the systems, somehow; all the sub routines in the tube are fused—and now us, too.*

Close on the sense of Sara came the intertwined metal-cool voice of station mind, always in Sara's head, part of Sara. Mind's voice felt different, had a different signature and sense—one not alive. It wailed warning, like an oracle: *Evacuate tube, systems critical, evacuate, overload imminent, terminal malfunction, evacuate.*

Under station mind, Esker sensed and heard the systems themselves, less vibrant and distinct, murmurs and mutters each with its own minor sound, but not individual: a chorus of gnats. Smudged now, no longer part of a working whole, they had fused into a jumble.

Overload imminent—that was station mind for things going bang.

Esker sought to move beyond the energy holding him, possessing his body.

He had to get them out.

Then another presence coalesced out of the luminous, echoing fire. As the feel of Darshun, Tomas, Sara, and Jhinsei was more vibrant than those of station mind or the tube systems were, so this presence was more vibrant than his team's.

Than anything, ever.

This voice, this presence, was not confused or inchoate, not babbling. It stilled Esker—all of them—in its need, encompassed and overrode all other imperatives.

Presence, feeding at impossible speed through all senses—touch, taste, smell, sight, sound, memory—into Esker's brain. Experiences that his brain only barely grasped, his frame of reference too limited for what the presence gave, or what it was.

Presence. Esker's mind, all of their minds together, tried to translate the presence into discrete, graspable bits. Taste of sweetness: honey, Esker's mind said—but not. Shades of color, leaves of light, saturated, illuminant. Warmth of touch. A caress, feathery, touching like dark blue velvet on his skin, on his mind, whispering in the air, a vibration along his eardrum, through every smallest bone in his hands, then—

Shift—

A prickle of cool vegetation. The low, singing sound of a voice made of thunder and continuum coming from the shadows and tall red fern-like shapes. A long stretch of dark, translucent sand.

Soft between his toes, but—not toes, not sand. Scent of heat and fragrant moistures. Beyond the sand, a deep, primeval wood, trees, but not. Columns of tangible light, living beings floating among the not-tree trunks.

He could taste, touch, hear, see, smell, but none of it was quite what his mind would make it—and all of it had the sense of presence behind and within it, the whole world a being they had been let into.

Terminal overload imminent, station mind sirened far, far away.

Like fairyland, he heard Darshun whisper in their minds, something from one of her esoteric stories.

Light of a harsher spectrum than the sweet illumination around them seared Esker's eyes as it splashed across his faceplate. The beautiful, haunting landscape broke apart as one curve of tube wall exploded inward. Sound, shock wave, debris, all reached them a beat later. Esker's eardrum shattered and he screamed, but couldn't hear himself. Tube panels and scorching hot board sections slammed into him. Broken bones, seared skin. Pain. He was thrown back into the entry, bodies under him, yielding on impact; he felt them, his team, crushed beneath him as he was crushed by a huge section of the tube panels. A rain of fiery debris buried him and Sara beside him in a hot, burning cave.

Immobilized, Esker stared through his scratched faceplate at Sara; her lozenge had cracked. Her eyes stared. Smoke curled out of a bleeding gash at her temple, her cybered brain fragged.

As the force of the explosion expended itself, the debris began to lift away. Esker felt himself float free, felt a distant, wearing pulse of pain. Then, mercifully, it all began to fade.

Through the fire and the smoke and the pain that fed into his brain from every nerve, the last thing Esker saw was a shimmer of energy fading into the ruined tube curve, into the depths of Termagenti Station.

Then there was nothing. All signals off line.

KIYR HOUSE AUTHORITY KIVE FILES –
REPORT ON ZEBULON TUBE INCIDENT (*Excerpt*)

From those few system readouts salvageable, explosion appears to have been caused by severe, but localized, energy spikes. Source and type of energy remain undetermined.

How systems reached this state of malfunction between the time of repair call and the time of the tube team's entry also undetermined.

Relay link with team lost approximately seven minutes prior to explosion. Reason: undetermined. Postmortem data extracted from Sara Mehet's cyber-relays indicates severe neural breakdown, hallucinations, which in turn indicate an overriding of the neuro-augmentation system theoretically considered impossible. Mind terminated her link when a feedback loop was detected; the loop channeled back and continued in both her bio- and cyber-synaptic pathways.

Fatalities:

Kiyr Esker James, 48 standard, Senior Systems and Op Tech.

Kiyr Sara Mehet, 38 standard, Senior Systems Analyst and neuro-augmented mind relay.

Kiyr Darshun Park, 32 standard, Second Op Tech.

Kiyr Tomas Oolambai, 28 standard, Mech Engineer and team troubleshooter.

In critical condition, under medical care of the head Thorough Order of Physic Arts obviary posted to station:

Kiyr Jhinsei, 19 standard, Kiyr House ward, apprenticed Junior Tech.

All aspects of culpability, system failure, and related questions regarding this incident remain unanswered or inconclusively explained.

Despite the inconclusive nature of the present kive file, Kiyr House Authority has requested no further investigation into this matter on the part of this office.

— File Kived by Kiyr Cecile Kolie-James, Kiyr House Authority officer on scene

Eighteen Standard Months Later

REVELATION DECK RESTED CURRENTLY IN STATION SHADOW, spangled in reflections off the solar collectors. Long glimmers cut through the high dim space in a slow dance. Revelation deck was a big space with open gridwork, gridwork being the bones of station superstructure hidden on other decks. Tall viewports and a lack of adult traffic made it a favorite haunt of station kids, four of whom sat clustered under a twenty-foot span of the grid arch. Likely there was someplace they were supposed to be, and strict regulations said they shouldn't be there, but it was a regulation never enforced.

Jhinsei, two-thirds of the way through sitting a shift at the automated shuttle monitors, liked the murmur of voices. He had been such a kid himself, not too many years past, listening to tales on Revelation; besides, they lessened the loneliness of the cavernous deck.

The monitors beeped softly with notice of a shuttle coming in. Jhinsei touched the work globe for specs, knowing it would be the shuttle ship *Teisco* with the quarterly Thorough Order supply shipment from their farms down on Ash. The Thorough Order of Physic Arts, which trained the obviaries who saw to the health of most of the wide-flung citizenry of the Aggregate—that was, the known, colonized, and governed universe, from planet to station to nomadic ship, all its star systems, single- or double-sunned, and all the spin drive-ship navigated substrates connecting them—owned vast tracts of land on many planets. Jhinsei, by close acquaintance with medlab and the head station obviary over the last eighteen months, felt a little too intimate with all things Thorough Order.

With one finger to the globe, he brought up the docking view, watched the small image in the globe as the *Teisco* tracked in and connected to the docking clamps. He checked all the readouts; everything was on the mark. As always.

You'd have to be more of a fuck-up than even he was to pull a regular duty more boring than sitting shift at the automated shuttle monitors, which handled routine, auto-piloted traffic between Termagenti Station and the planet Ash.

Fingers leaving small contact trails on the globe's surface, he keyed for refuel and system checks on the *Teisco*. He shunted the information to station ops and notified medlab of supplies for pick-up, then leaned back into a stretch, yawning. He stood to stretch some more, walked several times around the console, and then picked up the black paper rooster he'd been folding.

Quiet took shape within him as his fingers slowly formed the strange fowl, setting precise creases and subtle cantings into the thick paper. Roosters were an old world creature, lately being bred again down on the planet Ash.

"The Leviathan yawned," one of the kids' voices reached him. "And all the worlds and stars and systems of the Aggregate went dim, then flickered back to life."

"You need to find a new hobby," said a voice not belonging to one of the kids.

Jhinsei swung around, startled. Kiyr Cydonie Mehet-Kruez leaned on her elbows over the console, observing Jhinsei severely through narrowed green eyes, though one brow twitched upwards. Thick brown hair cut ragged over her shoulders brushed an old green jump; she wore chunky black sandals on her feet. She had a sober set of level brows over arched bones. Her lips, finely drawn, the lower lip wide, were chapped.

Jhinsei returned his attention to his folding. "Most people make noise on the grid when they come down here."

Cydonie made a low tsking noise, derisive. "A two-ton Kwai boxer in magnetic boots could sneak up on you; I don't know why they let you sit mons at all."

Jhinsei let that pass. "Origami is not a hobby, it's a therapy."

"Oh. Well, it's morbid. You only make things that are extinct or never existed."

The kids' voices rose suddenly. Jhinsei heard, clear as a chime, "—then the Leviathan said to the Drift Witch, 'I curse you and your line, down to a thousand thousand descendants, thus: your children will be subject to the drift within my bones, the void that is my heart. They will be lost, rudderless in the sea of stars, powerless in the substrate of time and space, at the mercy of the drift. And never will you find your way out of me.' But the Drift Witch laughed and stole the Leviathan's own bones to fashion a ship and—"

"The Drift Witch is our ancestor," another of the kids broke into the recitation. "That story's old. What about station stuff, our ghost—my uncle Phyl saw it when he was alone closing up his club on Semiramnis deck—he heard this music and said he fell into it and disappeared and when he came out the other side he had a nosebleed and the club's music systems were slag."

"It's not a ghost, you spinhead, it's just a glitch in the station systems."

"No, it's an 'other than human presence.'"

"Duh, if we haven't found any aliens yet—"

"It is too a ghost, my—"

"Shut it, we're not supposed to talk about it."

"What about the birdman, then, that walks through bulkheads and haunts the gridwork wearing a long cloak over a body made of glittering metal?"

"The what? Are you cracked?"

"No! People have seen it . . . him—whatever—lots of them."

Jhinsei glanced up at Cydonie, but she was turned away, listening to the kids.

There had not been another accident like the one to which Jhinsei lost his team. But uncanny things—sightings and unexplained computer glitches, energy spikes and random information strings with no clear origin—had plagued station for the eighteen months since.

The truth? Jhinsei couldn't say. Ghost, alien presence, freak accident—he didn't know. It was worth his freedom from psych ward not to venture any opinions on the subject, so he didn't.

Eventually, he'd received a clean psych bill. He chose another course of training and got posted to general ops, which was not the caliber of posting that tube team was, not the posting that his original test scores warranted. But after the accident, a dark place in his brain itched painfully whenever he came near the tubes, saw a dive suit, smelled the antiseptic and ceraplas innards of one, even heard the sound of a voice through suit link.

The collector reflections shifted minutely. The kids' voices rose and fell. Cydonie slid Jhinsei a glance. She was a ship navigator and worked off-station for long stretches of time. Jhinsei liked her, not least because she didn't seem to have the bias regarding lack of family association that so many in Termagenti's stratified society did. A benefit of time spent off-station, Jhinsei thought. It helped also that she had a dry, spiky sense of humor and seemed to like Jhinsei back. Her glance just now, though, held a kind of clinical interest that put all of Jhinsei's well-honed defenses on alert.

"What?" he said. It came out gruff.

Cydonie's eyebrows quirked. "Nothing." She picked up one of the troop of roosters Jhinsei had completed in the last six hours. They were in silver, grey, red, a holo paper that had stars shooting through it, and a transparent paper with eyes. Cydonie picked up the red paper one. She turned it, held it up. "What is this?"

"Rooster. Someone just started breeding a speciation down on Ash. So there."

She turned it in her fingers. "Can I have it?"

He checked to see if she was humoring him, but she looked genuinely taken with the rooster. Jhinsei shrugged. "Sure."

"Thanks."

Jhinsei smoothed a crease in black paper, doubled it back on itself. "What are you doing down here, Cydonie?"

"Came to visit. I'm off-roster for a few cycles. Possibly unemployed, actually." She shrugged. "I thought you might be lonely down here."

"Oh."

"Oh," Cydonie said, mimicking. "When do you get off?"

Jhinsei shook his head. "Got another four hours."

Cydonie groaned.

"You could go visit your family. Or stroll Semiramnis and Nicodemus decks—where the perversities and tarafiddle of the Aggregate universe all await your pleasure."

"Did you swallow a kive file cube with a station tour on it?"

"Or you could take a hop down to Ash and, I don't know, tour whatever exhibit the Thorough Order has in their Arts Center currently."

"Good idea. We can go together."

"Cydonie."

"I'm serious, Jhinsei. You've never been off this space hunk in your life, have you?"

"I came from off it. Somewhere."

"That you remember?"

Jhinsei slid one fingertip along a tricky fold and considered reactions. After a breath he decided he was too tired for defensive maneuvers and Cydonie hadn't meant anything by it anyway. She knew that noticing someone's unassociated state counted as insult, but had likely spent too much time off-station to care. "Thanks, but I don't have the cred for a hop to Ash."

"Well, how about a game of something fast and sweaty when you're off?"

"Sounds good. You sweat and I'll run rings around you."

"Ha. Hella you will, junior. Guess I'll go take some nutrition, the better to wipe deck with you."

Cydonie took her rooster and left. Jhinsei watched her up through the shadows over the grid.

He thought about the universe beyond Termagenti Station, and where in it he might have come from. His mother had been a visitor to the station, an outsystemer. She had stayed long enough to leave her four-year-old son in the Kiyr House nursery with his name and the clothes on his back, then left Palogenia System. For what reason, he didn't know. House Kiyr had taken him in ward because it was their nursery he'd been left in. He had been raised in ward, first in the Kiyr nurseries, then in fosterage, finally in operations, general pet to the techs and teams.

For a while he'd had Esker, Darshun, Sara, and Tomas, and the best niche a house ward was likely to get.

Here we are, self-pity central; may as well take the tour. It was an Esker-flavored thought.

Keep your tour, it's not going anywhere interests me. That was very Sara.

Jhinsei shook his head—though never, in the eighteen months since he'd regained consciousness after the accident, had the action dislodged their voices. Bits and pieces of his team's thoughts and selves had been left behind in that moment when the buzzing energy had flowed over them all, into and through them, filled them all with honey and lightning.

They'd become a part of him, fused into his brain, forming whole new sets of synaptic connections. Changing him.

No. Push it down. His fingers shook on the rooster and he stared at them, hard. Focus. I'm me. I like adventure flash kives, spicy fritters, and beer. Me, Jhinsei. I don't like exotic vegetables or opera or really tall men. That was Darshun, Esker, and Tomas.

Miss you guys, I do, but I'm me.

Like he had a hope.

He'd crushed the rooster. Everything had a strange dull gloss on it for a moment, a funny taste in his mouth, and all he could hear was a booming throb. Everything went distant, like thick glass separated him from the world.

He dropped the crumpled paper, squeezed his hands into fists, concentrated the overwhelming feelings there, squeeze—*Esker, Sara, Darshun, Tomas! Presence, strange, beautiful . . . Pain, alone, fear!*—release. He drew a breath, sweating, pushed hair off his suddenly damp forehead.

Slowly the world started to come back, shadows and cross-hatched light through the grid, dusky blue of the consoles, the kids' voices, hum of systems, black of space through the views, the steady state, distant stars, his hands shaking.

The sweat drying on his skin made him shiver in the chill air of Revelation.

He took a few more slow breaths and sat for awhile, just watching the slow scroll of numbers, letters, and symbols through the globe. Then he picked up the black paper, smoothed it out, and began again.

❊

The salon in Tiyo Studios held quiet as a bowl holds dark wine, rippled by surface tensions, opaque to the eye. Deep, form-responsive chairs segmented the wide circle of the salon at mathematically determined interstices, life-scale theorem. Almost no one ever sat in them. The heavily scented passiflora hedge vines running the circumference of the room tried to make Mheth drowsy. The vines were trained onto trellises and climbed high into the filtered light that fell from the collector array through the room's upper windows; drowsiness was the intended effect. It kept flash kive actors, producers, programmers, and distribution flams docile and blunted when they came with complaint or problem.

The salon functioned as a waiting room for Tiyo Studios, whose business was the making of flash kive entertainments. The studios themselves were a subsidiary of Tiyo Kive Industries. Tiyo Kive Industries' business was the manufacture and supply of kive technologies and the various formats they inhabited, from kive cubes to networked libraries, for everything from history and civstory kive files, scientific treatise, ancient lore, fiction, and philosophy, to flash entertainments made in Tiyo's studios and other studios across the Aggregate worlds.

Tiyo Kive Industries also produced the varied technologies for kiving the contents of those files, from standard shallow kive reading to deeptime, immersive kiving, a luxury indulgence of the wealthy. Tiyo Kive Industries, in fact, maintained something of a monopoly on the kive industry across the length and breadth of the Aggregate's star systems, planets, and stations. The Aggregate and its loosely centralized two arms of authority: Aggregate Control, Aggregate Oversight . . . and the hundreds of offices operating under those designations.

As Mheth waited for his brother Grath to unlink from conferencing with an outsystem trade consortium, he scuffed a hand idly through a biomech sculpture. It rubbed back, nubby dark red skin with a fine, velvety mist of pale green fur.

That Grath had requested his brother come here to wait in this fashion, rather than to the inner offices, was calculated insult to Mhethianne. So of course Mheth came, to be dutifully insulted so that he might then be sullen and difficult with righteousness. It wasn't really like Grath, who tended to rely on Mheth rather than antagonize him, so Mheth suspected their father was behind it.

A row of awards fortified one curve of Grath's sleek console. The sight of the awards weighed into Mheth. Slumping a bit lower in the form chair, he thought a pattern and triggered a shot of chi into his brain chem; the chi made a warm melt in his middle, made Grath an interestingly distant construct.

He'd originally gotten the chi augmentation years ago—illegally, because he'd been several years short of adult majority—as just another in a long selection of things done to irritate *the* Tiyo, Tiyo Sarsone Tiyo, Mheth and Grath's father.

When Grath finally finished his conference and sat back to receive his brother, Mheth met his brother's gaze with a sweet, heavy-lidded calm. Grath wore his blandest façade.

"Mhethianne, thank you for responding so promptly."

Mheth gave an inclination of his head. With his own well-sprung grace and the extra kick that the chi coiled into his muscles, he came out of the chair, across the salon, and settled to a perch on Grath's console. On the chi, his movements seemed to him infinitely slow while being, in fact, faster and more precise than normal.

"What's the kink, Grath?"

There was no shift of expression in Grath's face or body. He touched fingers to his workglobe. A row of small holo images sprang up along the console, a low, cacophonous scrawl of voices and ambient sound accompanying the vivid, minute mélange of figures and scenes. Along the bottom of each scene, glowing red alphanumerics gave brief indices. Grath moved a finger on the globe and the noise damped out.

"Studio B32. What's in production?"

Mheth felt his eyebrow curl up. "Having trouble with your eyesight?"

"B32."

"A very dry history of kiving and kive technologies, from the earliest pre-kive archival media known, things called film and discs and drives."

"And D17.7?"

"A heave-whacker, with no-name flash actors and two liters of pressed oil imported from outsystem."

"Yes. It will do well in fringe worlds, projections say."

Mheth shrugged. "They should have used effects for the oil; the director has delusions of art."

"L2?"

"Pseudo documentary. Feigned outrage and damning facts that won't actually hurt the industries under supposed examination."

"You're well informed."

"I'm the story coordinator, Grath."

"Yes."

Round over. Mheth watched his brother move his fingers and the studio views disappeared one by one until only one remained. G103.5. He knew without the index what production it was.

"That's what this is about?"

"It's unauthorized, Mhethianne."

"I authorized it, Grath."

"Not through me, you didn't."

Mheth lifted his chin. "Worried?"

Grath rubbed a hand over his face and finally made eye contact with Mheth. He opened his mouth to speak and was stopped by a voice from behind him.

"Mhethianne, get off the furniture."

Mheth looked over his brother's shoulder to see their father, Tiyo Sarsone Tiyo, come through the inner doors—without actually opening them. Sarsone hadn't been out of his vast quarters on Botree deck for over five years. He had become increasingly reclusive in the last ten years, his appearances outside of his quarters always holo, and even those seldom. Mheth knew, one of only a handful of people who did, the Tiyo had a rare nerve disease that was causing a slow, wasting attrition of the legs.

Their father's holo image came to stand by Grath's desk and peered at Mheth, projecting a convincing aura of refined menace. Grath's face, and Mheth's own, fifty years hence.

He remembered a time when, as a boy, he'd taken pride in the resemblance, and in his father. Remembered walking beside Sarsone, he and Grath small, proud boys, as his father greeted dignitaries from across the Aggregate worlds at a reception; their father quizzing them on the fine points of the philosophy of the Sinaiety—the fundamentalist sect on the planet Ash whose ties to House Tiyo dated back to system founding—and debating current events or the merits of the latest flash kive entertainments over meals, he and Grath competing for Sarsone's approval and laughter.

When they were boys, Sarsone had bestowed that approval, a warm and generous thing, without reserve.

That had also been a time when Grath was beloved older brother, confidant, friend.

So long ago, it all seemed as much a myth as the legend of the Drift Witch, Termagenti Station's favorite childrens' story.

"Mhethianne, your brother is merely aggrieved at your lack of respect in failing to adhere to protocol in channels of authority. And we're concerned at the outlay and occupancy of resources for what can only be an ultimately profitless piece of work, however estimable and civically minded it may be."

"Which of course is why Mheth is involved," Grath said, and it was not an unfair bit of sarcasm, Mheth had to allow. He spared his brother a glance. Grath was definitely peeved—more at their father, though, he thought.

Sarsone held up a hand. "Finally, my dear Mhethianne, authorizing some sort of lurid exposé on Tiyo and Kiyr's business axis and on new kive technologies, still being tested, isn't really an ethical act for a first son of House Tiyo."

"What are we afraid of?"

"Mhethianne, don't be a child." Then Sarsone looked to Grath.

Grath made a sound, a kind of weary grunt, and said, "Your authorization is cancelled until further considerations are made. Use of G103.5 is suspended; you and your partner are locked out and G103.5 systems will be purged."

"You—" Mheth started to laugh. "You're firing me?"

"Certainly he's not firing you," Sarsone said. "You're a Tiyo. Find something more suitable to do. The highest virtue of a strong species, remember, Mhethianne: singleness of purpose. And your purpose must always be one with Tiyo's." That was Sinaiety philosophy he quoted; it echoed down Mheth's memories like a bit of debris in an empty access shaft.

Sarsone smiled benevolently and flickered from view.

❊

"Point—mine!" Cydonie yelled.

Jhinsei ignored her, focused on the three globes in play—lucent, charged balls crackling with energy. All three hovered, then one darted left, one up, one diagonally. As they moved, Jhinsei moved, swinging his playing staff around in a circle slash. He caught the edge of the first, and connected solidly with the force center of the second. He missed the third globe but brushed close enough to change its trajectory; his point balance plumped and the game keyed him up a level. His staff went indigo, which indicated more charge.

Sweat dripped off his face, spiked his hair. He cast Cydonie a look, forbearing to yell back at her.

"Like that, is it?" Cydonie muttered as she slipped between the globes, turning, her blue-level staff held out before her in two hands, eyes tracking the smallest motions of the slowing balls.

Three plays later, Jhinsei had advanced to a black-level staff and the game was essentially over. In quick succession he destroyed each of the globes, taking their charges into his staff and into his point balance.

In the showers, on the other side of the waist-high partition, Cydonie was silent, puzzling over the game while she stood with her face lifted into the water spray. Eventually she sighed and gave Jhinsei a lopsided grin.

"You don't play enough," Jhinsei said. "Off-station too much."

"Thanks for trying to salve my wounded pride." She sighed under the spray, then palmed it off. "So," she said, standing under the heat current. "A meal and a drink to celebrate you trouncing me?"

"I'm wiped. And I'm supposed to meet Essca later."

Cydonie frowned.

"Cyd—don't."

"Sorry. I still can't get a conceptualization around you and Essca."

"I'm not her type?"

"Oh—physically." Cydonie looked at him from under her lashes. "But you're unassociated, you've got no leverage anywhere in station or system." She shrugged. "Definitely not a previously observed component of my half-sister's psych pattern."

"Psych patterns change."

She tilted her head. "Yes, but essential structures…" Then she shook her head, still-damp hair flinging water drops. "Jhinsei, she's my half-sister. Don't you think maybe I have one or two insights into her that—"

Jhinsei met her eyes. "Really. Don't."

Cydonie's hands went out. "Okay, okay."

It put a pall on things, though Cydonie grinned her usual grin when she waved Jhinsei farewell at the lift, on her way to find something more entertaining than he was.

He rode the lift with a Thorough Order obviary who stood silent and erect beside him, and three giggling House Toveshi brats who'd obviously been doing some rec substance. Jhinsei leaned against the back, barely able to keep his eyes open. He had several bruises from hitting the deck hard when he'd gone for reckless maneuvers in the game. He just wanted to crawl into a nest of blankets and go null.

The lift flashed past decks. He came to himself with a start as the Toveshi kids got off at Nicodemus deck, rubbed his eyes and yawned hugely. He caught the obviary glancing at him.

"'Scuse."

The obviary inclined her head: a small woman with straight black hair and dark skin that crinkled pleasantly at the corners of pale eyes. "Are you Kiyr Jhinsei, by any chance?"

He came awake then, surprised, but stayed slouched, examined the woman carefully from under his lashes. "Are you looking for me?"

She shook her head. The knot work in the inlay on her wrist placed her as a second level obviary, mid-way through her Thorough Order training, which meant she hadn't taken her arts yet. But she had the obviary expression down.

"My name is Zhou. I studied with Ramev Evans." She had a clipped, dropping accent that Jhinsei couldn't place. "You know Ramev?"

"Yes," he said, since Ramev was station's head obviary, under whose care Jhinsei had spent so many months.

The woman blinked at his tone. "Excuse me." She shook her head. "That was clumsy, wasn't it?"

"Hmm. It's okay. A little refreshing, actually. Usually obviaries are so..." He waved a hand.

"You find obviaries overbearing?"

"No, just too good to be true. Maybe you don't notice it unless you spend months under Thorough Order care while you yourself are a mess. Maybe I just have a complex." He listened to the pattern of his words and closed his eyes a moment, shifted Sara-sense out of his speech with an effort. He focused on the obviary. "Ever been on-station?"

She shook her head. "No. In fact, I think I'm a bit lost. I need to go to Tiyo Studios."

"That's Mignon deck; we just passed it. Abaccas and Botree decks are domicile for station juice, the wealthy and powerful elite, all houses, Cheval deck for outsystem juice, Dove for mid-level, mixed habitat. Echoria is worklabs, SciTech, and medlab; Faust is domicile for techs, mechs, and other working dross—like me. Mignon belongs to Tiyo Kive Industries, whole and entire, for flash kive actors, crews, studios. Nicodemus and Semiramnis decks are main bays, docks, and public trade—business, various worship temples, entertainment, food, and recreation; Phyndarial deck is the arboretum; Revelation deck for automateds and lost souls. Other than that the rest of the station through Zebulon is tubes, core, and collectors. House call?"

Zhou smiled at this rapid recital, as she was meant to. "Yes. Lost souls?"

"Station joke." Jhinsei examined the inlay at her wrist. A gold tri-braid edged by a black five-strand weave with green bits. That made her medical specialization neuro-interfaces and psych.

"Are you doing your arts in flash kives?"

"Yes. You know your Thorough Order obviary designations."

Jhinsei shrugged. Tomas had. He wanted to ask what was wrong in House Tiyo that they got an obviary shuttled special up from the planet Ash when station had its own full complement. But it was a question that went to confidentiality, one no obviary would answer.

The lift stopped and opened to the low gold light and dark plum corridors of Faust. "Just tell station mind Mignon. Enjoy station."

"Come to Ash sometime, I'll give you a tour of our Arts Center," Zhou said.

"Better than the one I gave you, I hope," Jhinsei said. She smiled as the lift doors closed.

His quarters were a tiny pocket in one of the hive clusters of quarters on Faust deck. Recessed biolumes in the walls and ceiling cast low light through the evidence of his existence.

Origami creatures in a myriad of colors and patterns crowded surfaces and hung from strings all about the small space. A collection of kive cubes was tumbled on the table next to the standard issue kiving unit in the wall. He didn't own any deeptime immersive kiving equipment.

One holo of Esker, Sara, Darshun, Tomas, and himself flickered above the table. The occasion had been Darshun's promotion to senior tech. They stood in a cluster, in their formal uniform jumps. Jhinsei had been fourteen and only recently adopted by the tube team. Sometimes he couldn't stand the hopeful vulnerability that showed on his own face.

Other than these details, and the incident collection on the shelf over his bunk, the quarters were exactly as he'd come to them four months ago. Nothing on the walls, no modifications to the standard fittings and systems. Watching a dragon he'd folded out of a thin sheet of metallic blue ceraform turn slightly in the air flow as the atmos came on, he pictured the words of a psych report: Subject engages his environment only minimally, has made no commitment to stay.

Where else, though, would he go?

The incident collection on the shelf over his bunk was comprised of artifacts and kived accounts. A holo of the crew of the Tiyo trade ship that found the derelict, standing around it in the bay: the derelict's strange, multi-ovoid, folded over shape glinted in the bay's dim light; some of the crew wore odd expressions—in the moments of the holo's capture shifting from grin to askant-eyed frown. Next to this was a kive cube with an account from the ship's pilot on their first encounter with the derelict, a halting confession made in secret against the express orders of Tiyo and the Khat. He knew part of it word for hesitant word: . . . *the first moment we came into view of it, adrift off the Penwei asteroid belt, something... touched my mind. Mother hell, I know how that sounds...but it was—like a deeptime kive trace left in your head. It was...huge, just vast, but also so intimate—like, under my skin—singing, velvet light . . . whisper-boom, like . . . I don't know, like a bloom of something indescribable, deep, deep inside of me.*

Other bits of Jhinsei's collection included a blurred holo of a scatter of light in a maintenance bay on Yang deck; a kive cube containing the voice record of how nine House Toveshi men had all woken with nosebleeds one shift, having had the same dream; a handheld with slagged, fused circuits that two ops crew had been using in the upper grid spaces when, by their account, a swarming energy had come down through the collectors. Several more neatly stacked kive cubes contained records of anomalous spikes, data strings, and other weirdness.

Since being released from psych, Jhnsei had hunted down evidence of the phenomenon, trading cred, shifts, beers, and once an interlude with a muscular Song woman who worked ship maintenance. They'd had sex in a maintenance bay, among the innards of a spinship drive. She'd been an experience; left him some nice finger-shaped bruises.

He'd collected it all carefully, but quite compulsively, under no illusions as to the psychology of the impulse.

He touched a kive cube with one finger, nudging it into line with the others. The first of the collection was a copy of the report of his team's tube accident, as well as copies of all the pertaining files he'd been able to acquire. He knew there were reports he hadn't been able to get. Beside the kive cubes was a fused and scored shard of wreckage from the explosion and a small vial holding a glinting sliver: a tiny bit of neuro scale from Sara's cybered brain.

Jhinsei sank down onto his bunk. The airflow, warmish and slightly stale, breathed over his skin. He wondered idly if the rumors of the bird-masked figure that had begun popping up could have anything to do with the other phenomena. Bizarre as it sounded he didn't see how it could be related to the energy that had taken his team—and left a bit of them behind in him.

The blinking of the message light by the kiving unit finally caught his attention.

“Through,” he said aloud.

Essca’s low, clear voice slid into the room. “Don’t forget mech, end of day cycle at Narcosin’s. See you.”

Essca clicked off. Another voice followed. “Jhinsei? It’s Cydonie.” A long hesitation and Jhinsei sat up. He’d just seen her, so what was this about? “I just found out—drift. I need to talk to you about something. I’ll be in the Blue Profane at oh-eight-thirty.” She’d drawn breath as if to say something else, then cut the link abruptly.

Looking at the dragon spinning lazily, Jhinsei realized that he’d left all his paper roosters along the console on Revelation deck. Which explained why Tadzia, his relief, had looked at him so strangely. “Forgetting something?” she’d called. He’d glanced back, shaken his head, kept going. Now he watched the dragon turn in the air and thought about things that had once existed and didn’t any longer, and things that never had. Maybe remembering those things, knowing of them, made them exist in some way.

It was a very Darshun-flavored thought.

⁂

Mheth left the Tiyo Main salon to stalk the halls of Mignon deck.

Leviathan’s bloody craw. So the whole point of his involvement in the documentary had been to annoy, where did they get off firing him? Not-firing him. They must really be paranoid. Or—Mheth slowed to a stop, standing in the middle of the corridor. Or there was something for them to be truly nervous about. Perhaps he and his documentary partner Kynan had actually found something damning?

He managed to keep to his usual saunter along the winding maze of the studio hive, but ignored the occasional hail from producers or crew who knew him—he was accustomed to check in on each production once every few cycles or so. Now he went right to studio G103.5 and palmed the globe lock.

A fizz of color, then nothing, his chemical signature recognized and rejected. Locked out.

Mheth swung around and leaned back against the locked entry, banging the back of his head lightly several times, wanting to curse out loud. Instead he pushed away from the door and headed to the lifts.

On Botree deck, in the haven of his quarters, he settled into a memform sling with a small vial of clear, chartreuse-tinted liquid from his private bar. Popping the vial's seal, he sipped the incredibly expensive neuro-catalytic liquor. It tasted only of warmth and light, with an after-sting of thick, deep infinity. After several swallows, he remembered he ought to leave word for Kynan.

There was already a widening, depth-edged gulf of light between him and the process of linking to station mind to leave a message. By the time his door signaled a visitor, he couldn't fathom the muscle coordination necessary to get up or even lift his head.

"Come," he gave voice permission without moving. The door opened to admit Kynan, who stomped in to stand over Mheth, scowling. Kynan's whole stolid self radiated righteous anger.

Toveshi Kynan Oolambai had evinced suspicion when Tiyo Mhethianne Tiyo had not only approved his application for license to work on his in-depth documentary on the Tiyo-Kiyr business axis, but offered help and finance. He'd declined both. But Mheth, highly sensitive to any opportunity to act as an irritant in the Tiyo eye, pursued him with the steadfast devotion of a lover. As Mheth could offer all that the Toveshi, as investigative documentarian, could desire, Kynan had been wooed.

"You can't lock me out of my own production! I don't know what the void you think you're playing at but I won't take it. I don't care who the hell you are, you're going to give me my work and get your void-cursed nose out of it!"

Mheth blinked up at the Toveshi. "Did you get my message?"

"Yes I got your message—after I found I was locked out of the studio. All it said was you had unfortunate news to relay. 'Unfortunate news.' You prissy juiced-up ass! Just like all station juice—you can't be trusted!"

"Oh. Suppose I should have said more than that. Could you sit down? You're in the light, just a shadow, you know."

Kynan huffed a breath, started to say something, stopped. Then he sat on a hassock float, bouncing slightly, muttering something under his breath.

Mheth stared into the nice infinity-glow with a sigh. "We've both been locked out. I've been fired."

"Balls. You can't be fired."

"That seems to be a technicality."

"Why, then?"

"At a guess, because we were sniffing too close to something."

"How do we get our work, the template, how do we get to it, then?"

Mheth rolled his head back and forth. "Can't. Been purged."

Kynan's mouth opened, closed; a soft moaning sound escaped him as he dropped his head into his hands. Then he came up spitting. "It's all right for you, you bastard, who cares—you can be calm, luce your stupid augmented brains out, but that's my work—mine. Do you know what it took to get some of that material, do you know..." He trailed off, dropped his head into his hands again, thick fingers clutching through his brown hair.

"Sshhh, Kynan. Darling man, it's okay: I have it all backed up. Here. In my private studio." He waved a hand toward the studio entrance, which was invisible, hidden in complex patterns on the walls. "I care, really, I do. That's why I've kept it backed up. See? I am a good partner. See? Kynan?" He levered his head up to see if the Toveshi were really there, or if he'd only conjured him out of the sweet infinite. Nope, he was there. Staring at Mheth, mouth open. Then he looked toward the entrance, which really was very well hidden, and sunk his head into his hands again.

"You ass, luced-out-freak of a fucking ass."

"No, really, Kynan. All here."

Jhinsei came awake suddenly, with Darshun's words, *like fairyland*, in his mouth, ringing in the air as if he'd just spoken them. A jetsam of strangeness faded from his head like deeptime kive files, a wash of wonder that left a vague imprint behind on his mind and senses.

He kicked off his boots and shrugged off his jump, rubbing his face. A glance at the chron told him he'd had an hour and a half of sleep. He considered trying for more, but both the fading, urgent beauty and the sense of Darshun, Esker, Tomas, and Sara in his head made him need to get out of the tiny space of his quarters.

Running the shower hot as it would go, he stood in the stinging spray and steam, tasting the dream still, a strange food whose flavors he couldn't decipher. He'd kived some cubes on fairyland, that thing Darshun had said just before dying. Quaint, twisty notion of ancient Earth that had left musty, oddly powerful thought impressions behind.

Superstition is the science of irrationality, Sara quipped in his head.

A wry take on just about everything from Sara, along with an aversion to talisters—the general term for fundamentalists of any brand—though Jhinsei supposed he shared in that anyway; from Darshun an interest in odd tales, esoterica, and the superstitions of various eras and worlds; a propensity to worry over other people's business and caretake from Esker; how Tomas loved to move, whether it was exercise, lovemaking, or a jig.

There were other things. Like how it had felt to Esker to kiss Darshun's mouth. Or Sara's occasional flashes of desire for Jhinsei himself, which she squelched in the conviction that she was too old—altogether it constituted a set of inner perspectives and awkwardness that had plunged him into a hot-faced tangle more than once.

Nothing quantifiable. Nothing the instrumentation in psych or medlab had ever been able to measure.

Just that I'm a disorderly committee of shadows and it doesn't go away and it doesn't fade.

Lying in medlab a year ago, his bed enmeshed in biotech support, Jhinsei had seen: in the faces of the Khat officers, hands on their weapons, in the small worried glances the obviary, Ramev Evans, cast from him to the Khat—he'd seen that they didn't want to hear about the bits and oddments of his team that he carried with him. *Authority wall*, Darshun had commented. *Wallheads, you mean*, from Tomas. *Wonder what could be going on in Khat to make them so hostile:* the Esker thought. *He's just being paranoid,* Sara scoffed, *Khat officers are always fondling their stingers.* An old station joke. *You've always been paranoid, Jhinsei. Comes with being unassociated in Termagenti's viper nest.*

Jhinsei had squeezed his eyes shut and agreed with Ramev and the Khat officers. Yes, he'd been hallucinating.

He willed his team to silence, cursed at them. Then he indulged the new interests now threaded, inextricably, with his old ones. His thoughts ran in patterns they'd never run in before and he didn't know himself half the time.

And sometimes, still, the words and thoughts of his dead teammates woke him from dreams, so that he surfaced from sleep with force.

Whatever that energy had been, shimmer of presence, memory, overwhelming sensory input for senses not human—it had blurred his team together and left them imprinted all through Jhinsei's synapses, muscles, and bones.

❋

The Blue Profane faced station core in the lower section of Nicodemus deck. A big dark cave with three levels of honeycombed seating pits around a central hollow, the lounge featured an ever-changing projection of environment flash kives that flickered through the dim. Currently it seemed to be in the middle of some gravity well kive files.

A vast bell of dark sky arced over couches and antigrav slings, stars spiked across the distance, their light glimmering through atmosphere—as it never did through station views. Winged things scryed hieroglyphs through the lucent dark, skreeking mournful song. The couches and slings were sparsely populated. Jhinsei scanned for Cydonie, but didn't see her. He ordered a tespa and found a table with a view of the entry.

The enviro changed, and the lounging pit now nestled in broad, rolling hills of long blue grass, rain hissing down. A wide, shallow river ran beneath Jhinsei's feet. Tiny flames of reflective red and yellow fish licked beneath the river's rain-pocked surface. A pale green sky and the smell of wet.

He nursed his tespa, the tea bitter with overlong steeping. Someone entered, rain reflections sliding and patterning over a face that resolved into Cydonie, still wearing her old green jump and chunky black sandals, hands stuck in the jump's pockets. She pulled something out of her pocket as she sat, setting a kive cube on the table. At least, it was kive-cube-shaped; but the material it was made of—a mercurially glinting, faceted substance whose color slipped from under his gaze, black, grey, lavender, verdigris, molten gold—he recognized from only one place: the holo of the derelict with the Tiyo crew who had found it and dragged it back to Termagenti Station.

He started to say something but she held up a hand as the barboy came by.

"Spindrift, please." The barboy went away. She folded her hands together on the table.

Jhinsei remembered the first time he'd met Cydonie. He'd accompanied Essca to a Mehet-hosted diplomatic falala. He remembered how unreal it had all seemed to him, how strange it was that he should be there, that he should be with Essca.

Cydonie had paused by their table, a little luced. Older than Essca. She passed a glance over Jhinsei and said to Essca, not really unkindly, "Who's the headcase?" Very coolly, Essca had introduced him. "Oh. Hey." Cydonie looked him over once more, waved a hand and moved along. Three weeks out of psych at the time, he'd seen himself in the mirror and didn't take offense at her words.

"You met my friend Touk, didn't you?" Cydonie said and Jhinsei came back to the moment. She looked very serious now, worried over something. Almost a different Cydonie than the one who'd bantered with him just hours ago.

Jhinsei nodded. "Bald, head tats? Kive tech tester?"

"Yes." One finger on the cube, she rocked it back and forth several times. "He's disappeared."

The environment shifted again. Jhinsei thought he knew why the place was half-empty; the shifts were nausea-inducing. A scintillant flutter of yellow birds skitted up out of low trees behind Cydonie. The riffle of many small wings filled their ears for a moment. He barely heard as Cydonie said, "This is a new prototype kive cube that Tiyo Kive Industries has been testing."

She waited while Jhinsei went over it in his head: Kive tech tester, disappeared. New kive cube tech. Tiyo. "What do you mean 'disappeared?'"

"Just—gone. I can't contact him through link; he wouldn't leave system without letting me know. Disappeared."

Jhinsei looked at the kive cube. Was it really made of the stuff of the derelict ship? It looked like it. "What does this have to do with it?"

"The material, it's not the casing. That's one of the new things about it. The kive cube's internals—the files themselves—are matriced into the material of the shell. It's highly conductive and—reactive—of and to human chem and electrical impulses. Tiyo calls the material lumin."

Cydonie pushed the cube to him, watching as he picked it up. He held it for a moment, a slightly rough, hexagonal-shaped kive cube, a little cool and oddly porous. Then the cube's planes and angles seemed to hum, or buzz—like a beetle had once in his palm on a visit to a biome in the Phyndarial deck arboretum. The cube grew warm and in a sudden flash of presence—touch, taste, smell, sight, sound, memory—fed into his brain.

Taste of sweetness: honey . . . shades of color, leaves of light, saturated, illuminant. Warmth, touch. Caress, feathery, touching like dark blue velvet on his skin, on his mind, whispering in the air, a vibration along his eardrum, through every smallest bone in his hands—

He dropped the kive cube, shuddering.

"Are you all right?" She glanced around.

He looked away, tucked his hands, still trembling, under his armpits.

"What did you feel?"

"It—too much—it was," his voice fell and the words rolled out, each a heavy thing of its own. "It was like the accident."

Her brows rose sharply. "I'm sorry. Void, I—" she shook her head, turned the kive cube in her fingers, frowned. "All I feel is a little tingle, warmth. That's the conductivity; it reacts to low-level electromagnetics, body chemistry."

"I don't understand why you wanted to show me this," Jhinsei said. He thought he did, though.

"Tiyo has been testing these for two months standard now. It took them a while to get the technology to the testing point." She stopped. Her brows quirked. "Jhinsei, would you not tell Essca about this conversation?"

"Why?"

"I just don't want it to get back to Ro right now."

Jhinsei felt his heartbeat pounding in his ears. "Dammit, Cyd, I asked you not to do that—it's not like that with Essca."

"Fine. Just don't tell her, okay? It's my business, not hers." She shook her head again. "Touk is an experienced, alpha-rated, safety-augmented kive tester. After running a test with one of these cubes, he began to see and hear things that weren't there; his testing supervisor checked him into medlab and made report to his supervisors. Hallucinations, nosebleeds, delusions. Therapies had no effect.

"Tiyo hasn't reported or filed any of it. Touk's supervisor deserted him. They're keeping it very secure—"

"Why didn't he report it to Aggregate Oversight?"

She folded her hands together and tapped one knuckle against her lips. "I think he did; he was going to, anyway. But I just got back from a ship run. I left him a message when I got in, before I went to see you. No reply. So I went looking. He's just gone. Vanished. He was off-station hire, not a lot of friends, but the few he had all have a different story, no one seems to really know where he is. As far as medlab knows, and station records show, he left Termagenti on a passenger hop, destination undecided."

"But?"

She shook her head. "He wouldn't. Not without a goodbye, a message, something."

The kive cube caught his gaze, glinting in the shifting light. "How long have they been working with this technology—this . . . lumin?"

"A year."

Jhinsei swallowed. "It's . . . it looks like it's off the derelict ship. It's all connected, the derelict, my team's accident, all the station hauntings . . . and now your friend's experience, his disappearance, and this," he gestured to the cube, "that's what you think?"

"Isn't that what you think?" She touched his wrist. "Jhinsei, isn't that what you think? That the station phenomenon is something related to the derelict and what caused your team's accident?"

He stared at her. "I've never told you that. I thought you and Essca weren't close."

Some thought moved behind her eyes. Then she said, with no inflection, "I heard her talking to Ro."

He drew a breath. Something hurt, like a tiny filament of bone breaking somewhere inside him. "Eavesdropping a common trait of your association?"

"The Mehet side."

Jhinsei shook his head and pushed back from the table. Her hand, still on his wrist, tightened.

"Drift—Jhinsei, I'm sorry, okay?" He subsided, still tense. "It's just, you've talked to a lot of people who've had . . . incidents." Her hand stayed on his wrist, her fingers warm and steady.

"What does that have to do with finding your friend?"

"I need more information, I need some kind of leverage." She looked oddly diffident for a moment. "Jhinsei, can you—would you tell me about the tube accident?"

He nearly flinched, then pulled his arm out from under her fingers, stared at her, probably blankly, as a sluice of emotion washed through him. He ran a hand over the back of his neck and looked away from her. "Why? How do you think it will help you—or Touk?"

"I'm looking for information. Touk gets fragged, then disappears. The rather alarming results of his test appear nowhere."

"What makes you Tiyo's conscience?"

One of her straight, dark brows lifted. "Don't care about anyone, is that it, Jhinsei? Poor orphan, who gives a drift about the rest of the universe?" She looked away, then said tightly, "You had a different, a stronger, reaction to the lumin than most other people. Some of what you said was almost word for word the same as what Touk said after the bad tests."

"I'm a headcase, remember," Jhinsei snapped.

The environment shifted out of the gravity well theme and into a nearly austere drift of glowing space rock. They sat in silence; he watched a muscle in her jaw work. She wouldn't look at him. Chunks of meteor glided by them, trailing improbable phosphorous lace in their wake. Jhinsei considered the conversation and was suddenly too tired to be angry.

"Look," he said quietly, "pursuing something that both Tiyo, and the Khat, incidentally, don't want pursued, is not a high-magnitude idea. For you or me. And yes, especially for me. No one is looking out for me. I've no blood to bail me out of stew if I get tossed in."

"I would. Athra's eyes, Jhinsei, I would."

He closed his eyes a moment, then said, "I have a copy of the kive file of the accident, and copies of some of the reports, including mine."

Cydonie blinked, which Jhinsei found minutely gratifying. "Those records are all sealed, totally locked down. I checked."

Jhinsei shrugged.

"Does Ess know about those?"

"No."

She raised a dark eyebrow and he shifted, uncomfortable.

"You'll let me kive the stuff you have? When's a good time? Now?"

He shook his head. "I'm meeting Essca in a while."

She nodded, slipped the lumin kive cube back in her pocket and stood. "I'll be in touch in a cycle or so then, okay?"

"Yeah."

She stared at him a moment more, then seemed to change her mind about whatever she'd been going to say. He watched her thread through the drift of space rock and out of the club.

❊

In the dim of the private editing cube off his quarters, Mheth ran Kynan's raw kive data, twigging out this and that thread as he sifted through it and dumping them to the working template where they would remix and fine-tune later. Kynan did info and stat feed layers less than an arm's length away in the cramped space. They'd lost their half-finished template, but they still had the raw data.

Half-light from the globes of the mixing comps filled the tiny chamber. Kynan hummed a Megrantian opera as he worked. At this point, Mheth could judge how the work was going based on what Kynan hummed. At the moment it was the role of a pivotal protagonist—at that point in the story where he pivoted to evil and undertook to murder.

"How's it coming, Ky?"

Kynan made a noncommittal sound through the humming.

"Don't sulk, Kynan. We've all the kive data; it's only time we've lost." He cycled through a series of feeds they'd tapped illicitly off the Tiyo testing lab down on Ash. Scents of antiseptic and sweat, air currents across the skin, visuals of testers hooking into the kiving equipment and neuro and physio monitors, murmur of voices.

"Some two hundred hours or so," Kynan interrupted his humming to say caustically. "Only time."

"Anyway, the template's back where it was; I'm into the new stuff now."

Kynan said nothing, but a while later the humming shifted to the second aria of the traveler Riella, who saves the Shanti Matrix from destruction, then seduces both the female hero and the male love interest. Mheth decided it was a good sign; Riella was certainly the most interesting character.

Mheth's muscles twitched at his long-held position and he triggered the chi, his breath deepening at its electric velvet push through his body. He sighed.

Kynan stopped humming to say, "I hate it when you do that; you sound so self-satisfied I want to spin you a new one."

Mheth considered responses, then shrugged. "Sorry."

Kynan's hand continued to manipulate his globe, strings of sub-level info feed moving through it. "How long have you been chemically augmented?"

"Mmm, sixteen years or so."

Kynan's disapproval radiated off his solid, stocky body. Mostly Kynan focused on his documentary and didn't take time for judging his unwanted, but indispensable benefactor. Mheth felt a slight pang, but it passed. He was used to disapproval. The kind and degree to which he was augmented clashed with the greater portion of moral and ethical philosophies. Besides the chi, he had an eye augmentation that allowed him to see in near-darkness. Getting augmentations purely for pleasure and advantage was not the same as getting, say, a cyber-relay augment for one's work. Of course, Mheth's augments were invisible until you spent time around him. Which only made the judgment harsher when it came, in Mheth's experience.

Not that he'd ever cared, or why had he gone ahead and gotten augments which categorized him, not legally, but in the minds of the many, as extra-human. On some worlds, that amounted to nonhuman. Not worlds of much interest, of course. Talister worlds with their fundamentalist mindsets—parochial, fanatic, dogmatic. No loss there.

"Why'd you do it?"

Mheth looked at Kynan's back; the man still wasn't looking at him. "Why do you think?"

"What do I think? I think you did it to piss off your father."

"Well, yes, but really, Kynan, all of humanity does chemical augmentation of some sort. For a crusading watchman your mind is a bit narrow. Oh, I suppose that's silly of me. Crusaders are always narrow, aren't they?"

"You're a prickly, prickish juiced-up prick with the reflexes of a super android and, as far as I can tell, not a shred of loyalty to anything or anyone." Kynan's voice, rather than judgmental, was merely curious. And, Mheth shuddered to detect it, a bit sad.

"I'm loyal to you and this project," Mheth said mildly.

"Currently."

Mheth laughed. "You're good for me, Kynan."

"I'm so pleased," Kynan said. A moment later he began to hum again, taking up Riella's aria where he'd left off.

Mheth settled back into a rhythm with the raw data.

More tests tapped from the Tiyo labs, this time the station facility rather than the one down on Ash; if Grath or his father knew... but what, really, would they do? He was a Tiyo, one of *the* Tiyos. Lock me away, ship me to Ash . . . well that would be unpleasant, certainly. His musings broke off abruptly.

He flicked the editing globe's time index back and ran the last moments again, not believing he'd seen what he'd seen.

It was an individual testing booth, which meant deep immersion kiving, high-level test. New tech. Mheth ran the index back further and slowed it down. Tiyo test designate number 531 was a man, he had a bony face with a kind of naked, surprised look about the eyes, a bald head tattooed with bold patterns. Mheth watched as tester 531 hooked up all his monitor feeds, settled back in the sling and slotted a strange, glittery, faceted kive cube.

"Tiyo experimental kive technology, file S-K137 BNW, test run alpha," number 531 said into the record. Then he closed his eyes with a sigh and began to kive. A bare moment later, viewer objective time, number 531 began to spasm, twist in his sling, hands grasping at the air. Sweat sheened his face; his lips moved around a string of words too broken and silent for Mheth to make out. His eyes moved behind closed lids. Acrid body smells filled the booth and a wet spot appeared on the upper thigh of number 531's red jump.

A Tiyo tech rushed in, disconnected the tester. But he continued to spasm, twitch, and mumble, eyes closed over a subjective time and space that surely held more than the few moments Mheth had watched.

The feed went dark as the tech cut power to the booth's system. A breath of darkness in the raw kive material, then the next set of data raveled through the globe. Mheth froze it and sat back.

"Kynan? Access the Tiyo public info reports, specifically new technology test results, index 13.29.3108."

"Just a sec, just a sec . . . okay. What of it?"

"Are there any anomalous results reported, any alerts, any notices of testing suspended on a particular new technology?"

"No . . . No. Not a one. Why?"

"Any such reports or flags for the whole of that quarter?"

Kynan ran through the info. Mheth tapped a finger over the frozen images in his globe. "Nothing. What already?"

Once more, Mheth set the time index back. Kynan stood at his shoulder. Leaning down, he touched the editing globe, set the kive data in motion, watched, listened. He hummed a bit, tunelessly, the bass vibrating in Mheth's ear, his lunch still spicy on his breath.

Mheth watched the pulse beat in Kynan's wide neck, under pale brown skin, a vein beating blue. The humming faltered. Kynan stood straight, ran one hand over his face several times, as if the texture of his beard stubble might tell him something.

"Tell me, is this something you were expecting to expose?" Mheth asked softly.

Kynan, one hand laid along the side of his face, shook his head.

"Ah."

Suddenly, both globes flickered and power to the editing suite stuttered. Then it died, low flares lingering a moment in the globes as the chamber was plunged into darkness.

"What the—" Kynan said.

"Technically," Mheth said, "the chances of this happening while station is still—judging by the relative quiet—intact around us, given that Tiyo backs up power relays to all its decks, are so small as to be virtually impossible. Highly trivial, in any case. Unless—"

"Someone did it on purpose," Kynan finished.

In the slight glow from the auxiliary panels, with his augmented eyes, Mheth could see Kynan, tapping his fingers to his cheek. "It could be the station ghost," Mheth said. "Many of the reported incidents include power failure or surges, general equipment craziness."

"Obviously," Kynan said, "it's not a ghost."

"Obviously," Mheth said.

A slight clatter echoed above them, in the grid beyond the ceraform tile ceiling.

"No, doesn't sound like a ghost," Kynan said.

"Right." Mheth went to the door and palmed the manual lock. He tried again. "It's stuck."

"Of course it is."

Mheth looked up as one of the tiles in the ceiling moved. A low grinding scrape and it was dislodged, then disappeared.

"What was that?" Kynan said. "Mheth?"

"Company." He watched in astonishment as a figure dropped down out of the dark opening in the ceiling, landing neatly with a thump and a whish of displaced air.

Like a fantasy from an adventure flash kive, the figure wore a hooded domino of deep, dark crimson over a suit of some unevenly faceted, faintly glittering material with, to Mheth's eyes, the same fleeting colors and surface texture of a pyrite compound. The suit covered the figure entirely, down to gloved hands and boots. The figure turned toward Mheth, revealing, within the domino hood, a bird mask, lurid and fantastic.

For just a breath, the domino bird seemed to stare at Mheth in the dark, then, so swiftly and easily Mheth didn't have a chance to think, it whirled on Kynan.

"Mheth?" Kynan's voice cut through his shock. "What's—"

Even as he leapt toward Kynan to come between him and the bizarre figure, the domino reached out to Kynan and wrapped two glittering, gloved hands around his thick neck. There was a gruesome dance, Kynan struggling with the glittering figure as they whipped around, Mheth trying to cut in, gripping the domino's forearms and pounding on the faceted suit.

Mheth was spun out of the fight abruptly and hit hard against a console. A sharp pain cut through his chest and he gasped for breath. His hands trembled, knuckles and palms lacerated from pounding and pulling at the domino's suit.

He raised his head blearily in time to see Kynan slump from the domino's grasp. The domino turned to regard him, bird mask tilted slightly. It set gloved hands on either side of the workglobe. After a moment, a glow fizzed over the surface, sparking thin arcs of electricity here and there, a deeper glow coming up from inside it, then a fizzle. The editing globe died, smoke curling up from its melted, fused hunk. Mheth blinked, eyes tearing at the smell.

The domino stepped back, arms out, palms turned up theatrically. Then a turn, cape skirling, one hand coming up with a stinger in it.

A tingling numbness spread coolly through Mheth.

He shot me. With a surprised squawk, Mheth slid off the console, unconscious.

Semiramnis' vaulted main causeway hung below the tiers of several lesser promenades, station's vast torus giving slant horizon in the distance. Vaulted arches gleamed blue-black in the filtered light, stars visible through the views between arches. The mural of the myth of the Drift Witch, part mosaic, part interactive hologram with embedded kive files, gleamed colorful and intricate along the inner, coreward side, interrupted by boutiques, clubs, eateries and emporiums of all kinds. Accelerated magnet trikes thhhpped by, glowing streaks of color. Association Council was forever trying to pass stricter regulations against the trikes, but House Kiyr held the import and licensing quotas and effectively stopped council incursions every time—despite the fatality and injury stats that concerned parents brought to bear. Foot traffic kept well to the edges, by the shops and eateries, or took to an upper tier, as Jhinsei did.

A shower of red petals floated through the air above a luxury boutique; tactile music drifted up from a club next to it, tingling over his skin as he passed; savory wafts from an eatery made his mouth water obediently. He barely noticed the ebb and flow of people around him. He had walked off the first flush of anger and frustration and felt inclined to laugh at himself, except a festering confusion lingered, grinding in his bones. All Cydonie had asked was what the accident had been like. Right. Reason enough for bad brain chem.

Pushing his hair back, restless and frustrated, he nearly ran into a couple of Khat officers. He jumped out of the way and fetched up hard against the arches along the view side of the promenade. The Khat officers cast him a look, but kept on their way.

He stood there for a minute, getting his breath, sure he must be lit up, a vile, freakish mutant, and, conversely, feeling he was disappearing from sight even as he stood there, a blip in the continuum.

He knew these for skewed thoughts, subjective to the point of dementia. Bad chem. Knowing helped. Some.

The arch was solid against his side. Vista through the view port was a magnified prospect of the smoke-green sphere of the planet Ash, its dark magenta and orange flecks vivid. People passed behind him, occasionally brushing close.

A lull in the foot traffic left him in relative silence and Jhinsei relaxed a fraction, tense muscles letting go. "Void, I *am* a headcase," he muttered.

In the absence of more immediate background noise, he heard something else: an echo of footsteps in the upper grid. Peering up into the shadowed spaces above, expecting to see an ops tech, he saw instead a swirl of dark crimson, a fleeting glitter, so brief he couldn't be sure he'd seen anything. Odd, to say the least; regulations restricted access to the upper grids: authorized ops tech personnel only.

Not that the regulations weren't violated on occasion, but only by ops crew not currently authorized. Darshun had liked the upper grid. Interstitial space, she'd called it. But glitter and crimson swirl . . . he couldn't fit what he'd seen with anyone who should be up there. Upper grid was dangerous; ops crew had fifty hours training before they were considered safe risk.

He craned his neck, peering up through the grid, into deep shadow, listening. Another step, then what sounded like a foot slipping, a clatter, an indistinct wumph. He couldn't see anything else.

He ducked around the arch and slipped through the promenade's railing to the access ladder, not looking back to see if anyone was watching him break about sixteen different regulations. The rungs were cold on his palms and through the soles of his boots.

The noise of Semiramnis faded further away. The air grew chill and shadowy, his breath puffing in the shreds of light. He reached the top, stepped onto the upper grid.

Jhinsei shivered, feeling the cold severely through his thin jump. Crew generally wore insulated suits when they came up here. Over the rail, Semiramnis' main causeway was far away, an indistinct stream of color and light. Almost no echoes reached him. So when he heard footsteps close by on the grid they came loud and startling.

He swung around, saw only the empty scaffolding of interlaced grid levels rising to conduits, collector panels, and access shafts, the upper reaches of the cavern of Semiramnis. The footsteps sounded again, from higher in the grid work. Jhinsei peered up into the crosswalks, seeing nothing, then a shadow, and after, a swirl of movement, color.

Down the slender walk a figure swung into view from the grid above, landing lightly. Tall, glittering, the golden face of some kind of a fantasy bird in the slanted planes of a mask. Unmistakably male, with a codpiece of the same rough, faceted material as the rest of the suit. Over suit and mask, he wore a long cloak. Crimson, blood-dark.

The masked face canted toward Jhinsei, so still that only the glittering of the strange material through the shadows gave evidence of breath. Jhinsei, caught in the stillness, hardly dared to move either. One of Darshun's stories—or the children's, on Revelation—had flared to life around him; he'd fallen into a flash kive.

Slowly, so slowly Jhinsei didn't register the motion for several breaths, the birdman came to Jhinsei, walking the thread of grid. The eyes in the mask were large, liquid gems. Jhinsei wondered, with a small, disengaged portion of his mind, what they did to the vision of the person behind the mask.

Then those eyes were an arm's length away, a full head above him. The cloaked figure shifted its weight, what light there was shivering over the greyish, rough facets of the suit. Jhinsei flashed on Cydonie's kive cube. The material was the same, taken from the derelict ship. What had she called it—lumin?

The hooded bird face tilted and a hand came up toward Jhinsei's face. He stepped back.

"It's you." The voice which issued from the mask was soft, cultured, utterly juice. He advanced and Jhinsei stepped back again, then stopped as the thin rod of the rail came into chill, rigid contact with his lower back.

The masked man put one lumin-gloved hand on Jhinsei's shoulder, a bruising pressure. Jhinsei strained back, feeling faintly absurd at the raw edge of his own fear, as the other glove came toward his face.

A rough-edged touch along his cheek and jaw. It felt like Cydonie's kive cube—and it began to sing against his skin, whispers flicking fire through his mind. He jerked back, hard, threw himself off balance and felt his feet come up off the grid as his momentum tilted him back over the rail. The moment unmoored from time, his stomach seemed to drop up, into his throat, and he felt himself falling.

His arm nearly tore out of the socket as the birdman caught him around one wrist, wrenched him up and back over. He slammed into the lumin-covered chest and was steadied, held, a grip to one wrist, the other shoulder.

Tiny blossoms and microscopic pricks of fire at point of contact, along one cheek, across his clavicle, on his palms, bursts of frisson, whispering of a thousand thousand voices against his skin. Heat and vibration sank down into him, contacted his blood, flushing through him. Light bloomed violently behind his eyes...the whispering opened up and he fell in.

Voice of thunder and continuum, saturated, illuminant . . . velvet fire at eardrums, through every smallest bone in his hands . . . shock of presence, other . . . and . . . pain, wrongness, voice and power feeding back on itself, visions twisted, hurting . . . all obliterated in pain...

He came up out of light and pain, into dark, blood-tinged shadow and chill. On his side on the thin grid walk, one arm and one leg hanging off, his head ringing, warm wetness on his face. The golden bird mask hung above him.

Jhinsei could tell by the hollow, sick pinch between his eyes and the taste in his mouth that the wetness on his face was blood from his nose. The masked man drew off one of his gloves, revealing a long, pale hand, manicured, ordinary. He put a bare finger to Jhinsei's face and drew it in a line along his jaw. Jhinsei nearly flinched at the plain, human touch. The birdman pulled his finger away and held it up, Jhinsei's blood dark and wet on the tip.

"Interesting," the man said. He brushed a piece of hair off Jhinsei's forehead, then pressed the bare hand to Jhinsei's throat. Jhinsei felt his own pulse beating hard and fast against the man's palm, heard his own breath, harsh and ragged in his ears. "Extremely interesting."

Jhinsei blinked, unable to gather a response. The man pulled a cloth out of his lumin sleeve and dropped it over Jhinsei's shoulder. He stood and inclined his head, the planes of the mask catching light, then he stalked away, cloak lifting and swirling behind him. He disappeared up grid rather than down.

Jhinsei lay there and listened to his head pound. Carefully, he shifted to his butt, one hand up to the rail, the grid walk suddenly way too thin. The cloth, forgotten, fell into his lap. A soft brush of whiteness; he wiped his face with it. The material bonded to the blood and lifted it from his skin. A very expensive hanky. He watched the blood as it appeared to erode into the air, though actually the cloth was digesting it.

In one corner a tiny symbol, holoed into the fibers. It glowed silver, then transparent, as he shifted the cloth. A stylized sigil, two interlocked triangles. Tiyo.

Mheth touched consciousness gingerly, as if it were a loose power conduit that might surge and blast him. Bitter taste in his mouth, ache in all his joints and muscles. Someone was shaking his shoulder.

"Ugh. Stop. You're killing me." He rolled away from the hand.

"Mheth?" A cough followed the ragged voice.

He opened his eyes and turned back. "Kynan? Thank bloody void. I thought—" He got a grip on Kynan's knee and used it to pull himself up as far as sitting. Kynan helped, though Mheth noted, becoming further aware, the Toveshi's heavy, capable hands shook. Mheth took a moment to examine him. Dark bruises circled Kynan's large neck, his eyes were shot with red.

Kynan likewise studied him. "You okay?" He coughed again.

"Will be. Stinger shot." Closing his eyes, Mheth thought the pattern and triggered the chi. Warmth washed through his muscles, melting through the ache. He still felt weak. "Need a couple, say ten, tumblers of something, say distillation of neutron star, to get this taste out of my mouth."

Kynan rubbed his face, his reddened eyes dull. "Everything's fragged. Your equipment. All my data. The raw stuff, the template. Backups. Everything." The flatness of his voice made Mheth feel vaguely desperate with an unfamiliar need to assuage. "What the Leviathan happened, Mheth? Who was that?"

Mheth shook his head, found it not a good idea, stopped. "I don't know. He was wearing…I don't know. Grath?" He waved a hand around the chamber. "Motive would indicate. But the extreme couture and mode of entry—not my brother's style. Too imaginative. A hireling, maybe, I suppose…" He pushed his fingers back through his hair, feeling helpless. "I'm so sorry, Kynan."

⁂

Jhinsei took yet another shower, his head pounding, then fell into deep, exhausted sleep. He was woken by a sense that the universe was sliding in toward an unfathomable density at its center, the dwelling of the fabled Leviathan, maybe. He opened his eyes to Essca, sitting beside him and leaning close, making a depression on the bunk mat.

She didn't smile, just watched him, her face very close to his. In Essca the Mehet family's clear features had come out soft, almost plain. The startling thing about her was her eyes, black in her pale face, under silvery brows and hair. Eight years older than Jhinsei, she held rank, title, and power in the world of Termagenti. A contained woman, strong-willed enough to have made a spooked, grieving, nightmare-plagued psych ward refugee act like he had a life because she wanted him to.

In the unguarded moments before he woke fully, Jhinsei wondered who really was behind her dark eyes, why she had ever been interested in him, what she saw looking at him now. Thoughts he didn't want to be having.

"So, where were you, mech?" Throaty, soft voice, her breath sweet on his face. He felt a shiver that was part apprehension and part arousal, neither wholly pleasant nor unpleasant. Compelling. Essca was always that. As he tried to figure where to come in on the day's events to explain why he hadn't met her, she leaned closer, slid her arms around him, her body along his. He touched his lips to a spot on her jaw, just below her ear. Silky, star-pale hair slid across his face. He was half aroused before she touched him and then her fingers found him out.

"Don't think," she whispered in his ear as their fingers moved at each others' clothes, "this means you're off the hook."

Hands, lips, teeth, tongues; pulse and muscle beneath heated skin. A fierce look came into Essca's black eyes, an occasional growled breath of pleasure puffed over his skin as she luxuriated in her effect on him. She wrestled him over onto his back, she on top, thighs clamped around his hips, and pushed his hands out of play above his head, holding his wrists with one strong hand. He let her.

"So?" Her husky, mild voice slid warm breaths over his jaw, into his ear; his skin prickled.

"Ess—"

She put her other hand over his mouth, shifted her legs, moved with a sinuous grind that made ripples of sensation. Shivers moved over his skin from point of contact; he waited to see what she would do, touched the tip of his tongue to her palm. She grinned, tightened her legs, pressed her palm more firmly over his mouth as he started to speak, whispered close to his ear, "I waited for an hour in Narcosin's, which Hedgar James took as permission to flirt me up. I recommend your excuse be entertaining."

She leaned close, sliding her palm from between their lips.

"Or what?" he whispered into her mouth.

"Well," her voice and breath slid along his jaw, to his ear, down his neck. Jhinsei bucked against her, cock hard between them.

Essca and his own body's heat and need almost smothered the distant but vivid whispers, nanoscopic shivers and sparks deep within his mind. The memory of otherness, echo of pain, a terrible blank breach of obliteration. Orgasm, when it came, was intense, incredible; and he had to bite down on a scream at the pain which burst behind it. If Essca noticed, she said nothing. She stroked the hair back from his face and pulled him, trembling, close.

A while later, they lay sprawled, limbs tangled. Jhinsei listened to the sound of his breath, of hers, rolled his head to find the liquid glint of her eyes through the dim. Her hand went to his wrist, tracing something. At the flare of pain as her fingers circled, not quite meeting, he realized what.

"Does this have something to do with why you didn't show?"

"Cydonie and I played globes; she got me with her staff and I had to wait in medlab." He said it offhand, easy, sighed and rolled to put an arm around her, press his face into her warm collarbone. He could tell by the tension in her body that she didn't believe him. Smart woman.

Her fingers moved up his arm. "You're not a bad liar, actually."

"I'm not—"

"Shh." Her fingers moved up to his face. Their bodies melded close, sweaty skin, legs twined, as intimate as bodies could be. But looking in Essca's face, Jhinsei shuddered. She smiled, a little sad. "We all have things not to tell." She shifted a thigh between his, stroked a hand down between them and lowered pale lashes over dark eyes.

Mheth and Kynan sat in a tiny bar on the bayside of Nicodemus deck. The Vendetta was an outsystemer hole in the bulwark between spinship docks. It catered to ship crew who lacked either time for or interest in forays further into station. The Vendetta was, particularly, not a place they were likely to see anyone Tiyo, Kiyr, or otherwise part of the Termagenti social system.

Mheth drank vaact, Kynan drank bluecottle ale from Ash, enough to color Kynan morose and light Mheth nova.

"Monolithic." Kynan nodded his head over the word. "Monolithic. Tiyo-Kiyr axis. How it fits into the larger intersystem trade and power complex. Whole Aggregate trade economy. Prosper at the expense of . . ."

"Pronouns. You. Me. Hims. Hers. Hirs. Thems." Mheth dabbed a finger at imaginary heads. "People. Prosper at the expense of people."

"Oldest tale in civstory."

"So we weren't really covering any new territory," Mheth said. He watched several newly arrived spinship crew exiting dock, small figures against the ship-sized architecture. They wore dark maroon jumps, a solemn-looking woman with thick, short black hair that stood straight up from her face; she was flanked by a plump woman with piebald skin and obvious neural augments glinting in her bald pate and a very tall, bronzy man with many earrings, hair black as the woman's, a rather antique, precise angling of beard and mustache on his bony face. As they passed by the tiny bar, Mheth squinted at the ship emblem riding their sleeves, a stylized holo of a shifting mist of stars set in a circle, a small ship appearing and disappearing through the mists. The bald woman's shadowed eyes met Mheth's briefly, then her roving gaze moved on, scanning and cataloguing.

"Right." Kynan's sad, luced voice recalled Mheth's attention. "No point in making the drift-cursed thing anyway. Waste of the last year of my life. Waste." He put down his bulb hard, waved his hand. "That guy, number 531. You figure there were others?"

"Yes."

"We . . . what should we do? This is serious stuff, Mheth. What they're trying to hide here is—"

"They. We don't know, do we, who 'they' are? Some strange creature in a mask, glittery suit and cape. Is it Tiyo, Kiyr, otherwise? Can't assume we know. What we do know is their mode is severe. Want to consider whether inviting more of such behavior into our general vicinity is something we really ought to do." He sucked the vaact's cool velvet burn between his teeth.

"So we just drop spin and hide in a well?"

Holding a last sip numbingly on his tongue, Mheth raised his bulb toward the barkeep. Kynan, taking his silence for answer, sighed heavily, slumping, chin to chest.

"I think," Mheth said softly, "you ought to consider that project you were offered on Megrant Five. I'll take up a less challenging pursuit or two. Let them know we're intelligent bodies who can take a hint."

Kynan's brows rose over bleary eyes. He scrutinized Mheth's face, skeptical. He opened his mouth to comment and belched instead, rubbed his eyes with pudgy fingers, looking suddenly very young to Mheth. Despite the alcoholic haze, bloodshot eyes, puffy cheeks, Kynan looked vulnerable and disillusioned.

Mollusk's was popular and crowded and not a place Jhinsei would frequent on his own, but Essca liked it. Jhinsei stood at the bar between a short, silver-ridged man and a tall ship's crewman in maroon. The silver-ridged man came as high as Jhinsei's chest, while the crewman towered over him. Essca, circulating, had fallen out of sight among a bristly flower of young Tiyo juice that Jhinsei wouldn't have gone near for much of anything.

The bar itself was the polished, pearly lavender, violet, and black shell once inhabited by a giant, speciated mollusk; the interior of the establishment itself was the even larger shell of what had to have been a truly monstrous piece of squicky conch life.

"Apologies," silver-ridge said in a melodious voice as he bumped Jhinsei's arm reaching for his drink.

"No harm," Jhinsei said.

The short man held out his opposite hand across his body. "Jaco Prawl, out of Piranesi. You are Termagenti?"

This, Jhinsei knew, was how much of the Aggregate outside of Palogenia System referred to station dwellers—by the name of the particular station.

Jhinsei nodded as he took the man's hand and shook. Jaco Prawl's silver ridges were hair, woven into sonic receptors. "Kiyr Jhinsei. Piranesi, that's in the Quadrangle, right?"

The man's light hazel eyes, fringed by silvery lashes, glinted curiously at Jhinsei's lack of family affiliation, but he clearly knew station protocol and did not remark on it. "That's right," he said. "Haven't been to Termagenti in a long jump; now I'm stuck on-station."

A server swept by delivering drinks and set out a fresh bowl of something that actually smelled appetizing—bowls of various sea foods imported from anywhere with some pickle water dotted the bar and tables of the crowded club; mingled with the crush of voices and body scents, they tended toward a damp, queasy-making garlic smell. Jhinsei picked a hot bit of spicy breaded fish out of the bowl and popped it in his mouth. Good. He reached for another.

"Thank Athra, something edible. Jumka fish," said the crewman on the other side of Jhinsei, reaching a long arm over him to sample the bowl's contents.

Jaco Prawl, out of Piranesi, mouth full, said, "Mmmm. That's the stuff. Jumka fish are actually kind of strong, but they know how to prepare it here."

The tall crewman smacked his lips in agreement, giving Jhinsei and Jaco Prawl a wide grin. The crewman was coppery skinned, rather ugly, but with an imposing presence. A precisely shaved beard and mustache slanted black across his knobby facial bones, framed by long hair that was equally black and glossy.

The ship patch on the crewman's sleeve was an expensive custom holo job: a circle with a moving star veil and a little ship playing here-not-here within it.

He nodded to them both, a shrewd gaze moving from Jaco to Jhinsei, and flourished one hand with a slight bow as he said, "Antoine la Savre, pleased to make your acquaintance."

"And yours, sir," Jaco Prawl said. "So, I'd taken passage on a triplite spinship with business in the dust belt. The biomechanicals in their spin drive caught a talister-bred germ and now they're in dock to cure the poor thing. Talisters," he said the word like a curse, shaking his head; Jhinsei found it a bit incongruous, given the somewhat fundamentalist views Piranesi was rumored to harbor. "Wouldn't mind," Jaco Prawl continued, "except I was due back home for a clone mate's joining ceremony."

The one thing everyone knew about Piranesi was its inhabitants' pride in—and fanaticism on the subject of—their genetic protocols, manifest in clone groups that were known as forms.

"How many in your clone form?" Jhinsei asked.

"There's five of us. Aural prospectors"—that explained the sonic receptors woven into his hair—"except Lacey, she's a composer. One getting joined is Beal; he's joining an off-world solitary, so it's going to be a farewell bash, too."

"Tried for passage on another ship?" Antoine la Savre asked.

"Nothing going that way on the current schedule." The Piranesian frowned and smoothed a ridge absently; they quivered in the constant noise flow. "Happens more and more lately; used to be there was always a ship going where you wanted. This keeps up, infrastructure all across the Aggregate, system-to-system travel and trade, will begin to degrade past reclamation."

Such pronunciations of doom weren't uncommon these days, Jhinsei knew.

"Do you happen to know," Antoine la Savre said, "which talister germ the biomechs in that triplite's spin drive caught?"

"No," Jaco Prawl said. "Never thought to inquire."

The crewman smoothed fingers over the precise angles of his beard. "I've been making a bit of a study, tracking the various ill-begotten, fundamentalist-minded children of the various talister factions."

"How curious," the clone said. "Would that be a hobby or some sort of vocation?"

La Savre laughed. "A bit of both." Then he went on, ugly face growing serious. "But it begins to be a truly alarming problem, these talister-bred bugs sidelining ships here, there, everywhere."

"Yes," Jaco sighed. "There are none so dangerous as those who claim to know the fundamental will of the universe." He seemed to be quoting something, but Jhinsei didn't know what.

"For talisters I believe it's more the fundamental will of the Leviathan's arse," la Savre said. He sipped his drink, wiped his mustache. "And yet, despite evidence of sabotage and anti-Aggregate feeling, talisters of various stripe have wormed their way into much power."

"Anti-Aggregate?" Jaco Prawl seemed to be examining the term.

"Insofar," la Savre said, "as the base philosophy of the civilization inhabiting the planets, stations, and myriad whatnot of space-going vessels gathered under the auspices of the Aggregate—and its authority—is accepted to be a philosophy of collectivism, respecting diversity and freedom of thought, yes: anti-Aggregate."

The crewman smoothed his mustache again, and continued, "One hears that some ship and trade magnates have even begun to strike deals with certain talister factions, in an effort to halt the depredations—at least on their own interests. Deals which ban travel to worlds the talisters deem untenable for one reason or another; deals which limit who may travel on a certain line, and allow for search and seizure upon those whose names appear on certain talister lists. Deals which prohibit certain activities—deep immersion kiving, for instance—during onboard travel time."

Jhinsei shifted as the crewman's words sank in, and said, "They can't really do that—it would limit business too severely."

"Better than no business at all and a sick spin drive, though, eh?" la Savre asked.

Jaco Prawl tsked, and said, "If one is short-sighted, I suppose."

"It's contrary to basic Aggregate tenets of civilization," Jhinsei said, knowing he sounded naïve.

La Savre nodded gravely, but said, "Sadly, that's never stopped anyone from doing anything." The crewman fell silent then.

On Jhinsei's other side, Jaco Prawl peered into his drink, silver hair receptor ridges quivering.

Together, Jhinsei, la Savre, and the Piranesian had almost finished the jumka fish. Jhinsei finally knocked back half his tespa, washing down the spicy heat of the fish. "What about a holo link?" he asked Jaco, going back to the clone's original problem. "Costs, but station mind has full system-to-system communication arrays."

"Piranesi's security regs," Jaco said. "System-to-system communications are strictly monitored and no full holo arrays exist on the planet. Why we travel so much. And why Piranesi envoys have union and state powers Aggregate-wide."

Jhinsei frowned; he hadn't known Piranesi was so autarchic. "No trespass intended."

Jaco waved a hand. "Don't worry it, no offense." His gaze moved behind Jhinsei; he sipped his drink, hiding a small smile.

A body came up close behind Jhinsei and pressed along his back, one hand sliding over his ass; a strand of Essca's hair slid across the back of his neck, over his shoulder, her scent around him. The hand slid around.

"Ess . . ." He shifted as she pressed closer; he could feel her grin against his cheek.

"What?" she said. Innocently. Her hand wandered; he gave up and turned into her embrace. As his hands slid up her body, he glanced over her shoulder and saw her uncle, Tiyo Ro Mehet, just behind her. Ro's dark grey eyes watched them without expression. He was Jhinsei's height with clear cut but heavy Mehet features, his face a little rough around the edges.

The heat Essca had kindled went cold and clutched ungentle fingers through Jhinsei.

Essca turned slightly, rubbing a hip over his thigh. "You remember my Uncle Ro?"

"Yes." Jhinsei managed a stiff nod. "Tiyo Ro."

"Kiyr Jhinsei." Ro smiled. "It's good to see you looking so well."

"Thank you, sir."

"Ro, please."

Jhinsei nodded again, leaning back from Essca. The spiced jumka fish swished fins in his gut. Sweat broke out on his neck and forehead; he could feel Ro observing all this minutely, eyes moving slightly.

Ro smiled again. "We don't see enough of you. Doesn't Essca invite you to family gatherings?"

"Jhinsei's shy, uncle. Now," she waved a hand at him, "displace. You're being a nuisance."

Tiyo Ro Mehet laughed and went on his way. All fine and friendly. Essca turned to look into Jhinsei's eyes; she could feel his trembling, he knew. She gave him a long, probing look, then set her cheek along his and dropped moist-breathed words in his ear, "What's the matter, something to hide?"

"Ess, you know—"

She stopped his words, predictably, with her mouth. Jhinsei stiffened, but, keenly aware of location and profoundly unwilling to make himself more conspicuous than he already felt, didn't push her away. He let her silence him, responded to the kiss, let his anger burn into sexual heat. Very fine for the self respect, a Sara-flavored thought ghosted through the back of his mind. He shrugged from it and focused on Essca, pliant and warm in his arms.

Lips and mouth tingled, lines of fire arrowing down and up his body by the time she withdrew. She licked her lips, touched his mouth, and peered past him into the empty bowl on the bar. "What was that, jumka fish?"

Jhinsei gave a breath of a laugh. "Yes."

"Mmm . . . see if they won't make another batch, okay? I have to imprint some grasp on a few more intellects. Then we can spin." Jhinsei parsed her slang-peppered words: She had to talk to a few more of the movers and shakers of Termagenti society present. Then they could leave.

She tapped his cheek and slipped away. Jhinsei sagged back against the bar with a sigh, then turned and scanned behind the bar for one of the servers, hyper-aware of Jaco Prawl and la Savre on either side of him.

"Of course," the clone said, raising his drink, "life still offers much compensation."

"Oh, indeed," la Savre agreed. "Such compensations are why we soldier on."

Jhinsei coughed to cover the blush that rose over his cheeks.

❊

Next day cycle found Jhinsei back on Revelation deck babysitting the automateds again. He'd remembered a sweater and had a new stack of ogu paper, a present awhile back from his obviary, Ramev. The ogu, made on a small world in the Nimbus System, was a pale rice paper with wandering shots of opalescent color in it. Folding the finely textured paper evoked in Jhinsei the grandiose sensation of humanity's ancient roots reaching to the far future through him. While inclined to scoff at himself for the fancy, he didn't deny he found it comforting. Or, almost-orphan that he was, delude himself as to why that might be.

All in all he was feeling rather pleased. Good brain chem; the Sara-toned thought didn't diminish the glow. Maybe it was just relief at being alone, on duty, and not at metaphorical sea, out of his depth at places like Mollusk's. When he was alone, or with one or two others, he didn't feel the *alienation* so keenly. Frowning over a difficult set of folds, Jhinsei chased that thought through a number of grim puns. Funny, he thought, that the human race had never found a better use for that word than one which referred to inner-species aliens.

Yet what was the station phenomenon if not an alien presence of some sort? A ghost? An alien ghost. What was the derelict ship? Was it not really a ship? A being, or a kind of bier, set floating in space carrying the genetics and—soul?—of a dying species? Had it only started to haunt the station after Tiyo cut into it, forcing it to search for a new vessel? It seemed to Jhinsei that the station hauntings all had the nature of something trying to make contact, but so alter to their human senses that contact always went wrong. Even the accident, at the center of that horrible, jagged memory, was an attempt at communication—communication that fused his teammates' minds and senses, even as it fused station systems. Trying to make them all work in ways they did not work.

An alien ghost. A chill crawled up Jhinsei's spine. They were a technological species, long passed far beyond the outer bounds of that ancient forest of superstition. Yet the forest had come with them—that was a Darshun thought. Jhinsei had kived a lot of esoterica in the last months. Every world had tales and legends of unexplained strangeness; horror tales in space endured, as persistent as ghosts themselves.

And then there was the bird-masked man in a glittering suit of lumin. What to make of him?

One of the monitors beeped; Jhinsei checked the globe and the ranks of lights on the panels. Scanning, he found a strand of data scrolling at the bottom of the docking schedules, a line of red alphanumerics interspersed with batti script. Batti was one of the languages that station mind used to communicate with itself. He recognized it from training, but he couldn't read it; for it to appear on an interface globe at all was highly unusual.

Jhinsei studied the scrolling data, half-folded ogu paper abandoned on the console. For the space of a breath he watched the scrolling script. A sweet, hot scent caught at the back of his throat and he licked lips gone dry. He stood and cast a glance around Revelation. Empty shadowed spaces.

Clearing his throat, he spoke to the link. "Termagenti, message through to ops control, priority one."

"This is ops control."

"Ben?"

"Yeah, Jhinsei. What've you got?"

"Anomalous string of data in the globe, mix of alphanumeric and batti code." He chewed his lip.

"Batti?"

"Yes. Someone been writing new interface protocols and you forgot to tell me?"

"Jhinsei—" He heard Ben James mutter an aside to someone. "You're not certified in batti, are you? Are you su—"

"Yes, I'm sure. I know what batti looks like, Ben. Could you maybe pull the data up to ops and get someone who is certified to kive it?"

"We're keying through the relay now."

Jhinsei took a deep breath and froze. The scent again, raking the back of his throat and the underside of his memories. He leaned forward, hunting the memory. As his hand brushed the panel, a surge at point of contact, in through his fingers and up his arm, burning cold, swarming light. All at once, he realized.

"No!" he shouted. "Ben, don't relay—" but the surge swallowed him down and his warning was lost in light.

Dimly, he knew that he flung his head back, that his hands rested on the panel, arms taut; distantly, he heard a siren and a shouting of voices through the link from ops. Then there was only energy that hissed and spoke over his skin, through his bones. It shouted into the synapses of his brain, flung shadows and struck light in the hollows of self and being at impossible depth, into otherness.

Alien.

Its presence opened through him, immanent being and landscape at once. A conscious, living vastness. There was heat and fragrant moisture, sand, dark, translucent, and hot. Low, singing voice that was air, breath, blood. Shadows and towering red fern shapes whispered around him—his brain strove for sense, understandable forms. He swallowed eternity in the mouth, not-mouth. Burning steam and a shiver of softness all through—

He came up gasping. Opening his eyes, he saw his own hand at the end of his arm, outflung on the cold deck, fingers twitching. He swallowed painfully, tasting blood. He felt fragile, emptied, a shell with cracks in it. Ache in his sinuses said nosebleed, in his cock, another fucked-up orgasm. *I'm bleeding light.* The thought, half-delirious, barely registered as his own.

He climbed slowly to his feet, using the console, wiping blood from his face, then just leaning there a moment, breathing heavily.

"Athra on a fucking stick." He coughed. Then, louder, voice rough, to the link, "Termagenti . . . " Jhinsei fell silent. The globe was a melted shell, internals half slagged, sparks running here and there throughout. Console and the rest, too. On top of the fused, crystallized, smoking slag of metal, ceramics, and plastics, the half-folded star shape of pale ogu paper was unsinged. A shiver of residual energy flushed through it, once, twice, then faded.

The arm he leaned on gave out, shaking, and he sank back into the console chair.

"Not supposed to do that, is it?"

Jhinsei swung around, then closed his eyes, wishing he hadn't. His blood thumped fast and hard in his throat, behind his closed lids. With a swallow, he opened his eyes and stared at the owner of the unexpected voice stupidly, nonplussed. She was short, squat, a metallic glint of kiving augments patterning the thin-looking skin of her bald head; she would be relaying info back to somewhere. Her skin was strange, brown fading to a pale, pigmentless ivory in odd patches. Her eyes, unnerving dark smudges, were ringed by shadows; she wore a dark maroon crew jump. Jhinsei squinted: with a familiar holo patch insignia, the same as the tall, bearded crewman at Mollusk's, with whom he and the clone from Pranesi had shared a bowl of spiced jumka fish. Jhinsei wiped more blood from under his nose, unable to draw any conclusions about that fact, to even think through the moment's empirical data.

"Quite a mess, isn't it?" Her eyes moved over the slagged monitors.

"Yes," he said, though clearly she wasn't looking for an answer. Maybe the name of the ship that appeared and disappeared on the holo patch was the *Rhetorical Question*.

Her gaze came back to rest on him, impassive. "You need medteching."

Jhinsei wiped his nose, causing a sting of pain and the wetness of fresh blood. He looked up then, at the tramp of several rapid sets of steps on the grid above them.

"That'll be help," he said, and suddenly remembered what he'd heard before the link fragged. "Ben . . . drift . . ." He looked back down and found the woman gone. Hiding, she must be. There was no way off Revelation deck but by the grid or the shuttles. He peered into the shadows by the grid arch, but couldn't find her.

Then the tramp of steps down the grid walk, too many and with no attempt at silence. Jhinsei watched as one junior ops tech, Song Ilya Kole, looking nervous and out of his depth, followed two Khat officers as they emerged from the shadows and bore down on him.

⁂

"How about here?" The vanessa trailed a silver-flecked finger through the sweat up Mheth's thigh, lifting an arched brow, lips curved. Her voice slid goldenly into the violet-dyed dim.

"Mmmm . . . what dimension shall we thus be spun into, you, I, and all the lightning synapse of our time . . ."

"What's that?" She added a finger, trailed higher, bent her graceful stalk of neck; impossibly long hair silked around him, scented of forest wind and gardenia. Mheth regarded the dark strands falling to either side of his face as she moved up, lowering exotic features and silvery violet eyes over him. Her eyes crossed ever so slightly, one of Bexi's better touches; it made the somatically modal flash analog hologram almost real. He ran a strand of her hair between his fingers.

"The silent walls of night they descend, all enclosed in endless heaven are we . . ." He smiled up at her. "From Rivas Grundy's 'Meditations on Between.'"

"Ah, poetry," she said. She slid back down, her hands dallying along the way towards their objective. She gazed along his body into his face all the while, the deep, empty passion in her eyes taking in his luced gaze and muddled needs and making nothing of them.

"Yes, and not very good po—eh—" He drew in a breath. "Ah. You are poetry . . . poetry in numbers."

She smiled, said softly, "I'm an illegal flash analog, a vanessssa . . . " She hissed the last warmly over sensitive flesh.

He felt a prickle at the self-cognizant words, but Bexi got her happies putting disconcerting routines into the analogs. The work in question flexed a thigh athletically between his and the prickle was outflanked. Several athletic maneuvers and a portion of time later, Mheth sighed in animal contentment; but too swiftly all his care and woe resettled.

He'd bankrolled Kynan into first class accommodations on an outgoing spin drive ship with Megrant Five on its route. Minimal goodbye and the best he could do to see to the man's safety. He'd made him promise to send word, to assure Mheth he survived and lived on to do his crusading work in relative health. Without Mheth, far from the mortal shadows of Tiyo, Kiyr, and Termagenti.

The vanessa, highly illegal—thanks to the Thespis Guild—somatically modal flash analog that she was, lay sweet-skinned and languid, long limbs entangled with his. Mheth sighed once more, stroked her silky hair, and said, "Key d-five-annie-two: discontinue." The vanessa went offline, disappearing from the violet-lit love nest.

He exited into the squalid, scuffed dim that comprised Bexi's place of business, an unregulated, literal hole between decks, formed of discard panels and power pirated from the conduits. Mheth leant against the wall. Bexi was dealing with a customer, telling the woman her key code and waving her toward an unoccupied nest. As the woman disappeared through a softly glowing entry, Bexi scratched her scalp through bristle-stiff brown hair and remarked to her assistant, Josh, "What do you lay she exits in a displeased lather before the time's used?"

Josh, twice Bexi's height and three times her width, rubbed a finger over his teeth consideringly. "Nah, she's more likely to frag the annie with overwork." Josh leaned on Bexi's console, a piece of disposable recyc-form. Bexi perched at the makeshift surface, working on an analog chip with some diagnostic tools. Bexi's nests were Megrantian prefabs, the whole operation motile. The Thespis Guild—which regulated all forms of performance service, from flash kive acting to waiting tables to prostitution—was a powerful entity. Mheth was willing to bet they had Bexi kived as a number one criminal menace. She didn't have to pay her vanessas and jimmies a thing—they, in turn, owed no dues to the Thespis Guild.

Bexi caught sight of Mheth and grinned, her smile glittering; her teeth had all been replaced with synthetic crystal at some point in her past.

"Told you to go for a jimmy," she said, "didn't I? Know your moods. You take it into your chemmed-up head to be perverse, though," she waved the coding stylus in her hand and shook her head, "nothing I can do." The needle beam of the stylus' data-manipulating ray flashed around over surfaces, glancing through shadows and the dim light from a string of biolumes. One of the biolumes was sick with the waste and the globe's slow, bruised blue descent into darkness infected the rest of the lighting unhealthily.

"Not asking for a refund, Bex," Mheth said mildly. "She was lovely. Beautiful work."

Bexi sniffed, cast Josh a glance, then bent back to her tinkering. "Want something, do you Tiyo?"

"Ah, Bexi, you're suddenly cold as Athra's vengeance. I'm hurt."

Bexi just scratched her scalp and waited.

Mheth leaned on the edge of the console. "Really, it's just a small matter, a bit of a key. Something untraceable, can crack a door as well as a private kive file?"

"Do such things exist?" Bexi snickered at her own appalled tone, then grinned. "Be expensive, such a thing; cost you more than, say, a ride on Athra's jeweled thighs."

A little while later Mheth, gloved in a low-key Dosgrianza holo-mesh formal, mingled with a selection of station juice at a Kiyr fete. They drifted and clustered over Kiyr Main's dark, silver-shot flooring, between the luminous, indigo crystal panels framing views. Sampling some tiny, liquor-filled delicacies, Mheth caught his brother Grath's gaze on him and tilted slightly to offer the suggestion of a bow. Grath gave a small inclination of his head and turned back to his conversation with Ro Mehet and an ice-haired woman. Mheth chivvied her name out of his memory: Essca Mehet, a Kiyr, niece of Tiyo Ro. A bit of a climber, if he remembered correctly, definitely looking to be serious station juice. She looked interesting at the moment, very dark eyes in a pale setting, wearing a provocative shimmer of silver, draped and baring.

A splash of color singed his peripheral vision and Mheth turned to find Kiyr Asia James, in reticulate plush woven of thousands of shades of scarlet. He looked well in it, if one could school the gaze to stay on him long enough to notice. Mheth squinted. "Red sun? Is it some sort of commentary on the health and life expectancy of the juiced class?"

"No, Mhethianne, it's traditional. This party is in celebration of Five Dragons Day on Jogun."

"Oh, why? That's a rather prov—"

"Because," Asia said patiently, "there's a small delegation of Jogun advocates on station to negotiate with Tiyo-Kiyr for trade upgrade." He raised his brows in the slightest gesture and Mheth followed it to find more red persons in a cluster near the latest sculptures.

"Ah. Bad of me not to know."

"Shriekingly." Asia sipped from a cobalt tumbler. "Despite the lovely suit, you look rather . . ."

"Of course," Mheth said, not too hastily. "Debauched reprobate younger son," he gestured with a delicacy between two fingers, "perceptions must be administered to."

"Mheth . . ."

"Don't frown, Asia, it ruins your appeal . . . wrath incarnate, the Seventh Shiva, a bloody menace with the nightmares of the Leviathan for a heart . . . actually, go ahead and frown."

Asia laughed, then frowned again, quirking his brows at Mheth. They proceeded about Kiyr Main salon, flirting pleasantly. Mheth was introduced to several Jogundians in varying states of red, sampled a variety of Jogun delicacies and goggled, frankly amazed, at the newest sculptures.

He was slipping core-ward, hoping to effect exit without note when a small woman in uninspired black walking with her head down bumped into him. She looked up with green eyes and an apology on her lips.

"Cydonie," Mheth said, steadying her.

"Mhethianne." She blinked, and seemed to recall herself from some deep distraction. "Hello. It's been . . . quite a while."

"An epoch or two."

She smiled slightly; it seemed an effort. "I'm looking for my sister . . ."

Mheth frowned. "Your sister?"

"Half-sister. Essca Mehet?"

"Great drift, I never even knew you had such a thing…though I suppose if I'd given it half a thought—I did see her; she's got some silver stuff barely clinging to her—there." He turned Cydonie slightly with a gentle nudge. "There she spangles."

"Thank you." Distraction overtook her once more; she squeezed his hand slightly. "I'm on-station for a bit…see you maybe." She left him, making for Essca, a slight silver blade in the midst of a blossom of red Jogundians.

Mheth watched her for a moment, scanned the salon to be sure no one was taking note of him, and slipped away.

✻

The bald woman stayed hidden. Jhinsei looked for her distractedly, while the Khat officers questioned him and Song Ilya Kole stood by staring, mouth agape, at the wreckage of the automated console and globe.

Jhinsei wondered why the woman would hide and if he should say anything about her. He knew the drift of his thoughts was fractured. He tried for a moment to pay attention to the Khat officer who was talking and failed; obviously in shock. Obvious to him, at any rate; which was funny, because the Khat seemed oblivious. You couldn't expect sharp observation from Ilya, who was clearly overwhelmed and very nervous. Jhinsei wondered why they'd sent such a junior tech. He worried at it.

"Ilya, what happened in ops? Why didn't Ben send a senior?" Ilya looked at him, mouth and eyes wide open, then back at the Khat officers. Ilya closed his mouth abruptly, swallowing. Jhinsei realized belatedly that he'd interrupted the Khat officer asking him questions. "Sorry. I'm sorry. What?" He wiped his nose, which still seemed to be bleeding. The taller of the two officers handed Jhinsei a cloth.

The other said, "I asked you what were you doing just prior to linking to ops."

"I—folding paper. What happened in ops?"
"Maybe we should get him to medlab," said the taller Khat.

"No, orders were clear. You need to come back to the Khat office with us, Kiyr Jhinsei."

"Freed, look at him. Medlab first, then Khat."

Freed, a severe sort of person, managed a very forbidding and implacable expression. He probably practiced it. Maybe there was a deeptime kive, *Expressions of Authority*.

"Khat first, then medlab. Not our call, Dell."

Dell, who clearly hadn't had the benefit of Freed's kive material, frowned. Ilya watched the by-play as if it were a game of force ball.

Jhinsei wondered idly if it would help if he passed out.

Light steps sounded on the upper grid. Revelation hadn't seen this much traffic, other than station kids, in some time. A flicker of liquid silver through the metalwork, a pale, sleek head. Essca emerged from the crosshatch of shadow, a graceful flame, a quicksilver angelfish gliding powerfully through deep waters. Jhinsei blinked. Losing it, definitely.

⁂

Bexi's key was a rectangle of transparent flimsy. It carried multipurpose codes. First Mheth used it on the lock on Grath's private suite in the Tiyo Studios salon.

The flimsy both cracked the lock and erased the fact of an entry from station mind. Inside, Mheth spared a moment's scan of the lush interior. Grath's inner sanctum of cover-up, graft, and corruption...his brother loved his work. Settling into his brother's chair, he inserted the flimsy between a kive cube and the cube interface connections in the console. Fingering a series of codes into the globe, Mheth, with the flimsy's aid, obtained access to Tiyo Grath Tiyo's private files and Tiyo Kive Industries' voice-sealed records.

The flimsy was the most expensive, illegal thing Mheth had ever touched. And he'd touched some pretty serious objects. To be caught with it . . . he shuddered slightly. In almost unconscious reflex he triggered the chi for an endorph spike; warmth stroked through his muscles and he leaned back, whistling softly to himself while he plundered the most secure files in Tiyo kives.

⁂

Jhinsei sat on a table in the gentle, cool illumination of medlab. Warm, fresh-smelling breeze drifted from the atmos vents, while barely audible scrubbers hissed, cleaning the air. The matte blues, greys, and sages of the color scheme all encouraged calm and relaxation. Jhinsei was anything but. He'd filed a brief report of events for ops, then, with Essca's intervention, been deposited at medlab rather than detained in the Khat office.

Now, nosebleed stanched, clean, divested of his jump and wearing medlab's all-too-familiar soft, coffee-colored pants and tunic, panic clawed the ramparts at the back of his mind. He needed to get out of medlab before it clawed free.

"Ramev, I'm fine. I'll go straight back to quarters, I promise."

Obviary Ramev Evans, once of the planet Ash, gave Jhinsei a look as he keyed settings into yet another scanner, preparatory to using it on Jhinsei.

"Deep breaths, Jhinsei."

"Drink void, Ramev."

Ramev shook his head. Tall, thin, with a bland face, gingery red hair and brows, Ramev Evans was quiet, thoughtful, and, as the head obviary and representative of the Thorough Order on-station, no small power in Termagenti. He was also the obviary who'd had care of Jhinsei after the tube accident.

"Do you like the new atmos scent?"

"It's annoying. I'm fine."

"Jhinsei—"

"Please?"

"No. You're staying the night cycle and don't ask again." He finished keying the scanner and came over to Jhinsei. But he held the scanner in his hands and regarded Jhinsei seriously for a moment. He had muddy agate eyes and short, dusty lashes, freckles across his face. "Here I have some control over who comes and goes. If you go to your quarters..." He lifted a shoulder, let it drop. "Or perhaps you prefer the Khat offices?"

Jhinsei shook his head; but the panic ripped and squalled. He shivered and wrapped his arms about himself to still it. Ramev studied him, then turned away to a cabinet, came back with a derm patch. He peeled the derm and pressed it to Jhinsei's neck with warm hands.

Jhinsei felt the panic fall silent, recede beneath a milky mist.

"I know," Ramev said quietly, "that medlab is hard for you. But you do understand?"

"Yes, I do . . . Ramev," he drew a deep breath and closed his eyes a moment, suddenly able to think again, "why is this happening to me?"

"That's a question I can't answer, Jhinsei." He fitted a scanning web over one hand, set the device's eye piece over one eye and cupped Jhinsei's jaw gently and firmly in his free hand. "Deep breath. Hold it." The scanning hand moved over Jhinsei's skull, taking readings through hair, flesh, bone.

Ramev finished the scan, managing to give Jhinsei a thorough head massage in the process. Not by accident; not much an obviary of the Thorough Order of Physic Arts did was by accident.

Jhinsei sighed; the head massage and the derm together left him drifting, the exhaustion of an abused body and mind going the rest of the way to make him sleepy. He stayed where Ramev nudged him, lying back on the foam table, watching the obviary as he collected his various scan data.

"I'll be in the lab analyzing. Sleep lights," he added to station mind. The recessed illumination softened to mere glow. He left.

Sleep slipped close, slid over Jhinsei with warm hands. But he couldn't, didn't quite, succumb. He hovered in darkness while just outside the calm pool created by derm and exhaustion, a synaptic storm flashed and sang. From out of the center of the storming light, Jhinsei felt the touch of the singing: a current of power reaching through the syrup of sleep. It ran over his skin, licked a slender thread of fire through him like a needle through a bead, and spoke into his mind in incomprehensible song—which he understood. Emphatically. It spoke, then withdrew, leaving essence of honey in his mouth, ache of longing through all his muscles. Every millisecond of the withdrawal imprinted through him, an endless thread of unutterable power through throat, esophagus, diaphragm, stomach, guts, cock, thighs, calves, backs of knees, soles of feet.

He shuddered, shifting, aware once more of the dim of medlab.

Someone stood beside him. Jhinsei blinked, swallowed the taste of honey in his mouth, focused.

Ro. Tiyo Ro Mehet. Standing by the lab bed with hands folded together. Jhinsei shifted, slid himself back and up to lean against the paneling.

"My niece," Tiyo Ro said, "is fond of you. I thought I'd see how you were doing." Nothing in his face, voice, or manner was anything other than benevolent.

Yet Jhinsei's skin prickled, his muscles tensing.

"It's perplexing, and a matter, I believe, for some concern. These events which keep befalling you . . . and others, of course. I have wondered if you might have insights which you've felt, perhaps, shy of sharing."

Jhinsei opened and closed his mouth. Nothing in Ro's expression changed as he nodded.

"I'm not suggesting, of course, that you unburden yourself to me." He smiled, his heavy features showing few lines, a bit of crinkle at the corners of his eyes.

Jhinsei swallowed. It seemed honey kept pooling in his mouth.

"Do you know you're bleeding?" Ro said, watching him. "There's blood on your lips," he said to Jhinsei's blank expression.

Jhinsei touched his mouth, brought his fingers away wet with a dark stickiness in the dim. He licked his lips, swallowed again. Tasted only pure, strange sweetness, which his mind made honey.

"Please come by the Khat offices during day cycle. Oh one hundred. I'll meet you there. Just a few details to set straight in the report. Rest well. Shall I call your obviary?"

Jhinsei shook his head. He watched Tiyo Ro leave, sat up over the edge of the foam and got to his feet. Shaky. He made his way to the lab, stood a moment in the doorway, in the spill of bright light.

It was blood on his fingers, dark red as it dried.

"Ramev."

Ramev turned his head. "Jhinsei—"

"I thought you said you had control of who came in here."

"I do." He straightened. "What happened?"

"And you thought Ro Mehet would be a good visitor?"

"Mind, who has entered this area of medlab in the last two hours?"

"Obviary Ramev Evans, Khat officers Song Juven Freed and Kiyr Misi Dell. Kiyr Essca Mehet. Kiyr Jhinsei."

"Ramev, I didn't dream Tiyo Ro Mehet."

"There's blood on your lips."

"I know!"

"Sit." He gestured to a low form chair. "Why are you bleeding? Ro—he didn't hit you?" He ran his palm scanner over Jhinsei, sounding slightly incredulous.

"No. I—" He swallowed again, wiped his mouth. "I was dreaming . . . I don't know."

Ramev considered, unruffled. For the obviary's calm precision Jhinsei felt a moment's nearly abject thankfulness, though in the past he had strongly desired more than once to shout at the man until his composure faltered.

"No internal injuries. Open." He played a light pointer into Jhinsei's mouth. "You bit the inside of your mouth. Hard. Hold on." Ramev left him and came back with a bulb and a small vial. He emptied the vial into the bulb, shook it. "Here, rinse with this, then spit it back." Jhinsei sucked a mouthful of slightly chalky water, then spit it back, bloody, into the bulb. The honey taste faded as his blood stopped flowing. He didn't remember biting the inside of his mouth. Why did his blood taste like honey?

Ramev's face had gone rather still and intent; then he frowned, bulb held up before him. Jhinsei had never seen that expression on the obviary's face before.

Oh joy of worlds, Jhinsei thought sourly, *in which I have disturbed the calm of such as Ramev.*

Halfway through kiving the data he'd flimsied out of his brother's system, Mheth stopped. He sat alone, kiving from a hand unit in one of Bexi's love-nests. The lava-veined green of the nest glowed unregarded. Mheth stared at the light blinking on the hand unit. His muscles bunched around a hollow, welling emotion for which there was no expression. He didn't trigger the chi. He wanted to, but didn't . . . some kind of self-flagellation for the rank criminality of the information he'd kived, the activities of thieves and murderers wearing a polite façade and the name Tiyo.

His brother. When had Grath turned from serious elder son and brother, the respectable one, for whom Mheth felt both love and exasperation, guilt and gratitude, to shadowy criminal covering up the murderous actions of their father?

And their father . . .

Mheth had played at being the bad son most of his life. But the badness here made him nothing more than a squalling dilettante.

He went back to kiving, mouth dry, mind a stinging blank. He'd see it through the end—the shape of which he could not see, or imagine. Only that it would probably require more of him than he was willing to give up.

❊

When Ramev finally released Jhinsei from medlab, night cycle and nearly another full day cycle had passed.

"You're going to have to come back," Ramev had told him quietly. "Your blood chemistry is behaving—strangely." Tantamount to saying he didn't know what was going on with Jhinsei. "However, you seem functional and lucid and otherwise healthy. Replace the patches every morning; that will replenish some of the essentials you're low on. Contact me if anything—anything—happens, any change, any more events. I'll be in the lab. Understand?"

"Yes."

"Jhinsei," the obviary had said slowly, "I should report this to council right now. This comes under the security protocols charter. I *will* have to report it, but I want to see if we can get a clearer idea what's going on first."

With these reassuring thoughts and a sheet of patches, Ramev sent him back to his quarters. Where he found two things waiting: a priority message ordering him to Khat offices, keyed to play on his entrance. And, sitting at the table, a woman with skin a shade or two deeper than Jhinsei's and a thick fluff of dark hair standing up from a serious, care-lined face. She wore a maroon jump which sported the now-familiar arm patch of a ship winking through a mist of stars.

Jhinsei stared at her while the message repeated through twice.

"Acknowledged," he said finally. "I guess the obvious question is who are you, how did you get in, and what are you doing here? Should I be scared?"

Her lip twitched just slightly, relieving the serious cast of her face. She only answered the last question. "Not of me."

Jhinsei narrowed his eyes and waited.

She'd been studying him right back. "My name is Sobriance Kohl." She pronounced it Sobree-ance Cole. "Captain of the *Oni's Wake*."

"And?"

She turned a kive cube in her fingers, set it back in the tumble. For a moment she looked slightly diffident. "I . . . it's not very hard, you know, breaching a regulation lock code. In fact, yours has been compromised a number of times. Lot of theft on-station?"

"My, that was an unsubtle redirect. I could just message Khat for security."

"I got the impression you don't really want to message Khat anything."

"Are there any more of your crew lurking about, or is it just the three of you?"

"There's a jo unit we leave on board. A roaming sentry 'bot," she elaborated to his blank look. "To discourage thieves. We're down a spinner at the moment." A spin drive ship without a spinner was pretty much stuck in whatever system they found themselves.

"You have a reason for breaking into my quarters, or are you just polishing your skills?"

The captain's ruby swinging from one earlobe glinted as she nodded, not responding to his jibe. "How much do you know about the Tiyo-Kiyr trading axis and the talister sect down on Ash, the Sinaiety?"

"I know they exist."

"And?"

Jhinsei thought about the derelict ship, Tiyo and its new kive technology, Tiyo Ro turning up in medlab, bland and threatening.

He said, challenging and defensive, "Why?" But then, as his indignation at her invasion and his protective armor faltered, found himself asking a genuine question, almost plaintive, "What does it have to do with me?"

He was too tired for this. Too tired for anything. He set the crumpled sheet of patches Ramev had given him on the table and sat heavily on his bunk.

Sobriance Kohl eyed the patches, acknowledging his question—or his tone—with a dip of her head. "Tiyo Sarsone Tiyo has, over the past few standard years, had increasing contact with members of the Sinaiety. Your name has appeared in their Termagenti to Ash coded communications, and in Tiyo-Kiyr inter-station communications, more than once, and with increasing frequency."

"What does that matter to you? Who are you?"

"My crew and I work for an office of Aggregate Control. We're investigating the Sinaiety's talister activities, and as an adjunct, Tiyo-Kiyr trade axis activities, Tiyo technology testing practices, and an underlying power dynamic that aims to disrupt the peace and productive functioning of Aggregate civilization." She recited this as if it were rote, then pulled on the ear with the captain's ruby. "My superior believes you may be a useful material witness."

"Witness to what?" Jhinsei squinted at her.

She gestured with a vague wave of her hand. "You're also an individual of interest to the whole investigation, of course, given how often your name has been coming up in Tiyo-Kiyr and Tiyo-Sinaiety communications."

Shaky and exhausted, Jhinsei just shook his head. "Look, I'm not up to this; I'm just...not. And you're right, I don't want to call the Khat—but the fact is, I have to report there shortly or they're going to come here anyway. I acknowledged the message; I should already be on my way. Are you going to—what, arrest me, put me in protective custody?"

He stalled out, stared at her.

"Nothing so dramatic. Let's just say I'd rather treat you as a friendly witness than end up having to deal with you as a casualty, a victim of the abuses we're investigating." She stood from the table. "I'll leave you to it," she stopped, staring at him with an expression—some emotion—he couldn't read. "Be careful with the Khat—they serve Tiyo interests more than you know."

A short while later, Jhinsei sat in the inner bowels of the Khat offices, hands on a bio-scan globe as he made voice report of the events leading up to the severe fragging of the automateds on Revelation deck, and, inexplicably, to the remote panel in ops through transfer of what should have been simple data.

He was trying very hard to breathe steadily and focus only on recounting events, training his mind from the things Sobriance Kohl had said, and the state of his blood chemistry. The bio-scan globe registered and translated everything for the tech to interpret. He stared at the room's inner core window which opened on the central well: view of collector reflections, abstract, slow-moving scatters of light.

"Go over the exact sequence again. Why did you shout warning to ops?" Four people occupied the high-ceilinged chamber with him. The questioner was Tiyo Anjou Balliard, recently promoted investigator; she paced slowly as she asked and redirected. Kiyr Argot Mehet, Khat Commander, sat across the wide expanse of table, while Ro Mehet leaned casually by the core window. A tech monitored the globe's readings.

"Because I . . . it was like, with the accident, when all the systems were—"

The tech looked up at Jhinsei, then back to the readings. Jhinsei stretched his fingers on the globe. Focus! In the cold room, sweat slid down the back of his neck, trickled down his sides. His arm itched under one of Ramev's patches.

Your blood chemistry is changing.

The tech looked up at Jhinsei again, then over at the Khat Commander.

"I'm sorry," Jhinsei said, a little desperately. "It's—a woman who says she works for Aggregate Control was waiting for me when I left medlab."

Anjou's brows rose. Argot Mehet frowned; Ro, as usual, wore no expression easily read.

"It's—she's captain of the *Oni's Wake*, in the spinship docks. Ask her yourself. That's why my readings are so looped. After everything else . . ."

Argot Mehet looked at the tech. The tech shrugged. "That could explain what I'm getting."

"So could a lot of other things," Anjou said. "Sir—"

Argot held up a hand. "Mind, confirm record of ship in station dock, *Oni's Wake*."

"Docking record confirmed, log of arrival, zero two hundred on five-two-three-one-oh-nine."

"Captain of record on the *Oni's Wake*?"

"Sobriance Kohl."

"System of origin?"

"Empala E."

Argot frowned. "Mind, record message for Sobriance Kohl, earliest delivery. Captain Kohl, please contact Kiyr House Authority to confirm some items of information for us. Our thanks."

"Message sessioned for delivery."

Argot, grey-haired with black, pocked skin, glanced to his investigator. Anjou was so short that, Argot sitting, she standing, their heads were almost level. "Continue."

Anjou thought for a moment. Then, "Let's go back, Jhinsei. Tell us again, in detail, what occurred in the moments prior to the incident?"

Jhinsei closed his eyes and took a long, slow breath. "I saw a line of batti code scrolling through the interface globe. Then for just a moment, I thought I smelled something burning. Then I contacted—"

"Did you check to see what was burning?"

"I looked around, but there was nothing."

"So then you contacted ops."

"Yes. I contacted ops. Ben was sitting link—"

"Tiyo Ben James."

"Yes. I told him about the batti and he decided to relay the data to ops for analysis. I'm not certified in batti." He paused for a moment to see if they'd ask again, as Ben had, if he was sure it had been batti, but Anjou simply watched him, waiting. "He was keying the data through and I . . . I smelled the . . . this burning smell . . . again.

It was familiar. I tried to figure out why, then there was a surge of—energy—up my arm from the panel and I knew. I just—knew. It was like what had happened in the Zebulon tube with my team. The energy, the way the mons were behaving."

Jhinsei watched apprehensively as Ro made a notation on his handheld and passed it to Anjou. She scanned it, looked oddly at Ro as she passed the handheld back, paced a moment. Then, "Describe your experience between the energy surge and the destruction of the automated panels."

"My—? I'm sorry, I don't underst—"

"Describe, as precisely as you can, what you perceived and how it felt." She glanced at Ro. "Did you see visions? Have strange sensory experiences? Taste something sweet? Hear music, voices?"

Jhinsei felt his face stiffen. He stared at a spot in the air. "I don't know what you mean. No."

"Ro," Argot said, "is there a point to this?"

Ro inclined his head.

"Answer the question, Jhinsei."

"I really don't know what you mean."

Argot and Anjou looked to the tech; he shook his head. "Not true."

Anjou leaned toward him, hands on the table. "Jhinsei, just tell us what you experienced; you've nothing to fear from the truth."

Jhinsei couldn't suppress a breath of a laugh or the words that followed. "I'd like to see your bio-scan readings when you say that."

The commander frowned, but Ro smiled.

Jhinsei closed his eyes. Nothing to fear from the truth. Except psych ward. Or worse.

. . . energy that hissed and spoke over his skin, through his bones . . . shadows and light flung at impossible depth . . . otherness . . . heat, moisture, dark, translucent, hot . . . a low, singing voice that was air, breath, blood . . .

"It's..." He tried to swallow, mouth gone dry. *Pull yourself together, Jhinsei.* Esker-toned thought, calm and wry. *Give them something and make it good. A little truth, that's all you need.* He opened his eyes and focused on his hands, dark against the gentle radiance of the globe. "The energy seemed to . . . smudge my senses, confuse everything and overload it at the same time, so I smelled burning which wasn't there, heard sounds that weren't there, saw and tasted—which is pretty much what it seems to do to comp systems, too."

Silence for a moment.

Then Ro's voice, friendly, but slightly suggestive, puzzled. "It seems to like you, doesn't it?" It was the first time during the interview that Ro had spoken directly to him. As a change in tactic it disturbed Jhinsei more than anything else. Because when Ro was ready to shed his friendly-uncle-of-the-girlfriend guise . . . Jhinsei shuddered.

"I don't know why. It's not like I want to get my brain fragged on a regular basis. Other people have had experiences of it."

"But no one so frequently as you."

Jhinsei shook his head, lips parted over a protest he didn't utter. His arms were tired. He looked at Argot. "Can we take a break?"

"Yes," Argot said, pinching the bridge of his nose and frowning. "I think we ought." He spoke in precise, round tones, no syllable shorted. "Fifteen. Anjou, get Jhinsei some food."

Jhinsei let his hands slide from the globe, not looking at any of them. His arms trembled, strengthless; he shook them out and leaned back in the chair, sighing. The tech rose and stretched, vertebrae popping, then followed Anjou from the room.

Argot rose, a tall and imposing man. "Ro, if you would speak to me in my office." He gestured the Tiyo out and Jhinsei was left alone.

❊

Mheth had paid Bexi to leave him use of the cobalt green nest, sans annie of any flavor, question-free, for as long as he wanted.

Want. What I want. He giggled, then laughed so hard he wheezed, breathless, the whole notion of want as ontological construct striking him as deeply and profoundly funny. Want. Want to be loved, cause trouble, find out secrets, help Kynan, uncover corruption, bother the family . . . want to know . . . then not know, be ignorant, get luced. One want cancels another. No want is a good want. *By your desires so shall you know yourself, by your engram and synapse, so you shall you be free.* What was that . . . oh, yes. Bynthonai Kree. Minor experimental augmenter who dabbled in poetry. Well, not poetry, stiff aphorism, really.

He'd studded his skin with patches and quick-puncts of various drugs, trying to put some distance between himself and recently gained knowledge. Then he'd forget why he'd made himself forget and trigger the chi augments, which then compensated, bringing the world back into lucid focus.

Mheth rolled over in the nest and watched glowing lava trails burning through the dark. Something hard nudged into his back; he pulled the hand unit out from under him and flung it. It dimpled the nest and bounced off, falling to lie unharmed in light-veined pillows. From the rack of puncts, Mheth grabbed up several slender, crimson-headed needles and slid them one by one into his arm. Hypnotized by his arm, he admired the pale golden skin, blue-stranded veins. Fine sculpture of bone, ligament, muscle. He spread his fingers, then flexed, watching the puncts move, little red-helmeted soldiers, back and forth . . .

Finally, the chi augment reached overload and gave up, his brain and body too soaked in foreign chem to respond. Distance widened, senses smudged, knowledge went fractal and abstract into meaningless patterns.

Sometime later, voices intruded on Mheth's nice, abstracted world. Voices which insinuated, demanding sense, attention, and answers, building bridges between comforting nowhere and hard, definite somewhere. Annoying. They should go away.

"He paid for unrestricted term." Burred rumble of a voice: that was Josh, Bexi's assistant. Then Bexi, "Maybe so; but can't and won't have Tiyo juice or Khat offies sniffing about for him and finding us. Void, look at him, will ya?"

"Fragged." Josh hmmed a little, reminding Mheth of Kynan. He groaned and rolled away from their voices. "We could dump him in the access between Phyndarial and Quant decks. Someone's bound t'trip over him there."

Bexi sighed noisily. "Knew he'd do me over eventually. All that juice and look at him, utter waste. Universe just ain't right in the head."

"That's because, dear Bexi," Mheth slowly wavered to sit upright and folded his legs crosswise, "the universe has the Leviathan for a heart. Black void of a monster. How could the universe be right in the head? We," he gestured to include them, nearly whispering, "dance about the deep endless, tiny gemmed moths to the dark flame of the empty infinite..." He illustrated the flame and path of a doomed moth with his fingers in the air, seeing trails of luminous light between his fingers. "Tracing our intricate dances, our lives a phosphor of fragile beauty and ugliness at the fine edge of the hoary monster's awful mystery... its great, evil eye, big as seven galaxies, half open in dreaming slumber, reflects our motions as the tiniest iotum in a depthless sea . . ."

Bexi and Josh watched him, his hands describing phantasms. Bexi wore a sneering expression of which Mheth took no notice.

"You see," he continued, hands tracing it all from the dim air as he spoke, as if he could wrest the images in his mind into being for them: a tiny insect star, drifts of time and memory. "It's phytonic, the universe: each smallest portion contains the pattern of the whole entire. In each of us, the Leviathan. Its universe-wide, chilly, chilly eye, like a poison, a virulent, ravaging disease, looks out of each smallest part . . . so, here, you and I, and Tiyo, oh yes, Tiyo and all the bits and parts of this monstrous replication of our darkest, ugliest heart . . . disease and poison, a rage of weeds to choke the scant light and warmth of distant stars . . . "

"What the jax is he looping about?"

"Well metaphors," Josh said, ". . . y'know, weeds and plants and such. Sort of. Bit mixed."

"Bit." Bexi snorted and ran a finger over her crystal teeth. "You've been missed, Tiyo, though Athra alone knows why. You're ejected. I'll keep the prepay for the loss of trade sustained by my having to shut down to avoid coming to the attention of your hunter seekers."

She frowned when he didn't move. "That means out, scut. Josh, give Mes Tiyo an assist."

Mheth climbed to his feet, unsteadily. He smiled up at Josh, then down at Bexi, bowed slightly. "No need, as you see. I'm—" Moving to sweep past them, his senses greyed, smudged. *Oops.* Desired effect at last. He slipped to his knees, but never felt the impact. *Fine,* he thought.

⁂

Waking had nothing much to recommend it, and it occurred to Mheth that he'd had a few too many such experiences lately; though this one he'd managed all on his own with no help from strange people in odd suits and bird masks.

Not so strange.

At this thought he frowned and pushed himself hastily to full consciousness, so as to avoid any further unwanted sallies from his unconscious on his unwary self.

Full consciousness entailed dizziness, a queasy stomach, and residual ache in all his joints. He really had messed with the chi; it would probably take the augment days to reassert chemical balance. He took in his locale. Just off Semiramnis deck. Well, Josh had been kind, in a way. Mheth had an idea he'd never see Josh or Bexi again, that his credit would no longer buy their location. Without co-ords, he could search the interstitial spaces of Termagenti forever and never find them. Probably find lots of other things though; perhaps run into a—

Ah, no. Mheth groaned and dropped his head in his hands, elbows on knees. No more thinking. Yes, that would work. Not at all.

With a sigh, Mheth folded his arms around his knees and raised his head. He felt the handheld then, tucked into his waist pocket. Pulled it out, ejected the kive cube. From the same pocket, he removed Bexi's flimsy key. Wrapping the cube in the flimsy, Mheth held it hard in his palm until he felt it begin to dissolve, the flimsy triggered to do so by his bio-chem. Then he set the little bundle on the deck beside him and watched it melt into slag with a wisp of chemical smoke.

He smelled the savory waft of food from somewhere nearby. He'd screwed with his expensive augmentation, found out things he really didn't want to know, and hadn't managed to upset anyone but himself. What a waste of cycle.

⁂

Being interrogated caused Jhinsei to miss a meal with Essca and his meeting with Cydonie. He'd tried to contact Essca when they finally released him a cycle and a half ago, but she had yet to respond. He was suspended from any duties pending further recommendations from Khat. After a long sleep, he considered what to do with his time.

There was the matter of the captain of the *Oni's Wake* and the things she'd said about Tiyo's communications mentioning him. Frequently. That he shrugged off as too much to deal with; it related, clearly, to the interest Tiyo Ro Mehet had been taking in him.

Then there was the matter of his own changing blood chemistry, his situation with regard to incidents of the station's haunting.

Investigation into the phenomenon and the incidents that involved it had become almost a comfort activity, an obsession exercised since release from psych months past.

He slipped into ops. It was main shift, the downtime lounge was mostly empty, just several off-shift crew taking in a news flash. Jhinsei ducked his head and ignored curious glances. The duty log showed Ben James should be sitting control. But in control, he found a repair crew at the innards of what had once been ops' central station. The melted slag of the outer shell sat on the deck beside them. Ben sat over at an auxiliary console, where communications and essential monitor feeds had been shunted. The repair techs, heads in the panel's guts, didn't even look up.

Ben, however, watched him come, then ducked his head back to his console. He gave no greeting. Jhinsei stood by, awkward.

"Ben, are you okay?"

Tiyo Ben James canted his head, rubbed a hand over neatly braided long brown hair. Then he folded his hands together and passed one thumb over a small scar on the back of the other repetitively. "As you see." He trained his gaze on the panel under his hands, light eyes steady, though slightly red-rimmed. Then he said, "How long did you have to stay in Khat?"

"Ben, I'm—"

"Oh, Athra's teeth, it wasn't your stupid fault, was it? I just…you know what sometimes gets said about you, Jhinsei?" He looked at Jhinsei finally.

Jhinsei shifted; he felt his face flush, then go stiff. But he kept Ben's gaze. Ben nodded.

"You do know, don't you? Doom of the doom crew. Death rod. Course, a thinking mech doesn't pay attention to that kind of thing, right? I never did." He shook his head, said more quietly, "and I don't now; but..." He rubbed his head again. "Clearly you should stay away from station systems." His lip twitched slightly, lopsided with the effort at humor.

Jhinsei heard the silence behind them and knew the techs had stopped working, listening. A moment passed, a general shifting and resumption of mutter and clatter as they went back to work.

Jhinsei flexed his fingers and unclenched his jaw. "You're probably right. Moot, though, looks like that'll be decided for me." He shrugged. "Not like sitting mons on Revelation is a big loss. Would you tell me what happened," he flicked a glance toward the slagged panel, "how it went down up here?"

Ben sat back. "You going in for Khat duty now?"

"Better than zero void. Please, Ben, I want to know."

So Ben told him, and, no more enlightened than before, Jhinsei went for a bowl of chirash at a stall on Semiramnis. Aromatic steam wreathed up from the nut and vegetable stew. He sat in a corner of the busy stall, anonymous. At the next table, a large man ate some chirash spiced so hot he sweated, red-faced, with an expression of bliss.

Semiramnis' causeway traffic streamed past beyond the entry. Washing the chirash down with cold tespa, Jhinsei savored the food and the anonymity. A check with station mind had told him that there was still no message from Essca, but several others awaited him. Cydonie, Ramev. Captain Sobriance Kohl. He hadn't answered any of them.

He tried to thread various bits of data and questions into some kind of order. Energy: confounding, inexplicable, untraceable, unscannable. He remembered the origami sitting unaffected on the melted console in Revelation. Energy that interacted with complex systems only; was conducted by them? That changed what it interacted with, slagged the simpler of the complex ones—if you could call Termagenti Station's systems simple—melted them together, set this charge down that path, for which it had never been meant, put batti in an interface globe, when interfaces weren't even configured for the script that systems used to communicate with other systems.

With more complex systems, human brains, something of the same effect. So far, not in itself lethal; it had been the chain reaction and resulting explosion that killed Jhinsei's team. He thought over his collection of incidents. Nosebleeds. Fucked-up orgasms. Somatic material the human brain couldn't process. Music that burned, visions that sang.

Your blood chemistry is changing. Blood tasting like honey. Was that because his blood was changing or because his brain's wires were so crossed he was experiencing a form of synesthesia? Everyone reported some of the same experiences of the phenomenon, yet for everyone they were a little different. None of the other people he'd ever spoken to had residual traces of other people in their minds . . . but one woman had reported feeling like she understood how the solar collector panels felt; she'd been bewildered but serious about it. Something, some *being*, Jhinsei was more and more certain, was trying to communicate.

It was a strand of strange, glinting beads leading back to . . .

A derelict ship hauled in by Tiyo.

". . . do you guys want to see it?"

Brinden's eyes narrowed, his gaze on Jhinsei. "I don't think—"

"Love to," Esker said, "—at least Jhinsei would, clearly—but we have to get to the tube and earn our keep."

"Maybe after?" Jhinsei said hopefully.

Sara snorted.

"Maybe."

"I'd like to see it, too," Darshun said and Sara snorted again. "Got something up your nose, Sara?"

"See you after, then . . ."

After. Not for Esker, Darshun, Tomas, and Sara. No tour of the derelict, no next meal, no anything.

His whole life now was an *after*. Shadowed, half-lived, no future, only that strand of glinting puzzles leading back to some answer, some source of the whole stinking mystery. At the end of the enigmatic strand, what? Understanding?

He finished the chirash, mopping up the last of it with a bit of flat bread. Washed it down with the last of his cold tea.

Understanding sounded good.

Revelations

Mheth's mother left when Mheth was six, Grath nine. Just kind of faded out of their lives, though Mheth had some notion that she'd tried to take him with her and been prevented.

Riding in the lift, head aching and full of serious thoughts he didn't want, Mheth squinted, trying to pull more from his memory than the vague impression he had of his mother's face, a pale line of cheek and chin, as she leaned close to him in the deep watch of a childhood night, and said—goodbye? I love you? He didn't know.

His father had always, in his memory, been the more vibrant presence, his mother just a background notion. Minders, tutors, and obviaries had been more present than he ever remembered her being.

Had his father changed after his mother's departure? Or had it been some intrinsic flaw in Mheth, and Grath, that had lost—or pushed away—Sarsone's interest? Mheth had watched his brother as he, too, grappled with the loss of their father's regard. To win that regard back, Grath took the course of the good son, the dutiful mainstay, support, and business clone. It hadn't looked satisfying or successful, or like much fun, to Mheth. So Mheth took a different path in his bid for the love and regard that had so filled the world and then—gone away, almost as completely as their mother had.

Mheth took the path not of the bad son, but a cognate: the jester, a ne'er-do-well prickly aesthete bent on pursuit of the frivolous and amusing.

This approach was even less successful than Grath's in capturing and holding their father's love or attention, but Mheth was engaged by his own performance and what began as a method of attention seeking became a defining motif in the architecture of his character.

At that moment, leaning in the lift watching the decks go by, Mheth considered the truth: these many years later of a life lived in splashy overstatement, he wasn't any happier than Grath and he had just that bit less of their father's regard. That remembered warmth of attention had never again focused on him as it had when he'd been a child. *My daddy doesn't love me*, Mheth thought, derisive. *Such a tired old trope, Mhethianne. Surely you can be more interesting than that.*

Tiyo Sarsone Tiyo lived these days at the innermost ring of Botree deck in a set of high, vault-roofed, labyrinthine chambers. Light-shot, marble-esque walls and real wood floors; many woods in intricate patterns, no two spots in all the rooms the same. Sarsone had his own discrete cell of station mind, a live-in obviary, and other privileges of which few were aware.

Mheth stood in the detam antechamber, studying a Megrantian sand painting set into the glossy marble wall. When the system green-lighted him and the door recessed, he found his father's obviary waiting for him.

"Hello, Kenit."

"Mhethianne." Kenit nodded, looking at a hand unit. "Your brain augment is strained."

He ignored her, peering across polished wood floors. His father's usual spot in front of his array was empty, though the globes flickered on. He raised an inquiring brow to Kenit.

The slightest suggestion of a frown crossed her face, shadowed her eyes, passed. "Your father retired to his sleeproom several hours ago."

"At mid-cycle? That's hardly like him."

The obviary snorted mildly. "How long has it been since you were even here, Mhethianne?"

He turned a shoulder to her and strolled down the hall. "I'll wait."

"Mhethianne—I don't think . . . " She stopped, giving up with a sigh, and came after him. She couldn't kick him out; he was Tiyo Mhethianne Tiyo. Mheth caught himself grinding his teeth at the thought and triggered his abused augments. Lucid satori gentled through him—followed by dizziness and a brief flush of soaring body temperature as he settled into his father's float chair. Yes, the chi was definitely strained.

Mheth kept still as the chair bobbed slightly. His heart beat hard. Sweat prickled his face; he drew a slow breath as the spike faded.

The float chair hung throne-like before a triple bank of view globes set in an artistic framework that matched the chair.

Kenit had come to lean by the array, arms folded. She studied him critically. "What did you do?"

Still ignoring her, he set a hand to the control globe in the chair's arm. His fingers shook.

Kenit made a disgusted sound. "I'll get my kit." As she disappeared into her room, Mheth allowed himself a shudder. He leaned his head back. In the globes, images of station life in various key locales, stats from the studios and kive testing labs, Tiyo business in other sectors, all flickered in minute detail. The array was an artifact of the last ten years, installed after the illness began to take hold. Before that, Sarsone had always been out and about, meeting with people, inspecting operations personally, making requested appearances, a commanding and charismatic presence in all circumstances.

His head pounded. Through slitted eyes, he saw unsuspecting people going about their business. He was watching the studio where the heave-whacker was being made when Kenit reappeared beside him, several hypos between the fingers of one hand, a special scan mesh keyed to the chemical signatures of Mheth's augments on the other.

While she ran the scanner, Kenit snapped the hypos in rapid succession, bursts of cool pressure on Mheth's neck. The scan hummed in the room's wide silence. Mheth watched the globes.

"Eilos' little sister," Kenit said after a bit. "You are an imbecile. Something in the attenuated Tiyo genome, I expect."

Calm settled through Mheth as the hypos worked to balance his beleaguered augments. The twitches left his musculature; his fingers stopped trembling.

"If I was your obviary, I'd tell you to take a walk to psych and request some eval."

Mheth closed his eyes and watched light trails.

Kenit surveyed her scans, shaking her head dourly. "There's going to be residual effects, Mheth. The chi augments are fairly resilient, but they're so well-integrated into your own neuro-chemistry and physio that anything which damages them has, by definition, damaged you. And you came very close to real impairment with all the drugs you for some reason felt it necessary to take. Do you understand that? Mheth?"

"Do you miss your homeworld, Kenit? Nentesh . . . fabled lost world down the rabbit hole . . . do you ever want to go back?"

"I did go back. Last Ingress, took passage on a Kiyr trader. That was twenty years ago. Next Ingress in another six."

"Not sooner?"

Kenit ejected a kive cube from the scan and shut it down. She handed the cube to Mheth.

"Why, thinking of going?"

Mheth regarded the cube. "Mmm. Tell me about it?"

Kenit cocked her head. "You won't be able to; you'd have to kill to get high enough up in the queue to make it at this late date."

"I am a Tiyo, Kenit . . . did you leave family there?"

"I believe we've had this discussion before. Just because you can't be bothered to remember doesn't mean I will repeat myself like a faulty system."

"That's right . . . a son and a father-in-law. Do you miss them?"

The obviary's lip twitched; she folded her arms. "If you could hear yourself, Mhethianne. On the one hand, you sound like a retro-cheapie, all sentiment and bathos. On the other," she gave a laugh, "you sound like a bad analog." She parroted him, "Do you have this emotion? How interesting, what does it feel like? Strange things, these humans. Which is very funny, because you're so twisted up in your emotions you're like an Ahmi infinity puzzle. No one, least of all you, will ever figure out which part goes where, where you start, where you end, what shape you ought to be."

Mheth blinked. Then he said, gently, "Do you know, you sound a bit like my father. Turn of phrase, brittle glint of inflection. Or like me, I suppose. You've been here too long, Kenit."

"Eilos, you're an ass." She turned on her heel to disappear into her chambers.

Left alone with his father's multiple eyes on Termagenti, Mheth watched a scroll of data without really seeing it.

Jhinsei had not been down to Zebulon deck since the accident.

The hum of station, the scuffed metal surfaces reflecting the unfiltered collector light up the curve of corridor, the smell of metal and the faint, lingering antiseptic of tube diving suits—all hit him hard. His breath misted into the chill air in rapid puffs. Shoulders knotted, hands fisted, cold sweat prickled his neck under his hair, blood needled under the skin of his face.

He shoved his hands in the pockets of Sara's old thermal jacket, hunching into it for comfort. It had a batti symbol stitched on the left shoulder and acid burns on the front. It had been her favorite. His mouth was dry and his knees trembled at the back as he walked past the smaller passages opening left, by the maintenance bays caverning off right. He was in dread of seeing a tube team. Two techs passed him, one so involved in describing to the other the latest frustrations of her love life that she didn't even notice Jhinsei. Her muscular companion, however, was familiar; after a moment Jhinsei remembered her as the tech he'd had sex with in exchange for an incident story. She met Jhinsei's eyes, giving him a small nod and a quirk of grin as they passed. He heard other voices down around a turn in the corridor and quickened his steps.

He didn't even know if the derelict was still there, where it had been, but then came around a curve and saw two Khat officers standing guard at the entry, just as before. Different officers, but the same positions. Jhinsei paused. He had no plan. Okay, recon, then. Darshun and Tomas thoughts urged deep, even breathing to calm the sudden violent pounding of his heart.

He approached, nodded greeting to the Khat officers, a man and a woman. Again, as before. He slowed his steps, peered curiously past them. The bay was a dark cavern with only suggestions of light that revealed nothing.

"Is it . . . would it be possible to just have a look at the derelict?"

Neither Khat said anything for a moment; they were looking at him a little oddly, the woman's eyes widening slightly as if she recognized him. Then they exchanged a brief glance.

"No," the man said then, "I'm afraid it's off limits."

The woman suddenly put a hand to her ear, eyes narrowing.

"Copy, sir," she said, responding to a message, "Corial and I are closest, we'll check it out." Then, to her partner, "A disturbance reported in storage bay three, let's go."

They both hurried off down corridor, without another glance at Jhinsei, as if he wasn't there. Very un-Khat like. Orders, they had orders, from someone, to let him through, though not, apparently, as a legitimate guest: *Sneak in now, we're not looking.*

With a deep breath and a feeling of idiocy that didn't override either his determination or the panic moiling just beneath the surface of his skin, Jhinsei pulled a palm lantern out of the thermal's pocket and squeezed it, then followed its wedge of clear light into the bay.

The arch and groin of support struts, stacked stasis crates and empty half-gee containers, all seemed to rise and fall under the lantern's beam. Shadows grew and slid away. The air smelled cold, dry, slightly sweet. The lantern beam passed over a workstation, monitors and a globe, a roll of tools on the console.

Then the beam found a grey glitter, splashed dully off a complex of faceting. An unfamiliar parsing of line, flow, and turn of shape that sat oddly between sight and mind.

A lattice of scaffolding stood about the derelict, platforms at various positions for study. He played the light over it slowly.

Parts of the grey, glittering form bore ragged holes where material had been excavated for Tiyo's new kive cube technology, the lumin. Words from the Tiyo pilot's account of first finding the derelict surfaced in Jhinsei's thoughts: *Something . . . touched my mind.* Words echoed by every one of Jhinsei's own encounters with the haunting, and the stuff of the derelict itself, the lumin, in the form of the kive cube and the suit worn by the man he'd run into up-grid.

It was bigger than he'd imagined it, but was still a smallish vessel—*no*, Jhinsei thought, *not just a vessel, a body*. Tiyo labs must have found some way to replicate the material if they planned to launch a whole new kive technology based on it.

Jhinsei went closer, circled, searching for an opening. The only openings he could see were the ragged holes, reminiscent of wounds. There didn't seem to be any pattern to them, as if they'd tossed magnet darts at the thing to decide what spot to mine, abandoning each site and starting on another just as randomly. He slipped between the bars of the scaffolding and approached one, a dark gape low on the derelict. The edges of the hole were jagged, as if they'd been unable to shear it smoothly. Facets glittered, casting jagged shadow teeth as the beam touched them. Jhinsei leaned forward, shining the beam into the hole.

The dull glitter continued several feet, uneven and raw-looking. His stomach muscles clenching, he hunched his shoulders and stepped through the hole—the *wound*—into the body of the derelict. Rough surface pressed up through the soles of his boots. Remembering his previous encounters with the lumin, he held his breath and moved carefully, avoiding contacting the ship with his bare skin. After eight tense, hunched steps, he moved into open space and stood straight, breathing hard.

The lantern beam revealed a large space, smooth curves and ovoid turnings, the upper reaches lost in darkness. Asymmetrically curved archways opened here and there into coiled passageways. The substance of the derelict was different here than the outer, faceted material. Where the light struck it was lucently smooth, a cloudy, iridescent suggestion of color moving beneath the surface, changing shade and hue relative to the light's passage.

It's like being inside an ear, a Darshun-flavored thought whispered through his mind. *It's beautiful . . .*

Creepy, more like. Make you queasy looking at it, Sara commented.

And suddenly they were all there, the sense of them, unbottled and flowing through him in rills. Esker's dry worry; Tomas' gentle thoughtfulness, quiet, as he'd often been in life.

Go in, deeper, Darshun whispered.

Oh yeah, that's a good idea; like he's not fragged enough. Such a waste . . . Sara's sarcasm ended with a flick of teasing lust. It curled through Jhinsei's belly like electric current. His cheeks burned.

Don't grind your teeth, Esker admonished.

Athra, not now. Please. Not now. The clamor subsided, but he could still feel them: inner ebullience of the dead.

He played the light over an ovoid archway, into the convolution of passage beyond, and shuddered at the thought of crawling through it. Instead, he kept to the most open area, trailing the lantern beam down a curving path which was itself made up of many curves and bulges. The surface under his feet rose and fell in smooth humps. Luminous streams of color swirled under the surfaces in the light's passage; cloudy blue, gold, burning yellow, a low note of indigo which pulsed beyond his visual range the moment he saw it. His boots made little sound; his breath husked, echoing. There was no scent that he could detect; just the cold of the bay; it smelled empty, like nothing.

And yet...despite the smell of cold which had come from the bay, it was not cold. Sara's thermal jacket felt too warm. It was at least twenty degrees hotter here than on the rest of Zebulon deck. Some remainder of power must still exist in the derelict's invisible systems; presence, energy, what? A phrase shadowed through his thoughts, Tomas-soft.

Relic biogenic activity.

Jhinsei considered it. Where had Tomas heard that?

Kived it in an old monograph.

The space went on, much longer than the outward size of the thing suggested, curling lazily around and inwards. Spiraling.

The curve tightened, the upper swells coming lower, the sinuous humps in the walls and floor flowing smaller; the colors fled from the light, running under the surface. Sweat trickled down Jhinsei's sides. He wiped his face on the arm of Sara's jacket, and then stopped abruptly, breathing harshly. The spiral had narrowed around him, no surface more than an arm's length distant. He appeared to have reached a blind end. He played the light around, turning in a circle. The runnels of violet veering off out of visible range were beginning to give him a headache.

He considered turning back. What, after all, was he doing? Tiyo and Kiyr techs and scientists had been all over this thing.

No sense giving up now, came the Esker-thought.

Sense? Nothing sensible about this little excursion; may as well be consistently stupid, though, doll.

Sometimes he wished he'd slept with Sara when she'd been alive. Maybe then he wouldn't be so unnerved by the thrum of her lazy desire burning unpredictably through his own synapse and muscle.

The roving beam fell over a deep shadow that seemed to shift into being as his light touched it. He directed the light back that way, then stepped to the undulation in the wall that had cast the shadow. The light curved around a fold in the surface. Around the fold, as Jhinsei moved closer gingerly, the beam picked out another passage. A snaking passage, the upper reach lost in darkness again, but the sides, as far as the light showed them, only an arm's length apart.

Jhinsei shuddered and stepped back. He wiped more sweat from his face, pushed damp hair back. The inner chorus fell quiet while he contemplated the passage. Finally, gripping the lantern hard and hunching in to keep from touching the close, petrified wave of the walls, he slipped around the crack.

His breath sounded louder than ever. The light bouncing across the surfaces and the gleaming colors moving beneath made him dizzy. He stopped at one point, closed his eyes, swallowed, and took several deep, slow breaths. When he continued, Darshun's thought signature trailed through his mind.

There's a tale, from the Chaldinni . . . during the third dynasty of Chaldinnian Sovereignty, a young woman named Coirtel undertook a journey from the lush enclave where she lived, known as the Grotto of the Nine Songs, to a desolate, failed area of the planet, the Meadow of the Sun.

As the tale whispered through his brain in Darshun's silk-soft voice, Jhinsei, though still gripping the hand beam white-knuckled and trembling as if he stood in a gusty wind, was able to continue. The close, tall passage contorted over and in and back upon itself. It was like walking in a giant puzzle box; he should have been prostrate with claustrophobic panic. But he listened to the slow furl of Darshun's tale and followed the gleam of blues, citrine, dark red, and violet that disappeared under his glance.

Unlike a puzzle box, the derelict offered no clues and gave no reward for correct decipherings. With no passages opening off the one he traveled, he decided it was more like the intestinal tract of the Leviathan's little brother than a puzzle box—or a ship of any kind.

. . . so Coirtel accepted the challenge of Kartome's game and began to make her preparations . . .

Beneath the glassy surface, the colors faded one by one, until only the violet ran from the lantern's beam, achingly vivid before it slipped out of range. Otherwise a lucid grey blackness rested below the surface all around, an endless depth sounded by shimmering, indigo-violet fractures.

The passage widened, opening out in long, flat facets planing the curves. Darshun finished her tale and there was silence, within and without.

Finally, the space widened out into a large chamber. Only the passage he'd just walked gave entrance or exit. He stopped in the center, traced the beam up, down, around.

This has all been very revealing; Sara-toned thought, so sarcastic it left whiplash burn.

Jhinsei wiped his face, sighed; he rolled his shoulders to relieve built-up tension.

Try turning off your lantern, mijo, Tomas soft.

Jhinsei looked down at the lantern, small oblong, warmed to his body temp so thoroughly it seemed part of him. "Why?" he whispered aloud.

But then he squeezed the lantern. The light cut off; darkness, utter as any Jhinsei had ever known.

And then . . .

Indigo-violet fractures pulsed and slid all around him, barely seen, like a flash kive of wet-world fish, deep beneath a dark sea. Mesmerized, Jhinsei found himself swaying with the intricate, endless rhythm that seemed to move the pulses. It began to feel like the indigo fractures moved through him, were speaking, their rhythm a language he could almost understand. Moments blurred into a flicking of indigo words through his blood.

A moment emerged from the blur and he found he'd slipped to his knees, crouched over the surface he couldn't really see; just the elusive blips of color. His hand hovered inches away from a bare-fingered touch. Jhinsei blinked and drew his hand back. He crouched there, suddenly icy with fear sweat, unsure how he'd come so close to doing something he'd resolved not to do.

Get real, doll; you're going to have to touch it.

Sara's right, Jhinsei. Why come all this way otherwise?

Go on, it'll be all right. We're here. Jhinsei blew out a breath, that the Darshun ghost within him should consider this fact a comfort.

Still, he crouched there, arms folded about himself, eyes scrunched shut. *I am in here, I am in here, me, Jhinsei, I'm in here. Me. I. Am. In. Here.* The litany calmed him slightly, his own inner voice, small hollow of quiet within his blood and bone that was himself; which, questionably valuable commodity though it seemed, he found suddenly he was very afraid of losing. It wasn't the inner sense of his team which threatened, they were part of him. It was the overwhelming, obliterating voice of something entirely other.

Slowly, eyes still closed, Jhinsei lowered one trembling hand.

The sweaty skin of his palm melded to glassy smoothness. It was warm, nothing more for a moment. Then tingling soaked up through his hand in fine, electric threads, into his arm, slow trilling of warmth. He took a breath, let it go, and the warmth snapped into a fizz of heat and shot through him faster than thought. A burning blink, a dizzying edge . . .

. . . and he was elsewhere. That low, singing voice made of thunder and continuum came from the rustling shadows and tall red fern shapes all around. Dark, translucent sand stretched into long distance, silky grains between his fingers, against his knees—but not knees, not fingers. A scent of heat and fragrant moisture curled through him like ink in water. Beyond the sand there was a wood: trees, but not. Among the not-trees floated columns of tangible light. He knew it was living, all of it, sentient and full of being, could touch that knowledge like skin.

His brain worked at making unfamiliar things apprehensible, sticking now and then like a nano-glitch in a kive's data stream.

"You're trying too hard, Jhinsei," a voice and whisper of breath in his ear. Darshun. And she was there, dark skin shining in the soft light as she lay back in the sand and dug her toes into the clean, darkly luminescent grains. "Just relax." She smiled contentedly, flash of white teeth.

"You should try it with a cybered head," Sara said, and she was there, standing a few feet away, stark and pale, light glinting in her hair.

"You're not cybered anymore, Sare." Darshun picked a handful of sand and let it fall, watching the play of light and color as it hissed gently back down.

Sara grunted. "Guess not. Still feels like it, though." She walked over to them, eyes scanning the surroundings. When she reached them, she crouched down, reached out, and ruffled Jhinsei's hair with a grin. He felt the sting of a blush all the way down to his toes.

A laugh drifted across the sand; Jhinsei looked around to see Tomas and Esker strolling from the wood, not-wood, barefoot, the legs of their jumps rolled up. Tomas was gesturing widely and snatches of his voice reached Jhinsei; it had been Esker who laughed.

Jhinsei blinked at tears, felt them caught in his throat. Esker's laugh, that he'd missed so much. Sara leaned close and traced a tear as it burned down his face to his lips. "I think Jhinsei missed us."

"But we've been with you, all this time; I kind of thought you were sick of us." Darshun came up from rolling in the sand. Glimmering grains of sand clung to the wool of her hair.

Sara's fingers were still on his face, cool-warm, gentle. She touched his lips and canted him a knowing look.

"Not the same, is it, doll?"

Jhinsei caught her fingers in his, raised his other hand to her face. Soft flesh over the curve of jaw and cheek, the fragile, finely webbed skin under her eyes; Sara's eyes, which had always been shadowed, hagged.

"Hello, Jhinsei," Esker said, and he and Tomas stood behind them. Tomas grinned widely.

Sara withdrew her hand, surveyed it a moment. "Of course, it's not really us."

A shudder made Jhinsei shift back; he took up a handful of the warm sand and squeezed it in his fist, feeling the grains shift. "What do you mean?"

Darshun lay back in the sand. "Sare's right; we're dead, I guess. In you courtesy of the—this—" she swept her arm through the air in an encompassing gesture, "life-form, energy. Whatever."

"I'm not sure it's actually still alive, either," Esker said thoughtfully. He settled beside Darshun and put his head in her lap.

"It is a ghost, in some ways." He reached a hand up to trace the underside of Darshun's jaw. "It's just a very potent one—a ghost that carries the DNA of an entire race, a race that itself must have been more potent than us by far. The derelict was never a vessel, not in the sense of being a ship. It's a reliquary. Or, maybe this," he waved a hand, "is just a latter stage of this being…these beings…" he rolled his head in a shrug, "a natural stage of its collective life span."

"Or a natural stage as manifest in collision with humanity," Darshun added softly.

"Relic biogenic activity," Tomas said as he moved around them, his feet tracing patterns in the sand. "Alien ghost energy."

The middle distance beyond them was the violet-shot black-grey depth of the derelict's inner surfaces, larger, vaster, deeper. The sand seemed to turn into liquid at some distance, glinting heat and depth. The not-wood reached crescent arms around them, the not-trees soaring to immense height and the columnar, gently glowing lights dappled back through it beyond Jhinsei's sight. Why he knew they were alive, he couldn't say. The red-edged fern spikes rustled in the windless air. *Air?* Jhinsei thought, then let it go.

"So it *is* a ghost," he said, looking at Sara.

She frowned. "Still not what I would call it."

"Relic biogenic activity," Tomas said again as he did a slow backwards arch. He flipped his legs over his head and came upright again, trailing a spray of sand.

"Semantics," Jhinsei said.

Sara snorted and threw up her hands. "Okay. You win, orphan boy. Happy?"

"Sara," Esker said mildly. Then he got a funny look on his face; he started to laugh, softly. Darshun, watching him, drew her brows together, then raised them. She, too, began to laugh, head thrown back in the sand.

"What?" Sara demanded.

"Well, semantically speaking, what are we?"

Darshun laughed harder, then gasped and sighed, snickering. Sara scowled. "I am not a ghost. There's no such thing as ghosts.

We're some kind of chemical trace, a . . . living syntactic intaglio," she looked pleased with the phrase, "left by our encounter with an alien life form."

Opening his hand to let the sand flow back, Jhinsei found it had melded into a thing the shape of a kive cube; it looked, in fact, just like the lumin kive cube Cydonie had shown him. He dropped it as if it had bitten him, watched it melt back into formless, glittering dark grains. A pulse of fear hollowed him; he curled up beside Darshun. Her arm came around him. The shifting warmth of the sand and Darshun's comfort held him. With an ear pressed against her side, he listened to her breath and heartbeat.

"So what about this Sobriance Kohl woman, huh?" Her voice vibrated under his cheekbone, the question floating above him.

He'd actually forgotten her existence for the last while. He shrugged against Darshun. "I don't know."

"Look," Tomas said softly. He lifted his chin toward the not-wood. The beings were moving, red-tinged shadows blurring around them.

"What's going on?" Jhinsei whispered, pushing up on one arm.

"I think it's a...some kind of anamnesis," Esker whispered back. Jhinsei glanced at him; the columns of floating light were reflected, tiny flares in Esker's eyes. Anamnesis. Jhinsei fished a definition out of deeptime kive knowledge, *a recalling to memory*.

He glanced around at each of them, their faces rapt, even Sara's. Darshun sat up; she gripped Esker's hand, her other hand on Jhinsei's ankle. He closed his eyes a moment, but it closed nothing out.

A sound, which seemed to have been present all along, now grew gradually more audible. It rushed, infinitesimally slow, boomed, too low and too high and all through every mote of being. It sang.

Out of sound, came wind, picking at their hair and clothes, swirling the sand up into fluid, hissing veils. Jhinsei blinked and squinted; sand caught in his eyelashes and starred his vision with dark, violet glitter. It brushed against his face, warm grains flung by the wind's force.

The beings floated through it, unperturbed, hundreds, thousands of glowing columns. All around them now; it became clear to

Jhinsei to what point they were all spiraling.

"We appear," Tomas said, "to be the center of some sort of whirlpool."

"I don't think they even know we're here." Esker's gaze tracked the spiral. "As I said, I think it's a memory or something."

"And we just happen to be sitting right at its focal point?" Sara's hair whipped about in the wind.

"No," Darshun said, her voice almost lost in the rush of sound. Jhinsei jumped as her fingers bit into his ankle. "Jhinsei is. We're just along for the ride."

The columns of light filled Jhinsei's sight. He wanted to say stop, enough; wanted to lift his hand, pause the endless motion. But his want fell away, swamped by the spiral's imperative. It was a gravity so heavy Jhinsei felt every molecule's weight as the spiraling columns flashed slow fire into his brain.

A great spiral, astronomically slow at its outermost, a slow, slow turning, spiraling in, from time and motion measured galactically to measurement in terms of a star's life, a system's life, a planet's. In and down, turn, spiral. Down into turns in the scope of a planet's geologic time—

—closer, tighter, the columns of luminosity an infinite-seeming garland about them now—

—into time measured by the passage of a species through the turns of existence.

The beings were close, the edges of the first of thousands blurring and burning across their faces. Jhinsei felt the rushing of wind—thunder and continuum.

Darshun, Esker, Tomas, and Sara began to blur around him. Blurring, stretching in the immense weight, burning, fading into light.

"Mother hell," Sara said, and they were gone, and the beings spiraled in on Jhinsei alone.

In and into. Down, turn and turn, the passage of ages, civilizations, eras, faster now, into turns measured by century, decade, years and days, faster, faster, the brush of an eyelash, pump of a heart, burn of blood beneath skin . . .

He threw his head back abruptly, gasping a scream as the spiral snapped taut into itself; dense howl of implosion, nova core of urgent radiance in a single flash.

Pain, everywhere, then nothing. Nothing.

Jhinsei dropped his head down into his hands. He swallowed the taste of metal, his throat raw. He sat in the sudden, stunning emptiness of his own head, the dark derelict, the humming station.

❋

"You're in my chair."

His father's voice levered Mheth from sleep mid-dream. He woke in a cold sweat and opened his eyes. The Tiyo's flinty expression was at ludicrous odds with his petulant tone.

"I was waiting for you," Mheth said.

Mheth climbed out of the chair, reduced to the role of difficult child.

Sarsone folded his arms. He leaned slightly, an effect of the anti-grav assist braces he wore, discreet metal filaments with small hover devices at the joints, on arms and legs. They made his motions ever so slightly odd, stick-like and weirdly articulated. Bird-like.

Everything dropped back into place, all the revelations kived in the last day and a half. Athra's eyes, why had he thought it was a good idea to come see his father? Because—it had become clear that much of his brother Grath's energies were involved in covering up their father's activities. Down on Ash and here on station at testing labs, in the larger realm of Aggregate Control and Oversight. It had become clear that while Grath was the originating agent of much ill, it was all to deal with things their father had his hand in.

Sarsone settled into the float chair. His hand curved to the control globe in the arm, fingers spidering darkly over its glow. Every so often, the assist braces clicked together at his knees.

"Father, I need to talk to you."

Sarsone turned to regard him. Mheth fancied he could almost hear the tick of an unaccustomed movement in his father's neck. How, Mheth wondered again, had the father he remembered, the charming, compelling man whose love was a warm embrace, become this querulous, cold man?

"I know . . . " Mheth said, looking past his father to the bank of screens above them. "About all the bad tests and the problems caused by the new kive tech, the covered-up results, the disappearance of kive testers." He didn't look back down at his father, but felt his gaze. Mheth continued his recital. "The fact that the new kive tech is still going to be released in beta on Ash and then more widely, despite unresolved one-in-twenty impairment scenarios and the recommendations of half the senior scientists in tech.

"All on your insistence." Mheth looked back down, searching for a sliver, a remnant, of that lost father in the man before him.

Sarsone turned back to the monitor screens, hand working the globe.

"But . . . why?" Mheth heard the plaintive note in his own voice. "What possible . . . Why?"

First one, then another of the screens shifted focus, fading to different views. A number of them were of private quarters. Was the shift his father's answer, or just disregard for Mheth's presence? These views, which hadn't been part of the monitoring system last time Mheth knew anything about it, were illegal, prohibited by laws of human conduct older than the Aggregate. Mheth couldn't say he was very surprised, though.

"You don't understand," his father said. He sighed. "It was your brother who could have benefited from the time you spent outsystem, I believe. Ah well. He cares too much what others think, and doesn't comprehend that the true bottom line has nothing to do with wealth, but at least he understands that the priorities of House Tiyo are his priorities. Though his recreational activities are rather disturbing.

"It's not that I don't understand your concerns, Mhethianne. But there are overriding factors of which you are not aware."

"Enlighten me, then."

"Change, Mhethianne. Fire and rebirth." He touched Mheth's arm and directed his attention to one of the globes in the array. "You've reached for perfection, for betterment yourself, with your augments. Trust me, Mhethianne: I've seen the pattern and found the key."

Mheth stared at him, then followed his gaze to the globe. Private quarters, probably on Faust. Small, undistinguished, a strange clutter of paper sculptures being the most remarkable thing about the space. A figure lay on the bunk, fully clothed, wearing a thermal jacket and foam-soled work boots, curled toward the wall panel, nothing visible but the clothes and dark hair. Light flicked over him, briefly, quarter doors opening and closing, and another figure moved into view. A spill of silver pale hair over an elegantly clad shoulder...she knelt on the bunk and leaned close, sliding a hand over the sleeping person's hip. He woke violently, one hand flinging up and into the woman's chest.

As she turned away, Mheth recognized Essca Mehet and the illusion of watching scenes from a flash kive in progress faded abruptly. He looked down.

"And that," he asked. "What's your reason for viewing private quarters?"

"The same. There are those whose function it is to be catalysts, matches to light the fire that will burn away humanity's imperfections, the fire of our evolution. Evolution of species, Mhethianne. Nothing more or less."

A sick ache went through Mheth at his father's words, as he watched Sarsone watch intimacies acted in private. Mheth was hardly a model of proper human conduct. But this was over a line. Coupled with his father's words, it was more than disturbing.

His father seemed to forget him and never moved as Mheth backed away, turned, left.

❋

Sara's voice whispered to Jhinsei from a great distance, yet so near she was all around him, a pale heat of words that he couldn't quite hear. He strained after her in a vast nothingness, darkness pregnant with light. The more he strained, the less he could hear her. He made himself still, stilled even his breath in the echo of darkness. Listened for her; if he could only hear her, if her words could slip into his ear, he knew everything would be all right.

Something touched him in the nothingness, slid over his hip and intimately around his cock. He jerked, hitting it aside with a shout of incoherent panic.

"Void—Jhinsei, what the utter empty is the matter with you?" The words were pained, very close, and not whispered at all; all the weight of blood, bone, spit and flesh was behind them.

Essca.

Jhinsei became aware of his body, lying on his bunk in quarters, a pain in his shoulder and back from twisting violently to…to hit Essca. Impact jarring up his arm, the sound of it, her surprised grunt of pain. He didn't want to, but he opened his eyes.

Essca sat on the edge of the bunk, a hand to her chest; her expression, startled and hurt, showed more vulnerability than Jhinsei had ever seen in her. Even as he took this in, her face hardened.

She came at him, landed on him solidly, got a trained grip on his wrist and bent his arm above his head, pinning him. Catching her opposite wrist, he held her still, but didn't resist her.

"Ess—I'm sorry. You startled me."

She hung above him, hair falling to either side of her face, curtaining them in pale silk, both breathing heavily.

"Bad dreams?" Her voice came out husky, her eyes very dark, half anger, half desire, lips parted. Her breath smelled of anise. She shifted, one tense thigh going between his.

Jhinsei arched slightly to push back; neither of them loosened the bruising grip of their hands. Essca stared into his eyes. Slowly, she smiled, then leaned closer, lips to his.

The link chimed with a message; she pulled back. Something in her expression told Jhinsei to answer.

"Through."

"Jhinsei," came Ramev's voice.

As Jhinsei started to reply, Essca moved in close and stopped his words with her mouth; she tasted of anise, too.

"Jhinsei?" Ramev sounded puzzled. "I guess you're not there… odd. Must be a glitch in mind's messaging routines. Please get back in touch with me soonest." He terminated the link.

Jhinsei groaned and let go of Essca's wrist to wrap an arm around her and pull her closer, kissing her hard.

The link chimed again and she pulled back.

"Forget it," he whispered.

"Answer it."

She relaxed on top of him, fingers gentling on his wrist.

"Through."

"Jhinsei?"

Cydonie's voice came into the room.

Essca stiffened, her fingers tightening so hard Jhinsei winced.

"Answer her," she said, toneless.

Jhinsei searched her face. Then he said, "Cydonie. What's up?"

"I—" she drew a breath, sighed it out, a soft whisper through the link. "You missed our meeting. Can we reset?"

Essca's eyes, all pupil, stared into his; he felt strangely calm. "When?"

"What are you doing right now?"

"I can't right now. How about…18:00, chirash stand on Semiramnis?"

"Okay. See you then." The link chimed off.

He looked up into Essca's face, her dark eyes. "She's your sister, Ess, I wouldn't—"

She twisted his arm. Pain burned down into his shoulder. "Half-sister."

"Essca—"

"Shut. Up."

He got a grip on her hand and peeled her fingers off his wrist. She resisted until the last, then let go, pulled away. Her eyes closed and her face twisted with an inner turmoil Jhinsei could not read. He sat up.

"Ess—"

"Shut it! Just shut up." She flung out a wild punch, catching him on the jaw, just under his ear, without real force.

"What the drift, Essca? You can't think I'm cheating on you."

She turned away, drew in a shuddery breath. Her shoulders shook; if Jhinsei had been able to credit it, he would have thought she was crying. But she turned back, eyes dry.

"So what are you doing with Cydonie?" The words hung in the space between them.

Jhinsei scrubbed his face. He was suddenly finding it hard to stay focused in the moment. He felt shuddery, empty, the fading hard heat in his cock underlining a far more profound emptiness.

There were no extra voices in his mind at all now. No acerbic commentary, no nudging, dry wisdom or helpful insights.

Esker, Sara, Darshun, and Tomas had evaporated as utterly as water into dry heat.

"Jhinsei."

"She wanted to talk about something, didn't say what."

"Uh-huh." Which said clearly she didn't credit that. But she let it pass and said instead, coolly, "Where were you earlier?"

He blinked, opened his mouth, shut it; opposing impulses warred, to tell her and maintain some semblance of the relationship, against the feeling that he shouldn't tell her. He forced the words out. "I went to look at the derelict." He scrubbed at his face again. "I've wanted to for a long time. Look, Ess, I'm sorry about . . ." he gestured to his own chest. "I guess it made me think about my team and I got a little . . . jumpy. That's all. I'm sorry; it's not you—"

"I know it's not me," she snapped.

She leaned back, regarding him from a distance that seemed suddenly so great Jhinsei could not imagine how they'd ever touched at all.

Her gaze faltered slightly, slid away, uncertain or troubled. He tried to pinpoint what had just flickered in her eyes, in her movements. Then, again, she shut down whatever it was, folded her hands together and draped them over one knee, lean arms crooked. The look in her eyes assessed him coolly.

"I don't know what we're fighting about, Jhinsei. You need a shower, you stink. I'll see you later?" She made it a question, not the Essca norm. Jhinsei decided to take it for apology.

"Yeah. Ess, I'm sorry."

She slashed one hand in a curt gesture. Forget it. "Since you have an appointment with Cydonie, we'll say 21:00."

"Okay."

She stood and looked down at him a moment, the troubled something flickering through her eyes. She stared at him intently; then, without another word, turned away and left.

Unable to apply anything more than limp thought processes to the matter of Essca's peculiar and fleeting expressions, he let it go. Contemplating the emptiness in his mind, he groaned, rolled to his feet, headed for the shower.

For nearly a cycle, Mheth sat in his quarters, lights at minimum, distilling set and a bottle of unrefined grellwach on the table before him. Husky, dark-toned voices, with the occasional rise of lucid soprano, sang through the air, a six-hour opera.

There'd been a message from Kynan. By now his erstwhile partner was enroute to Megrant System. That was a good, anyway; Kynan gone, safe, away. Doing what made him hum the happy arias.

Mheth carefully poured a thread of the silvery grellwach distillate.

As the steaming sting of the grellwach melted down his throat, a section of the data he'd kived from his brother's personal files uncoiled in his mind. *Test subject 531 is no longer an issue. Analysis is that the subject was unstable. The lumin will go to beta on Ash, despite my attempts to put a hold on it. Father is insistent that it also space more widely to other beta markets. While the modeling on profit is undeniably stellar, the fallout over time is unsupportable. But Father . . . He will see it done, one way or another. Damage control is essential, tracks must be covered.*

Mheth squinted through the dim, his brother's voice echoing in his head. He rested his head against the wall, the thin tiles cool against his cheek and temple.

He hadn't entered his editing suite since the . . . attack. The door was closed, seamless and invisible on the wall. Mheth pictured the wreck in the studio. Pictured the bird mask, the cloak, the suit of lumin.

Another bit from Grath's kives unfurled in his head. This one tasted of metal, blood, flesh. Full immersion somatic hurt and fuck flash kive, with Grath on the administering end. Sweat sliding over skin, nubile body arching under his hands, under the stroke of strange tools, restraints at ankles, wrists, the twist of neck, ridging of muscles, fall of hair over a lush, pained face . . . all observed with the close attention of fetish. The 'partner' was a young man, but there'd been others with women. Mheth had only kived a bit of one, then scanned quickly over the others in order to dismiss them from his investigation of the files. The stench of fear sweat, pain, and his brother's excitement made Mheth's muscles tighten; with an effort, he stopped the kive memory. How had he never known his brother's tastes in sex ran to sadism?

. . . *not brother's style*, he'd said to Kynan. *Too imaginative.* Mheth snorted. Clearly there were depths to Grath that Mheth had never suspected. But did that make him the birdman? It just didn't fit in his head. No, he was certain now it was his father.

He set another batch of grellwach to distill, thinking that he really should be more careful what he kived. His brother's immersion sessions with full somatic hurt and fuck kives wasn't something he wanted in his head.

He had a sudden memory of Grath, age eleven standard, patiently helping Mheth, eight, with a civschool presentation on gravity well insect species, fine-featured face intent, hair falling over his forehead as he and Mheth fashioned mock specimens from wire and paper and pinned them to a board.

A fog of condensation formed momentarily on the silver metal of the distiller, obscuring Mheth's curve-distorted reflection. The device gave a chuffing hiss, soft under the mordant strains of opera.

⁂

Jhinsei threaded the traffic on Semiramnis deck feeling like a dustbelter—overwhelmed by the sounds, the colors, the motion. Things he'd seen and known most of his life seemed amazing to him, things as familiar as station mind, coffee, the colored streak of mag trikes thpping past.

It had started in the shower, something stirring to wakefulness inside, something not-him, excited by the needling of water spray on his skin. It reminded him of how, when he was a kid in Kiyr House nursery, they'd gone to the arboretum and watched accelerated seed-to-flower displays in the biome study center. He'd imagined swallowing one of the seeds and having the little green seedling emerge and uncoil into the humid air within his belly, then burst into a blossom that would live inside him.

Now something was using his skin to feel the air, scent, see and hear everything, rising to it with wonder. Behind this whatever-it-was, Jhinsei was terrified and jittery as hell.

He missed—missed desperately—Sara's acerbic commentary on the situation, the comfort of Darshun, Tomas' insight, and just the sense of Esker. Though he'd spent nearly two years trying to get them to shut up. And now this . . . rider.

Washed, changed, and occasionally just himself, he found Cydonie leaning against a scrolling wall display, watching traffic. She wore the same old green jump and black ship sandals she always seemed to wear. The skin under her eyes was smudged a delicate blue with weariness. She fell into step beside him and they continued along.

"Huh," she said, looking at him sidewise.

"What?"

"You look . . ." she shrugged. "I don't know. Different."

Jhinsei considered responses, found none. "Find anything on your friend?"

She shook her head.

"You look wiped. What have you been doing?"

"Running sims."

"Not of lumin kive cubes?"

"No. Told you, I'm not at all self-destructive. I'm taking the spinner's upgrade exam soon. Getting certified for deep runs."

Jhinsei looked past her as a trio of mag trikes streaked by, gold and blue. "What Tiyo's doing—they don't understand what they're using."

She nodded, studying him. "Do you?"

"No. But it's not just a derelict ship. It's . . . Here." He slid the kive cube of the Zebulon tube accident out, proffering it to her. She picked it off his fingertips without comment, slid it into her own pocket. She had small hands, little scars and scratches marking them, the nails short.

They passed a frittery; the scent of spiced bread and seared peppers drifted between them. Cydonie watched several Khat officers pass them, silent for a moment. Then, "Have you heard any of the reports from Diva's Palm?"

"Isn't that a village down on Ash?"

"Yeah, one of Tiyo's beta market sites."

"Right. No, I haven't." Jhinsei suppressed a rising urge—not his own—to run and examine a view arch more closely. He focused on what Cydonie had just said. "They shipped the lumin kive cubes to Ash for public use?"

"Yes. Whatever happened down there has been concealed, as well as whatever happened to my friend in the tests; the reports are just rumors of rumors. Strange behavior, in just a few people… like a selective infection. Escalating. Symptoms: hallucinations and nosebleeds."

Jhinsei stopped against a railing, looked out through the views to the star-pricked deep. Cydonie turned to lean with her back to the rail, chewed a thumbnail.

"I saw a man," Jhinsei said softly, "up in the grids over Semiramnis, wearing a whole suit of it. The lumin. A whole suit, with a bird mask and a—" he gestured "—cloak. When I touched the lumin . . . " He swallowed, staring so hard at distant suns his eyes burned. "It's not an inert material. That ship . . . is, was . . . alive. Or, not truly dead. It's alive, and sentient."

Cydonie dropped her hand. "What are you saying?" Her mouth hung slack for a breath, considering. Then she shook her head. "No. It can't be sentient, Jhinsei. Alien, maybe. But not alive, not—conscious. Conscious." She shook her head, rejecting the idea, though not, Jhinsei thought, as sure as her words. She shook her head again, then her eyes narrowed. "A whole suit?"

"Yes. I know I'm pretty cracked, but this was much more profoundly cracked than I can aspire to. And—" He hesitated, about to describe his experience in the derelict, but unsure where to start. As he looked at the side of her face, gentle arcs, shadowed eyes, an impulse yearned through him to trace the line of her jaw, lick her ear, touch her all over. His fingers stretched with it while he ruthlessly throttled it, an impulse not his and not sexual; but nearly overwhelming in its ecstatic, curious affection for first this, then that.

"Juice, though," Cydonie said, "have to be, to have a whole suit. What did he do?"

Jhinsei curled his fingers into a fist and rested his hands on the rail. He related the encounter in detail, and described as clearly as he could what had happened when he touched the lumin.

Her brows crooked down and then up in disbelief. She folded her hands together. "Jhinsei," she began when he'd finished.

"There's more," he said. "I—look, kive that cube—then tell me I'm a driftcase or whatever you're about to say. I don't necessarily disagree, you know." Knowledge—or delusions?—like suppressed subliminals, shivered in his bones with the hum of angry bees. And though he restrained it, the little flower of otherness continued to breathe gleefully through every one of his senses, reaching for experience. "Sentient," he whispered. Cydonie didn't hear.

"All right." She rubbed her eyes. "I really wish you hadn't told me about this person in the suit. Find my friend. Pass my upgrades, get taken on a likely spin drive ship as a spinner, and spin deep—I want off of this bitch of a station for a turn or three. But how I can leave with you being stalked by birdmen?"

Something in her words struck a pang in Jhinsei; self-pity, he decided. Here Cydonie was, associated, part of the infrastructure of station life, supported, nurtured, needed, constrained, inspired, and empowered by it; and all she wanted to do was leave. But would she have had the necessary tools to become a spinner otherwise? Not likely. The family mojo behind a spinner had to be pretty solid.

As a house ward, he'd spent a lot of his life feeling like a discarded bit of flawed personhood. He'd just begun to experience belonging, to experiment with trust and a feeling of insiderness, when the accident happened.

He knew his psych. He'd kived plenty of it. But deep structure change, everyone knew, was tricky. Consciously decided shifts of life practice, attitude, expectation, reaction, had to be implemented over time.

In the absence of their actual inner presence and voices, he supplied what his team would say to these thoughts. Nothing so great about being an insider, Sara would snipe. It's yourself you have to live with, from Esker. Darshun: it's okay to feel that, but don't beat up on yourself about it. And Tomas: you need to relax, Jhinsei-gi, ree-lax it; no prosper in being wound so tight against life.

Jhinsei sighed. "I didn't realize you meant to go away for so long. Nothing to stay for, huh?"

Color rose in her cheeks a moment; she didn't reply.

"You will come back?"

"Of course."

The answer, and her certainties, depressed him. For some reason, an image formed in his mind: Sobriance Kohl, captain of the *Oni's Wake*.

As if he'd called her up out of a holo matrix, she said behind him, "Jhinsei." He turned; she was accompanied by the piebald woman, both in their maroon ship jumps. While her crewmember scanned the immediate surroundings, Sobriance Kohl studied him intently, hands clenched together. She was a bit taller than he was. The captain's ruby swinging from one ear looked good against her skin, her dark hair.

Cydonie looked back and forth between them and when Jhinsei didn't volunteer an introduction, stuck her hand out. "Kiyr Cydonie Mehet-Kruez."

The captain took the offered hand. "Captain Sobriance Kohl, *Oni's Wake*." She touched the shoulder of the piebald woman. "Dragon Hidalgo, my cyber-tech. Filling in for spinner, currently, too."

Cydonie nodded to the woman. "I'm doing my upgrades for deep spin runs soon."

Dragon Hidalgo grinned, which made her strange face friendly and oddly attractive. "Spin lucky."

Captain Kohl's gaze slid back to Jhinsei. "Can we talk? There's something important I need to tell you."

He wanted to talk, to know what she had on Tiyo and what Tiyo wanted with him. He followed her to the relative privacy of a small viewing alcove off the main causeway, waited as she chewed her lip, staring out at the brush of distant stars through the deep.

He waited to hear the details she'd omitted earlier. But when she spoke, her voice low and intense, it was just to say, "I think you're at risk here, on-station. I *know* you are. Tiyo's interest in you—no," she said, to his indrawn breath, "I don't know why, exactly, but I do know that the interest isn't friendly. More, we've tracked militant talister activity that could put the station in danger."

Jhinsei blinked. "You've warned the Khat, right? How do you know this, anyway?"

She glanced around before answering. "Kiyr House Authority has been briefed, but declines to take the threat seriously; I know because it's part of my job to know. The Aggregate Control office we work for is . . . obscure, but powerful."

Jhinsei regarded her. "I still don't understand why you even care what happens to me."

She tilted her head back, looking past him. "Jhinsei, I'm being honest with you—and breaking some rules of secrecy to do it. I know you have no reason to trust me, but, talister threats aside, Khat and certain agencies of Tiyo are showing a disturbing interest in you, from what we've been able to gather. Let us get you off-station."

A variety of thoughts and responses contested in his head. "I—drift, I can't deal with this, not right now."

"Jhinsei—"

He shook his head, turned sharply away and escaped back the way they'd come. Passing Cydonie at a fair clip, he said to her, without stopping, "I want that kive cube back when you're done with it," and kept moving.

It was the middle of station night when Mheth decided the thing to do was go and find his brother. Activity on-station was in reality only slightly less than day cycle, with alt-shift station personnel, those who preferred night cycle to day, and ship crews, who all ran on their own cycles.

His brother's quarters on Abaccas deck were empty and he wasn't in the private bar where he usually ate.

Mheth gathered, obliquely, through a conversation with the proprietor of the bar, that Grath had just obtained a new deep-immersion flash kive. Which meant he would probably be in his private suite off Tiyo Studios salon. Mheth considered the irony briefly, leaning in the lift as it sped past decks, then dismissed it, making his way down the corridors of Mignon deck to the Tiyo Studios salon.

Lights on low in the salon, the ambience hinted assignation, mystery. Grath's sleek jo unit patrolled, multiple eyes ticking and looping through data freshets. It ignored Mheth as indisputably Tiyo, as it had earlier, when he'd used the flimsy acquired from Bexi to break into Grath's suite.

Standing at the entry to the suite now, Mheth paused with his palm over the entry request, memories slipping from lost depths. It had been a long time since he'd come to see his brother unsummoned. Once, before Mheth went outsystem, he and Grath had been close. But Grath had changed and Mheth had. When Mheth returned, augmented and at odds with much of his world, he found his feelings were greeted with censure by a Grath grown well into his role as inheritor of Tiyo. All the questioning and exploration of their childhood and young adolescence had been tucked far down and turned in on itself, turned into something twisted behind Grath's smooth, arrogant façade.

Mheth put his palm to the request globe's cool, semi-porous surface. It flexed lightly against his skin, reading chemical signatures, transmitting his presence inside the suite.

Seconds ticked by; the jo unit prowled. Of course his brother wouldn't admit him. He waited anyway.

The door slid open and there Grath stood, ale-pale hair mussed, wearing a supple, full-body leather robe with voluminous, rucked sleeves that ended in tactile-gloves. The gloves dangled loose from the sleeve-ends. The close, detailed rucking was present in other strategic areas. The robe, currently blush-green, was made of bianth leather, grown in vats on Piranesi. It was a highly conductive, reactive material.

Grath also wore an expression Mheth had never seen on his face: satisfaction. His whole bearing smiled with it, though his mouth did not. He stood aside and gestured Mheth in.

Inside, more low lights. The whole scene was making him twitchy and Mheth resisted the urge to trigger his beleaguered chi augments. Grath settled into a deep-immersion kiving sling, where he'd clearly been before admitting Mheth. There was no reason he'd needed to get up to admit Mheth. He'd done it for effect. He waved an arm toward the line of bulbs and bottles that caught the soft scatter of illumination. Mheth walked a half-circle around his brother and turned, ignoring the offer.

"Well, get me something," Grath said, good humor undiminished. "The antuille," he said, watching Mheth for reaction.

The word, like an invocation, stiffened Mheth's spine, but he concealed response, deliberately relaxed into an elegant slouch. He went to the bar and studied the bulbs and bottles. He picked out a slender gold bottle, opened it, the ceraform cork cool and smooth in his fingers. As he poured the antuille into a delicate bulb for his brother, the scent reached out to memories of his time outsystem and drew gentle yearning through him with a shudder. He swallowed down memories and vulnerability together, turned to his brother with an easy, shallow smile, and offered him the bulb.

"You were wanted earlier, Mhethianne. Where were you? I actually sent a few people out searching for you."

Mheth watched his brother sip the antuille. "I've been wondering, Grath, what exactly was the 'disposition' which you made of number 531?"

Grath took another sip, silent. Mheth continued. "And the other anomalous responses, how did you cover those up? Whatever did you put into the reports to Aggregate Oversight? Or the Thorough Order monitors on Ash?" He ran his fingers over Grath's kiving unit. "It incites the synaptics…just why, Grath, is it so important that an alarmingly unsafe new technology be put into spin?"

The smile faded from his brother's bearing, the glow of sex-warmth going chill. "So your delicate sensibilities were actually stirred by your little documentary project. And I thought you were only doing it to get up Father's nose." He tilted the translucent bulb. "I didn't think you'd gotten that deep into things; not all of that information was in your raw data." He shifted, one hand moving in an aborted, frustrated gesture. "Fine, you know. Maybe now you could start to help me cover Tiyo's ass instead of trying to expose us. Somebody has to keep Tiyo safe from Father's," he stopped abruptly, clamping down on whatever he'd been about to say.

Mheth walked a slow circuit of the room. Dark, ilganite paneled walls, lights inset like gems in a deep cave in random-seeming patterns. A wall of Soli masks, lurid colors glittering, intricate images shifting on the surfaces of the grinning faces as Mheth moved. A Quinteppi sculpture of a young man, a little less than life-size, interactively poseable, the skin biomech, softer than the real thing over supple ceraplas musculature.

"How long have you known? Does he keep it in a secret compartment, like an agent in a Chaldinni sleuthing epic?"

"What are you talking about?"

At his brother's tone, irritated and baffled, Mheth looked up.

"Mhethianne, what are you luced on? Do you know how seldom I get to indulge—" Grath stopped, shook his head. The bianth leather streaked to bone white.

Mheth studied him. "You don't know," he said, "do you?"

Grath just looked at him, shook his head again. He got up from the sling and went to pour himself more antuille. "Explain yourself, Mhethianne."

"Have you heard any stories of the birdman of Termagenti?"

Grath's brows rose.

"Or maybe—tell me it's some flash actor you've hired, for some bizarre reason, to do some of Tiyo's ass-covering?"

His brother laughed, sharp and bitter. "Lucky for Tiyo, your sleuthing skills aren't terribly good."

"You don't care, do you?"

"About what, an anomalous one-point-five tester, a backwater planet that Termagenti Station may as well own?"

Mheth scrubbed his hands over his face. He felt like his skin was trying to crawl away. "The Thorough Order might have something to say about it—or the farming collectives."

Grath sipped the antuille. As he regained composure, the jagged white streaks in the suit mellowed to warm cinnamon. "As though you do, Mhethianne—care? Really. Tiyo has been conducting business with more or less the same moral tenor for the length of your life. I do not believe you have suddenly grown—"

"You really don't comprehend me at all, Grath. And I can't believe you don't know." Looking at his brother, however, he did have some doubt. Was it possible? Could he not know that someone was creeping about the guts of Termagenti in a suit of unpredictable materials with a bird mask, looking after Tiyo's interests by destroying evidence of their misconduct? Mheth looked at his brother, rich hair slightly disheveled over pale, high forehead, long fingers caged about the exquisite bulb of expensive drink, waiting to get back to his hurt and fuck kiving.

Something broke in Mheth; he felt it, a quick echoing pain, like a dying tone in the ear. His breath shook, caught on the painful bones of it in his throat.

"I don't know what? You have my attention, Mhethianne. Curiosity piqued; if you don't intend to satisfy my pique, then you may as well leave so I can satisfy it elsewise."

Mheth touched his throat, feeling the heat, palm to skin, the knot of his larynx; finally he swallowed, drew breath.

"Are you going to pass out?" Grath asked in a nearly avid tone. Mheth closed his eyes; he wanted to trigger the chi, but resisted.

Idiocy upon idiocy. He looked at his brother. All Grath was doing was being Grath. Covering for their father's business practices and keeping the family power intact. And finding ways to indulge his own needs—with kives, not people. About what had happened to number 531 and related issues, yes; he knew, but considered it acceptable loss.

Grath said, then, "Would you help me, if I asked you?"

"To cover up public endangerment and murder?"

"To do your duty to House and family."

Mheth opened his mouth, then closed it. He stared at his brother.

Grath raised an eyebrow, then twitched his head in disgust. Acid green streaked into the mellow color of the suit. "As I thought. Are we finished?"

Mheth pushed himself to his feet. "Yes, I suppose we are."

He headed back to Botree deck and his father's quarters. There seemed no other spin, no other set of numbers, only this quest for knowledge he didn't actually want.

Kenit let him in; she was neat but hollow-eyed and had a crease on her face from a wrinkle in her bunk sheets. Clearly woken by his request for entry.

"Athra's bones, Mheth, twice in one set of cycles?" She studied him critically a moment, then shook her head and disappeared into her room, leaving him to the empty main room and the many eyes of his father's globes, the only light in the dimmed space.

He approached the entry to his father's sleeping chamber, stood before it, feeling an unhappy sense of portent, then pressed his palm to the request. The door slid open as, inside, his father granted entry. Heat came round the door edge, a blaze of bright, effulgent light. As it spilled across Mheth's face he flinched back, squinting.

His father's voice came out of the burning. "Get in if you're getting."

One hand shading his eyes, though it hardly helped, Mheth went into the light. He heard and felt the entry slide shut behind him. Stifling heat enveloped him. Eventually, through the brightness, he was able to make out his father—his father's face, eyes closed, above a glittering, faceted suit. In the crook of his arm, resting on a gloved hand, was the golden bird head. The light bounced and ran, heated and rivered the air around the surface of the suit. On a sleek biomech lounger lay the mirror-chipped swath of domino.

The glow came from a bizarre assemblage of multi-spectrum biolumes which had clearly been altered in some way.

With the burning of light around the suit, something else weighed into Mheth. A heaviness, a subtle wrenching that pulled at the properties of space around them. Galvanic tugs at his skin, through his muscles and gut; blinks of vertigo—and a whispering sussurration at the edges of aural sense, not heard, not really, but indisputably there, both distant and right up in the bones of his jaw, the filament of inner ear, a miasmic buzzing.

Eyes still closed, his father said, "Well?"

"You . . . I . . ." Mheth shifted his shoulders, gathered a few of his wits. "Why the bird head?" His hands were trembling and he swallowed hot saliva.

Sarsone drew a deep breath, almost a sigh. He said, "Nourish cycle complete." The biolumes shut down, the punishing glow faded.

Mheth blinked in the sudden dim, after-trails burning in his retinas. With the fading of the light, the strange tugging at his skin and the skips of vertigo also faded.

Sarsone moved out of the circle of biolumes, sat elegantly on the lounger, the bird head mask still perched in the crook of one arm. "It's a phoenix, of course."

"A . . . oh," he said, dredging the relevant ancient mythology out of his brain. "Are you trying to ignite, then?"

"Please, don't be tiresome, Mhethianne. Now you know: I have revealed myself to you. I'm pleased, actually, to be able to share this miraculous thing with my son." He held up a gloved hand, turned it.

"Miraculous," Mheth echoed. "In what way exactly?"

"The lumin allows me freedom of movement—revitalizes my body's damaged nerves—reconnects them, or obviates them," he smiled at his own play on obviaries. "And it is more, much more. It conducts wonders to me. Whole new realms of sense experience."

"I don't understand."

Sarsone smiled benignly and moved his gloved hand, tracing images on the air. "You step into another place, into a deeper set of equations . . . do you know," he drew in a breath, closing his eyes, "I can feel you, the heat signatures of your chi augments, the sweat on your palms, taste the grellwach you drank several hours ago. All your apprehensions, your fear. Your love. I sense it all as though you were a part of my body and being.

"This, this is what must be shared with the rest of Aggregate humanity. In our new lumin kive techology lies the miraculous. Small tastes of what I've found here. Now do you understand why this new technology must be shared? It is no danger—"

"But the tests—number 531—and—"

"Statistical anomalies, those few; defectives, that this wonder should affect them so. If we are to evolve, Mhethianne, then the recessives will have to be filtered out."

Mheth blinked at his father; he felt for a moment as though the station shifted off its axis, gravity offline. Things drifted, then resettled, askew.

His father was insane.

Not just cold and unrepentantly exploitative where once he'd been warm and brilliantly successful, but mad. Cracked. The most powerful man on Termagenti was a headcase.

The whispering susurration pressed on Mheth's senses. Screaming. That's what it seemed like. A muffled, but horrible, tortured screaming. The lumin was screaming. Couldn't his father hear and feel that? He looked at his father's face. Apparently not. Or maybe that's what had turned him into a headcase.

"I'll have a suit made for you."

"That's...generous. But I came to tell you, I'm thinking of taking a spin, to Megrant, or Samdjadsit Station; I've always wanted to see it, the Coreyal Sea. A little hejira."

"No."

"No?" Mheth started to say something, stopped.

His father watched him through half-lowered lids, still benign. "My dear Mhethianne, this is too important. I can't have you darting off about the Aggregate upsetting officialdom and such with your misguided concern for a few anomalous defectives. No. I've already seen to it, as soon as you began your little between-decks investigations. You'll find it quite impossible to get passage on anything in the ship bays."

As that settled into his brain, Mheth had a brief, terrible thought. "...My—Kynan? Is Kynan alive?"

"Yes, yes. Don't worry. Really, Mhethianne." As if Mheth's concerns were unsuitable. He didn't move, only sat, upright, the phoenix mask in his arm like a ceremonial icon.

Mheth backed a step. "Can't you hear it screaming?"

Sarsone frowned. Annoyance, sadness, shaded his expression. "Don't tell me my son is defective, Mhethianne."

❋

Jhinsei tramped the length of Semiramnis on a steam of anger. The captain of the *Oni's Wake* wasn't really the cause of it, but she'd managed to focus all the unfocused loss, confusion, and fear churning inside him nicely. He barked a deck name at the lift and found himself on Phyndarial in the arboretum. He fetched up under a Brody elm, leaned his back against its rough, solid trunk and looked up into red and silver-gray leaves. Filtered collector light, heavily bounced and re-bounced, clung to the edges of things, a pearled and fulgent glow. Scents of soil, dusty leaf debris, and recycled air.

"I should have just punched her out, I'm sure I'd feel much better," he muttered, mouth twisting. What was she about anyway, trying to scare him? What did the woman want of him?

"Talking to yourself, Jhinsei?" Cydonie approached from the other direction.

"I'm a headcase, remember? What are you doing here, anyway?" Jhinsei flung a hand out, a gesture to the depth and breadth of the arboretum and station beyond.

Cydonie shook her head. "I followed you, idiot."

After a moment Jhinsei dropped his head back against the tree, then pushed away from the trunk. He and Cydonie fell into step, walking deeper into the arboretum's towering tree mass.

"So?"

She tucked hands in pockets, shrugged. Then she said, "I just wanted to make sure you were okay."

Jhinsei laughed. "I'm just great."

"Yeah." She snorted. But she didn't press, just walked with him.

Jhinsei's thoughts skittered about. The rider. A threat to station. Secrets—his, other people's. Essca. Ro Mehet. Someone in a bird mask. Tiyo and Kiyr and a derelict alien hulk.

The path wove through a grove of jali trees, thin bent brown branches and pale yellow seed pods flourishing under the gathered light of the solar collectors. Pebbled shadows covered the ground and patterned the air. Bell-shaped yellow pods skithered in the wind programmed into the atmos. A small flight of finger-sized grey birds lifted from the upper branches, looping up in fluid formation, stirring the air with wings and cooing.

"Jhinsei?"

He blinked and looked down, finding Cydonie several steps ahead, looking back at him. He realized he'd stopped, watching the birds, his whole body straining towards them in rapt transport. The rider's.

He made an inarticulate noise and scrubbed his hands over his face.

"What is it? Tell me what's going on with you."

He gnawed at his lower lip, stared up into the collector-lit distance. "I don't know if I could explain it, given eternity to talk and all the language in the universe."

"Try."

Closing his eyes, he saw bird trails and felt the rider's euphoria in his bones. Eventually, haltingly, he began to tell her. They walked through the jali grove and came to a small meadow. Long, salt-pale grasses feathered in the artificial breeze. Beyond this the woods trailed off into small clumps amid rolling park. At theoretical distance a mountain rose, holo vista over real flora. The perspective was an acclimatization tool for Termagentis preparing to go wellside.

Other people dotted the landscape, alone, in pairs, and a few groups of children with jo units.

Jhinsei trailed off, glancing at Cydonie anxiously. She had yet to say a word. Something like despair washed through Jhinsei; he swayed and sank slowly to sit in order to avoid falling. The grass prickled coolly against his skin, whispered in the breeze around him. Fresh, sap scent; the rider lifted, thrilled, and his own exhausted gloom fizzed off in a frisson of joy.

It was making him dizzy; the more buoyant the rider, the lower he seemed to drop each time it receded and he found himself again, a vessel in space, farther and farther adrift, drained of motive force.

Cydonie dropped down beside him and stared toward the holo mountain. She picked at the grass. Jhinsei thought back over his stumbling recitation and shook his head. A warm grip on his knee pulled his focus back to Cydonie.

"Just processing." She released him and wrapped arms around her knees. "What's it…I mean, are you aware of—?" She gestured, a vague wave of the hand to her own body and head.

Jhinsei ran his palm over the prickling grass. "Sometimes it's all I'm aware of. Then it's just me, until some other wonder, like," he picked a blade of grass, held it up, "or bits of the architecture, someone's bone structure. There's no telling." He stared at the mountain vista until it blurred. "Drift, what am I going to do?" He dropped his head into his hands, over the hollow in his gut and the fear in his bones.

"Jhinsei, have you eaten recently?"

He had to think about it a moment, then shook his head.

"Hungry?"

He was, he realized. Maybe that was the gnawing in his gut.

"Let's go eat. Chath's? I could go for a pile of khet with hot chutney. And a few bottles of something cold and lucing."

"Khet's an outsystem gravity well import, it's expensive."

Cydonie gripped his arm. "Don't worry it, headcase, I'm buying."

They left the arboretum, catching the lift from Phyndarial to Nicodemus deck and heading for bayside, to Chath's, outsystemer-run and out of the way. As the savory, rich aroma of khet reached Jhinsei, his mouth watered. He hadn't realized how hungry he was. Before, when he'd forgotten to eat, Darshun or Esker had spoken acerbic remonstrance in his head. Before that, they'd said the words, when once they were living beings.

Now he had the rider, who lifted to the scents, curious and eager.

Foot traffic and ship bay transports traversed the wide periphery of the bayside arc. A mosaic of color and motion took them in, amongst ship folk from across the Aggregate worlds. A tight knot of Sinaiety members drew more attention than anything else. The Sinaiety were Palogenia System's very own talisters, split off long ago in isolationist fervor down on Ash, during the settlement of the system. Their beliefs were somewhat opaque to Jhinsei; he only knew they disapproved of humanity's failure to evolve in some way, and kept themselves to themselves while sending small groups of representatives to mingle with the corrupt rest of humanity and see to Sinaiety interests in the wider world. This group wore hooded cloaks in muted colors off which the light sheened, a fabric that was probably sensitive to its wearer's core temperature. Woven into the robes were intricate patterns of metallic bits that caught and turned the light. They walked in close formation, expressions forbidding approach or contact. Anyone Termagenti-raised knew enough to leave Sinaiety alone, but Jhinsei wondered how they kept curious outsystemers from crossing their taboo line and talking to them. It was unusual for them to be up on station and off of Ash at all.

Between the group of Sinaiety and the flow of outsystem activity, Jhinsei felt anonymous, which was its own form of relief. A part of him knew the anonymity was an illusion. For the sake of food and some sense of normalcy, he accepted the illusion and tried to ignore the rider. He wondered if he'd get better at it with practice—or if the rider would grow stronger and he'd disappear altogether.

They found a standing table and keyed in orders. Jhinsei leaned his elbows on the table, scanning the other patrons. Cydonie had talked inanities all the way here and was now silent; Jhinsei knew she was overwhelmed and unsure what her reaction should be. Believing him, he thought, would be hard.

The Sinaiety had followed them in, congregating closely around one small table. He thought about the Sinaiety, then, recalling something Esker had once said, about close links between the reclusive Ash sect and House Tiyo. House Tiyo and the Sinaiety, Ash and bad beta tests of lumin kive cubes, covered up. Cydonie's beta tester friend. Lumin . . . the derelict and what had happened to him on it . . .

What was the connection between all these elements? He studied the group of Sinaiety a moment more, then let it go. It was too vague. He put it down to his general state of over-stimulated, underfed anxiety and abandoned thought as their food arrived, a large steaming pyramid of khet, the river crustaceans' shells boiled bright blue, several bowls of spicy chutneys, and two sweating cold bulbs of dark, sweet ale.

❖

In the cross-hatched shadows on the grid above Revelation deck, Mheth leaned against a strut, his thoughts spiraling around like doyenne moths over a shaft of light. Doyennes were silvery blue moths that bred in untended conduits and fed on the dust of biomatter. Called doyenne because that was the name of the ship on which the moths first appeared, larval riders in some well cargo.

He'd settled on the simplest course of action. Run away. Simple, craven, textkive Tiyo Mhethianne Tiyo, despite the juice at his disposal, connections, endless options.

Perhaps his father's obviary was right; he was an imbecilic ass. Surely he could do something. Of all people, he was in a position to . . . to what? Get his father some help, psych-mod, adjustment. And why not his brother, too, while he was at it? And himself, as well. They were clearly all in need of it.

Why else, really, had he been helping Kynan with his documentary? Expose the nasty, the sick parts, call down the searing laser scalpel of Aggregate Oversight, cleanse the house, the blood, and body that were Tiyo.

"Impasse and muddle, good my celestial friends," Mheth whispered. It was a line from Hanumar's soliloquy in *The Lament of Three Planets*. That had been a good flash kive, droll and full of unemphatic meaning. Years ago now, that they'd made that flash, when Mheth had been story coordinator for only a short while, after coming back to Termagenti from outsystem.

Soft footfalls sounded on the grid steps. Mheth glanced down through the grid at the tech sitting monitors. She didn't glance up; one hand on the globe, she leaned on the other, dozing or gazing out at the views, Mheth couldn't tell which.

His friend Asia appeared above, dark head bent as he passed through shadows and light.

⁂

Jhinsei drank from his third bulb of ale. The rider, more involved in the experience of food and drink than Jhinsei was—and he was pretty involved in it—was currently manageable. The decision now was whether getting totally luced would be a good or a bad idea. Actually, the question might be whether it was possible. Three ales and he didn't feel them at all. He felt pleasantly full of khet and hot chutney. He had to piss; but the warm dissipation of sharp edges, the filling in of anxious, hollow places with alcoholic glow, not at all. He felt better for the food, but more or less exactly the same otherwise. *Your blood chemistry is changing.* Perhaps the alcohol couldn't touch the alterations to his body chem which had already been affected.

An edge of raw panic crested through him. With a shaking hand he set down the bulb.

Cydonie looked at him. "What?"

"What do you think . . ." The words dried up in his mouth.

Tiyo Ro Mehet stood in the eatery's entrance with two Khat officers flanking him. One of the Khat officers was a cyber-relay. The clientele, mostly outsystemers with no idea who Ro was, ignored him, though there was some shifting in response to the Khat uniforms and holstered stinger weapons.

Then Jhinsei saw that just behind Ro stood Essca. She looked at Jhinsei, her face hard and closed. She touched her uncle's shoulder and pointed. Ro's gaze followed her gesture and came to rest on Jhinsei with a finality he felt down to his bones.

Chath's wasn't very big. Essca, Ro, and the Khat were upon Jhinsei before he did more than blink.

"Kiyr Jhinsei," Ro said, quietly, only to him, "you are hereby quarantined under the Bromah Dictate. You will accompany us, please."

The blood drained from Jhinsei's face. He blinked at Ro, in whose hard, bland expression no trace of the affable uncle remained. He couldn't bring himself to look at Essca, felt everything going distant, strange.

"The Bromah—" Cydonie said. "But that's—" She laughed. "That's ridiculous. He's no more an alien than you are, Ro."

"Cydonie," Ro said, barely glancing at her, but his mouth thinning, clearly not pleased at her presence, "your objection is noted. If you wish to kive a formal protest on Kiyr Jhinsei's behalf, you may do so."

Jhinsei leaned on the table. "It's all right, Cydonie..." He tried to think what else to say, but then Cydonie was speaking harshly to Essca.

"This it, Ess, consolidating your power? Is this the last hoop?"

"Don't," Jhinsei said, his voice coming out strained and rough. "Cyd—don't."

"Essca is merely doing her duty to House and station," Ro said. He met Jhinsei's look, his own expressionless—except for the slightest hint of something smug. Essca's ice-blond hair caught the light and Jhinsei dropped his eyes before he had to see her face again.

He couldn't seem to catch his breath, or hold a thought.

"Athra's shit, Ro. Essca," Cydonie said, low and angry. "You're bastards."

After a moment Jhinsei moved to join Ro and the Khat officers. His limbs felt animated by water—or something even thinner, air and promises. He felt the focus of everyone in Chath's. He didn't look at Essca; couldn't. "Let's go then," he said, wanting to get out of the eatery, wanting to move, and lacking any other graspable motivation at that moment.

"Jhinsei," Cydonie said, stepping towards them.

A new voice interrupted. "Isn't the Bromah Dictate more the province of station's head obviary? It's to be administered only at the discretion of qualified Thorough Order of Physic Arts personnel." Antoine la Savre, the tall bearded member of the ***Oni's Wake*** crew, Sobriance Kohl's's crew, appeared seemingly from nowhere. He looked down at Ro wearing an expression that matched his reasonable tone.

"Senior Obviary Evans," Ro said, just as reasonable, "withheld report of information and is suspect as compromised by possible alien presence."

"No!" Jhinsei burst out. "Ramev was just waiting to gather more data, he was going to report it, he told me he would. I'm not—for drift sake, this is ridiculous!"

"That is to be determined under observation," Ro said.

"I'll get you an advocate," Cydonie said tightly, still glaring at Essca, who had yet to speak.

"No," Ro said. "The Bromah Dictate precludes advocacy."

"Bromah Dictate be singularized," Cydonie said. "The damn thing was kived over four hundred years ago."

"Aren't you rather exceeding your authority as House Tiyo adjunct to Kiyr House Authority?" la Savre asked, still reasonable.

Ro acknowledged him more fully. Something like a smile curled his mouth. "Because Tiyo retains ownership of the derelict vessel from which this phenomenon is suspected to have originated, Tiyo also retains responsibility for any contaminants that it carries. We take that responsibility seriously."

Cydonie gave a breath of a laugh. "Right."

Then they were moving, Jhinsei between the two Khat officers, Ro and Essca before them. He saw as they turned out of Chath's that Cydonie and la Savre were staying with them.

Suddenly Sobriance Kohl and her short, piebald-skinned crew member Dragon Hidalgo were there, too. They got right in Ro's way, forcing the party to come to a halt.

"Remove yourselves," Ro said.

To either side of Jhinsei, the Khat officers' hands went to weapons. Jhinsei's gaze fixed on Sobriance Kohl's face. Things she'd said earlier made more sense. The look she gave Jhinsei had a kind of calm solidity and competence that carried a promise—one that felt like more than air. Something in it fortified him, gave him a sliver of grounding.

"You can't invoke the Bromah Dictate without bringing the attention of Aggregate Control," Sobriance Kohl said. She held Ro's gaze. "Are you sure you want to do that?"

"And you are?" Ro was beginning to sound testy.

"Sobriance Kohl, captain, *Oni's Wake*."

"Ah." Ro waved a hand to the Khat, who subsided fractionally, stingers settling back into holsters. "The Termagenti office of Aggregate Control is on Semiramnis deck. You're welcome to lodge any concerns with them."

"Kiyr Jhinsei recently accepted a post on my ship." Captain Kohl lied with authority and ease. "By spacer law, as a member of my crew he has full rights to all resources of reply and defense—rights which cancel the Bromah Dictate's preclusion of advocacy of council."

A member of my crew. The words, lie though they were, caught Jhinsei hard.

"Kiyr Jhinsei," Ro Mehet said, "is a member of House Kiyr and a naturalized resident of Termagenti Station. This is station business. You may take your concerns up with the outsystem liaison office or—what office of Aggregate Control did you say you were with? Take it there. For now, you will clear the way." He gestured to the Khat again and the weapons cleared holsters this time. Regulation Khat stingers weren't lethal, but they would knock a person on their ass and out of commission for hours.

Sobriance's gaze shifted past Ro to Jhinsei. She seemed to be trying to communicate something. Then she nodded to Dragon and they stepped aside. One of the Khat officers jostled Jhinsei into motion again. He lost sight of Sobriance and her crew, and of Cydonie, glimpsing Essca every other step as a gleam of silver-gilt hair in his peripheral vision.

He could smell his own sweat; see the pores and individual hairs on the back of Ro's neck above his collar. It felt like roots had suddenly grown in his ears, sounds booming at a distance. His heart thumped laboriously, the space between each beat a long void. His legs moved more and more slowly, heavy and too light at the same time. The tastes of honey and fear pooled in his mouth.

He thought it was somehow a part of this personal perceptual malaise when the lab-grown biolumes all along the corridor, that augmented the collector light, began to sink to bruised dimness one after another as some sickness branched through them rapidly. Collector light in this section of the station arc was insufficient and in moments everything fell into dusk and shadow around them.

Traffic fell still for a breath; the Khat officer who was a cyber-relay paused with hand to ear. He said, "Systems failure originating in medlab, some kind of sabotage, they're saying; causing a ripple failure through station—" and a deep, deafening alarm sounded, overriding his words.

Outsystemers began running for their ship bays, yelling over the pulsing of the alarm. Ro grabbed Jhinsei by the arm, a hard grip. The Khat officers closed ranks to either side.

"Come on," Ro shouted; Jhinsei only heard him because he was so close.

Someone barreled into them from behind. One of the officers was pushed into Jhinsei at the same moment a transport brushed close on one side, clipping the other Khat officer, who stepped hard into Ro. Jostled and pushed from several directions, Jhinsei landed on his side, hip and elbow jarring into the deck. Bodies passed over him, someone tripped over his legs.

He tried to crawl out from under the tangle. A hand grabbed his arm from above and pulled. Thinking it was Ro, he struggled.

Then he looked up into the piebald face of Dragon Hidalgo. He grabbed her hand and let her tow him up, then away, into a headlong run. He heard Ro's voice as he followed Dragon, then nothing but the booming alarm. They dodged outsystem crew, another transport, station ops techs. He barely registered anything as they wove through a tangle of traffic and stopped against the corridor wall near an access hatch. Dragon paused, scanning, her expression inward on the information she was getting from her cyber-relays. Jhinsei pushed aside a momentary, overwhelming memory of Sara and touched her arm.

"This way," he said, taking the lead. Through the hatch, then down, into the interstitial grid space between decks. The alarm, shouting, and tromping of feet were muted. Their breath sounded loud. After five minutes of clambering up several grid ladders, over cold, metal-slatted walkways, then down another set of ladders, they came to a pocket alcove and Jhinsei stopped, leaning back. Then he slid down to a crouch.

He looked at Dragon. "Thank you."

She examined the area, then him. "What are you going to do?"

"I don't know." He rubbed his palms on his thighs, pushed his hair off his face.

"Is there some way you can get off-station?"

Off-station. Jhinsei blinked at her. Of course. "What about with . . ."

Dragon shook her head. "We'd meant to leave here with you—if you'd elected to come," she said. "But now, given the connection, they're certain to insist on thorough ship-check when we leave. Also, now that the sabotage we were meant to prevent has happened—we have work to do. Our boss isn't very forgiving." She shrugged. "Any other ideas?"

He shrugged off various emotions with a deep breath, focused. Off-station. "There's the automated shuttles," he said. "On Revelation deck."

"That means the shuttles between here and Ash?" At his nod, she went momentarily into infofugue, then came out and nodded. "You can work the clearances?"

"I think so."

"What happens when you get to Ash?"

"I don't know." The weight of it all—Ro, Essca, the possible truth of Ro's accusations; the empty echo where Esker, Darshun, Sara, and Tomas had been—threatened to sink him. He drew a breath. "I'm hella fucked."

"Pretty much," Dragon said. "But House Tiyo and Khat authority don't extend down to Ash, right? And once the *Oni*'s free to leave station, we can come down and collect you." She paused. "If you want that."

He didn't answer her, because he didn't know. Instead he asked, "Won't you get pulled in for helping me get away?"

She shrugged. "In the confusion, I doubt anyone has a clear idea what happened. But even if they do peg me, Sobriance is working on a bit of legal, to haze things up enough to make it unlikely they'd pursue it."

He thought about it. "You said—sabotage?"

"Yes." She shook her head.

"It may have been the station . . . phenomenon."

"No." Dragon looked down at him, then lowered herself to sit cross-legged beside him. "It was sabotage, aimed at the Thorough Order, via medlab. It's been happening all over the Aggregate. We were sent to investigate." She said it in such a way as to tell Jhinsei it wasn't an employment with which she was particularly pleased. "Now we've mucked it up and there's cleanup to do. We can't just leave." She studied him a moment. "You look like fried shit, kid."

"Sounds about right."

She traced two fingers over the patterns on her face. "This Bromah Dictate flap, it's just an excuse, right? To pull you in? They want something from you?"

Jhinsei met her gaze. After a moment he said, "I don't know. I've had—something's going on. My—I've had a lot of—contact—with the phenomenon. I'm." He dropped his gaze. "Something's happening in my—" He swallowed and closed his eyes, trying to follow one thread of words to their end. "I'm still me." Eyes still closed, he whispered it to himself again. He opened his eyes and said slowly, "And Tiyo does want something. They're not afraid of alien contamination. Not the way they gutted and—cannibalized—that ship to make it into a kive technology that they've already shipped down to beta market on Ash. When they could see—they must have been able to see . . . " He shook his head again.

"Oh yeah, that's some attention span."

"That ship, the derelict, it was—is...was—I don't know—alive. And very . . . It's sentient."

She met his gaze. "From what I've accessed of station mind and kive files, I'm inclined to believe you. But that's not our problem right now. Yours is to get off-station, and ours is to deal with the fallout of the sabotage situation and try to salvage some information from it, at least. There's a good possibility our investigation will take us down to Ash, though. Can you remember a contact code if I give it to you?"

Jhinsei nodded.

She told him the code. "So you can link to us privately if you need us. Now, what do we need to do to get you on one of those shuttles?"

Shuttle

THE LAST THING JHINSEI EXPECTED WAS ANOTHER STOWAWAY ON the *Rainsquall*. That this other stowaway should be Tiyo Mhethianne Tiyo—the face and slouching arrogance unmistakable—rattled him badly. He watched the Tiyo from across the small space of the shuttle's confines while they waited for departure.

For his part, the Tiyo eyed him once, brows raised, said in a half-asleep voice, "I had no idea this was a popular mode of travel," closed his eyes and leaned back. His legs stretched across all there was of deck space.

Jhinsei made himself smaller as his thoughts grew paranoid and panicked. It was a trap; the Tiyo was there to tag him. Watch him. Down on Ash he'd be seized by other Tiyo agents and locked away.

The lights of the *Rainsquall*'s boards flashed and patterned through ship checks, as directed by the ops tech sitting monitors on Revelation deck. The hum of power engaged, vibration a low note through Jhinsei's bones. His thoughts raced in an ever tighter circle. He stared at the cargo-wide entry hatch, eyed the Tiyo again. This was a mistake. He had to do something else. He had to get off the shuttle. Now.

He dove for the hatch, palmed the exit pad; the long door slid open. Cold air wafted through the hatch from Revelation. A warning sirened silently above the hatch. Jhinsei took a step.

An arm caught him around the chest, a foot hooking one of his knees, the man who a moment ago had been indolently sprawled and seemingly asleep caught him, tripped him, and drove him back into a sling with trained efficiency. Jhinsei blinked up, seeing the door slide back shut, hearing the hum change as the *Rainsquall* shifted in preparation for detach.

He struggled to fling free of the Tiyo's hold as the Tiyo struggled to hold him there, both of them near silent but for grunting and huffing. Jhinsei heaved and twisted, but the Tiyo held him down, one arm across Jhinsei's chest, the weight of his body trapping one of Jhinsei's arms. The Tiyo held his other arm with a grip on Jhinsei's wrist that felt likely to crush tendon. The man leaned close, sitting on Jhinsei, his own desperate intensity the equal of Jhinsei's, his training, weight, and strength superior.

"I'm sorry," the Tiyo said, staring into Jhinsei's eyes. "I truly am. Entitled to second thoughts and all that. But if you draw attention to us now, you void my opportunity and I can't let you do that." The crush of his grip never changed as he spoke or as the *Rainsquall* disengaged, maneuvered, and passed out of station shadow.

Jhinsei twisted, the man's weight on his chest making him gasp. The world narrowed to the closeness of their breathing as they struggled, Jhinsei trying to fling the Tiyo off, the Tiyo shifting as Jhinsei shifted, holding him fast with the hum of the shuttle, the mutter and beep of shuttle system to itself and station mind as background noise.

Once, the Tiyo said, softly, "Don't look back."

As the shuttle approached orbit field terminus, Jhinsei made himself relax, his muscles go slack. He drew in a slow, even breath, held it for three counts, closed his eyes, then shouted, butted his head up into the Tiyo's face, and flung upwards. Finding himself free and crouched on deck, he dove for the shuttle's control boards.

A grip came down on the back of his neck, fingers like pincers. A sliver of something colder than ice bit into his neck. Freezing touch, up into his brain, then down into his body, sting of it in his nose. He focused on the slowly blinking lights of the board and tried to keep moving. But the lights seemed further, not nearer. The air opened up into warp and wave. Jhinsei turned slowly, falling. The man rose above him. The air opened further and darkness rolled out of its seams, reverse vacuum. There was too much, too much of everything, the universe flooding slowly, so slowly, into the tiny space of the shuttle, squeezing him out of existence. There was only the flood of air and the darkness.

Jhinsei came to in the sling, vibrating gently with the *Rainsquall's* hum. His limbs were chilled, like things left out in the black of space, his chest and neck ached. His mouth was dry, lips unable to move, eyes tearing even in the low light of the shuttle's tiny cabin. He blinked and the tears trailed down his face. After a moment he tongued some of the salty moisture off his lips, to moisten his dry mouth.

The Tiyo lounged in the position in which Jhinsei had first seen him. He had a little frown on his face and stared at the globe which relayed images of their fore and aft passage.

In the small space he was close enough that Jhinsei could have touched him easily, if Jhinsei could have moved. The heavy chill in his limbs told him that soon his body would be all ache as things came back to life.

He closed his eyes a moment and, in the way of testing for a sore tooth, looked for the presence of the rider. It was there, quiet. He thought of a small creature sheltering in a corner when the environment went haywire—Jhinsei being the environment.

He opened his eyes again and looked at the globe, felt the steady hum of the shuttle. They were fully en route, long gone from station. From help, from harm.

From everyone and everything Jhinsei had ever known.

He must have made a sound. The Tiyo shifted to lean forward, elbows on knees, studying him.

The other man was ten, maybe fifteen years older than Jhinsei. A thin face, mobile, sculpted lips and brows. Dark gold hair, eyes soft blue.

With an easy move, the Tiyo shifted to the sling beside Jhinsei, set them both rocking a moment.

"I'm sorry," he said. "But I really did have to leave, and if you'd gotten us discovered—" He gestured.

Jhinsei made a sound and shifted. Pain sang slowly through him. He stared up into the dim of the cargo-crowded shuttle. It hurtled on full auto through Palogenia System, along a set course, a much-traveled route that left no discernible impression whatsoever on the universe.

Beside him in the other sling, the Tiyo shifted and Jhinsei's sling echoed the movement. A strand of his hair slid, caught in his eyelashes. He tried to lift a hand, but it was heavy, and pain coursed like a thousand stitches, lacing him through and through. He forgot everything momentarily, where he was, who, gasping at the intensity of it.

A hand moved the hair out of his eye, a face leaned over his. The long fingers of the hand still lay against his face, gently. The hand stroked back into his hair several times.

"I didn't want to use the icepick, truly. Its after-effects are especially unkind. But you would persist." The blue eyes did look repentant, the thin face unhappy. "I'm sorry," he said again. The stroking fingers touched Jhinsei's lips. The Tiyo disappeared for a moment; Jhinsei heard a rustling, shuffling, then the man was back. He lifted Jhinsei's head and put a bulb to his lips. Water, cool, flat. Jhinsei swallowed several mouthfuls. The bulb was removed.

"My name is Mheth."

*

The trip between Termagenti Station and the planet Ash was six cycles for an automated shuttle. It was clear that the small space would have been too small for Mheth even if he were alone. That first cycle, as the pain slowly went out of Jhinsei, he watched Mheth—Tiyo Mhethianne Tiyo, he didn't forget that—pace from cargo stack to entry hatch, to system boards and back. Watched as he slumped long-legged in a sling, flung himself up again, paced, flung himself back down.

Jhinsei rested and watched, keeping his thoughts from settling anywhere. Not on his lost-anew team, the rider, Essca, or Ramev and what would come to him of all this.

Instead, he thought about the planet Ash. A gravity well. Another place entirely from the one he'd known all his life. He thought about Ash, everything he knew about it. All the things he'd kived on the push of Esker's interest, which had lived in him.

Humans had been messing with Ash for generations, planet shaping, land reclamation, deep seeding. Three regions of the planet were inhabited; those areas constituted only a small percentage of the planet's overall land mass, which was separated into three parts by an ocean and a high desert mountain range. The central region was given over to farms and ranches growing and raising speciations of ancient agricultures. Then there were the lands, farms, schools, retreats and centers belonging to the Thorough Order of Physic Arts, the planet's only real juice.

Jhinsei thought of the obviary he'd met on station lift, on her way to consult with Tiyo. Zhou, who had studied with Ramev. Ramev was from Ash originally, he remembered. Had he left family there?

Other bits of kived knowledge bobbed to the surface of his thoughts. In the central region the light of Palogenia fell silvery-green across the farming plains and river deltas. Ash had three seasons, called Reave, Sow, and Trouble. It rained for most of Sow, all of Trouble, and parts of Reave. They were still finding new life forms in the edge regions and in the waters—vast ocean, rivers, inland lakes.

Dragon Hidalgo had given Jhinsei a small supply of Aggregate scrip; his own station credit was inaccessible to him. He'd come with nothing; he had nothing. No home, no work or position, no inner collection of ghosts. The contents of the shelf above his bunk in his quarters on Faust were the only possessions he regretted. And Sara's ragged thermal jacket with the batti patch. It got cold on Ash, so the kive cubes said. And . . .

Essca.

Jhinsei made a small sound and shifted restively. Essca was a thought that didn't bear weight; spiny and spiked, it stabbed back at the least pressure of notice.

"Are you in pain?" the Tiyo inquired.

Jhinsei shook his head.

"Speak, for Athra's sweet sake. I'm so tired of the inside of my own head."

Jhinsei considered the Tiyo. Suspecting he wouldn't answer, he asked anyway: "Why are you here?"

Mheth smiled. "Ah, it has teeth."

"Kiyr Jhinsei."

"No association?"

Jhinsei just stared at him, which seemed to amuse the Tiyo, who continued, answering his own question. "No blood association, then. House Kiyr, one Jhinsei; not a Termagenti name. It's a neomythic catholicist name, isn't it? None of those insystem. Foundling orphan?"

Jhinsei thought of Esker, Darshun, Sara, and Tomas. "That's me."

The Tiyo studied him inquisitively. "An interesting story?"

Jhinsei shifted, leaned his head back. He ignored the question and repeated his own. "So why are you here?"

"Oh, just a little vacation to Ash. Inspect the local watering holes, maybe indulge in a bit of a well-side fling."

"I think," Jhinsei said, "that the Termagenti-Ash Passenger Line offers tours. And meet-and-greets at all the best spas on Ash."

Mheth nodded. "Actual berths, private quarters, all of that, no doubt."

"No doubt."

Silence fell, and Jhinsei felt himself sinking back to sleep. He roused at the sound of the Tiyo on his feet, pacing the small space.

"I'm running away, really," Mheth said. He wasn't looking at Jhinsei, his voice quiet and serious, inward. "I poked at the undersides of things…and can't stomach what I found." The Tiyo scrubbed his hands over his face, back through his hair. "I love my father, you know. But he's . . . drift, Father, what happened? Was it," his voice dropped, ". . . was it my fault?"

He looked at Jhinsei suddenly, one hand over his mouth, and then just as quickly looked away again, continued pacing.

"I'm running away, too," Jhinsei offered into the silence that hung in the wake of the Tiyo's words.

They regarded each other. Jhinsei cast about for something else to say. The Tiyo flung himself back into a sling.

"This is so much more real," he said after another silence, with a gesture to the shuttle's cramped interior, "don't you think? Authentic," Mheth said, rolling the word in his mouth. "Much better than a passenger line tour."

"Authentic." Jhinsei let his eyes close, a slow wave of exhaustion, sluggish velvet tide, pulling through him. "Yes, I see what you mean," he murmured. "Passenger transports are for wimps."

"Spineless juiced-up wimps," Mheth said.

"Exactly." Jhinsei found himself thinking about his mother, for the first time in a long time. His mother who'd left him on station like an inconvenient parcel—his mother, who had come from off-station, somewhere, as Jhinsei was now, for the first time in his memory. He sank below the tide of icepick-induced exhaustion a moment, resurfaced, some words in his mouth—you know Termagenti's haunt? It's here, inside me, I'm haunted—that he never managed to say as he sank once more.

❋

Mheth watched his traveling companion fall into sleep like a pebble into heavy gee. He was not surprised. The icepick packed a lot of nasty. He'd been saving it for the possibility of a more threatening sort of adversary—but nothing generally went as planned, did it?

His own thoughts were without order, a packet of over-excited molecules. Focusing on another being, engaging another mind, that stilled the twitchiness somewhat, and began to settle things into a familiar order. And now the other had removed his mind to the inaccessible reaches of slumber.

"'He sleeps, great Mother, he sleeps and all the Earths sleep with him.'" He quoted the words aloud, to fill the humming silence, the next moment flung up and paced, to keep himself from grabbing the Jhinsei person and either shaking him awake or squeezing him like the nubby-furred, bio-form kirrikian-beast he'd had as a very small Mheth.

Thinking of the kirrikian-beast made him think of his father, a water-clear flake of memory, Sarsone saying dryly, "Ridiculous attachment." Yet who had given him the toy, if not his father? He couldn't remember. Had it been one of his minders, a tutor, his mother before she disappeared from their lives?

Nudged by these thoughts, the image of a golden phoenix mask rose before his mind's eye. He stood still in the middle of the shuttle's thrumming, claustrophobic shell and stared unseeing at a stack of ceraplas crates until they blurred. Tears stung and flowed, but they may as well have been someone else's; he didn't know what he felt.

He knelt by Kiyr Jhinsei-no-association in the sling. Watched him sleep. It came to him, then, that he'd seen this person sleeping before, on one of his father's monitors.

Strange.

Mheth frowned. What was the Jhinsei person doing here, then? Running away, he said, like Mheth. From what? He studied the Kiyr; he was the only item of distraction about. Attractive, at least. Currently all warm and pliant, limbs in abandonment. Dark hair, lips parted over dreaming breath, angled architecture of bones. Not very tall; a nice package taken altogether, though.

Bexi had been right, of course, he preferred the jimmies somewhat over the annies. And sex was his preferred method of avoiding unhappy thought. He wasn't sure Jhinsei would be terribly amenable, though.

Mheth propped chin in hand, considering.

There was a whole new planet, all of Ash—which was a joke, of course. Barely settled but for the Thorough Order colleges and retreats, the rest of the planet was farms, mines, and the Sinaiety's outré tribal enclaves. The spas Jhinsei had referred to were mere volcanic piss holes. No civilized life; it was all well-grubbers at subsistence level. But the Thorough Order colleges would be tolerable. Just. Except for the self-righteous perfection of all those obviaries-in-training. Hundreds of Kenits who would tsk and find him pitiful, just as his father's obviary did.

The Thorough Order of Physic Arts, though, also possessed their own deep space port, for the ferrying-in of students from thither and yon in the Aggregate, and later deployment of new-made obviaries. He'd be able to find passage away from Termagenti, out of Palogenia System.

Mheth heard a strange, gasping sound and put his hands over his mouth to stop it. Sweat prickled along his sides.

His father's obviary Kenit would say he was having a breakdown.

The glittering-eyed bird mask floated above Jhinsei, tilted slightly to inspect him. They hung together, him and the birdman, in the weightless drift of an abandoned, broken Revelation deck.

The giant spangles of collector reflections slid through floating wreckage, across dark blue console, ragged sections of grid, whole struts of the grid arch, and the melted slag of the work globe. An empty tube diving suit brushed across his arm, cracked faceplate flashing through the collector reflections as it tumbled in a slow dance. Heavy limbs, the helpless struggle of nightmare.

The birdman put a gloved hand on his chest and pushed him. It took his breath away, pulsed through him from point of contact and cast him, drifting, slowly back and back.

He sailed through the spangled light among the other flotsam until his back met solidity, the hard surface of the view. Pushing off with one foot, he spun slowly and found himself in darkness. A brief kaleidoscope of images, Sara, Tomas, Esker, Darshun, the derelict, a vast net of light . . . A voice, booming deep and endless, yet whispering quietly . . . so quietly.

Straining to understand it, he surfaced to wakefulness, to the utilitarian dim of the *Rainsquall*, the slight sway of the sling.

The Tiyo, sitting on the deck like a lean, pale Buddha, contemplated Jhinsei as though he were a meditation exercise.

"Bad dreams?" he inquired, making it clear he'd been watching for some time.

Jhinsei frowned and reached for the water bulb.

"The angel frowns." He sounded slightly mad, the Tiyo, like a character in a flash kive entertainment. "Although—angel . . . hmm. No, actually, you look a lot like Tempah-maya in the Fujit Cycle. A dissolute but still pure slut-angel."

Jhinsei stared at him a moment. "Kive a lot of that sort of thing, do you?"

The Tiyo's lip curled in a slow smile. "I'm a connoisseur."

"Of ancient, pre-flash kive scoria?"

"Sad, isn't it?" The Tiyo sighed. "I'm a great disappointment to everyone."

Though Mheth's tone was light and arch, sadness and trouble weighed behind it, plain to Jhinsei as a bitter taste on the air. It was a different perspective for Jhinsei, on familied, associated life, the expectations of others that might be difficult to meet. His team, ad-hoc family that they'd been, had always been proud of Jhinsei.

“Are you hungry? We’ve been in this hopper for a touch over a cycle now and you haven’t had a morsel.” The Tiyo gestured. “There’s some lovely q-bars and rations here.”

“I know. I brought them,” Jhinsei said, eyeing the stash the Tiyo had plundered.

Mheth gave him a smug look, one brow curving up. Jhinsei laughed, he couldn’t help it.

A while later, sensing a slight clearing in the weather, the rider emerged, sampling the q-bars with him, peering at the Tiyo, stretching into his senses to make the cramped shuttle a palace of marvels.

With the Kiyr awake, the time passed somewhat more agreeably. They played kish-bei, the ancient spacers’ game, without a board or pieces: “Questor star to lost planet.” “I see that with evolved fish and take your wager tiles.” “What? You can’t play evolved fish, you never pulled the mutagen.” “Yes I did, it’s right here, right beside my invisible meteor field marker.” “If you’re not going to play seriously—”

They talked about ancient tales of the supernatural from pre- and post-diaspora eras and worlds, of which the Kiyr knew an inordinant amount.

They talked about food.

“The Ascony? The spicy fritters are edible, I suppose,” Mheth said. They sat on the scuffed, chill decking, leaning against crates.

The Kiyr shook his head. “I could eat them every day. Drift,” his throat moved over a swallow as he tipped his head back. “Now my mouth is watering.”

“Zurka’s, now, their chirash—”

“Do you mean that little dive between decks that moves every few cycles?”

“Yes,” Mheth sighed. “Euphoric.”

The Kiyr knew little of epic poetry, so Mheth recited all of “Meditations on Between” for him. That took nearly a whole cycle, with breaks for tepid water and increasingly detestable q-bars.

Jhinsei also fell asleep once, and then pretended to twice more, snoring loudly through several stanzas.

Several times Mheth had seen the Kiyr's gaze become abstracted as he touched the sling or a q-bar wrapper wonderingly, or stared at the views of space in the globe, or at Mheth himself, with an almost reverent shine in his eyes. Mheth started to ask, but the Kiyr's expression shuttered so completely he thought better of it.

Later, the Kiyr began to tell him, hesitantly, about growing up in Kiyr nursery, being adopted in ops by his team. He fell silent after, fingers folding and refolding the fabric of one jump sleeve, brooding. Then he said, "I have no real memory of my mother, but now that I'm out here, with no home to go back to…it's like a rope in the darkness; I have no idea if it goes anywhere worth going, but it's there."

"My mother," Mheth said, "disappeared out of our lives when I was . . . five, I think. I don't really know what happened. I asked, but my father . . ." He shook his head. "Sarsone Tiyo excels at the non-answer. Not long after she went away, I think—it all blurs, doesn't it?—I had a terrible dream.

"My brother said I woke up whimpering. I know it left me scared and," he touched a hand to his chest, dragged it down to his gut, "hollow-feeling."

"What was the dream?" the Kiyr asked.

"I was standing in a station reception hall with my father, the lights off and the starfields through the views cold and distant. A shadowy group of Aggregate dignitaries surrounded us. One reached out and touched him and he just—disappeared. Out of the world. Gone."

Even now it gave Mheth a shudder to remember it. The dream had stayed with him all down the years, and had come true, in its way. It had probably been coming true when he'd dreamed it, his subconscious already well aware of things his waking child's mind could not, or would not, encompass.

❊

Planetfall. The *Rainsquall* beeped, chirruped, clicked. In the interval between orbit and infall, when weightless zerogee floated them briefly in the slings, the Tiyo went sickly pale and sweaty. Eyes closed, his throat worked, swallowing against the nausea that often affected anyone not trained for zerogee. Jhinsei did not feel smug, however. He was far too preoccupied with his own concerns.

I could just be going insane. He watched the relayed images of a growing Ash in the shuttle's globe.

Nonsense, you're perfectly sane, I can tell; sane enough, anyway. You just have a tendency to obsess.

It was the rider; its first fully formed thought communication. And it had a distinct familiarity, yet not. Sara, yet not. Not-Sara.

And then it added, *This is what it is; just deal,* which tasted of both Darshun and Esker, yet—not. More, less. Other. But with . . . borrowings.

Borrowings? the rider echoed, considering, and seemed to laugh. *If you like.*

I don't like, the thought flared through him, harsh and angry. The rider withdrew abruptly. Leaving him alone in his mind, free. Still there, he knew, but not in his consciousness. Great. Inhabiting the wreckage that constituted his unconscious: mazes of buried memory, deserted, airless corridors, strange, neglected forms and monsters.

The *Rainsquall* coughed and jerked as infall caught hold. The Tiyo gave a small sigh. Then he asked, his voice quiet, "Have you been to Ash?"

"No." He watched the globe, which the Tiyo studiously ignored. "I've kived a lot on it, though." He glanced at the Tiyo. "If you close your eyes and follow your breath, it may help."

The Tiyo did that, his face vulnerable without its usual veneer.

Jhinsei searched for a talking distraction. "In the Suerell Mountains, on the southern polar continent of Ash, infall is prohibited by the Mavira Pact. The peoples who live there are isolationist—violently so in the past. Deep in the Suerell, they have a temple known as the Pearl Biscuit." He picked his way into the story, pulling bits from things Darshun had told him and from things he'd archived at the urging of the now absent Darshun-within. "Very few people outside of the Suerell have ever been there, but there's an account by Hidras Vin, a Quinteppi anthrotographer..."

The *Rainsquall*'s hum changed tone as atmospheric navigation systems took over; vibration shuddered through the hull, the cargo, slings, Jhinsei and Mheth. Jhinsei closed his eyes. The images relayed through the globe at this point weren't of much use, just blurs and tears of planetary cloud and land.

"Hidras Vin tells of a ritual more strange and beautiful than any he had witnessed elsewhere in all the Aggregate worlds he'd visited . . . " As he spoke, Jhinsei sensed the rider, back from the nether regions of his mind, hovering just on the edge of his consciousness, like a child on Revelation deck, listening to story.

⁂

The shuttle settled into berth with a chunk and hiss of couplings, followed by the dying hum of systems powering down as it went passive in the grip of Ash Base.

Mheth considered his lack of practical knowledge about this, the inhabited planet nearest Termagenti Station, and was offended at his own ignorance. But then, Ash was widely considered a backwater. Though there were some who considered that sort of thing exotic, Mheth was not one of them. Except for the presence of the Thorough Order enclave here, and it was one of the Order's smaller such, Ash's only distinction was the planet's proximity to Termagenti itself.

Yet here he was. Whether it had been the most brilliant idea—well, Mheth had thought a lot during their six-cycle trip. It was clear to him, on reflection, that he'd panicked, and behaved, overall, most unsatisfactorily.

Fragging the chi had been the first stupidity. He'd knocked his whole chemical profile seriously off kilter; no wonder he'd panicked. So his father was insane and dangerous; it wasn't really a very different characterization than Mheth had assigned him in the last ten years, just, with the lumin suit and phoenix mask—more so.

Maybe he wasn't quite to terms with that one.

Whatever the conspiracy his brother was trying to keep decently covered, however, it was certainly no big shock to Mheth that such a thing existed. Why else had he been helping Kynan with his exposé?

The chi seemed to have stabilized. Except for the bout of soul-wringing nausea, now past, Mheth felt well. It was going to be lovely just to get out of the barbaric and amenity-less metal pod of the shuttle that smelled very much of unwashed people at this point, despite both of them washing with antibac cloths several times. Rainsquall indeed. Who named the shuttles anyway?

Though it hadn't been all bad, the shuttle trip.

Mheth looked thoughtfully at the Kiyr. Sweet of him, the bit of story-telling distraction. Jhinsei, clearly feeling his glance, turned his head from some inner contemplation.

"Just a little longer now," he said. "They have to do a contaminants sweep. Then we offload with the rest of the cargo."

"Will there be security of some sort, do you suppose?"

"By now they know the ship weight is above mark; usually that means a passenger. It's fine, though. Except for those areas interdicted by pacts and accords, Ash is an open planet. Standard physical and psych check for bad bugs or bad chem, and then they won't care what we do. At least," his mouth quirked in a wry grin, "that's what I've always been given to understand. I worked the automated monitors on Revelation for the last six months."

Mheth controlled his expression. He could see Jhinsei waiting for reaction. Not a coveted post, Revelation deck; anyone raised on Termagenti knew that. Ops crew rotated through it and never had to sit the post more than once every couple of months. To be posted there regularly for six months was almost reason enough in itself to stow away on a shuttle.

For all they'd shared in the forced intimacy of the shuttle, Mheth realized he still didn't know why the Kiyr had fled station, though he'd inferred it had something to do with the loss of the Kiyr's ops team.

Suddenly it clicked into place, his memory at last surfacing the relevant data. The Zebulon tube accident, the whole team killed but one, their orphan ward: Kiyr Jhinsei. The accident had been station gossip for a month or so. Jhinsei had been psych warded for a goodly while. Ravings about an alien presence, mental telepathy, his whole dead team being with him.

Mheth recalled one odd exchange he'd overheard between his

brother Grath and Ro Mehet. *I'm still not sure I see the necessity*, Ro had said. *He's useless, a waste of resources.* And Grath had shaken his head. *Father is quite clear on it, Ro. The Kiyr is important.*

"I wondered how long it would be before you figured it out."

Mheth looked up from his memory.

"Took you quite a while," Jhinsei added. "Not the swiftest Tiyo in the pack, huh?"

"Simply not a gossip monger," Mheth said, archly. "Stowed away with a celebrity and I had no idea. So, did you just get tired of Revelation duty?"

The Kiyr's expression closed up. "Something like that."

The shuttle link chimed.

"*Rainsquall*, we got some tourists aboard?" A woman's voice, with a burred accent.

"Yes, Ash Base. Two to disembark, with permission." He cast a glance at Mheth, hesitated, and then said, "No armaments hard or soft." Mech or bio, that meant.

"I recognize that voice, don't I?"

"Yes, Ash Base, I expect you do."

"Well, well, nice of you to come and visit, Termagenti."

The entry light went green and the hatch unsealed with a hiss.

Ash Base was the original site of first planetfall, many gens in the past, after a previous many more gens of planet shaping. That, at least, Mheth knew, as well as any other person raised in Palogenia System.

It wasn't much to look at so far. They came out of the *Rainsquall* onto a deck, high up in a wide empty space studded by walkways and decks with mostly empty shuttle bays.

The air, though. Warm and very different from station air, close and thick and full of unfamiliar smells, it seemed to cling to the skin.

Vertigo blackened Mheth's senses for a swaying moment. He felt a presence beside him, a hand at his elbow.

The Kiyr's slate-green eyes appraised him.

"It's only going to be worse outside," Jhinsei said. "Haven't you ever kived any well-prep somatics? Spent time in the arboretum?"

"I've been on a planet before," Mheth said. He saw the ice of his own tone in the expression which crossed Jhinsei's face before he turned away.

Mheth followed.

The lack of station or ship hum under his feet made everything flat, made his balance feel strange. The decking and walls were scuffed and shabby, the light dim. It took Mheth a moment to see the three Ashlings standing at the end of the walk by an open lift platform. A burly woman with bristling grey hair, owner of the burred accent and metonymic title "Ash Base" and two people who retained little individuality for Mheth, as they were immediately left behind to begin offloading the *Rainsquall*.

The lift's downward movement bore little resemblance to any motion Mheth had ever experienced on Termagenti. Ash Base remarked, without looking at them, "You'll be feeling that extra bit of gee."

The lift jolted to a stop at the bottom and they followed the woman into a small alcove off the larger open space. She went to a console and globe, leaving them at the one tall window of semiperm—the transparent, porous material favored for windows on any planet with a vaguely temperate climate. This pane gave them a clear view of land and sky.

Sky . . . a lucid ivory in patches visible through bulbous dark grey and roseate clouds. Rich air came through the pane of semiperm: warm, wet, full of scents.

Even through the loginess of extra gee and the stringy ache left in his muscles by days on the shuttle, Mheth felt something, like a head lifting within him, to the touch of something deep, exotic and homely at once, something he'd missed and needed without knowing it was missing.

"I thought you said you'd been on a planet before." The Kiyr stood by the window with him.

Mheth had been on exactly one other planet, a heavily populated and developed hub of Aggregate trade. It hadn't been like this. He spared Jhinsei a glance, but the Kiyr, too, was focused on the outside view, eyes wide as Mheth knew his own were.

"And you said you'd kived well-prep," Mheth said.

Jhinsei didn't respond. Immediately outside the base hangar stood a grove of trees, rough-barked with spreading branches. But the grove sheered off and opened out into a wide stretch of terrain, running out and out to distant horizon and a rise of mountains disappearing into a veil of cloud. The land went on forever, ochre and greenish blue with low grasses. The sheer space... Mheth swayed and closed his eyes.

"Look," the Kiyr said. Mheth dragged his eyes open.

A large, rough-furred creature lounged under a tree, its yellowish color nearly disappearing into the general dun of the sandy dirt path. It lay on its side in a state of abandon. Large, fur-tufted ears twitched slightly. Its stomach was a lighter dun, almost the ivory of the sky's clear bits, and pads on the bottoms of the large paws were also pale, dark brown fur thick between them.

"That's Atrook," the woman said behind them. "He's the second gen of a cross speciation of sun bear, ocelot, and St. Bernard—that's some kind of canid—adapted for all-weather conditions. Woman who developed the beasts calls them sundogs.

"Now, if you would," she gestured them back to the console.

Two quick extractions from each of them, arm and behind the ear. The Kiyr, it interested Mheth to note, went quite pale, hands fisted and knuckles white. Ash Base appeared not to notice and moved on to Mheth.

A puff of cold air and a sting, then her samplings went into a scanner. Mheth saw the woman raise an eyebrow when his augments registered on the profile, but she said nothing. He wondered briefly what a profile of his father's psych chem would show and just as quickly abandoned the thought.

The profiles linked to the Aggregate database and in a moment the woman knew pretty much everything official—and many things personal—there was to know about them.

Jhinsei was watching the woman. And the woman looked up over the globe at the Kiyr, a sober, but, to Mheth, otherwise unreadable expression on her weathered face. She had light, dirty-ice-gray eyes.

"It's not . . . it's . . ." the Kiyr started to say, and stopped.

The console popped out two small kive cubes. The woman scooped them up, handed one to Jhinsei, one to Mheth.

"Your visas, good for three months standard. At that time if you fail to report to this or another official Ash office, you will be in violation of Aggregate Standard Law."

She met the Kiyr's gaze, and added, "Ramev Evans sends regards."

Jhinsei's just-light-enough-to-show-it skin blushed deeply. It annoyed Mheth to be in the dark as to why, to what was going on in the by-play.

The woman turned to him. The look in her eyes reminded Mheth of Kenit. "So, Ser Tiyo, Termagenti royalty as it were. It's not every day we get the juice of the old witch down here at all, much less arriving stowed away on an automated."

Mheth folded his arms and leaned back against the table. "Yes. Well," he said, and winced at the limpness of the comeback.

Ash Base then delivered what sounded like a rote speech. "You have passed scan and profile, and such can be guaranteed of all persons on planet who have passed through a Base point, but no promise can be made for the entirety of the population currently resident."

"How reassuring."

Unexpectedly, Jhinsei laughed. "Tiyo to the nines, aren't you?"

The woman's eyebrows went up. She didn't smile, but the tension Mheth had been playing against disappeared. She turned and gestured them to follow her.

They did so, across the wide, dim hangar space. Mheth thought about being called juice of the old witch. Nobody called Termagenti "the old witch" on station. He was out, seriously out, of his depth here.

This, he realized, had been a colossal mistake.

Adventures in the Gravity Well

Jhinsei wanted to ask Ash Base what else Ramev might have said, but not in Mheth's hearing. In their time together he'd formed a connection with the Tiyo, an unexpected friendship, but he was still wary of Mheth's link to House Tiyo and all that might come with it.

The rider, having emerged from the half-dormancy adopted during the latter portion of the shuttle journey, now leaned out over his mind like a kid over the haft bar of a magnet trike, joy riding. Its interest and distraction added to Jhinsei's own and filled his mind with chatter.

At the same time, his thoughts jittered around the question of what exactly his profile had told the Ashling, what Ramev had said, what his status in the universe might now be. Alien threat, infected fugitive, wanted for questioning? It was a measure of Thorough Order power on Ash that a link transmission from Ramev could make someone ignore whatever anomalies his chem profile must have shown and—seemingly without qualms—let him onto her planet.

They exited the hangar through a short corridor into a welter of light and they were outside. Jhinsei swayed, but the rider rose to the onslaught of sense input even as he was overborne by it.

It was the air, first, and overwhelmingly. More alive on the skin, in a way station air never was, full of tastes and scents—the pollen and sap of the trees, the microscopic grit of the dust of organic matter—soil, rain, life borne on winds which crossed mountain, field, forest, and ocean. Jhinsei felt an urge to pull off his clothes and run naked through it, this rich air.

He wasn't sure if it was his impulse or the rider's.

Then there was the light, which fell from so much further than the solar collector light on station, fell through deep cloud and thence into the trees differently—a world differently—than collector light through the jali groves in station's arboretum. This light had weight and heft, rich with water and the dust of minerals, bent by atmosphere, utterly unlike light as Jhinsei knew it.

Leaves on the trees whispered against one another in the wind, tossing shadows in confusing curls and leaps.

Jhinsei heard a small moan beside him. Mheth's face had gone pale and greenish; his eyes were tightly closed, fists clenched at his sides. His throat worked as he swallowed repeatedly.

Though Jhinsei registered the overwhelming, vertigo-inducing sensations, he was not overwhelmed. Not because of sojourns in the arboretum for well-acclimatization, nor because of all the Esker-inspired kiving, or any particular stamina of his own.

It was the rider.

Stretching into his fingers, pulling in sensation through Jhinsei's eyes, nose, skin, listening through him. Sucking in the world like a maintenance octo snorting scum.

Glancing at the Tiyo's pale, sweating face, Jhinsei supposed he should be grateful.

Ash Base looked at Mheth with the first signs of amusement Jhinsei had seen in her. "Shuttle hitchers never are prepared." She pointed across a small cleared area, then abandoned them, retreating back inside.

One arm of the hangar looped around to connect to the structure huddled across the clearing, an awkward, domed building. Behind it and on the other side of the clearing were the waving arms of the trees. A road, tracked and rutted, terminated in the clearing.

Wind sung in the distance. Shadows passed over them as the clouds moved. Jhinsei squinted into the glare of Palogenia as the sun appeared briefly, marveling at the heat that came with the light.

The Tiyo nearly leapt out of his skin when a leaf touched him, twirling through the air on its way to the ground. He was plainly miserable and said nothing at all.

A scythe screen veiled the vehicle-wide entrance of the domed building. The screen shimmered palely as the wind blew occasional leaf debris against it. There was nothing to be seen of the inside of the place from outside, just the pale singeing of the screen across a dark well.

Jhinsei met the Tiyo's gaze. Still greenish and sweaty, Mheth nevertheless managed a lift of one eyebrow. Jhinsei grinned; he knew, in a central, currently distant place within him, that it was as much the rider's grin as it was his.

The screen hissed over their clothes and skin, cleaning sweat and grime from them. It tickled a bit down Jhinsei's sides and back. The rider wanted to laugh. Mheth was a step behind him, the low static of the screen rising with passage, falling.

As Jhinsei's eyes adjusted to the dim, he made out a loading dock, crates and platforms lined up along the left going back to a wide load door at the other end and into the hangar. A motley collection of transport vehicles were parked just inside.

In the main, domed portion of the building, an ad-hoc lounge area held a number of people, as well as a holoscreen, a collection of tables and chairs in wildly varying styles, many of them looking like someone's art project, a bar, and several work globe consoles, two of them ancient.

Most of those present sat in a group about the dark holoscreen, talking. One woman sat by herself near the bar. She also stood out for her attire, a hooded mantle of fine, sheeny fabric, probably sensitive to its wearer's core temperature. Woven into it, an intricate pattern of metallic bits caught and turned the light. She was a member of the Sinaiety, Ash's reclusive, clannish talisters. Jhinsei remembered seeing the several Sinaiety on station, at Chath's, before Ro Mehet and the Khat officers descended on him.

Jhinsei glanced at Mheth. He seemed somewhat better now they were inside again. Lips compressed to whiteness about the edges, but the blue eyes were tracking details.

Jhinsei didn't think the Tiyo had much more of a plan than he did. Right.

"I'm going to ask around about work. You might be able to hire a vehicle, or a ride—wherever it is you want to go." He assumed the Tiyo had access to cred, which Jhinsei did not, but left a note of question in his words.

"I . . . Can I look for work with you?"

Jhinsei nodded and the look of panic on Mheth's face eased, a little at least.

A man wearing a jump bearing Ash Base insignia sat at the newer work globe. A woman leaned on the other side of the console, speaking quietly to him.

Looking at her from the back, for a moment Jhinsei saw Darshun in the cant of shoulders, tilt of neck, and tight, wooly fingers of dark hair, standing out every which way. This woman had a lot of silver and grey in her hair, though, her skin lighter than Darshun's had been, and she carried more height and weight.

And, of course, Darshun was dead.

His knees began to shake. Everything went distant, seen and heard through a half-solid thickness of air. Drift, not now. He clenched his hands tight into fists, drew a deliberately slow, deep breath, let it out, uncurling his fingers.

Several repetitions and the world came back into present focus. He ached in a familiar, hollow way, still shaky.

A soft singing shivered through his bones. It soothed. Echo of velvet, effervescence—just the slightest touch. Taste of honey. A vast pooling depth of energy within.

He felt better. He felt wonderful—euphoric.

Bloody void.

Developing an addiction to the alien ghost riding his blood and mind was probably not a good thing. But he did feel better.

He waded in among the small gathering, Mheth at his shoulder. Glances were flicked their way, brief; conversation carried on.

It reminded Jhinsei of being the new kid walking into a room in civschool.

He met several of the glances thrown their way with a polite, open nod, and approached the base worker talking to the woman, waiting for them to finish.

The woman cast a look over her shoulder and stepped aside. "Go ahead, we're just trading gossip."

Jhinsei inclined his head and said, "I'm just wondering if you know of any work—anyone looking for an extra hand—well, four of them," he gestured between himself and Mheth.

"There's a few calls on the list," the base worker said with a nod. "I'll pull 'em up for you."

"Actually," the woman said, "I'm looking for some temporary help." She held out her hand. "Ophedia Evans."

Jhinsei shook—her hand was warm and very strong. "Ki—um, Jhinsei. This is Mheth."

Ophedia Evans was a large, imposing woman with a round face, strong bones, and skin just light enough to show freckles across her broad cheeks. Her eyes were the startling green of raw coffee beans.

"You all squared away with base? Got your visas?"

"Yes," Jhinsei said. "We're cleared."

She looked at Mheth and hesitated, about to say something else, then shook her head. "Come on and we'll load up." She gestured Jhinsei and Mheth to follow her and headed to one of the parked vehicles, a hybrid monstrosity that looked like it had been pieced together from the innards of a mining ship and the discarded ceraplas skin of a maintenance octo.

It gave a good hum when started up, however, and she backed it to the cargo dock. They loaded cereplas crates and packing cubes, some of which Jhinsei and Mheth had been staring at for the last six cycles, into the capacious back and sides of the vehicle.

At one point Jhinsei felt a prickle across his shoulders and looked around: the lone Sinaiety woman in the hooded mantle was watching them.

No, watching him, the rider said and Jhinsei glanced at Mheth. The Tiyo heaved a stack of plats, having recovered a portion of his sangfroid—or pretending to it, at any rate.

Ophedia Evans supervised the loading, with particular instructions about where this or that crate went. When they were done she waved to the base workers and some of the others and then directed Jhinsei and Mheth into the abbreviated crescent of the vehicle's drive-pit.

It smelled like wet dirt and cereplas and was not really large enough for three. In fact, it reminded Jhinsei of a tube diving suit. He was sweating, his anxiety level lapping higher, before the vehicle even passed through the scythe screen's hiss.

Then the woman hit a button and the pit's bubble closed over them.

Jhinsei suppressed a small moan.

The woman keyed in auto-nav and they took to the road through the trees. Beads and holo-chips swung from a handhold above the seat crescent. More holo-chips, bits of brightly-hued ceraplas, and other trash tiled the console and interior a multi-textured, glinting mosaic.

They cleared the trees and the world opened out around them. Green and russet furze, tender looking with flushes of pink, rolled away to a distant swell of hills, and the hills to mountain-edged horizon. Heavy clouds had closed out all view of the lucid ivory sky.

It began to rain.

Jhinsei forgot his suit-associated anxiety. The hiss and scatter of rain against the bubble, the hum of the transport, everything faded. There was only the distance, even darkened and dampened by Ash's ever-present weather.

The spectacle of perspective.

Jhinsei felt Mheth shift, breathing deeply as he took it all in. Then the Tiyo looked back and Jhinsei followed his gaze.

The yellow creature they'd seen earlier—the sundog, Atrook—broke from the tree line and ran after them for a ways, bounding with ungainly grace across the rain-dimpled furze. Then it stopped and stood, watching them go.

Ophedia Evans finished with her onboard checks, settled back, and said, "So. You are Kiyr Jhinsei. My brother-in-law Ramev Evans—your obviary, I take it?—asked his brother—my husband Taebit—and me to find you someplace to be. Plenty of work on the ranch; never say no to free labor. What I don't know," she turned to Mheth, "is who the hell are you?"

*

The dark air of planetary predawn was cutting and raw with cold wind. Mheth followed Ophedia's barely seen form into the goat enclosure, a roomy shed of dark stone and ceraform fittings. The turquoise-coated brenner goats smelled rank and warm, bumping against him. Their salt-white eyes caught stray gleams from the biolumes overhead. They had rough, slightly oily fleece, one of the oldest and hardiest of all human-bred speciations, more gentle in nature than any of their long-gone kin.

They were still rambunctious enough for Mheth.

The feeding process was automated, but long experience dictated human presence and interaction on a regular schedule. Also, as far as Mheth could tell, Ophedia liked the rough beasts. As the feed poured out of ceraform shoots into neat troughs, they moved among the brenners patting backs, checking bodies and legs for general health and well-being. This one, Snepo, needed a bone-knitting booster for a recently broken leg; that one, Jasper, was pregnant and needed her vitamin hypo. Mheth eyed the dark, nearly indigo coat of a small male that seemed to have taken exception to him, then bent to feel over Jasper's round body as Ophedia had showed him, checking for lumps or excessive heat. The goat butted him gently in the chest, impatient to get to her feed. Done, Mheth applied the hypo shot. He let the goat go, grunting, then fell flat on his face, butted from behind. The dark goat nodded its head back and forth with a stuttering baa.

"That's Digger five, Mheth zero," Ophedia said.

"Charming." He climbed to his feet, dusting off hay and detritus. "You're on their side, of course."

They spent a while longer, poking and prodding, checking teeth and the programming of the octos that cleaned the enclosure, then moved from the goat house to the gardens to check on the happiness of various micro-organisms in the soil.

Next they gathered a variety of readings from the monitors which rooted, right along with the vegetables, deep in the soil, for the monthly report to Aggregate Planet Shaping Oversight. Apso, Ophedia called it, as though it were one of the goats. Finally, they finished and went to join the other humans for their own breakfast.

Out on what Ophedia and Taebit called the terrace—a flat bit of the dark native rock from which the ranch's buildings had mostly been hewn—they breakfasted and watched the sunrise.

Palogenia ascended ardent white through an ice-green sash of clouds. There was, to station-bred senses, a comforting sameness to the daily event. Only sometimes, it was tinged with a glace of other hues, yellows, pale rose, purple-blue.

Mheth took it as esthetic consolation for having, barbarically, to be up while this world in its gravity well still wallowed in night's darkness.

A river ran to the south, marked by the light-caved mist rising off its surface in the early chill. Following the river's path with the gaze led to a slow rise of the land from fertile, lush fields into steppes and thence to distant mountain ranges with names, Mheth had learned, like the Slow Mountains, the Grape, Spoon, and Sestina ranges.

In the other direction, small crop groves, of spice and fruit speciates, cradled the ranch.

The terrace, as the rest of the ranch, had been quarried, sheared, and fitted by Aggregate well robotics to Taebit's design specs. The dark, white-veined stone had been tortured into complicated, vaulting curves and geometries.

Looking around the day after they arrived, Mheth had observed that the inside of Taebit's head must be a somewhat frightening place.

"Truth," Taebit had allowed, nodding placidly.

Mheth lifted a hand to Jhinsei, already sitting to breakfast after having finished whatever it was he did out in the fields before light. Breakfast this morning was eggs from the quail flock—speciated quail, apparently they hadn't been a flock creature back in the long ago—with goat cheese. Mheth took nugatory pleasure in eating the tangy mellow cheese; it was the only way he seemed likely to get his own back against the goats. Rolled biscuits with herbs. Spiced tubers and peppers from the house garden. Fields of the same vegetables stretched off to the west.

The early day smelled of soil, savor, coffee, and, occasionally, goat. The sound of forks on plates, Ophedia speaking quietly to Taebit on their side of the table. Jhinsei sat beside him, both of them so hungry there was no conversation for the first while. The dawn offered its pale green gentility, slightly sullen with a thin underlining of burning gold. The curve of the house bulked behind and to their left, patinaed by the low furling light of the sunrise.

Taebit cooked all the food. A small man, with wooly, reddish hair and pale skin stained by long hours under the sun, he was younger than Ophedia and dryer than dust.

Mheth scooped up a bit of vegetables and egg with a piece of biscuit, sighed in satisfaction as he chewed. "You know," he said after swallowing, "you could do serious prosper on station making food like this. Call the place Taebit's Tenders."

Jhinsei snorted into his coffee.

"Yes," Mheth said, "I suppose that does sound a bit like you might be offering something besides food. Taebit's Treats. No—Taebit's Transcendent."

"Glad you're liking the comestibles, Mheth," Taebit said. He tore a biscuit in two and mopped his plate with the delicacy of an obviary surgeon. "Jhinsei, how's that response unit coming?"

The Kiyr swallowed, set his coffee cup down. "It's reacting to climate shifts, but it still isn't reading moisture, chem, or microbial changes. The chips are a gen or two out of date."

Taebit nodded. "Can you do anything with them?"

"I'll work on it." He fiddled with his cup. "Taebit, why can't you get new chips? They're cheap. And jp sensors or kick-relays? You have plenty of other up-to-date tech." He gestured out at the fields, back at the house, looked from Taebit to Ophedia. "It's not the cred, so what is it?"

Ophedia glanced at Taebit. "Those particular chips," she said, "are made with an ore that's mined on Quintep. Elements in the ore are vital to the life cycle of half the biology in that ecosystem, but Norton-Creel, which runs the mining op, won't consider alternative ores—they have exclusive rights to that area, for one thing, and the expense is higher, so it would lower their profit. So they're destroying a singular, ancient habitat. Not a particularly new story."

"Older than god," Taebit said.

"Tiyo has ties with Norton-Creel," Mheth said.

"Mmm-hmm," Ophedia said. "And it's Tiyo that's blocked Palogenia System from trading with alternative producers and suppliers. So we have old chips, or trade in the gray market and take the chance we're getting junk chips. Then there's the embargoes the Sinaiety puts on things, for its own reasons, which are labyrinthine. Sinaiety seems to be in with Tiyo, too, tell you the truth. It all gets up my nose."

Mheth toyed with a biscuit. He knew all this from the research Kynan had done when they were working together. Trade blocks, odd partnerings, indiscriminate pillage of well systems even when long-term reason indicated alternative courses of action. It had not seemed very terrible to Mheth, particularly against the knowledge of other transgressions. Hacking up a derelict ship even after evidence of its sentience had been made clear. Disappearing test operatives when they had unpleasant reactions to the material made from that ship. Covering up possible fatalities and data and putting the lumin kive cubes into further test circulation here on Ash. And though his brother Grath was merely corrupt, his father Sarsone was truly mad. *If we are to evolve, Mhethianne, then the recessives will have to be filtered out.*

How had he not noticed his father going mad? That thought had wracked him, in the several weeks of gravity well nights since they'd come here. With that thought came memories, examined and turned through his mind like cards in the hands. He'd remembered it had been his father who gave him the nubby Kirrikian toy, telling him the legend that went with it, of the beast that could sail the deeps of space free and unconfined by a ship. It had been not long after Mheth and Grath's mother disappeared. In the memory, his father was distant, sad.

Even as he drew away from his sons emotionally, though, Sarsone had been sane, still a power on Termagenti and a force beyond it. Diplomats and trade consortiums, visiting dignitaries and celebrities, all had sought out Tiyo Sarsone Tiyo.

In Mheth's time outsystem, he gained a different perspective on the power and influence Tiyo wielded. That new perspective, combined with anger and hurt over his father's withdrawal, helped to make him the droll and eccentric profligate he'd become.

He thought now with some shame of his petty rebellion, while Grath had been left to bear all the responsibility.

The conversation had moved on without him.

"—hardly a matter of virtue, Taebit," Ophedia said.

"The Sinaiety believes it to be."

Ophedia snorted. "Power's what they're concerned with, Tae, just like everyone else."

"There's not much kive material on the Sinaiety," Jhinsei said. "Even though you see them on-station sometimes." He was leaning forward, and frowned now, at some private thought.

"The Sinaiety," Mheth said, "are the descendants of Gavald Rivas. Who believed, let me see, how did it go, 'Single-mindedness of purpose and a dedicated disregard of those whose purpose runs counter or at irrelevant attitude to one's own is the highest virtue of a strong species.'"

"Huh," Taebit said. "Never heard that." He dipped his head, nodding. "Makes a certain sense of them though. The doctrine in the generations since has spun a bit; the oddest thing about them, I think, is that no one ever leaves; no children rebel. There are no 'former' Sinaiety."

"It's not odd, it's scary," Ophedia said.

Jhinsei was looking at Mheth. "How did you know that?"

Mheth shrugged, then said, "Gavald Rivas and Harthon Tiyo, the esteemed Tiyo ancestor who helped to establish Termagenti, were cousins. It's in Tiyo ancestral kive files."

Jhinsei squinted, but said nothing.

They all fell quiet. Wind hissed across the fields and the bean crop waved silver, then green. Palogenia, which had risen and then got caught in clouds, let down a delicate light across the long horizon.

It still seemed to Mheth an optical illusion, the wide endless horizon. It still gave him moments of vertigo. The scent in the air, though, textured of blossom, soil, water, and sap, was an intoxicant.

A sound grew, moving in from the distance. Taebit glanced at Ophedia. "Be Ramev."

"Mmm." She glanced at Jhinsei, peering out toward the road. Then she nodded to Mheth, hefted herself up and moved off, leaving them to clear the table.

⁂

Mheth lounged on his bed mat, smoothing two fingers over the thin, temperature-sensitive blanket repetitively. Three walls of the room, which Ophedia called the back porch, were semiperm.

The sky outside was filled with well night. Scents of soil and green, darkness, moisture, ozone. Earlier, Taebit had tasted the air and said, "Going to be a moud storm."

Whatever that was.

Light came in from the corridor, making shadow and cross hatch of the room. A corner of it had been given over as quarters for him and Jhinsei. Jhinsei's mat lay empty, the blanket folded neatly.

Mheth stared out at the lowering sky, thinking back over the evening, over the images and memories of his father still hovering close as breath. Whatever else, even as he hurt over his father's disregard and questioned his power, Mheth had still respected Sarsone; he'd been the bedrock against which Mheth rebelled.

The panic he felt now, beneath all, the craven need to run and hide, was because that bedrock and the certainties against which he'd always acted, had crumbled, gone rotten at the core: if his father was insane—not just crotchety, distant, and authoritarian—the world made no sense anymore.

As Taebit had prophesied, Ramev had arrived—and turned out to be none other than Termagenti's head obviary, Ramev Evans. Who happened to be Taebit's brother. Obviary kit in hand, he'd peered up at Mheth, his eyes, the same light color as Taebit's, full of the same wry humor. Mheth had never met him because the Tiyos of House Tiyo used their own private obviaries. Mheth, braced for the criticality of Kenit, found he was full of nervous energy with no sparring partner. He triggered the chi and watched Ramev's trained eyes take in the physiological changes that marked its passage. The obviary's expression did not change and he made no comment.

Between necessary tasks and respect to the organism of the farm, Ramev, Ophedia, and Taebit shared news of the sort which never came through link. Trivia and politics of Ashling society, Mheth found it interesting in the way of a flash kive drama. He didn't quite believe in it, but it was colorful and engaging. After supper, Taebit's weather prediction, and an evening check of animals and field systems, Jhinsei had disappeared with the obviary, the Kiyr's face taut with a set of emotions Mheth could not read, though he thought fear was among them.

Jhinsei fascinated Mheth, in part for want of other distraction, and in part because he had allowed himself to form an attraction and an attachment to him. Mheth's thoughts turned up a memory now: the screen in his father's mosaic of prying eyes, showing Jhinsei and Essca Mehet in a twist of passion.

Though the bond they formed on the shuttle had deepened during their time on the ranch, there were things Mheth had not asked Jhinsei, likewise things Jhinsei did not ask Mheth. They talked, here in their makeshift quarters, in the depth of well night. About flash kive entertainments, dreams, bizarre fringe cultures, Ophedia and Taebit, growing up on Termagenti—about more than Mheth remembered talking to anyone about in his life, except his brother in that long ago time before things changed.

He prodded at the little knot of feelings developing within him, sighed, and set his mind on other things. Sifting through bits of the news Ramev had shared, he tried to chase down something that had been bothering him since the subject of the Sinaiety had come up. Something about Tiyo, and about the state of relations between the Sinaiety and the Thorough Order.

Tiyo and the Sinaiety, and that old connection. Mheth remembered his father speaking of it on more than one occasion. Then he thought of his father's words some weeks past, about evolving, and set that alongside the Sinaiety belief in the inherent failings of humanity as it was.

Mheth rolled over abruptly to one side, physically trying to shift away from thoughts of his father's madness and deadly meddling.

Ophedia and Taebit had link access, of course, but it was often down. Mheth suspected that Taebit actually preferred it so. He imagined the Ashling sneaking out to calmly sabotage the workings—which were, after all, fairly basic and generally immune to failure. Then, in the morning, he would give a philosophical lift of his shoulders. Not working again? That's the will of things, eh?

In any case, there would be nothing on link about Tiyo, about Mheth, or lumin kive technology cover-ups. Tiyo very much did not advertise their business and saw to it that no one else did. What Aggregate citizens at large were to know about them, Tiyo Kive Industries controlled: the newest flash kive, the most highly charged immersive kives. Now Mheth had a better idea of the rigorous methods employed by his brother and his brother's associates in that filtering.

A shift in the air and the scuff of steps announced Jhinsei as he came through the room's lucent shadows. A curious combination of want and tenderness tangled in Mheth's gut.

He sat up and leaned against the room's one solid wall, looked out at the sky. A murky, verdiginous flickering roiled through distant cloud mass. Mheth squinted at it; his experience of planetary meteorology was slim, but it didn't look like lightning. The air about them, outside the semiperm and over the fields, had gone dull, still.

The Kiyr lay down, one arm over his eyes.

"You know Termagenti's head obviary?"

"Think about it."

"Oh, right. The accident."

"Right, that." He spoke from under the crook of an elbow.

"Mm. Did you ever kive Secaucus James' *History of a Station*?"

The Kiyr was silent for a moment, and then quoted, "'The simplest explanation for the naming of the station is that the thing is a bitch.'"

Mheth continued the quote. "'Though there is something to recommend the commentary of one visiting ambassador in the early days of habitation, that the "mind of the place is as painfully inexplicable as an ingrown toenail."'"

Wind splashed, sudden and violent, across the fields and against the semiperm. Stronger winds moaned behind it. The roiling, flickering murk Mheth had seen in the distance was almost upon them.

"What exactly is a moud storm?"

"Mouds are some type of insect. I think—"

Flickering murk hit the semiperm, with a huge rush of wind. It went over the building in a wave, filling the air with little lightnings and smudges of color in the murk. There was an odd pattering Mheth thought must be rain, but then thousands, hundreds of thousands of bugs began tumbling into the semiperm, pitching along the roof, spitting colored light on impact, chartreuse, verdigris, dark gold, angry reds.

Jhinsei sat up, eyes wide. It seemed to go on for a long time, droves of insects hurtling on the wind, gusting torrentially into the semiperm and everything else in their path, flashing stains of gleaming color all around. The noise dinned and drowned. It wasn't just the sound of insects pummeling semiperm, walls, and roof, but a sibilant clicking washing through it all from the insects themselves.

A scent like cardamom and hot sand burned the air. The moud storm raged for maybe ten minutes. Then, slowly, the noise of wind and pummeling insect bodies lessened. The sound of rain came, gentle in the wake of the violence; occasional straggling insects, tiny turning flecks of colored light sparked and disappeared. Scents of cool and mineral rain washed through the semiperm.

"There are no full-immersion kives of moud storms," Jhinsei said after a while. "I knew what they were, but . . ."

Mheth studied the Kiyr unobtrusively. His face had eased of the wary tension he'd brought with him from conferencing with the obviary. Cleared by wonder.

"'It can be a deeply weird universe,'" Mheth quoted from an obscure cult flash kive.

"'And for that we cherish it most of all,'" the Kiyr returned and Mheth felt a flush of pleasure.

Then Jhinsei said, "Do you know what the Bromah Dictate is?"

"Of course."

"I'm under it."

"You're . . ." Mheth squinted. "The Bromah Dictate—"

"Tiyo, in the person of Ro Mehet, with the cooperation of Khat, wanted to quarantine me."

"Ro." Mheth flashed again on the surveillance screens in his father's quarters. "If . . ." He stopped. "The Bromah is an antique relic of the Expansion. You don't look like an alien. What did the obviary say to you?"

"Ramev says that while I'm neither contagious nor dangerous, my blood chemistry is undergoing radical alterations and I have been affected by. . .something. Which, when you think about it, is a frighteningly imprecise diagnosis from an obviary."

"And?" The Kiyr looked at him. "Well, child, augmentation, rec substances, genetic trifling—there are many ways in which the chemical structure of your average human critter can be messed about, yes?"

Jhinsei's gaze moved from Mheth, a restless shift that told Mheth he didn't want to talk about his situation anymore. The Kiyr confirmed this impression by attempting to shift the conversation, saying, "Do you always talk like that?"

Mheth laughed. "Don't try; you're a rank amateur. You started revelation time." He leaned over his knees. "Give. It's not as if I'll turn you in to anyone."

"I know," Jhinsei said.

Mheth felt another flush of pleasure at the implied trust.

Blowing out a breath, Jhinsei said, "At first I wasn't sure, but now."

Rain washed through the night. Soothing, Mheth decided, that sound.

Then Jhinsei's voice slid into the air again, quiet, weaving and hesitating through the rain sound. "I boarded the derelict—you know, the ship of 'unknown origin' House Tiyo brought in a few years ago."

"Yes." Where the lumin came from, Mheth thought, on a complicated knife twist of feeling.

"Something . . . something happened. Though it had already begun. I was, I don't know, primed, or something, when my team—in the accident. That ship was alive. Did you know that? Did anyone at Tiyo SciTech actually know that? Dying though, because of all they did to it. Alive for millions of years, Mheth, millions."

"Why do you think so?"

"Because it's in me, its . . . consciousness. Funneled into me like a universe into a drink bulb. And it's . . . drift, I don't know, developing. Graduated to full sentences a while ago. My rider.

"So you see, I am infected."

"Or delusional," Mheth said. "Because of the chemical changes in your body, you know, delusional."

"Possibly."

Silence again. Mheth picked over recent events. Then, "My father was watching you. On one of his spy globes. And a lot of scary testing results with the lumin—the kive tech they developed from the derelict—were self-effacingly labeled 'anomalous.'"

"Your father was watching me?"

Mheth nodded. "He's . . . my father's . . . dangerously cracked." He looked away, overwhelmed for a breath by loss and fear.

Rain whispered into the interval of silence. Then Jhinsei said, softly, "That's why you ran."

Mheth let the silence stretch. It hadn't been a question and Jhinsei didn't push him for an answer.

"Did . . . do you know if Essca . . . " The Kiyr made a low sound of misery and anger.

"Essca Mehet? I doubt she knew about the nature of my father's surveillance, but I'm fairly sure, given her relationship with Ro, she...well. What were you doing with the ice queen anyway?"

"Apparently, being reported on to Ro." The words carried a weight of anger and hurt.

The Kiyr shifted suddenly, looked at Mheth in horror. "What do you mean—the nature of your father's surveillance?" Then he groaned again. "You can't mean—that breaks the most essential codes of Aggregate civilization."

"I told you, my father," Mheth shook his head. "Somewhere along the line, he fell—hell, he waltzed—over the edge. Now, he wants humanity to 'evolve'—and he's prepared to force the issue." Mheth stared at the rain blearing and pocking the semiperm walls. "Somehow he thinks you're a key component in that plan." He listened to his own words. "I love my father, you know. He was . . . when I was very young, he made me feel like anything was possible, that because he loved me, I was the most competent, able being ever to exist."

Mheth closed his eyes. More words, about the suit of lumin, the phoenix mask and cape, fell silent on his tongue. Evidence of a whimsy turned to true madness. It was this that frightened him, in a very personal way.

Whimsy, in Sarsone, who had never before demonstrated this attribute so basic to Mheth's own nature.

He lay back down and stared into the rainy dark.

"I'm sorry," Jhinsei said, voice quiet. "I think . . . I wish I could have known my mother, but if I ever did meet her . . . I don't know." He shook his head.

"I know too much, you know too little." Mheth contemplated it. "I'd trade you, I think."

"No," Jhinsei said. "What you had, even though it went away, that's," he fell silent, and then, "you don't know how amazing that sounds. Better to be abandoned as an adult than a child, I think."

Mheth considered it. "Maybe."

"Still. I can't imagine having that and losing it, either. I'm sorry. What are you going to do?"

"I don't know. What are you going to do? Look for your mother?"

"I . . ." The Kiyr blew out a breath. "Maybe? You know," the Kiyr shifted, some thought energizing him. "That captain, of the *Oni's Wake*, and her crew, they're agents of some kind for Aggregate Control, investigating the Sinaiety, your father, and the Tiyo-Kiyr trade axis. I guess I'm not supposed to tell you that, she said it was secret, but," he shrugged. "They gave me a private link code. Maybe you should tell them? About," he waved a hand, conjuring, for Mheth, Sarsone, Grath, beta tester 531, and all of Tiyo's nefarious activities to hover in the corner of the room.

"If," Jhinsei deflated a bit, "I mean if you want to do that."

Mheth felt his head nod, though the motion felt distant as he considered, picking in his mind over the ruins of his understanding of the world. *Really*? he thought, but, "I think I do," he said, and heard the shake in his own voice. "That's a plan—or a place to start. Maybe," he echoed the conversation's recent refrain.

"The certainty in the room is reassuring," Jhinsei said.

"Decisive and heroic."

❋

The next morning mounds of moud husks littered the ground, heaped against every structure. After breakfast Ophedia handed cereplas rakes with round-edged tines to everyone, including the obviary.

Smells like light, the rider said. Jhinsei sniffed the cool morning air; it smelled like spice and ozone to him. The husks were blue, veined with glints of other colors.

Mheth said, "So they don't die when they hit things and make colors in the air?"

"No." Ramev stood next to him. "It's how they shed their skins." He nodded to the husks. The obviary's resemblance to Taebit came clear in the way both men's red hair borrowed fire from the morning light.

Mheth looked blankly at the rake in his hand. "Don't you have an octo that can do this?"

Taebit leaned on his rake. "The husks are delicate once they're shed. They're loaded with things are good for the soil; gotta harvest them careful so they don't start to break down until we're ready to use 'em."

"Oh." The expression on the Tiyo's face drew a snort of laughter from Jhinsei. Mheth's expression changed and he slid Jhinsei a look from under lowered lids, which only made Jhinsei shake his head.

He started raking, the Tiyo following his lead. The spice and ozone scent rose around them; it was mildly intoxicating. Between one of Mheth's arch comments and the next they were both laughing and the work passed on a blurred high.

By the time they were finished, the moud husks raked into twelve large, airtight stasis containers, Jhinsei was sweaty, his clothes damp and smelling of the husks' pungent spice. Palogenia rode midway up a cloudless sky, its long stretch of pale light casting stunted shadows. It was the first clear day Jhinsei had seen.

He leaned on the rake. The horizon, a distant, rough line of mountains, drew his gaze. More precisely, it drew the rider. Jhinsei still found the distant expanse unsettling. But the rider leaned into it. *What do you see*? Jhinsei wondered.

Possibility, the rider said. *Life.*

You see that in everything.

The rider's *yes* sang through his whole body. He shivered afterward at that fact, and at the fact that he was standing here having a conversation with the whatever it was sharing his body.

I have a name. My essentiality.

What is it?

I don't remember . . . I'm not fully me yet. He's watching us.

Jhinsei looked to find Ramev watching him. The others were putting the rakes away, Ophedia explaining something to Mheth while Taebit got the loader going to shift and store the stasis containers. But the obviary was watching Jhinsei and met his gaze, his expression trenchant. As if he could see the conversation in Jhinsei's head.

Ramev put his rake up and joined Jhinsei. "The expressions crossing your face are not far from those one might observe on a headcase."

"Headcase? Obviaries don't say headcase. *You* don't say it."

He shrugged a shoulder. "It's not Thorough. But it conveys. Would you prefer 'someone suffering from alien infection'?"

"You're different down here." Jhinsei squinted into the distance. "If you're worried, why didn't you just send me to the Thorough Order main headquarters on Ash?"

"Termagenti agents have already ensconced themselves in the visitor's wing."

"Agents? Were they Khat?"

Ramev lifted one shoulder, let it drop.

Jhinsei rubbed at a blister on his hand. "They'll figure out where I am."

"Likely."

"Drift."

"It should take a while; no one will really be helping them. Somewhat the opposite. Discreetly, of course."

Jhinsei stared across the newly raked grounds at Taebit setting the loader to work, Ophedia and Mheth leaning in the shade under a dark-leafed tree. "I have to leave. I can't stay here."

Ramev gave a nod with a head tilt, much the way Taebit did.

Jhinsei rubbed a hand over the back of his neck. Despite his planning session with Mheth the previous night, the prospect of leaving had still been theoretical—the work and routine of the farm, of Ophedia and Taebit's nonjudgmental acceptance, had been a comfort, a haven.

❋

Out in one of the groves later that day, Jhinsei worked alongside Taebit, shooting nutrient sticks into the soil among the roots of fruit tree speciates. Clouds were moving in from the westward mountains but hadn't dimmed Palogenia's simmer through the trees yet. His thoughts flew in circles while the rider stayed quiet. He could feel it, a presence in all of his senses, however silent at the moment.

The grove was a fruit speciation called gualems, a sweet-sour fruit. The trees, on the late side of fruiting, filled the air with a pungent bloom of decay. Taebit worked along the next row. The long, hollow heat of the day was silent but for the sound of his and Taebit's injectors, the slow sigh of an occasional wind through the leaves.

Taebit had loaned him leggings and a tank made of temp-regulating mesh, but even so sweat crept along his hairline and awareness of the heat made him pause just to draw breath and squint through the trees into light-struck distance.

"They say station-bred never do get used to it," Taebit said, without breaking rhythm. "Horizon, distance, the air, the light."

"It's big. And . . . empty." Though the rider didn't think so.

Taebit cast him a look, jiggled the injector through a jam. "You seem to have adjusted pretty well, actually. Better than Mheth."

Jhinsei looked down at the soil between roots. His hair fell in his eyes and he pushed it away for the hundredth time. "Have to cut this stuff off," he muttered. Something soft hit him in head. He caught at it as it fell: a length of braided mesh. Taebit nodded to his hair.

With the mesh holding his hair back, Jhinsei bent again to his task. As he worked, he replayed their conversation and wondered what Taebit knew. He didn't think Ramev would discuss him with anyone but another obviary; but Taebit was observant, thoughtful. Knew his obviary brother, well enough at least to add up sudden working guests with his brother's prolonged visit and come up with questions. But he didn't ask whatever questions he might have, nor did Ophedia. Never asked; just worked them, fed them, gave them a place to sleep out of the moud storms. Generally kind and friendly. Taebit with his drier than dust humor, Ophedia gruff and gentle together.

Jhinsei found he'd stopped working and was staring into the distance, at that rough, mountainous horizon.

Jhinsei sought out Mheth and filled him in on what Ramev had said. He found the Tiyo amenable to putting their plan, such as it was, into motion. He meant to announce their decision that night and send a message to the *Oni's Wake*, but the farm received another visitor, making the supper table crowded and precluding that conversation.

Tandred Adasanand, a block of a man, arrived on an unlovely beast he called Bliss, a thoroughly inappropriate name for the creature, apparently a hybrid known as a cambull. Taller than Jhinsei, it spit green mucus and reached its long neck to bite anyone who came close. They stabled the cambull near the goats, and it and the goats spit and sneered at one another.

Over the meal, Tandred held forth on subjects from weather to animal genetics, finally coming to the subject of the Sinaiety and the reason for his visit. He lived, Jhinsei gathered, in the Choudow, a valley region just within the first mountain ridges to the west. There, the rumblings of Sinaiety-Tiyo conspiracy and trade corruption to which Taebit and Ophedia had alluded had erupted into outright accusation and threat. Finally, there had been a violent altercation on the grounds of Tiyo's kive-tech beta-testing site, when a group from Tandred's settlement tried to demand answers regarding the disappearance of one of their own who worked as a tester. They were intercepted, none too politely, by a small band of "verten" Sinaiety, the members of the tribe who traveled and conducted trade negotiation. Apparently the verten now took it upon themselves to protect Tiyo interests outright.

"The verten were different; the arrogance they usually hide under a veil of manners—it was foremost, and they were contemptuous with it," Tandred said, pausing to take a deep sip of ale, wipe foam neatly from his facial hair, and belch. "Something's changed; they've come to some new agreement with Tiyo. Something which gives them what they want—which has always been power and land. Land already occupied. The Choudow, or some portion of it."

"You think they've found a way to breach Aggregate accords?" Ophedia said, incredulity in her voice.

"Yes."

A beat of silence. Then, "What's the proof?" Ramev asked.

Tandred held up one finger. "One, the coalition hedged and hedged on the supply deal, then stopped communications entirely. Either intimidated or co-opted. Two," a second finger, "Ashki knows all the verten, and she says there's a non-Sinaiety agent among them. Highly unlikely—unless it's to their extreme advantage. And three, what are they doing playing guard dog at Tiyo's beta-testing facility?"

Jhinsei glanced at Mheth. The Tiyo had been listening closely. Now he shook his head slightly, staring abstractedly at the blinking ochre glow of the link in a dim corner of the room.

"Could mean several things, that," Taebit said. "Not necessarily conspiracy. Could have nothing to do with land in the Choudow." At the looks he received, he raised his hands. "It's disturbing, yes. But considering all possibilities is only common sense."

"True enough, Taebit, but I've made my reading of the situation. I've already contacted Aggregate Oversight."

"And told them what?" Ophedia asked.

"Essentially what I just told you, with a statement from Ashki and kive record of all our communications with the coalition. Now I'm making the rounds. Don't trust the links."

Which would have seemed paranoid to Jhinsei once.

He missed, suddenly and acutely, Sara's mordant attitude, Darshun's gentle presence, Esker's solidity, Tomas' curiosity, felt the lack of them all in a strong, pulling wave.

"You should have contacted the Order first," Ramev said. His voice was mild, but there was tension in his posture, his neck muscles corded.

"The Thorough Order," Tandred said. Nothing else for a moment, then he looked at Ramev over his glass of ale. "The Order takes entirely too much upon itself," he said, and drained his glass. "Ah, Taebit, that's a fine brew. Some sandberries in the mix?"

"Sandberry honey, actually," Taebit said. "Have another?" Thus, and with several dry, off-subject comments, Taebit somewhat diffused the tension.

Tandred left in the early morning; Tandred's news worked like yeast through their company. By the evening of the next day, Taebit had decided to head for the Choudow to assess matters. After further consultation, Mheth and Jhinsei decided to hold off on contacting the *Oni's Wake* and accompany Taebit so that Mheth could investigate the situation himself.

After supper, Jhinsei sat on the floor at a low table in the main living space, working on refitting one of the ranch's response units, little monitors that sat out in the fields collecting weather and soil data and adjusting feeding and watering mixtures and schedules in response. Taebit sat on the long memform couch that took up a third of the room, restringing an intricately carved and ancient instrument. He called it an oud. He had oiled it previously, and the scent of the oil hung in the air.

Ophedia came in from the garden; she sat beside Taebit, close, the memform redistributing to her bulk. There was a sigh and a giggle—from Taebit—and Jhinsei closed his focus down to the work in front of him.

The oud gave a complaining twang and was set aside. After some shifting and more giggles, Ophedia sighed and made a hmm sound, then said, "Those north field sensors running okay now?"

Taebit grunted. "Good enough."

"'Cause I'll be handling things alone while you're off to the Choudow."

"Oh?"

Ophedia looked over at Jhinsei. "Seems Tandred's talk struck a nerve."

Jhinsei set the response unit down. "Mheth already talked to you?"

She gave an affirmative grunt. "To look into the Tiyo situation, he said. And that you'd be going with."

Jhinsei flipped the screwdriver back and forth between his

fingers, looking down at the table. "It's better if the people looking for me don't find me here." He didn't look up to see what their reactions might be.

"Appreciate that, Jhinsei," Ophedia said, and then, "But it's not like we couldn't tell there might be some trouble attached to you." He looked up then, met her gaze.

"We got some good work out of both of you," Taebit said, by way of benediction. He pulled the oud back into his lap and plucked a string, the low note crying through the room. "And Mheth's interest gives some weight to Tandred's theories. Shaping up to be an interesting trip."

Ophedia leaned close to Taebit, tracing a finger down one of the oud's strings; it gave a whisper-whine of sound. "While you're at it, you can take some of the west field crop, a few bushels of seelies, last of the fruit, and a couple flats of the ale, trade for components and medicines."

Taebit picked out a plaintive phrase. "Suppose I can. Have to take the bubble instead of the speeder."

"Suppose you will."

Taebit sighed, then looked over at Jhinsei meditatively, a slight gleam in his eye, startling him.

"What?"

"Ramev's planning to head for the Thorough Order retreat up in the mountains; we'll be going in the same direction for a spell. Might as well caravan." He smiled on the edge of that observation. "Athra knows I love a caravan." He leaned back into Ophedia and tilted his head for a kiss.

❋

Later, when Mheth was not in their makeshift quarters, Jhinsei found him out on the terrace. He joined the Tiyo at the table and they sat, quiet, held by the simultaneous breadth and closeness of planetary night, the arc of patchy clouded and star-pinned night sky somehow more vast than ever the dark of space seemed on-station.

The air, conversely, touched close, a slight chill of evening dew, the scent and taste of more rain, the river, trace sweetness of bean blossoms and fruit trees, a rank whiff of goat. The occasional caprine bleat and the hum of house and ranch systems did little to impinge on the echoing silence of well night.

Mheth shifted, making a small sound, half-sigh, half-mutter. Jhinsei could see a sliver of the Tiyo's cheek and jaw in light from the house; the rest of him was a suggestion of shape, angle, shadow.

Jhinsei just waited.

"I don't think I can do this," Mheth said, eventually. He bent his head, leaning forehead to fisted hands. "I don't even know what I'm trying to do. Be Tiyo's conscience? Me?" He snorted.

Jhinsei drew a breath, unsure what he was going to say, but then Mheth continued.

"I should just stay here. The goats and I are coming to an understanding."

"I imagine Ophedia can use the help," Jhinsei said. He traced a finger over the stone of the tabletop. "But without me and Tae here to . . . ameliorate . . . she'll probably kill you within a week standard and feed you to the goats."

Mheth snorted on a laugh. "They'd enjoy it, too, the nasty blue items." He folded his arms and laid his head down against them.

One of the Tiyo's eyes caught the light now, and he looked at Jhinsei. Jhinsei looked away, out at the grey roll and ruck of land under night-lucent arc of sky. The rider thrilled through him. For a moment he felt he might lift to soar the air above the endless-seeming stretch of world.

A dropping, empty moment followed, frightening, as he fell back into himself, unable to encompass the rider's ecstatic reach.

The rider fled back into bone shadow. Jhinsei's hands shook, his whole being uncertain for several breaths.

"I'm scared, too," he said then.

✻

They set out the following morning. When Tandred left, he headed south on Bliss, further into the plains. They would retrace his route across the steppes and into the Slow Mountains.

It didn't seem like much of a caravan to Mheth—though he couldn't say he'd ever been on one. His impression of the term, however, included a more substantial collection of travelers than he and Taebit in the loaded bubble and Jhinsei and Ramev in a Thorough Order land cruiser.

The first day out, heading from the plains across the green, terraced fields and dark soil of the steppes, they traveled along the river. The land grew steadily steeper, the course of the river cutting more deeply into it. Tall grasses hissed along the bottom of the bubble. They passed through dark, threatening storm systems, rain hissing and popping on the bubble from above, then into brief breaks of white sky, light sheeting down before the next system filled the sky again.

Mheth took it in through the bubble's semiperm. A part of his brain wanted to make it an immersive flash kive. The sounds of the rain, texture of scents, barest touch and taste of that air through the semiperm: the planet invaded his senses as nothing on-station ever had. He thought back to the night before, and Jhinsei's admission. Scared? He was terrified. Yet he felt more than ever determined to take this into his hands, to do something to stop Tiyo becoming a name synonomous with awful behavior.

When they stopped to set up camp, Palogenia was sinking toward the tops of the Grape and Spoon Mountain ranges and the packed soil of the road's track was well above the river's fast flow. Tall, pale grasses made the high banks and the hills shaggy. The sky held clear for a bit. Wind ruffled constantly through the grasses, making the hills look like rough silk in the biscuit-pale light, raising a soft whisper from all around.

Mheth breathed the sweet, fresh air and leaned on the warm side of the bubble while he waited for his legs and gut to understand that they had stopped moving. He triggered the chi and listened to Taebit and Ramev bicker about whether they needed to set up shelters.

His thoughts had been flipping in repetitive patterns ever since Tandred's visit. That Tiyo had an agent or agents in the Sinaiety, he was certain, not just from what Tandred said, but from things he'd learned while working on the documentary kive with Kynan.

What Tandred had said, plus the brief altercation between him and Ramev, had brought several disparate bits of data together in his mind and given Mheth a very bad feeling. Tiyo had been using the Sinaiety, to put his father's dangerous new kive cube technology into circulation, the Sinaiety using Tiyo to grab at land and power. Now he began to wonder, were they also working together to undermine the Thorough Order presence in Palogenia System?

"Mheth!"

The sharp shout brought his head around and he realized Taebit had said his name several times already.

"Put it in motion, skyboy. Get the cooker out of the bubble and set it up, then start prepping some of those onions. Unless you don't want any dinner."

Jhinsei appeared beside him with a raised brow and a hand to his shoulder and they set to work.

⁂

A fire crackled warmly in the ceratile cooker, an old-style mobile hearth. The last of a thin, burning green sunset smoldered between the dark peaks of the mountains. Already the sky was heavily ticked with stars. The air off the river and down from the nearer Slow Mountains was chilly and smelled of more rain coming.

They lounged about the hearth fire on camp pads, conversation having fallen into a lull. Some kind of bird called, *lu-woot, lu-woot,* out in the night over the shush of the river.

In contrast to the fear of earlier, Mheth felt a sense of contentment so deep in his bones he wondered, mildly, if he ought to be alarmed by it.

"Taebit," Jhinsei said into the silence, "why is it you like caravans so much…I mean," he faltered a moment—briefly unsure of his forwardness, Mheth thought—and then finished, "what was Ophedia teasing you about?"

Mheth leaned forward to peer at Taebit through the flame-picked dusk.

"Well," Taebit said softly, "happens that Ophedia and I met on caravan." He looked toward his brother, currently a shadow beyond the bulk of the hearth, then away. "Caravan was out of Farplains, to the south. More than twenty years ago." He fell silent, gazing into the past, and then went on. "I was going to the coffee plantations to look for work. Our father's ranch had taken fatal damage in a planet-shaping convulsion; non-beneficial microbes toxified the soil and the crops were ravaged by a variety of plant diseases. Apso took it over. Ramev'd already gone for the Order. Until I could get a stake together, migratory was about the only option.

"Ophedia was new come from outsystem. She'd bought a piece of land in the steppes. She had some plans, knew right enough what she was after." His teeth showed white in a grin.

"Lucky for you," Ramev said softly.

"Lucky for me," he agreed. "Long travel, the Farplains-Vichou route. Days for talking and…learning. Nights all sweet with sage and vebrillia, mists over everything. By the time we reached Vichou, Ophedia'd hired me as a hand."

"Hired you?" Mheth broke in indignantly.

Across the fire, Ramev chuckled.

"Sure enough. But by then I knew what I wanted, too."

Mheth glanced at Jhinsei, but the Kiyr's eyes were lowered, his focus inward. He opened his mouth on a comment, but an echoing boom rolled across the night, drowning all sound.

Ramev and Taebit were up on their feet, Mheth and Jhinsei following. They peered toward the mountains.

"There," Ramev said, pointing.

A red glow, where recently green sunset had reigned, smudged the dark sky between peaks of the Slow Mountains.

"That's in the Choudow," Taebit said.

By the end of the next day they were in the mountains. The bubble hummed between cliffs, over long rises, down deep inclines, lime-white sunlight flashing across the semiperm dome in the patches between mist and rain.

The light was warm on Mheth's skin, the air cool in the cloud patches. Ramev had taken the lead here, the cruiser some ways before them, occasionally visible around bends in the twisty road. Taebit guided the bubble with one hand, seemingly relaxed, humming softly. It reminded Mheth of Kynan.

What reports they'd been able to pick up over the link told them that a store of chemicals near the Tiyo beta-testing facility—which was in the central hub of the Choudow's settlement areas—had gone up, violently. How exactly this had come about was not clear from what came over link. Meth knew Tiyo, in the person of his brother Grath, must be somewhere in it, covering up more of their father's activities with the lumin. Everything he'd heard since coming to Ash, combined with the knowledge gleaned from his activities on-station, told him there was a Tiyo presence within the Sinaiety, for the purposes of land acquisition, trade control—for power. Specifically, the power they were aiming at would weaken the position of the Thorough Order on Ash and in matters of system trade and policy.

Planet shaping had transformed only ten percent of Ash into viable land—land which had already been worked and proven was especially valuable. The Choudow grew coffee and speciated plants whose properties were used in Thorough Order medicinal compounds, held and produced minerals and ores used in various techs. It was owned and worked by a consortium of longtime settlers and Thorough Order personnel, and it was more than valuable. It was one of a series of keys to the balance of power in Palogenia System.

Add into the mix his father's lumin plans and now the beta-testing site going boom. His father's push with the lumin was something Grath was working to keep a lid on . . . but might his father have his own connections within the Sinaiety—acolytes ready to help humanity evolve through use of the lumin kive technology?

It was a tangle. Mheth looked toward the dark shadow of smoke in the distance.

"So, will Ramev go with us to the Choudow now, to the disaster site?"

Taebit left off humming with a sigh. "Don't think he's quite decided yet. He's been on link to the Order; there are obviaries on-site already. But he'll have to make up his mind soon."

"Why?"

"Cut-off's coming up for the only land route he can take to the retreat."

Soon they caught glimpses of the valley, down though fertile gorges, across narrow ridges, and between plunging crests of land, opening and closing and opening out again.

Taebit slowed the bubble. Up ahead, Ramev had stopped the cruiser on an out-sweeping jut of land with a clear view across the valley. The valley stretched out like an endless rolling bowl, stranded through with the glint of rivers, light chasing rain and cloud in patterns all across it. But smoke hung in a shadowing pall near the center, a rufous smolder only barely visible below. Here was where they'd say goodbye to the obviary; Jhinsei would join Mheth and Taebit in the bubble.

The mountain air was cool and sweet; the smoke too far away for them to smell it yet, with the wind in the other direction. Taebit's normally wry, gentle face was grim.

Mheth's eyes had trouble with the perspective, the distances making little sense. It didn't seem quite real to him; when he tried to grasp its reality, vertigo sent echoes through his head.

He turned away, and saw Jhinsei, a little behind the rest of them, eyes closed, arms folded tight against his chest. He thought at first the Kiyr was only experiencing the same vertigo as he was, but then saw how tightly his fingers gripped his own arm, clawing, how grey his skin looked, shining with sweat in the cool air.

Mheth opened his mouth to say something, and then fell silent as a sheen of light licked from Jhinsei's skin, a glowing suspiration that slipped out of the Kiyr then back in, moving over his face, body, limbs.

The Kiyr's eyes opened and he seemed to look straight at Mheth. Then his eyes rolled up in his head and he pitched forward. With a startled step, Mheth caught Jhinsei as he fell, entirely unconscious. Slipping to the ground with the Kiyr resting half in his arms and lap he felt a slight heat, a tingling along his arms, in his hands, gone almost as soon as he felt it.

Ramev was by them in a moment, peeling back Jhinsei's eyelids, checking his pulse, feeling over his limbs. The obviary reached into the small kit that every obviary carried and pulled out a derm patch. Taebit stood by, frowning.

"He . . ." Mheth started, then trailed off, instead asked Ramev, "Is this because of what's . . . in him?" The obviary didn't answer, reaching to put the patch to Jhinsei's neck.

Before he could, the Kiyr spasmed and gasped as he came to consciousness, hands clutching at Mheth's arms. He opened his eyes a moment, closed them again, and then, using his grip on Mheth's arms, pulled himself up to a sitting position.

Ramev sat back. "What happened?"

The Kiyr's glance flickered up to the obviary and then dropped.

"Jhinsei?"

He shook his head and pulled his arms in tight.

Mheth sat back. "Probably just the vertigo," he said. "I'm a little queasy myself."

"Right," Ramev said, making the word into a whole sentence.

"I think," Jhinsei said tightly, in a strained voice, "I need to go with Ramev to the Thorough Order retreat."

The Thorough Order cruiser had a different hum than Taebit and Ophedia's bubble; it rode lower to the ground, nosing its more powerful head along the terrain. The heavy friction and planet-bound vibration were the same as the bubble's, however; both made Jhinsei feel, after several hours, as if his bones were breaking apart—which was actually a welcome distraction from what was going on inside of him.

This latest episode had decided him and he'd told Mheth, Ramev, and a somewhat nonplussed Taebit—he needed help of the kind only obviaries would offer, if even they could. Jhinsei was beginning to have a premonition of serious unpleasantness.

So he and Ramev were on their own now, having parted with the others an hour back at a fork in the trail. Taebit and Mheth were going on to the Choudow, Ophedia's trade goods now to serve as aid packages. Ramev had given them oxygen derms, filter masks, and instructions to be vigilant of their well-being.

Taebit shook Jhinsei's hand. Then Mheth had stared at Jhinsei and Jhinsei at Mheth.

"I'll come with you," Mheth said.

Jhinsei shook his head. "You have something to do—sorry I won't be there to help."

Mheth looked like he would argue, a familiar expression of recalcitrance twisting his mouth. Then the Tiyo pulled Jhinsei close, gripping him hard. Jhinsei hugged him back. They gripped hands a long moment after.

"Be careful," Jhinsei said.

"And you," Mheth said.

They parted.

Ramev navigated, focused on the road which took them higher and deeper into the mountains. Jhinsei glanced at him sidelong, keeping his eyelids lowered. He wasn't really pretending exhaustion—but he wasn't ready to answer the obviary's questions, either.

Ramev, for his part, didn't seem ready to ask them.

The two half-moon seats in the cruiser's forward cab were made of sueded memform, soft against his neck. Light stuttered through trees and rock formations, flicked over his eyes, red through lowered lids.

He'd been standing there, taking in the dark pall of smoke and the distant evidence that things were still burning, despite the rain. Then—

Everything spasmed, flashed . . . the distant roll of the valley, the presence of Ramev, Taebit, and Mheth close by, his own insides and outside, guts and skin, sound roaring and whispering at once, unbound light and resonant darkness, forever and the smallest fleck of moment flashing through him. It was—whatever it was, it was too much and he'd gone blotto.

The rider was quiet now, felt almost contrite in this after-silence. Too quiet. Jhinsei didn't understand what had happened, and the rider was his only source of information on the subject.

He closed his eyes all the way. *Hello*?

Nothing. He could feel the rider, but the rider wasn't talking. Brilliant. Chasing a figment through his imagination. Except the rider was very much more than that.

Talk to me—what was that? What happened?

The rider slunk out from bone shadow and synapse. It didn't stretch out onto him as it usually did, reaching to touch the world through his senses, but hovered, oddly contained.

I believe the correct term would be . . . growing pains.

Ashes to Dust

Taebit maneuvered the bubble down out of the mountains, picking up speed as the valley opened out around them. The road passed through thickly grown fields, groves, and clustered settlements. From the valley floor, the distant sullen burning could not be seen, only the towering, still-spreading cloud of heavy smoke. It was several hours before they actually came within its shadow.

As the transport took them within a netherworld of smoke, Mheth glanced back once through the shadow toward the lucid valley they were leaving behind.

Grey soot in the air, grit hissing against the semiperm. Taebit keyed filters that made the semiperm less permeable, but the acrid burning still reached them. The bubble's lights cut only a short distance into the dim, an eerie landscape of otherwise undisturbed fields and dwellings, covered in ash and debris.

Mheth's eyes began to sting, his throat to burn. Taebit's eyes began to tear as well, and he gestured to the supplies Ramev had given them.

"Get out those filter masks; guess we should do some of the derms, too."

He found them in the neatly ordered box. Taebit slowed the bubble and stopped, lights flashing. He snapped one of the masks open and put it on, covering his nose and mouth with the filter, his eyes with lozenge goggles.

Mheth snapped a mask open as Taebit had and it took shape in his hands. He put it on, pulling the band over his head, drew a deep, filtered breath, another, feeling the constriction ease in his throat and lungs. They each stuck on one green-gold derm. The derms went immediately a deeper green, shading to blue.

In the short time they sat there, a thin layer of gritty soot had silted onto the bubble in little piles and smears. Taebit set them moving again, keying the semiperm dome to a low vibration to shake off the worst of the silt.

The rest of the journey was tense and eerie. Things rose out of the raining soot and murk—buildings, fields, abandoned equipment, groves of trees—then receded.

Unable to relax, Mheth sat on the edge of the seat, peering ahead. Time stretched into subjective fugue; it seemed they would be forever on this road. By the transport chron, it was a little under an hour later they stopped.

They were still several kilometers from the smoldering site when they hit a makeshift line of old ground vehicles and storage drums cordoning off the area beyond. Fire still raged in what had been a huge compound of buildings.

"Chemical," Taebit commented through the mask. "Has to be."

Flame and smoke roiled in towering rage. The heat hit them, so intense they weren't likely to have traveled much further anyway. They watched as air vehicles moved in from the northern ridge of mountains and dropped small objects into the smoking inferno, sweeping away sharply as soon as their loads were dropped. The only result Mheth could discern was a thickening of the smoke.

A warehouse building loomed to their right with more ground vehicles parked by it under an awning of slick metal-silk tarps set on stasis poles. Taebit backed the bubble from the cordon and took them over to park among the others, hidden from the raging glow in the shadow and shelter of the building. The rain was beginning again, mixing into the soot in the air, turning it into sludge.

Several cruisers with Thorough Order markings sat among the vehicles. Taebit grabbed a case of seelie nuts, pointed Mheth to a box of gualem fruit, and headed for the scythe-screened doorway. Mheth hefted the box, a whiff of clean, tangy fragrance rising from it, incongruous in the present environment. He followed Taebit through the screen; it hissed and sparked as they passed through, removing a portion of the sooty debris dusting them.

Inside, air filters hissed quietly from above and after he set the box down, Mheth unclipped the top of the mask and slid it off his face to dangle around his neck. The air wasn't exactly fresh, but it was breathable. Stacks of storage pods and huge crates had been pushed over three layers deep to line one wall, making space for a temporary shelter and med center. Biolumes on stands pooled light through the nearer half, panels of ceraplas separated out shadowed sleep space at the farther end, nearly two-thirds of the floor space filled with cots and mats, most of them occupied.

Mheth found himself staring at a woman with half her face covered by healing mesh, and half her arm on that side missing. An obviary sat by her, changing the mesh on what was left of her arm, the old mesh browned with blood. On the mat next to her, a small child of indeterminate sex watched solemnly. Beyond them were more injured—many, so many. An obviary sat with a man covered head to toe in mesh, a breather over his nose and mouth; another sat before a line of mobile but singed and bloodied people. Mheth turned away slightly, feeling a bit like someone had sucked his insides into the void.

What was he doing here? He should have gone with Jhinsei and Ramev. The Kiyr was at least familiar, a Thorough Order retreat would have been…restful, or something. Anything. There was nothing here for him, Tiyo Mhethianne Tiyo. Nothing he could do, for himself, for anyone else… Mheth stiffened his spine. Don't be craven. Someone had to do something about his family's crimes.

"Taebit." A man approached them.

"Trinam." Taebit shook his hand. "Trinam Ribacci, Mheth."

With a brief nod to Mheth, Trinam went on, "Got your link. Any supplies are of course much appreciated. Much appreciated. I think what we'll do is hook you up with Ashki, she'll know where best to put you to work. It's terrible." He shook his head, met Taebit's gaze, and dropped his. "Nineteen confirmed dead—so far—in the initial incident, the wounded," he raised a hand to gesture, "you can see." He was an older man, pale-skinned, with a weak chin somewhat hidden by a precisely trimmed beard, dark eyes. He wore well-fitted clothes, somewhat soot-stained now.

As they followed Trinam between rows of mats, Mheth kept his gaze on the back of Taebit's head. He resisted the urge to put the mask back in place. Blood, medicines, unwashed flesh and other things he preferred not to analyze permeated the air. The crying of several children and huskier sobbing from one or two adults drifted to them from different parts of the huge space. He felt trapped in a horrible full-immersion kive feed, the kind you didn't want full somatics on.

Trinam led them to a small alcove created by several panels of lurid, touch-sensitive ceraplas that looked like something left over from the set for a heave-whacker, or one of Grath's hurt and fuck kives. That evocation evaporated as Mheth saw a small, stout woman sitting at a console before three work globes, a link, and a pile of hand units. While she worked a globe with her left hand, the right reached without looking for a heavy mug, sipped, replaced it; that hand went to work on another globe while her left still worked the first. She had a cap of disheveled pale hair, a full round face red in the cheeks. Her busy hands were inelegant and pudgy.

"Ashki."

She jumped at Trinam's voice, looking up at them, blinking watery brown eyes. She settled quickly, though: magisterial in a round, red-faced sort of way. "Trinam?"

Her gaze passed over Taebit and Mheth, came back to Trinam.

"This is Taebit Evans," Trinam said. "Lives over to the steppes. And uh, Mheth. Taebit's brought supplies from their farm and they're both ready to lend a hand."

She nodded, looking distracted, her attention going back to the globes, then said, without looking back at them, "Relay and comestibles can use them, one each."

❊

The terrain heightened and sharpened around them, the cruiser taking stomach-dropping turns over deep precipices, nosing up, then down. Sharp peaks crenellated the pale green sky, steeping the plunge of narrow valleys in deep blue shadow. The vegetation was thick, brisk scents reaching them on chill air through the semiperm. They passed through clouds, deep grey mists, and out, into wafer-thin light.

As they plunged ever deeper and slowly higher, Jhinsei saw waterfalls slinging down to form pools far below; unexpected meadows dotted by violet and blue flowers; birds with wingspans wider than arms outstretched, riding high currents of air. Once, as Ramev maneuvered them slowly through an area strewn with mossed-over slabs and boulders like Leviathan play blocks, he looked up to see an animal, small and sleek and still, perched above them, watching their progress.

The rider, reticence abandoned, pressed up into his senses. He found his fingers spread against the slightly porous surface of the semiperm, nostrils flaring, eyes tracking. The dread drop of shadow and water down and down, the craggy lift of rock towering above them, the trembling of a fantastically twisted tree that had grown in a continuous downshaft of wind, and the flame lick of something glowing indigo fire, glimpsed far below in a pool of water, guarded by enormous pale ferns—he absorbed and was absorbed utterly by all.

"Not behaving like any stationer I ever saw planetside."

Ramev's voice startled him and he sat back, blinked, and glanced at the obviary.

"Ought to be cringing in the seat with your eyes shut about now," he continued.

Jhinsei considered responses, settled on "Are you doing a study?"

"They've been done. The definitive work is Xoixan's." He spoke without looking at Jhinsei, eyes on the terrain. His manner was pure obviary, calm and inquisitive on a note of receptive concern—not too pushy, but opening the door for confidences which might help in an eventual diagnosis and treatment.

"Obviaries," Jhinsei said. "Is there a course for that expression on your face, or does it come naturally?"

Ramev's lips pursed over a smile. "Extra credit; you stare into a mirror while kiving true stories of horrible things happening to nice people." He glanced at Jhinsei again, lips pursed over something other than a smile.

Jhinsei waited for the questions, but they didn't come. Eventually the tension of waiting eased and his attention drifted back out through the semiperm. Light and shadow flicked over his face. Then Ramev's voice came again.

"It's becoming too much for your body, isn't it?"

He swallowed. Sun burned over his eyes and he stared into the white-gold glare. "Growing pains, apparently."

"Apparently?"

"It talks to me now."

Ramev couldn't seem to find anything to say to that.

The cruiser climbed higher. Jhinsei let his head fall back against the warmth of the seat. Sun and shadow now, light thinning even more with the atmosphere. The rider soaked it in through his skin.

Jhinsei leaned forward, intent on the scenery, in a kind of fugue as the rider poured through him into the passing landscape. The sudden cessation of the cruiser's movement jolted him; the bone-melting constancy of vibration emptied only slowly out of his limbs. He felt a touch of light pressure at his neck and turned to see Ramev bending close. He blinked at the obviary.

"Oxygen assist," he said. "It's thin up here."

Jhinsei slid his fingers over the derm under his ear and nodded.

Ramev shifted back to his side of the seat and Jhinsei sat up with a yawn.

Up here didn't really cover it.

A sweep of land wide and tall and deep, like waves of verdure and rock frozen in the act of crashing into the sky. Above, in the breaking wave of the mountaintop, a long, slope-roofed structure hugged the crags. White walls curved to the land and rose to carved and peaked lintels. The many windows, round and rectangular, were set with carved screens. Tiled and painted terraces laced through the wandering structure and towers of varied stone stood at several of its many ends. Turbine wind towers and solar panel arrays outrigged the structure, reminding Jhinsei of the Quinteppi ships that put in at station.

The mountain rolled down to a shallow valley, steeped at the moment in late sun over the sage and honey colors of plants and flowers carpeting the ground in patterns. Stone walks made part of the pattern and after a moment, he could see a person here and there, walking, or bent over the vegetation with a basket beside them.

Ramev set the cruiser moving again. Pale blue brenner goats

dotted the slopes between them and the retreat, bleating as they leapt up or down away from the noise of the cruiser, their hooves clipping on rock. A thin silky air filtered through the semiperm.

The rider pushed up through him; for a moment there was radiance, joy sweeter than breath to starving lungs. Then the radiance turned to burning behind his eyes, pressure under his skin. His senses blurred, and blurred further, sickeningly: the taste of goat cries, overpowering scent of wide-open light, the colors of the flowers and the green verge singing through his bones, too deeply, burning echoes bleeding into his brain, his blood . . . he was a world, a universe, an eon . . . but he couldn't . . . he wasn't . . . *I'm not big enough.*

Distantly, he heard a voice. "Bloody void," it cursed. He wanted to agree.

*

His adventures in the gravity well of Ash, Mheth mused, seemed fated to revolve around the preparation and dispensation of food. He balanced a tray of broth, fruit juice, water and supplements in his arms and followed behind a short man named Tariq, who carried another tray of nuts and fruit, circulating among the wounded and grieving. There was a self-serve area set up for volunteers, the displaced, and those waiting for news of the missing.

Tariq was a poor choice of ministering angel; the few words he spoke, to Mheth and patients alike, were delivered with terse, directionless antagonism. Mheth realized he probably wasn't much better, but at least he found it in him to be gentle, his voice pitched like an obviary's to a reassuring range of calm concern—which was really only a defense against sunken, blank, or hopeful eyes, burned hands and bodies.

There were no Sinaiety among the wounded; Mheth was looking out for them. He'd seen several among the volunteers, recognizable for their heavy, complex robes and lack of interaction with anyone who wasn't Sinaiety.

He and Tariq made the rounds until it seemed everyone was fed and watered. Then Ashki set Mheth to the task of putting together kits of personal hygiene supplies, tiny sonic depilatories and hair cleaning combs, tooth cleaning tabs, insta-bath cloths, and vitamin derms. When he next looked up, Taebit had disappeared to somewhere or other.

Mheth missed the Kiyr, last bit of the familiar. He felt hollow and heavy at once, as if he might either float away or sink without a trace. No one would miss him, no one remark upon the phenomenon. This tragedy, these people—was Tiyo really responsible for this? And if so, why was it his responsibility? He hadn't set it in motion, wasn't doing any dirty work to cover for his father's madness. He was the irresponsible, black-marked Tiyo, out of the loop. What was it he thought he could do here? Some vague notion of expiation had been in it somewhere, to right the wrongdoing of his family. Great yawning maw of the universe, how ridiculous. Clearly he'd been overseeing flash kive features too long, to have such simplistic and null-headed notions. Or perhaps he'd been inspired by the company of Taebit and Ophedia, fine humanoids that they were. But he wasn't an agent of Aggregate Control or Oversight, to investigate and make arrests.

He wasn't Tiyo's conscience, was he? He'd been fired from the only position he had ever held in the family business.

And yet. Hadn't he benefitted all his life from the power shifting that had gone on, beneath his notice, out of his sight, but underpinning his place in the universe, a place of unexamined safety and privilege? And didn't he have a way to contact some agents of Aggregate Control, Jhinsei's Captain Kohl and her crew?

When the kits were all assembled, he avoided Ashki, who had emerged to confer with several soot-covered rescue workers. Mheth looked around for Taebit, but didn't see him in the building. Snagging a food container and some water, he found a quiet spot at a table beyond the screens.

The food was surprisingly good. He didn't recognize the marking on the container's side, a plump man with a bird perched on his hand, so it was most likely local, something that never made it out of the well.

A low murmur of voices preceded a small group of Sinaiety, three men and a woman, by their robes and hoods. They fell silent on seeing him, brushed past him with bare courtesy and settled at the far end of the table. There they began speaking again, in low tones whose words Mheth couldn't make out. He sighed into his food, feeling tension creep its cramped fingers into his muscles. Finally, though it somehow felt wrong in the face of all the suffering around him, he triggered the chi.

Warm wash of relaxing muscles, clarity, the brain chem of well-being. Thus, rather than hunch further over when Ashki appeared behind the screens with food container and mug in hand, he smiled on her as she sat across the table from him.

She seemed different, somehow, out from behind the work globes, and Mheth realized it was simply that her face and body had unknotted from intense concentration. Wide brown eyes regarded him intelligently from her round, red-cheeked face.

"Don't worry," she said. "I'm not going to assign you to another job. Eat in peace."

"Where'd you spirit Taebit off to?"

"He went with a crew to the areas where the fire's out and they're digging the rubble for survivors and casualties."

She lifted a shoulder at his look. "He volunteered."

It was chill in the cavernous warehouse, despite heaters. Ashki wore an antique style of long, split seamed coat over heavy leggings. Made of equally out-of-date heat retaining bio-silk in a dull metallic brown, the floor-length coat's sleeves ended in half-gloves. Mheth had the chi to impart warmth, the Sinaiety their robes and layers. Mheth considered them, the Sinaiety, sidelong, tapping his utensil on the food container.

"Do they ever mix with anyone other than themselves?"

Ashki's pale brows lowered a moment over the question. Then she shook her head. "No. The only interface, even among the verten, is with the vert, by their law. This is as mixed up with the rest of us as they ever get. To be eating at this table, you know, that's actually treading on the edges of legality for them; but, in extraordinary circumstances..." She trailed off with a gesture.

Mheth raised his own brows. "Why are they here at all?"

"There were Sinaiety in the complex where the beta-testing facility that went up is located. Regularly are. It's the trade center hereabouts, after all, and they certainly don't trust anyone who's not one of them to protect their interests. Matter of fact, the vert was there and she hasn't been found among the survivors yet. Likelihood of finding anyone else alive gets slimmer every hour. So."

"How are you—interfacing—then?"

"Oh, there's always a vert in training. This one's young and male and quite an arrogant little prick."

Mheth found himself grinning. They spoke softly, keeping the conversation private.

"In fact," her nose wrinkled, "if the other vert isn't found, the new one will represent a serious shift in Sinaiety relations. He's come up from a different faction, with a very different set of priorities and attitudes on relations with the Choudow and the rest of Ash—and, one supposes, the Aggregate at large."

"They don't have names, any of these verten?"

"They have them." She shrugged. "Not for us to know."

Mheth chewed on that, along with the last of his stew, while Ashki dug into hers.

"You know," he said after a bit, "that sort of cohesion to a founding principle at such a stretch of gens…it's rather statistically impossible, from what I understand of cultural drift theory."

"Mmm. Tell that to them."

"Mmm. Apparently, that wouldn't be very politic. What would they do, anyway, if I talked to one of the verten other than the vert?"

Her brows rose, as though no one ever ventured such a thing.

"Oh, come now, surely? Don't you have any sociopaths, children?"

"We've been living in proximity to the Sinaiety for all our lives, Mheth. And gens back. There were feuds with them once, territorial wars. We've learned."

"Have they?"

"No doubt. Off-worlders have been known to make the mistake—the verten just ignore them utterly." She inclined her head slightly down table. "Give it a try if you don't believe me."

Mheth smiled again. "Gracious, woman, don't bait the freshies." He shifted slightly, toying with the wilted edge of his food container. "What about Sinaiety lands proper? There've been visits by anthrotographers, Aggregate reps, I know there have."

She finished her stew and flattened the container with its little man and bird for recyc. "Awfully curious, aren't you?"

"I've been told. What do you think happened?" He gestured beyond the shelter's walls, the high windows and laboring filters, toward the unseen, still-smoldering ruin.

Her eyes flicked briefly down table again. Mheth suspected it was an involuntary reaction. "Something exploded," she said.

"A bomb? Which begs the question, planted by whom?"

She gave him a very direct look. "We don't know yet if it was an explosive; the site's been too hot for investigation."

"Well, that kind of tells its own story, doesn't it? What I don't get is, if this was cover-up for something going on in the testing facility . . . well, it seems excessive."

She shook her head.

"The shift in the Sinaiety, then, maybe," Mheth went on, softly, musing to himself more than to her.

But she caught his hand, hard, in her pudgy fingers. "Don't meddle. This situation is a chem salt waiting for a catalyst."

He had to think for a moment to realize "chem salt" was well slang for a primary planet-shaping tool. He gave her a brief nod, but said, "Seems to me the salt's already been catalyzed."

She released his hand and then patted it, which Mheth found rather effectively incongruous to her tone. When she stood up, she was not much taller than she had been sitting.

A dark cave. The derelict ship, Jhinsei realized slowly. He sat at its center, the warm, dark glassy smoothness shimmering with indigo-violet fractures of light, at that spot where he'd touched the strange skin of the real derelict on-station, weeks ago. A universe ago. At the edges of this derelict, though, cosmos skirled, a forever of drifting space. Shadow melted into eon, the dust of cosmic life. Before him, hovering in the air, deep radiance in the form of a flame: the rider. Then, as if they'd been there all along, forever, Esker, Darshun, Sara, and Tomas in a half-circle about him.

"It's a conundrum," Darshun said, cross-legged beside him, leaning forward, hands clasped under her chin.

Sara snorted. "Hardly."

"Self-preservation above all, Sare?" Esker's voice was mild.

"Damn straight."

Jhinsei couldn't take his gaze from the radiant flame, the rider. They were connected, inextricably linked. Warmth, luminosity, like a sticky flux of blood, flowed between them.

"It's his choice," Tomas said. "Has to be. No one else's."

"It's not just another life form, a squalling human babe," Esker said. "It's more."

"No," Darshun said. "How can you say that? A different life—ancient, the last, vast—maybe beyond our comprehension—but no more precious."

Sara snorted again.

"Something up your nose, Sare?" Darshun said.

"It's killing him. Him, Jhinsei. Who knows what it will be, or if it should be. But Jhinsei deserves to live."

"Yes," Esker said. "Yes."

"Still his choice," Tomas said.

The rider did not speak, only very gently began to disengage from him, withdrawing warmth and luminosity, breaking the connection filament by gossamer filament, as he could not. So slowly he knew he would barely feel it drawing away.

". . . has to be his choice, Zhou, you know that."

"It's killing him, whatever it is."

"Zhou, this has always been your worst—Jhinsei, hello. With us again?"

He blinked, slow to focus. Then a familiar, freckled face, red hair: Ramev.

Someone else sat just beyond the Termagenti obviary at the end of the pallet. A small woman with straight black hair, pale eyes, severe cheekbones. She looked vaguely familiar.

"Jhinsei, this is Zhou. She trained with me and I've asked her to consult on your case."

Mountain air came through a long window running the length of one wall, the view shaded by fretted overhangs. The room's colors and character suggested a space carved from some ivory dawn in another age, one which favored high ceilings, arches, and latticed screens of translucent, roseate stone. Ramev's hair clashed.

"We've met, actually," the woman said, and her voice brought it back to him, the brief interaction on a station lift.

"You'll," he paused at the croak of his own voice, then continued, "have to give me that tour of the Thorough Order Arts Center." His gaze dropped to her wrist. "You took your arts?"

"In flash kives, yes."

Jhinsei looked back to Ramev. "My case?"

Ramev looked down. "With her arts in flash kives, Zhou has knowledge specialized to neural conditions."

"Is that what we're calling it?" He coughed again, croaky voice giving out.

"Here." Ramev held a clear bulb in front of his face, water beading its interior; his desperate need for liquid registered and he opened his mouth to sip, then took the bulb from Ramev. His mouth came unstuck somewhat, the simple cool wash of the water everything for a moment. He sipped in silence, not watching them watching him. Felt the rider, back in the shadow of his bones, a luminous presence.

After a while he didn't like all the silence. "Two obviaries, just for me. I must have gotten some heavy juice while I wasn't looking."

"Yes," Zhou said, "but not the kind that brokers Aggregate trade or alliance."

"And just where did you pick it up?" Ramev contemplated him. "Time to tell us the whole story, Jhinsei—the whole thing. You're safe here. There's no Khat, no Tiyo, no Ro; and we need to know if we have any hope of helping."

In the pale light of the gracious room, all of this seemed indisputable. So he told them. They drew more from him with a well-placed word or gesture than he'd known he had in him to say. When he came to the end of the words, another bulb of water and a bowl of some sweet, white-green fruit later, they were silent. Zhou stared fiercely into a middle distance while Ramev tapped one finger against the side of his face with his gaze on the floor.

"Well," Jhinsei said, "I feel so much better now. Very reassuring. Fine form. You've relieved me of my annoyance at the intimidating perfection of obviaries."

Ramev smiled, but Zhou frowned. “I still say,” she said to Ramev and not to Jhinsei, another breach of obviary finesse, “system suppressant is the best course of treatment.”

“System what?”

“System suppressants,” Ramev answered him, somewhat restoring natural order with the reassuring calm of his voice, “are a kind of treatment which has been used widely at various times in history. It is, however, a treatment at odds with the tenets at the base of Thorough Order teaching and rarely used now.”

“Except in cases involving absorbed sensory dysfunction,” Zhou said. “Which is my area of specialization, you’ll recall.”

“He’s not a kive testing casualty.” Well, there went Ramev’s composure.

“No, but that’s the closest model we’ve got.”

Jhinsei’s attention drifted as the rider simmered to the surface of his awareness like a spinship’s drive heat melting up from his bones. From the corner of his eye, and in the reflections of both Zhou’s and Ramev’s gazes, he saw the flush of shimmering energy that licked from his skin and then faded back in. Scent and song filled his mouth and colored his sight.

Then words, as the initial surge subsided. *Let them treat you. You cannot hold me, cannot . . . your material is not right, for me to grow further, to become—neither of us will survive.*

Jhinsei took this in, aware of both Ramev and Zhou watching him with equal parts avid fascination and concern. Aware. He was aware, of so much, through the rider, as the rider through him. How sweet life, how amazing.

There must be some way.

No.

But—

“There must be some way,” he echoed his thought aloud. Zhou’s lips thinned; Ramev raised a reddish eyebrow.

“To what?”

Yes, Jhinsei said to the rider. There’s some way. How do you usually . . . do it? Become? Silence, a floating in his senses, low thrum in his bones. Then, *I need the ship, that which was myself, as well as needing the material of your body and being. With the stuff of the ship, yes, perhaps I would survive to be reborn, but you would not survive the transformation.*

The ship. The derelict on Termagenti.

"I have to go back to the station," Jhinsei said.

There is no time. No time. I cannot control my growth for very much longer. You must let them treat you.

"Jhinsei, you can't. If you go back to Termagenti now, you'll be arrested and quarantined."

He took in the concern in Ramev's eyes and nodded. "It's too late, anyway," he said softly. He looked down at his hands. His hair, grown long, hung forward over his face. The moment seemed to detach, in silence, from the flow of time. Eventually, he looked up at Zhou.

"So this treatment will do what, exactly?"

"Isolate, suppress, and ultimately destroy the foreign elements in your body."

Destroy.

I don't want to kill you, Jhinsei. Without the stuff of the ship, I would die in the process anyway. We should stop the process so you do not have to.

Simple really.

Yes.

A breeze sifted into the room, the air crisp.

"Jhinsei," Ramev said, "you don't have to decide this moment. There isn't even a guarantee that it will—"

"Okay."

"Okay what?" Zhou asked.

He met her gaze. "Let's try the treatment."

She held his gaze for long time and then echoed him, "Okay. I have to make the derms. It will take a day."

After Zhou had gone, Jhinsei watched Ramev fold a blanket, stack dish and bulb on a tray, peer out the window toward the land unrolling below. Eventually he came back to the pallet and sat at the end of it.

"We don't know if this treatment is going to work. It's simply the only treatment we can come up with."

"What's wrong, Ramev?"

The obviary's lips curled. "You learned a bit of obviary manner in all your time with us." He sighed. "System suppression is not a beneficent treatment. It will attack your systems as much as this 'rider.' Making you more ill to make you better goes against all I believe in."

"Oh." The mutter-cry of a goat drifted up from the mountainside. "Would you show me around the place—if you're not too busy?"

"You should rest."

"Uh-huh." Jhinsei just looked at him.

Ramev shook his head. "Come on, then."

Mheth idled at the table, slumped over, head resting on arm, listening to the low voices of the Sinaiety at the other end, his thoughts running after conspiracies that slipped before him like smoke and shadow. If Tiyo was using the Sinaiety, or members of the Sinaiety, to cover up testing gone wrong at the facility here, what did the Sinaiety get out of it? Well, Ashki had answered that. Did that mean a faction within the Sinaiety itself had done this, taking the assignment for the cover-up from someone in Tiyo as an opportunity to serve their own purposes—namely getting rid of the current vert?

Land and power. Could Tiyo really deliver on a promise of already occupied Choudow lands to the Sinaiety? Would Tiyo—in the person of who, his brother, his father?—make such a promise? Why? To secure the support of the Sinaiety; but, for what? Surely they had more efficient ways of covering up alarming testing results.

He sighed and straightened. Through the lurid screens, he glimpsed Taebit, returning with a search team.

Slipping out of the dining area, he negotiated mats, people, and med equipment, making his way toward the entrance. It looked like the search party had only brought out one person, a soot-blackened figure on a hover-stretch, even now being transferred to a mat, an obviary standing by.

Taebit gave little more than a grunt in greeting. The filter mask hung around his neck, though his face wore a reverse imprint, clean skin around his eyes and nose, a layer of grey everywhere else.

The scythe screen had cleaned some from him, but wet ash and grit were etched into every thin crease of skin. He wore a hooded oversuit of some thin, shiny material that glowed slightly. For visibility, Mheth supposed. Dirty, ashy water still beaded the suit. Two other searchers had come in with him, likewise damp, gritty, and exhausted. Taebit pushed the hood off his head, exposing the orange wool of his hair, and dropped down onto a bench, elbows on knees, rubbing at his eyes.

Mheth slipped to the food table, grabbed a stew container and some water, came back and set them and himself on the bench beside Taebit.

Taebit nodded, took up the water. His grimy hand left smudges on the bulb. He muttered something and then began to shake. After a moment, Mheth realized he was laughing, almost silently, the kind of laughter that was close kin to crying.

"Ash," he said. "We're Ashlings." Slowly the laughter subsided. Suddenly he drew a deep breath, as if he hadn't remembered to breathe for a while, and rubbed a hand over his face.

He didn't seem to have any more words; Mheth sat beside him in silence, casting about for something useful to say or do.

"Taebit," one of the other searchers called, "this way to clean up; then we get some rest." The woman plodded off without looking to see if Taebit was following. The Ashling sighed, nodded to Mheth, and hove to his feet, trailing the other two searchers in his party. He gave a last glance in the direction of the person they'd brought in, and then disappeared beyond another of the various makeshift walls of screens and crates.

Mheth felt a kind of sinking, an awful hollowness in his gut.

The entry opened, shadowy figures beyond the scythe screen moving into it. The screen hissed and sparked and the newcomers emerged, one, two, three, and four of them. Mheth went very still, every hair on his body standing up as if someone had plugged a live wire into him, his pulse beating a sudden lightspeed thrum. Then he shrank down, slid off the back of the bench, and retreated to the shadows.

Peering out between screen sections he observed the party, which included an Ashling official wearing a suit and an anxious expression, an Aggregate official with an Immersive Technologies

Oversight & Investigations patch on her black uniform jump, and—his brother Grath. A Tiyo lackey stood at his brother's shoulder, cybered and scanning.

Of course. The Tiyo beta-testing site had been in the center of the complex taken by the explosion and the chemical fires that followed. A Tiyo had to make an appearance. Of course Mheth was already here, but no one knew he was a Tiyo. And he didn't represent Tiyo interests. Mheth watched his brother. Grath's eyes, heavy-lidded, did not so much take in the surroundings as dismiss them. He wore an appropriate expression of somber concern, but his posture and body language told Mheth other things. He was wary of the Aggregate investigator, offended even, at her presence. Immersive Technologies Oversight & Investigations was a branch of Aggregate Oversight. Which made Mheth think of Jhinsei's ship captain and her crew and, looking at his brother, gave Mheth an idea. From what Jhinsei had said, Sobriance Kohl and company were in the system investigating for some obscure office of Aggregate Control, the sterner half of the Aggregate's two regulatory arms, control and oversight. Because, perhaps, as such they could do things that the official presence, the agent accompanying Grath, couldn't?

Tandred's report about Tiyo's new kive tech beta results must have reached at least somewhat receptive ears, though. The Immersive Tech office had sent this officer before the explosion happened; there hadn't been enough time for her to be there otherwise.

Except that now, of course, there was no evidence left for her to investigate. Just an explosion and the fires it had caused—those had quite effectively wiped out the beta-testing labs. Which made the case for Tiyo being behind the explosion a bit stronger.

Mheth's thoughts strayed to Kynan and he promised himself to double check that the Toveshi was truly safe and away. His attention came back to his brother's group as they began to move around the shelter, stopping to talk to an obviary. He was torn, wanting to hear what they said, but unwilling to be seen by his brother or the Tiyo lackey. Of course, hiding out where he was the whole time Grath's party was here might prove difficult. An obviary had already come back to poke through some supplies, scrutinizing Mheth but not saying anything.

He watched as the small group worked its way around, the investigating officer and the Ashling taking the lead more and more. With some brief word to them as they disappeared beyond the panels and crates marking Ashki's territory, Grath hung back, the lackey at his shoulder. His brother didn't appear to say anything, just inclined his head, and the lackey slipped off between cots and out of Mheth's view. Grath then disappeared beyond the screens, rejoining the others.

Mheth considered, watching the lackey now, as he slipped back out through the scythe screen. The quality of the light coming in at the entry and through the high windows seemed to indicate that the day was waning. But he wasn't certain. He hadn't been on-planet long enough for the light to make that much sense to him. He didn't relish the idea of being outside under a rain of wet ash and debris in the dark.

Making his way, with frequent glances toward the lurid screens sheltering Ashki's alcove, Mheth passed Taebit, hard asleep on a mat, a thin, silvery line of drool across his stubbled jaw. Taebit's fingers twitched momentarily, eyes moving under the thin skin of lids. Mheth moved on, to the scythe screen and through its brief, scintillate friction, then out.

Cold, humid air enfolded him, gritty and clinging, the smell of wet ash strong after his time in the relatively clean, filtered air of the shelter. Moisture beaded the ground transports near him, and thick mud had spattered the hover guards. The day was waning and a steady drizzle popped and hissed beyond the canopy. The directionless salt-colored light held in the cloud cover left the land beneath adrift in leaden twilight. Mheth peered out from under the canopy, scanning the dim landscape, the smudged distance.

There was a suggestion of movement, midway into the distance, in a small grove of trees huddling in the ashy milieu like a widow at a funeral. Mheth glanced left and right, then set out across the field. He was wishing for one of the suits Taebit had worn, or at least a hood, before he'd gone ten steps. The rain was barely coming down, but the air itself was grubby and clinging.

Up close, the trees looked like thin, misshapen pillars. Or the Drift Witch's many-fingered hands. They retained a thick leaf canopy though and little of the falling grit and rain reached him once he was under their cover, only an occasional drip or creak of branches. Triggering the chi, he was able to move slowly and silently from the cover of one trunk to another. He peered into the murk, his eye augmentation aiding his night vision.

Something rustled in the leaves, a branch cracking, and Mheth fell still. The heavily swathed figure of one of the verten Sinaiety emerged out of the gloom between boles. A twitch of swathing and the verten showed a delicate female face. She glanced around. Then another figure emerged and Grath's Tiyo lackey joined her. Mheth wasn't close enough to hear them, but either this was an unlikely illicit love affair, or it was simple proof of Tiyo's involvement with some among the Sinaiety—an involvement they felt the need to keep secret from both the Ashlings and, possibly, the rest of the Sinaiety.

Mheth edged slowly closer, alert to the slightest notice in either the Sinaiety woman or the Tiyo agent. Finally, he could hear them and fell still again, leaning into one of the knobby, smooth-barked trees, listening. Sweat pricked along his neck and slid down his face.

"—very explicit. You've placed Tiyo in an unbelievable position. With the report that just went in to Aggregate Oversight, it now looks like we could very well have done this to cover the evidence. You've made it necessary for Tiyo Grath Tiyo to come down here. And you still haven't explained your actions satisfactorily. How does a simple instruction to eradicate kived testing results and remove several individuals become a fireball that takes out the entire Choudow Trade Center?"

The woman's head lifted slightly. "The pattern required and we interpreted. Tiyo knows this is our priority. The pattern."

"The collateral damage of your 'interpretation' was too high!"

"We have always and will always do as the pattern compels. Tiyo should not be surprised. The Tiyo understands." The emphasis she placed on *the* told Mheth that she meant Sarsone, and that Grath was a pale second in the Sinaiety's view. So what had his father been up to with the Sinaiety? Just what was the pattern?

His father's evolution of humanity?

"Tiyo Grath will be *the* Tiyo one day. Tiyo Sarsone can no longer be the sole voice of Tiyo's role in the pattern—"

"The Tiyo still performs the pattern; he is with us."

"What?" The Tiyo agent blew out a breath. "So you're in contact with Tiyo Sarsone, of course. Your people need to understand this: If you expect your objectives to be honored, it will be with Tiyo Grath Tiyo's aid or not at all. No further 'interpretation' is to be made. You must answer to Tiyo Grath."

In the Sinaiety woman's silence, the creak of overburdened branches could be heard; the spatter of water to leaves; and then the distant thrum of an air vehicle. Water, or sweat, dripped into Mheth's eyes. The bark of the trunk was wet, too, and cold where his palm touched it.

The woman seemed to be weighing some thought or set of equations; she stood unmoving, delicate face raised to the Tiyo's. It was too dim for Mheth to read her expression. Eventually she said, "There is no cause for concern."

"So your people always say. But here Tiyo Grath has had to come and answer awkward questions from an Aggregate investigator when, without your interpretive actions, he could have met with them on-station and in a position of power."

Mheth thought of the people, the wounded people, in the shelter, and Taebit's exhausted, dirty face as he laughed instead of screaming. He had to swallow back bile, sure he was going to be sick. As he hung against the tree, another set of footsteps approached. Another Sinaiety arrived, this one tall and bulky within the robes. The two Sinaiety conferred low-voiced and Mheth lost their voices under a sudden rise of wind that sent accumulated rain splattering to the ground.

Mheth remembered saying that he wasn't Tiyo's conscience; but he was beginning to think, as under-qualified as he was for the position, it was his. Whether he wanted it or not.

As one, the two Sinaiety turned from the Tiyo agent and walked off into the gloom. The agent stared after them, cursed softly, and set off in the opposite direction. After waiting a little longer, Mheth followed in the direction the Sinaiety had gone.

The world had grown darker, the last of the day's light draining from the cloud cover and out of the landscape. In the grove it was now almost truly dark, leaving Mheth's eye augment little to work with, and he moved slowly, hands out, the trees just shadowy shapes that he felt as much as saw.

The sound of a step, a rustling in the leaves, and he went still. He listened, breath suspended, tense. There was another step and suddenly he was facing the Sinaiety woman, emerged from the gloom, the sheen in her eyes giving her away more than anything else. They stared at each other.

A loud crack yanked his gaze up to the darkness, out of which a branch appeared, falling from the upper reaches accompanied by a flotsam of debris. He dove into the woman, hit the ground with her and rolled them both away as the branch crashed down. Sludge and twigs splattered over them. Slivers of wood stung Mheth's face and his knee smashed into a tree root. He cursed as pain shot up his thigh.

The woman shifted, small under the layers of robes. She pushed an elbow into his side and pulled away, sitting up on top of him. He had a brief view of her face, her eyes all iris, then he gripped her arms hard to stop her motion for what he suspected would be a weapon.

"Wait," he said. "I've come from my father, Tiyo Sarsone. I'm Tiyo Mhethianne Tiyo."

The woman hovered over him, then she nodded and stood, giving a short, shrill whistle.

Yes, Mheth thought, *of course, don't mention it, glad to save your life*; he climbed to his feet, rubbing at scrapes on his upper arm.

There was a whistle from a ways away. With a jerk of her head she gestured Mheth to follow her. At the far edge of the grove from the building housing the rescue operations, the large Sinaiety man, a big bulk in the dim, stood beside a large, beaten-looking transport.

The woman leaned into the transport. Voices, over the hiss of an open link, back and forth with the low-voiced words of the Sinaiety woman.

He caught his brother's voice, then, coming clear for a moment over the link: *Oh? All right. Bring him to the tower. I have a pick-up to make . . . for my father. In any case, the Oversight agent is satisfied for now. I'll be at the tower before you.*

Mheth strode forward with all the hauteur of *the* Tiyo and took a seat in the transport. The vehicle shifted as the large Sinaiety man boarded. The vehicle's dome closed with a rasp and the transport began to rumble, moving. Mheth couldn't see anything outside but occasional flashes of light in the night and rain splattering on the scratched dome.

⁂

They began Jhinsei's treatment that night. Back in the high-ceilinged, rose-ivory room, Zhou pressed the first set of derms along the inside of his left arm. Jhinsei watched her dark, slender fingers. The derms looked like any derms, three greenish ones, four pale yellow, one a dark, bruised red. Outside, the sky showed stars, but was taken over by dark cloud in the distance. Lightning flashed in the clouds, illuminating layers of the system; thunder reached them, muted. Closer, night insects churred and a hunting bird called from a perch in the eaves of the retreat.

Zhou rolled up the rest of the derms and sat there with him, looking out at the distant storm.

Ramev had gone off to attend to some other business after the evening meal. They'd eaten all together with the other thirty or so obviaries at the retreat, in a half-open hall on the inner oval of the compound.

"Once," Zhou said, "while I was studying for my arts, I spent a month on the *Matilija*."

"The org—the full-immersion ship?"

"The orgy ship? Hardly." She tilted her head slightly. "That reputation is not truly earned. Though it helps keep their cruises full. It would more aptly be called the party-of-one ship."

Jhinsei snorted on a laugh, shook his head. "So, what was it like?"

"All very discreet . . . a little like a floating morgue. Even in group immersions, there was no physicality, though the passengers' memories of such confused more than one couple when they were out of immersion and taking cocktails on the observation deck. I did a monograph on altered states of physiology and the oneiric psychology of kive echoes."

"Oneiric psychology of kive echoes? So . . ." Jhinsei squinted, "how kive echoes in dreams affect our physical functions?"

One corner of her mouth quirked up. "I may have been somewhat intellectually pretentious." She tucked the roll of derms under one arm. "You should sleep."

"Hmm." Jhinsei nodded.

"Any questions about what to expect?"

He shook his head. She'd gone over it: Dizziness, nausea, aching muscles, dry mouth.

"You know where I am, just down the south corridor?"

He nodded again, summoned a smile. "If I wake you up will you tell me stories about growing up on Ash?"

"What, no more tales of the obviary-in-training?"

"Ruins the mystique."

After she'd gone, he touched the biolume to darkness and sat on the bench carved into the windowed wall. The planetary night outside gained visibility and depth, the sweep of land down from the crags in which the retreat was built, into the bunched slopes of lower mountain, the valley indistinct beneath the dark smudge of storm. Above, the lantern of the sky, so different from the ink of space in which Termagenti Station floated. He could see the station, a flickering light among the stars in the south quadrant of the sky. A bird hunted below, a dark streak he could just see as it went from glide to swoop before he lost sight of it.

Air breathed through the room, the insect churr riding it like vapor. His skin itched a little under the derms and he shivered. A soft, thin blanket of bio-silk fiber was folded on the bench; he pulled it around himself and leaned back against the carved window frame.

He must have slept, because he woke with the clutching anxiety of nightmare. He couldn't remember dreaming, only the fading voices of his team and the sense of something essential—lifeline, muscle, bone—snapping. He remembered pain, the vibration of it ringing still in his blood, caught in his throat, a metallic taste in his mouth.

The rider hovered, its presence lighter than the brush of a moth's wings.

He abandoned the blanket and the prospect of more sleep, stretched aching muscles. Out in the corridor, he stood still a moment. It was eerie how no one stirred during well night, everyone sleeping, or keeping to themselves. On station such a thing never happened. A silent station was a dead one, a ghost hulk. A story told on Revelation.

Shaded biolumes glowed at intersections and turnings of the corridors, through the lattice of some doors and windows. He turned the wrong way once, ending at a long terrace overlooking the eastern vista, sky over cragged land, with no sign of the storm that brooded westward. Backtrack and retrace; eventually he came to a small temple, set within an outer wall of the retreat, which Ramev had shown to him on their tour.

The near-constant rain in the lowlands didn't plague them here; instead clouds rolled through, dense fogs that watered the land. The temple, dedicated to one of the Thorough Order's more obscure tenets, was partially open to the elements, with a half dome of tinted semiperm giving way to open sky over flourishing gardens. There were no biolumes, but luminescing vine flowers blooming over rocks and up carved lattice and walls glowed a descant to the dark.

A float bench sat among some tall rushes. The bench's memform gave to his body and warmed quickly. Air breathed across his skin and into his mind, so different, so mingled of coolness, moisture, flower, and herb scents, it was either intoxicant or misery to the station-bred. For the rider it was intoxicant, and so for Jhinsei.

Everything, it seemed, was intoxicant for the rider. It reached for life, for the textures of darkness, the hue of light, skin, and breath, the tiniest touch of scent and sound. There was…joy in it, reminding him, in a way that their echoes in his head never had, of his team. Darshun's delight in exotic fauna and good food; the intense pleasure Tomas took in the ambit and articulation of his own muscles; the heat and engagement in Sara's eyes at unexpected moments; Esker's curiosity about everything people did, his joy in Darshun and in his team.

Now the rider hovered in the shadows of his bones, drawn into itself to keep from overwhelming Jhinsei's ability to contain it.

He leaned back, the sky a deep, wide dark above him, star-specked in patches clear of cloud cover. Watching the flicker of those distant cosmic bodies through gravity well atmosphere, his thoughts called up a ship, the *Oni's Wake*, and from there, its captain, Sobriance Kohl. Working for some mysterious office of Aggregate Control.

Who was she, this woman? Why had she offered him a place on her ship? To be wanted—such an old, primal part of him, that need. To be wanted, when he was sure that he was not enough, never enough, not somone to be wanted, needed.

With the rider, in the rider—there was so much potential, so much more than enough.

Jhinsei realized it just wasn't in him to kill that potential, nor to abandon it, as he'd been abandoned.

Holding his arm out, Jhinsei looked at the derms, barely visible against his skin. He began to peel them off, a brief pull, not quite stinging, and the sound of them coming unstuck. He pressed each one to the last in a neat stack on the memform.

That done, he laid back and watched the distant stars glitter, as they never did when viewed from station. He felt the rider stir.

I won't abandon you, he said.

Something in the tenor of his thought, the things behind it, made the rider subside, silent.

His mind wandered, over faces and events, coming to rest on Essca. The quirk in her lips as she leaned over him; the warmth of her against him. Ro's face when he said *she already knows*. The look in Cydonie's when the subject of Essca came up. Everyone knowing, apparently, but him, that it wasn't love, or even affectionate lust, Kiyr Essca Mehet felt for the twice-orphaned headcase House Kiyr ward. She'd worked him, and watched him. But why? What did they want?

The rider?

His mind turned up the image of Mheth, then Darshun, Esker, Sara, Tomas. He found himself crying, throat tight, nose snotty, the tears sliding down his face, just like that.

A low hum drifted through the air, almost a whine. An air vehicle, sounded like; but the sound barely made an impression on Jhinsei. He wiped his nose and face and his thoughts slid back to the question of what they wanted, Ro Mehet and whoever in Tiyo gave him direction—Tiyo Sarsone Tiyo, it seemed. If it was the rider, had they had some plan to see the rider . . .birthed?

It would need the ship, the substance of the ship, that process. Jhinsei took a breath, realizing after he had this thought that it was the rider, whispering in his mind.

"Don't do that," he murmured.

What?

Sneak up on me that way.

Silence, hovering, then, *Put the derms back on.*

He rolled his head against the memform. *No.*

There is no point to it. It needs both—a body like yours and the stuff of my old self. Without my ship—myself, it is myself—I cannot become again, but neither can I stop the momentum of my progress. It will destroy your body. Pointless, useless. Waste.

He stared up at the stars, saw one moving, perhaps a ship. What was life like on a ship? Cydonie seemed to prefer it to life on a station.

Don't be a headcase.

You sound like Sara.

Thinking of ships brought the *Oni's Wake* again to his thoughts. What handle did they go by? *Oni's Wake* seemed a mouthful. Just *Oni*, maybe. It might have been nice to get to know her, Sobriance Kohl, and her crew.

The sound of a rushing wind with a roar and whine in it came up the slope out of the night. A ship landing, maybe, someone arriving for urgent Thorough Order care? He didn't feel stirred to investigate; he was leaving the world.

I won't abandon you, he thought again.

A sound at the outer gate of the garden brought him sitting up, however, peering through the dim.

"Is someone there?"

A man shadowed by another emerged from the dark, into the small glow of the flowers. His hair glinted gold. He looked a lot like Mheth, but there was no mistaking him: Tiyo Grath Tiyo.

"Hello," Grath said, smiling.

Something small and sharp was pressing into Mheth's back. The two Sinaiety, gargantua and the woman, were faceless swaths of hooded robes, only their breathing and occasional speech, about the route or food, and once some joke about the rain that Mheth didn't get, marking them. The smell in the transport was truly horrible. It seemed to consist of old animal shit, grease, and rotted, half-eaten food—he'd had the time to analyze. He was sure they usually used it for transporting livestock. The Sinaiety were uninterested in speaking with him; the quality of the silence that met his words made silence preferable.

He watched through long hours of dark, the rain and lightning splashing on the transport dome. Eventually the sky began to pale behind the heavy weather systems. First the soft green that most characterized Ash's sky; then a band of glow with an orange blush through it. Occasionally branches obscured the view, and then tilting walls of rock as the transport began to climb into the mountains.

The transport link signaled a message coming in. The woman gave voice permission and Sarsone's voice came through.

You left a marker in the system for me, Chei? What is your news?

"The pattern has been shifted," the woman—Chei—said. "Your sons' motions interfere with each other's and the pattern."

That's where Mhethianne got to, is it? Of course . . . Hmm. There was a moment of silence. Then, *Grath was very upset with you, you know.* His father actually giggled.

"We have the younger," Chei said. "We are taking him to the Dosi Crags, where the elder has his base. That one portends something with the catalyst."

Does he? No trace of laughter in that.

"It is not the pattern."

Leave it to me.

Tight silence. Finally, Chei said, "As the Tiyo says."

The pattern simply moves of its own, Chei. Faith is all.

"As the Tiyo says," the woman said again. The link terminated.

Catalyst, the woman had said. Mheth chewed on it. What did that mean? What was this catalyst . . . or, perhaps more importantly, what was it meant to catalyze? Oh, of course: his father's evolution of the species. Which meant the catalyst was not a what, but a whom: Jhinsei.

That bloody derelict, the accident, the new kive cube tech, lumin . . . His father's ravings about the next step in human evolution.

What was Grath doing with Jhinsei, then?

Void and drift and damn the Leviathan's bloody craw anyway.

⁂

Jhinsei took a step back from the men facing him, and another, backing toward the door into the retreat. The large man at Tiyo Grath's shoulder moved to the front.

"Let's not be tiresome," Tiyo Grath said. "Just come with us. No fuss."

Jhinsei paused, then pivoted on one foot and broke for the inner door—

—and found himself on his knees as the rider pulsed through him, leaving him gasping. Weak and trembling, his chest and body ached as if something were trying to expand the cage of his bones beyond their capacity. He wheezed, blackness wavering through his vision, tears sparking at the low light in the temple. He hung there, leaning on one hand.

Steps, close beside him on the sand path. He tried to gather himself to stand but wasn't ready, legs strengthless and aching. A hand caught him under one shoulder and hauled him up to face Tiyo Grath, who peered down at him.

Something flickered in the Tiyo's eyes that made Jhinsei flinch back, but the other man was a solid wall at his back, gripping his elbows to keep him upright. Brief visions out of adventure flash kives flickered through Jhinsei's mind, of snapping his head back into the man's face, using him as leverage to plant his feet in Tiyo Grath's gut and kick the shit out of him. But his head just fell back and his legs trembled, his breath wheezing.

That something in Tiyo Grath's eyes intensified once they had him out of the retreat and into the sleek shuttle craft perched on a narrow strip of mountain. The Tiyo's expression was mixed avidity and speculation, with a total blindness to him, Jhinsei, at all. It was an expression that scared Jhinsei more than his own impending death and made him want to run far, far away.

The shuttle took off, a vacuum suck of sound. As the ground dropped away and the shuttle banked through the night sky, Jhinsei pressed himself back into his seat. *Now would be a good time*, he said to the rider. *Maybe we can take out Tiyo Grath when we go*. The rider didn't answer, but Jhinsei felt it, remorse and stubborn hope a luminous weight in his bones, a depth of possibility not to be. Too vast for his mind—he felt it like fire and storm deep within the quantum dust of his being.

The flight passed for Jhinsei in flurries and grindings of that dust, in seeking breath, in forgetting to breathe, falling into the chasms the rider had opened behind his blood and losing himself there. It passed in a forever that blinked by like a moment. As the first green of dawn shredded the sky, the Tiyo agent set them neatly onto a platform cut halfway down a black tower of rock. The shuttle's lights cut harsh shadows from the crag's heavy foliage, glinting on the rough, striated stone. Jhinsei entertained a brief, colorful thought of throwing himself from the platform, but the Tiyo agent saw him through a small door in the crag with an implacable grip to his arm.

Inside the crag, they herded him into a round globe of a lift bisected by a flat floor near its base. The sphere slid down through the crag, coming to rest so gently Jhinsei didn't know they'd stopped until the curved door slid back, revealing a windowless room made airy by the lighting—it looked disorientingly like a room on-station. As they stepped out of the lift, the Tiyo agent slid the tip of his little weapon up and shot a slender needle of pain into the back of Jhinsei's neck. It dropped him as if all his tendons had suddenly been cut and he fell neatly over the arm of the agent, who then hauled him to a pale, vat-leather lounger on the other side of the room, rolled him onto the long piece of furniture, and left the room. Presumably they hadn't wanted to carry him all the way but had thought he might, finally, balk effectively at a couch?

As Tiyo Grath sat beside him, his eyes veiled by that avid, furtive anticipation, Jhinsei realized they might have been right.

He was aware of the thinness of the bedclothes provided at the Order retreat, which left his arms bare and, for all the thermal intelligence of the cloth, left him feeling chilled and vulnerable now. Tiyo Grath leaned close, and then moved one hand, doing something that sealed Jhinsei's bare flesh, at arms, neck, ankles, to the leather of the couch. Panic fluttered, birdlike, in his chest. The Tiyo turned away, pulled something out from a drawer in the bottom of the lounger, and then sat straight with a glove in hand. It was made of the same vat-leather as the couch, rucked here and there with filaments of some kind woven all through it, tiny light beads blinking here and there at the tips and on the cuff. Grath pulled it on slowly, watching Jhinsei. Then he sat back a little, mouth twitching.

"I've never done this with an actual person, you know. Only analogs . . ." He blew out a breath. "I'm a little nervous."

Feeling his motor control beginning to come back, Jhinsei tugged at the bonds sealing him to the leather. There was little give. His whole body tense, he squirmed, trying to get just one arm free.

Grath shifted, watching him, leaning closer.

"You should stick to the analogs, then," Jhinsei said, still tugging to get a limb free. Grath lifted the gloved hand and Jhinsei flinched, strained to roll his head away as the Tiyo leaned closer, his mouth open almost vacantly. As Jhinsei twitched, Grath closed his mouth, swallowing.

"You're going to die anyway, aren't you? There's nothing anyone can do now. Relax, you may enjoy this. Let go."

"No," Jhinsei said, and then yelled it as Grath trailed the gloved hand over his chest and down his stomach, into the loose opening of the sleep pants. "I don't want this! Stop—" His voice failed on the word, rising into a cry as the glove snapped stimulation, lashing pain plaited with pleasure up through him from multiple points of contact, the stroke of Tiyo Grath's fingers a precise insertion of the two together wherever they passed. Grath's mouth hung open again as he pressed his gloved hand between Jhinsei's thighs, pushing thin cloth aside, ripping it when it didn't give way quickly enough for him.

Jhinsei panted, trying to find breath between bone-wringing assaults, his body, everything, out of his control. He felt tears on his face and tensed, anger surging behind the pain, growling through the unwanted arousal. But as it continued, pain, pleasure, pain, anger bled away, into a hollow of exhaustion. Jhinsei longed to follow it, to bleed out of himself, into that hollow, into nothing.

The rider had fled long since, tucked up somewhere in his bone shadow. *Wrong*, Jhinsei's thoughts repeated, over and over, *it was all wrong.*

❋

The Sinaiety brought the transport down into a valley, into a landscape Mheth found hard, visually, to parse. Looking up through the transport dome, he saw sky and towering things furred in dark foliage. It took him a while to resolve them into rocky crags that were like giant pillars throughout the valley, towering far above the spiky trees foresting their bases.

The transport stopped with a groan and a shudder.

Then gargantua opened the transport. There was a smell of water and Mheth took a deep breath of clean air. The crags were shaggy with vegetation of a green so dark it appeared black. They stood tall, linked by deep flora and trees whose densely needled boughs bent and twisted tortuously in every direction. Large for trees, but small in comparison to the steep turrets of rock. All of this was doubled and upside down, along with the arc of sky, in a stretch of calm water. A deep mineral smell came from the water that made Mheth's head ache. Something else, the trees maybe, supplied the air with a tang. A slight haze softened the distance, making mirage of the far stretch of flat green punctuated by crags until it merged into mountains.

The woman spoke into the transport's link unit and received a brief response.

"The catalyst," Mheth said, and the woman turned sharply. "He's important to me, too," Mheth continued. "I don't think my brother means him any good."

The woman waited.

"Maybe I could use your link?" She studied him, glanced at gargantua, and then lifted a hand. Quickly, before she could change her mind, Mheth sent a brief message to the coded contact Jhinsei had given him for the captain of the *Oni's Wake*, *Help needed at coordinates of message origination.*

The Sinaiety seemed content to stand by the transport, waiting. The sky arced wide and high, a pale shell over the valley.

A figure emerged from among the trees, barely stirring the brush. As it came closer, Mheth recognized the Tiyo agent, the one from the shelter and grove in the Choudow. Grath had traveled considerably faster than Mheth and the Sinaiety had.

The agent ignored Mheth and spoke to the Sinaiety, "Tiyo Grath thanks you."

The woman and gargantua exchanged a glance. They inclined their heads. Then, without a look at Mheth, the verten Sinaiety climbed back in their transport, that did indeed look as though it was mostly used to carry livestock, and rumbled back along the suggestion of a road. Mheth squinted after them, thinking back on his father's words over the link.

The Tiyo agent gestured, still without actually looking at Mheth. "This way, please."

The tang in the air became heavier as they came among the twisty limbs of the trees. Some kind of huge juniper speciation, Mheth thought, long-ago kive information from civschool surfacing.

In the green dim, the rustling of small creatures and the soft stip-stip-stip of some insect were loud. Dark needles, faded to grey here and there, cushioned their footsteps. A bird screeched, earsplitting and strange.

The ground rose slightly and they reached a smoothly curving structure, nestled into the base of one of the crags. Seen closer, the rock and soil of the crag were striated black, the clinging trees, scraggy shrubs, vine, and mosses a patchwork of dark greens. He gazed up—and up—and after a moment saw what was probably invisible from above, from space. A small landing pad cut into the crag, camouflaged by its colors. A shuttle sat on it, chameleon-skinned.

And what, Mheth wondered, a lift down through the rock? In any case, this was clearly Grath's "tower."

The Tiyo agent went in through a blue-tinged scythe screen and Mheth followed. Inside, he was met by a purely familiar décor, the subtle colors, metallic ceraforms, and extrinsic textures that his brother favored. A large room, diffuse light from above: they might have been on-station. No sign of Grath. Another Tiyo agent very similar to the first sat on a form chair identical to those in the Tiyo Studios salon; he was kiving from a hand unit. The agent who'd come in with him gestured Mheth to another form chair.

An almost closed door led to another room. All Mheth could glimpse through the crack was shadow sifted by a faint scatter of gold light. A brief sound, like an indrawn gasp of air, cut off, another. Other, indistinct sounds, a rustle, a whisper. The first Tiyo agent met Mheth's eyes a moment, looked away, expressionless. The other continued kiving.

The form chair's comfort relaxed him, the light did. Familiarity.

The occasional sound from the other room and the shifting of shadows rasped through his thoughts.

He levered himself back up and made his way to the door, glancing at the agents. The one watched him, but made no move to stop him. Rather than pushing the door open, Mheth slipped through it, widening it only enough to do so.

A room like the one Grath had on-station, in his quarters. Spare but opulent in its spareness. Jhinsei lay on a molded recliner, clothes half off, like something out of one of Grath's hurt and fuck kives. The recliner had skin bonders that held his arms and legs. The Kiyr was breathing heavily, eyes closed and face turned away, flushed and sweating. Grath half sat on the edge of the recliner, just watching him.

Mheth saw it all in hyper-bleached clarity, an edge of something both horrified and fascinated wiring though him. All around the void in his gut. He must have made some sound, Grath turning. He wore a patterned robe, long, open, a strange glove on one hand, away from which Mheth's gaze slid quickly, to focus on his brother's face. He looked beatific. Not merely sated or avid, but glowing, like the icon of a saint, with love and grace.

Mheth stared at him, unable to find anything to say. Jhinsei made a sound, between a moan and a grunt; Mheth saw his hands strain briefly. Like a signal, it released them both, Grath to stand, Mheth to shudder on a surge of rage, and find his voice.

"Are gravity wells somehow exempt from Aggregate law, or did you just not bring any kives with you?"

Grath shrugged and turned back to Jhinsei. "He trespassed on Tiyo property, now he is Tiyo property. And, sadly, not long for this universe."

"What do you mean?"

"Don't get hysterical, Mheth. I'm not going to kill him; nothing in that for me."

Grath's gaze strayed down to the Kiyr. "It's different with a real person, much different than a kive," he said quietly, almost revelatory.

A red tide washed up through Mheth, a cold prickling all over his skin, his fists clenching. Through gritted teeth he said, "Grath, there are places—you could find willing partners."

His brother's mouth thinned, the skin around one eye twitching. Not a happy expression. "That would be a game." He sighed, waved his hand, the subject, aside.

"It's a waste, really," he said then, "the whole thing. And a damn nuisance. Kiyr Jhinsei went on the derelict, Tiyo's derelict, he got some sort of thing in him, and *it* is going to kill him. And Father is down here somewhere, being insane, and I don't want the two to meet—it will only make Father worse."

Mheth was in Grath's space, arm back and swinging before he knew he'd made the decision. His fist connected hard with his brother's jaw. Grath stumbled sideways and back. Mheth shook his hand out, the red wash of anger still high, Grath looking at him with one hand to his face, stunned expression on his face.

Turning away, Mheth crossed to Jhinsei. He knelt on the floor on the other side of the recliner. He was a little afraid to touch the Kiyr, who didn't seem aware of his presence. As he began breaking the bonding of the seals at Jhinsei's arms with one finger, Mheth voiced his anger without looking at his brother.

"How convenient for you—you can watch the Kiyr die, have some fun, and clean up the mess the Sinaiety made cleaning up your mess all at the same time. A lovely time for all down in the gravity well."

"Father's mess, Mheth," Grath said acidly, "not mine. And someone has to do it." The last had some tinge of pain in it that

Mheth didn't understand—then he did. That Mheth had abandoned him in the fight for House Tiyo's health and sanity. Mheth almost snorted at that thought—that either he or Grath should be responsible for anyone's sanity.

Grath climbed to his feet, stepped close, and lifted a hand toward Jhinsei.

"Leave him alone," Mheth said sharply.

Grath dropped his hand and studied Mheth. "What exactly are you doing down here?"

"Running away. I haven't quite got the hang of it, apparently."

"You confused my Sinaiety a bit. They don't respond well to confusion." He smiled slightly, and then winced, touching the rising welt on his jaw.

"I think you'll find that they are Father's Sinaiety," Mheth said.

Grath shrugged. He was maddeningly calm—thus it had always been, Mheth raging, Grath the cool and level-headed elder brother, indulgent of his brother's failings.

"What's your percentage in the Kiyr, anyway?"

"He's my friend."

Grath's brow furrowed.

"For drift's sake, Grath, it can't be that extraordinary a concept."

"Since when, exactly, has he been your 'friend?'"

Released, Jhinsei rolled away from the sound of Grath's voice.

"It's not—bloody void." Mheth took hold of his rage, said evenly, "I'm taking him out of here. And I'm using your link to get us transport." He drew a breath. "If he's . . ." blew out the breath, "going to die anyway it shouldn't make any difference to you."

A number of expressions washed across his brother's face, then he shrugged. "You're right. There's nothing anyone can do at this point, as I understand it. I intend to be certain, however—Father is about somewhere and I don't want him getting ahold of the Kiyr. I do insist that he remain here." He gestured magnanimously. "You're welcome to stay and say farewell."

"Get out."

Grath folded his arms. "This is my room."

Void, it was ludicrous; they were like little boys squabbling over a toy. Mheth moved to shoulder Jhinsei to his feet. As he got one of the Kiyr's arms, a radiant glow pulsed from Jhinsei's body, licking over his skin and along his limbs. The burring energy reached Mheth; he tasted it up through his bones. After the pulse faded, he leaned forward for leverage and lurched to his feet, dragging Jhinsei with him. He swallowed the taste of ozone in his mouth.

Jhinsei's eyes were tightly closed, fists and body clenched. He stirred with a gasp as Mheth levered him up, a deep juddering tremble all through him. He wouldn't meet Mheth's gaze, eyes lowered, but gripped Mheth's arm. His skin was warm, limbs trembling.

After leaning against Mheth for a moment, he pushed away, taking his own weight. "I'm all right," he muttered.

"Oh, yes, me, too. Just brilliant."

The Kiyr gave a husk of a laugh.

"Another room," Mheth said to Grath stiffly, flicking a glance at the recliner.

Grath's eyes narrowed. "Yes, of course. Do come this way."

Jhinsei walked beside Mheth with his gaze on the floor; he wouldn't look at Grath, barely at Mheth. Grath led them past the two Tiyo agents to small quarters off the main room. One pane of semiperm gave view into the thickness of the twist-limbed trees, their scent on the air. Jhinsei sat heavily on the sleep platform. He shuddered, wrapping his arms around himself.

Grath looked uncomfortable. He turned abruptly and left. The door slid closed behind him.

Jhinsei began to rock slightly. The scent of the trees itched at Mheth's nose. That same raucous bird, or one like it, screeched a call. Suddenly Mheth sneezed, three times in rapid succession, his eyes watering.

He saw Jhinsei shaking even harder. Alarmed, he took a step towards him, and then realized the Kiyr was laughing. His own legs trembling, Mheth sank onto the other end of the bed mat.

"He's right," Jhinsei said, still not looking at him. His voice was rough.

"Grath isn't right about anything. On principle."

The Kiyr's breath hitched a little as he drew it deep and let his arms drop, hands falling to his thighs, sitting straighter. He reached out a hand, gripped Mheth's arm, a brief, warm touch, though he still didn't look at him. "Thank you," he said quietly. Then, "How did you get here?"

"Commandeered a ride in a transport smelling of speciated shit. You can probably tell."

The Kiyr almost looked at Mheth, sidewise, then shook his head. "What . . . what happened? Where's Taebit?"

"Still in the Choudow helping. The explosion was bad, chem-fed, the fires were still going. Lot of casualties and wounded." Mheth paused, then said, "The Sinaiety did it, at Grath's instruction—he just wanted the testing results with the lumin kive technology covered up, but the Sinaiety also wanted their current vert killed. Needed a regime change, I guess. My brother's also trying to cover my father's tracks. My father is obsessed with the lumin. He even has a suit of it, you know." He wiped a hand over his mouth. He was rambling, he knew. "And he's down here, somewhere, apparently."

Jhinsei looked at him then, an odd expression on his face. "Your father is here, on Ash? Do you think . . . would he have . . . would he have the suit?"

"What? Why?"

The Kiyr shook his head. "Where would he be, do you know?"

"No. Why, Jhinsei?"

But the Kiyr wouldn't look at him again. "Never mind; it doesn't matter."

Mheth was finding it hard to look at Jhinsei, too. "I left a message for the *Oni's Wake*. For help."

"Good—you're seeing it through—making things right. That's good, Mheth."

"That's not—Jhinsei, please don't give up." Mheth waited for the Kiyr's nod. It was unconvincing, but it was all he was going to get. "Right now I'm going to find us some water and food. I'll be right back. Don't, um—just rest, okay?"

"Get cleaned up," Jhinsei said. "You do stink."

Mheth found the water room, cleaned the worst of the stink and grime off himself and put on a spare set of clothes he found in the cupboard. Then he went and found his brother. Grath lay in the recliner where he'd had Jhinsei, composed, ankles crossed, lids half lowered.

Mheth leaned against the wall just inside the doorway.

"Father's . . . he needs help, Grath."

"I'm aware."

"So while you're messing about with the Sinaiety, breaking Aggregate laws like toothpicks, he's just going slowly to hell."

"What the void do you think I'm doing down here, Mhethianne?"

"Why don't you tell me?"

"Father wants the Kiyr—he has some notion of rebirth, evolution or transcendence or something. That suit of his, the lumin—the testing trials with the cursed stuff had to be covered up. The Sinaiety just took it too far. And to convince Father the lumin technology had been shipped and was in circulation while moving core and cosmos to see the shipments went exactly nowhere—do you have any idea how hard this has been? The Kiyr had to be removed from play, out of Father's range."

"Wasn't down the well far enough?"

Grath threw out a hand. "It should have been, but now Father's down here! For all I know I only just got the Kiyr out of the way. I can track a kinless station reject because of the tags we had the Khat put in his blood, but one old man in a crazy suit with a bloody bird mask I can't find anywhere."

Mheth considered that, of half a mind to go back to Jhinsei right then. Instead, he said, "Do you really think Aggregate Oversight—or Control—won't get onto what you're doing down here with the kive test cover-ups, with the Sinaiety?"

Grath closed his eyes a moment. "Void, Mheth, what do you care?"

"That explosion killed people, Grath. Real people." The smoldering air, blood-greased limbs, half-meshed faces flashed through his head.

He looked up as Grath rose from the recliner. "Someone has to look out for Tiyo interests. Father stopped when he became obsessed with the derelict and his vision of a new humanity. You certainly have no interest. Or aptitude."

Mheth shook his head. He thought about his father and Jhinsei. Jhinsei was going to . . . die? That thought, which hadn't fully penetrated before, kept distracting him.

Jhinsei. Mheth dropped his head into hands. There had to be something. Something.

"Aggregate Oversight couldn't care less what we do," Grath said. "Palogenia System is a speck in the larger universe, Mhethianne. How have you never realized that?"

He felt his whole face thinning with anger, nostrils flaring, and fisted his hands tightly. Finally he said quietly, "Don't you even care? You just forge illegal alliances with a proscribed well culture and take out any people in your way with explosions?"

Grath turned away, arms folded against anything further Mheth might have to say. So Mheth went back into the quarters where he'd left Jhinsei and stopped just inside the door.

Jhinsei was not there. A breeze frisked over the disordered bed clothes. The semiperm had been breached, a ragged hole letting in the full flow of cool, sap-and-needle scented air.

Mheth sneezed.

When Mheth left him, Jhinsei went to work on the semiperm immediately. Breaching a pane of semiperm required knowledge of sub-harmonic sound frequencies and currents of outer-spectrum light. Esker had known one, Sara the other. Usually, it also required tools—a frequency gauge, or at least a laser needle.

Using knowledge that both Esker and Sara had possessed, the rider sussed the specs, nudging Jhinsei to put his hand to the slight vibration of the pane. Wait, the rider said, and they waited for the rider's next surge—every one of which brought them closer to the end of his body's endurance and the rider's ability to get control of its growing self again after the surge.

It was fairly unspectacular; all the fireworks were from the rider. The semiperm simply fragged where the rider's energy touched it, melting out from there, a steady slag marked by a leading edge of pale, heatless burn.

He waited a few breaths for his shuddering to subside and the world to unblur.

Don't think about Grath. Not staying here, that was all he knew. Mheth had done what he could to get him out. He had to do the rest.

Sarsone. The name threaded through his thoughts, with visions of a figure in a glimmering, faceted suit of lumin on the grid work between station decks.

He went out the window, scraping hand, arm, and hip on the slagged edge. Hit the soft mat of needles on the ground and the scent nearly knocked him over. Crouched low, he ran in a hobbling lope, deeper into the tree cover, away from Grath's hideaway.

When he was out of sight of the hideaway, he straightened and continued at a pathetic jog. Everything hurt, particularly his thighs and groin, like slivers of glass had been left behind in the wash of strained and aching muscles, courtesy of Grath and his void-cursed glove.

Don't think about Grath.

He ran, breath ragged and feet stumbling, until the rider spasmed. Then he lay where he'd fallen, face in the layers of needle mulch. They were humusy and cool underneath, slightly damp with their own decomposition, prickling into his skin. He slid his hands down into the cool of it, holding on as the wave receded.

You could have done that earlier, during Grath's little joy session.

Every time I lose control we come closer to—

—I know.

He leaned up on his elbows, and then rolled to his back. The twisty trees went on forever, dark corridors of them. He couldn't see the crags anymore. Palogenia, risen high enough to trickle light through the trees, pooled and flickered furzy shafts through the shadows. Tiny birds, like specks of blue fire, dove and darted among the trees. Wind rustled the topmost branches. The deep needle bed grew warm to his body. Jhinsei closed his eyes a moment, felt shadows and light, wind, play over his face. He opened them to see the same shadows and light tossing about, patterning the air. The sky glowed high and far away, endless.

How long?

The rider stirred from their contemplation, from sensual stupor. *Not long.*

This seems as good a place as any.

No reply, simply the filling of his senses, his fingers and toes, lungs and skin with murmurous lightning. The world spun stillness above and below.

Then the rider spasmed. Convulsion of space, air, senses. Infinite smell of the sky, too close to breathe. The waving tree shadows and pooling light echoed and boomed hugely. Jhinsei gasped at the pain, hands to ears, curling into a ball; nothing he did lessened the onslaught. The rider's incandescent glow poured through his closed eyelids. He could taste it. It pummeled through his mind, histories and eons he couldn't voice. His muscles screamed, straining to hear and see. His bones burned and the world howled, huge and rushing, endless and crushingly empty.

In its wake, as the rider contained itself once more, the surge left Jhinsei wrecked, more than any previous episode. His limbs ached distantly, breath rattled, heart pounded so fast it felt ready to burst. He knew suddenly, that that was what would happen, the rider's next spasm, or the one after.

He just lay there, tasting honey blood in his mouth, barely forming thoughts under the agony in his head. His eyes teared steadily, blurring trees and sky, blink, the clarity blurring again.

When a face bent over him, strange, glittering, and angular, it took him several harsh breaths to understand what, who, it was.

❋

Mheth contemplated the slagged semiperm and the empty quarters. Then he climbed onto the bed platform and leaned out, peering through the trees. The silvery, needle-covered ground showed him nothing at first. After he'd stared at it for a while, though, he could see the fragile impression of passage, broken needles and dark patches of stirred matter.

He sat back, eyes closed. Oh, for a civilized moment. A hot soak, an aperitif, a languorous meal, intelligent, congenial company. A proper horizon that didn't challenge one, going on for bloody ever. Air which was air, not so ridiculously full of scent and moisture.

He opened his eyes and looked at the closed door to the main room, through which waited the Tiyo agents, Grath. Then he climbed out the slagged window, landing in a crouch.

Jhinsei's path was easy to follow, uneven, the graying mat of needles dug up into dark ruts. He'd gone maybe fifty paces when a glow seared through the trees, a pulse that flooded, then receded. Close by.

The Kiyr hadn't gone far. He found him, among the trees, lying on the thick needle bed, a glittering man sitting beside him.

Jhinsei stared up at the bird mask. Phoenix. The thought floated up from information kived when he'd had a Darshun-within. Ah. It made more sense now. His gaze wandered over the glittering suit that was made of the derelict ship material—the rider's former self. He tried to gather enough breath to speak, but failed.

Slowly the figure settled to the ground beside him, and then the gloved hands lifted the mask off. Jhinsei stared at the man who reverently set the mask aside and turned back to him, a somber smile on his face, as if they were sharing the greatest and most wonderful secret.

Older, thinner, the bones so pronounced he looked almost cadaverous; the same hair, the same eyes as Mheth. Tiyo Sarsone.

The Tiyo, *the* Tiyo, laughed—giggled—in delight at the expression on Jhinsei's face. He sobered slowly, taking in the blood on Jhinsei's face, from his nose and mouth, the ragged hitch of his breath, heavy sweat on his skin.

"You shouldn't have run," he said, in his juice accent. "It needs the ship, yes? Was the ship . . . I begin to understand only too late. To me, it should have come. To me. Together, we would have risen, transcendent. New. Ancient. Glorious.

"But you," he finished, shaking his head. He looked up, then, and waved. "Mhethianne."

Jhinsei rolled his head to see Mheth as he dropped down beside him, opposite Sarsone.

Mheth said, his voice cottony, "Why did you run? I told you, help's coming."

Jhinsei rolled his head back and forth once. The air crackled in his ears and light whooshed across his skin like a physical thing. "No—no point. We'll just go. Me and the rider. No place. Can't . . . become. I'm tired, Mheth."

"Leviathan's ass, Jhinsei. That's, that—that's void fucking shit." He sounded so angry. He'd never heard Mheth sound so angry. "Fuck you. No." He had a hard grip on Jhinsei's wrist.

"Become," Sarsone said softly. "Perhaps we still can."

Mheth looked up at his father, sucking in a breath. "What?"

"Become. I am here, the ship is here, with me, its material." He raised one gloved hand into a shaft of sunlight, scattering glittering reflections. "What do you say, Kiyr? Shall we try?"

Jhinsei blinked up at him, and then closed his eyes a moment. He'd been so ready. So tired. Then he let his gaze go to Mheth, felt the heat of the Tiyo's hand on his wrist, the insistent weight of Mheth's anger. At him.

Slowly he flexed his hand, turned it, got Mheth's hand gripped in his own.

Can it work? he asked the rider.

I don't know. Maybe. If it's enough.

He looked back to Sarsone. After what seemed a long time, but could not have been, he said, rasping, "Try. Yes."

Sarsone set one gloved hand over Jhinsei's chest, to feel his heart's frantic, labored beating. Jhinsei's shirt askew from Grath's attentions, it was lumin glove to bare skin.

The rider surged.

To point of contact, into the glove, up through Jhinsei's heart, a velvet, burning rush through his blood and bones, dragging up through his groin in orgasm, from his limbs in convulsing arc, down from his brain and through his throat.

A radiant snap, a moment of time so dense all time fell into it.

Nets of coruscating light, endless nets, fine, flushing, chorusing, raveling and unraveling space . . .

. . . and then, for Jhinsei, nothing. Endless light folded into quiet dark.

All signals offline.

⁂

This time the flash of light bled so searingly that it burned through Mheth's one upflung hand—the other tightly gripped to Jhinsei's—burned through and through him. Wind pushed around them, so strong it swirled the mats of tree needles off the ground and up into the air. The trees creaked under the wind's power.

Etched hallucinations, after-images burning through his mind: a figure of bone and raging light, Sarsone, lit from within as a universe flowed up into him and took him bit by bit down to molecule, particle, pure energy; he disintegrated into a rush of cosmic radiation, which, eating him, then fell back, darker, fading, as if eating Sarsone quenched it. Then the light was gone, quenched indeed.

A scent—honey and ozone, lightning and flowers—deep and strong in the wake of the light's passage. The wind slowly died away.

Mheth blinked, haunting image and light burned into his retinas. When he could see again he couldn't comprehend what he was seeing. Jhinsei lay where he'd been, unconscious or dead. The pigment had been stripped from his hair, all of it that Mheth could see, hair, brows, sparse facial hair, all lucent white as an albino's against the Kiyr's olive skin. Mheth still gripped Jhinsei's hand in his.

There was no trace of Sarsone but the phoenix mask, on the ground by Jhinsei. Instead, a figure lay sprawled across Jhinsei's legs. Its hair and eyelashes glittered dark grey and flickering with color like the lumin. As far as Mheth could tell it was neither male nor female. Or maybe both.

Mheth sat there for a time, unable to assay even Jhinsei's name, afraid. Then a normal gravity well wind soughed through the trees and he sneezed. The figure across Jhinsei's legs opened its eyes and Jhinsei shifted beneath it.

Relieved on Jhinsei's account, Mheth found he was still afraid. His father was gone. What was this glittering creature?

⁂

The first signal to start up again was one from Jhinsei's leg, telling him something was lying across it and his foot was falling asleep. A hand gripped his. Mheth.

He twitched, tried to move, then did, slipping his hand from Mheth's, rolling over and dragging his leg out from under something warm. He gained his hands and knees after what seemed a long time, hung there a moment, feeling too void awful to be alive.

Then he sat back as it sank in. He was alive. He cast his attention inward, a silent call into the bone shadow of his own self. The rider was gone. There was only ache and emptiness.

He looked at what had been lying across his leg, expecting to see Tiyo Sarsone Tiyo. Instead he found a naked person with hair, eyes, fingernails, toenails—all the shifting, glittering dark-light of the lumin. Of the derelict ship. As Jhinsei stared, the figure's skin luminesced, from dark to pale, then back.

Male and female, the figure, both, more, neither, either. Herms were not unknown. Hir and se were the pronouns used in most places, or their, or some form thereof. But this being—more than herm, or less, or just—different.

Hir mouth was slightly open, chest rising and falling, eyes open, looking up into the trees, the sky. Hir face . . . Jhinsei sucked in a breath. Sara, Tomas, Darshun, Esker and . . . Sarsone.

Of Tiyo Sarsone Tiyo, there was nothing but the bird mask and the mirrored cloak, half fallen across the newly born being's body.

Slowly hir gaze came to Jhinsei and they stared at each other. Se sat up, looked around, then back at Jhinsei, sitting in the puddle of mirrored domino.

Jhinsei looked past the rider at Mheth then, who spared him a glance, but then returned to watching their new companion. He was a little pale about the eyes and mouth—terrified, Jhinsei thought.

Jhinsei couldn't say how long they might have sat there that way, none of them moving.

A sound ripped the air and they all looked up: a ship filled pale sky, glimpsed piecemeal through the thick trees. Quickly out of sight, the ship's path over and down was audible, a roar of landing, then a fade of sound, until slowly the birds and insects took up the silence again.

"You said," Jhinsei coughed, voice thick in a throat dry as ash, "you said you messaged the *Oni's Wake*? Mheth?"

Mheth's gaze had gone back to their companion. It took a long moment before he looked at Jhinsei, his face somewhat vague as he nodded, "Yes." Some expression beyond fear and vacuity came into his face and he sat a little straighter, teeth clacking once and his whole body shaking slightly. "Yes," he said again, "I did. That ship, you think?"

They were silent walking through the woods. Mheth continued to shiver so hard his teeth were chattering.

The new being, the was-rider, walked on the other side of Jhinsei, calm and strange, so clean and…new. Glittering, literally, skin uncertain of its hue, first pale, then dark, then somewhere in between. It was hard to look at hir. And hard to look away.

Jhinsei leaned on Mheth and Mheth on him. The Kiyr provided a warm anchor point against Mheth's shivering. When they'd stood in the clearing, surveying their new companion, the bird mask, and the lack of Sarsone, Jhinsei had gripped Mheth's shoulder, and hadn't let go since.

Beside him now, Jhinsei slowed, stopped, Mheth perforce stopping with him. He was aware of the being on the other side of Jhinsei, hyper-aware, as though se were in constant contact with Mheth's skin and thoughts.

A woman stood several feet away among the trees. Her bald head was pigmented in several different shades, some of them glinting metal, and her maroon ship jump was baggy on her squat body, a weapon slung casually over one shoulder.

"Dragon," Jhinsei said, voice still rough.

"Jhinsei." The woman surveyed them, brows rising. After a long moment she said, "Dragon Hidalgo, *Oni's Wake*."

Mheth clacked his teeth together. "Mheth, um, Tiyo Mheth Tiyo. I sent you the message."

"Tiyo Mhethianne Tiyo," Dragon said, with a nod. She seemed to be thinking. Mheth found himself studying the metal glinting in her scalp. With another nod—to the voices in her head, Mheth suspected—she swung around, saying, "Well, come on. There seems to be a lot to sort out.

"We were already en route this way, as it happens," she said as they joined her, "when Mheth's message reached us."

"You were already—?" Jhinsei said. "Why?"

Dragon Hidalgo slid Mheth a glance. "We're here to arrest Grath Tiyo, under authority of Aggregate Control."

Mheth chewed on that a moment and said, "Good."

Bird calls and the rustle of wind in branches filled silence that followed as they walked. Mheth let the tossing light under the trees and the scent of the needles and humusy earth distract him.

They came out of the woods, the full light of the day nearly overwhelming. A spinship, the Oni's Wake, sat on the green verge by the lake, and though it was huge, it looked small beneath the crags.

Grath and the two agents sat on the ground under the weapon and guard of a tall, broad man with an antique affectation of facial hair. Grath looked...Mheth couldn't decipher it. One of the Tiyo agents wore a darkening bruise on his face. They were somewhat rumpled. A dark-haired woman paced by the water. She stopped abruptly as they approached, waited.

She was the captain, Mheth saw as they reached her, her ship patch and the ruby visible at one earlobe marking her. Mheth thought she looked a lot like Jhinsei, even with his hair now white. When she looked at Jhinsei, her brows rose high, but she said nothing. Then she turned to Mheth.

"You're Tiyo."

Mheth sighed. "Yes."

"He's not with them," Jhinsei said. "He's with me. He sent you the message." To the coded contact—by which he meant, I trust him.

The captain—Sobriance Kohl, Mheth remembered—pursed her lips.

"Actually," Mheth said, "I want to give evidence to the appropriate authorities—information on Tiyo's illegal doings." He looked at his brother, then away.

The captain's gaze sharpened. "We can connect you to the appropriate authorities. When we got your message we'd already collected enough on Tiyo Grath to warrant his arrest, but there's still a lot to unravel."

A clatter on the shuttle's entry stair was accompanied by clunky black ship sandals and a silver jump appeared, then a head ducked out under hands hooked on the entry overhang. Kiyr Cydonie Mehet, of all people.

"Captain, message from your Oversight contact in the Choudow; she says..." Cydonie fell silent, taking in the tableau. Then she grinned. "Hey Jhinsei—nice hair. Hey Mheth."

"Cydonie?" Jhinsei said, sounding more gobsmacked by her appearance than everything else. Last straw, Mheth thought, as Jhinsei said, "Cydonie . . . what . . ."

Mheth found himself thinking of the quote he and the Kiyr had once shared, *it can be a deeply weird universe . . .* "'. . . and for that we cherish it most of all,'" he said softly.

Sobriance Kohl blew out a breath. "Look, we have a report to make, people to deal with." She didn't look at Grath or his agents. "All of you, I suppose, had better come aboard."

Washed, full of spicy fritters and beer—*what would you like,* Antoine la Savre had inquired, throwing an arm wide in extravagant gesture, *anything, anything in the wide universe, from the starry swaths to the darkest wastes—spicy fritters,* Jhinsei had interrupted, *and beer*—Jhinsei now sat on a low couch in the *Oni's Wake* galley and lounge, a space off the spin drive deck.

They'd eaten alone, Jhinsei, Mheth, and the rider. The rider had eaten, and eaten. And eaten.

Cydonie joined them for a while. She'd apparently hit it off with Sobriance and been hired to the *Oni*'s crew as their new spinner. She tried to talk to Jhinsei and Mheth, but the wordless exchanges between Mheth and the rider, and the way everything she said met with limp exhaustion from Jhinsei, eventually left her adrift in their collective silence. When the rider's skin luminesced from pale to dark, then to indigo, where it hovered before pulsing back to dark, Cydonie stared, emitted a small, squawkish sound, and left.

The *Oni*'s galley contained an era-spanning array of shipyard salvage. The ancient cook-stove and other equipment looked retro-fitted from an Okuta class hauler, not pretty, but the counters were light-shot ilginite, straight off a luxury cruiser. A jumble of couches, tables, grav chairs, and slings were lit by a set of biolumes clearly pirated from a dance club somewhere. Herb and food smells mixed with those of metal, recyced air, and grease.

The rider sat beside Jhinsei, had stayed close as a child to its mother, almost following him in to bathe. Se wore an oversized ship tee and shorts, sat with one knee crooked up, arm wrapped around it. Tomas had used to sit that way. Hir nails and hair gleamed under the biolumes.

Jhinsei and Mheth both wore old maroon crew jumps, complete with the holo patch of a ship through cosmic veils. Jhinsei's jump hung on him, rolled at sleeves and ankles, likely la Savre's.

The rider's eyes kept going to Mheth, with knowledge in them, some proprietary feeling that spooked both Jhinsei and, he could tell, Mheth. The rider's pleasure in the fritters and beer, though, had been familiar to Jhinsei, and he found that the rider's wonder and rapt engagement of the senses lingered within him.

Watching the rider, he kept seeing a plane of cheek, turn of hand, the set of hir shoulders, and fleeting expressions all echoing the remnants of Esker, Darshun, Sara, and Tomas that Jhinsei had carried. Taken with an overall physical aspect that recalled Tiyo Sarsone Tiyo to an uncomfortable degree, the glittering hair and nails, and the luminescing skin, Jhinsei could barely grasp *that* the rider was, let alone *what* the rider was.

Except that he felt—and it was clear the rider returned—a sense of kinship. As though the rider was, truly, Jhinsei's child or sibling. They were family. Given the presence in hir of Sarsone Tiyo, Jhinsei thought the rider probably saw Mheth that way, too.

"How are you feeling?" Jhinsei said, watching Mheth put aside his own plate of uneaten food. Clean, the Tiyo still looked haggard to Jhinsei. Haunted—a state with which Jhinsei felt quite familiar.

Mheth rolled his shoulders, drank from his bulb of beer, rubbed fingers over his forehead. "I told Captain Kohl to put Grath in the brig," he said, instead of answering. "But she doesn't have one and she said she couldn't do that anyway."

A shudder passed through Jhinsei, clammy and gut-hollowing. "So," he said, "where is he?"

"He and his lackeys are locked in Dragon's quarters."

Jhinsei considered that and then decided not to think about it.

After bathing, when he had confronted himself in the mirror, the sight of his white hair and brows startled him, his face strange and familiar, with no one looking back at him but himself. He hadn't looked for long.

"I'm going to file report with Aggregate Oversight of what I know about Tiyo's activities," Mheth said then, "on Ash, with the Sinaiety…the lumin testing. There's no proof anymore, but I'm going with Captain Kohl to Aggregate Prime. There I'll give Oversight testimony about my—about Grath, and my father." The Tiyo's gaze flicked to the rider and he fell silent.

The rider looked up from a fourth serving of fritters, gaze on Mheth. Mheth said, "Yes, well, some things about my father," he said. "Then . . . then, I don't know. I need to check on the well-being of my friend Kynan. Beyond that . . ."

"Beyond that?" Jhinsei prompted.

Mheth made a face at him, but persevered. "I, well . . . I mean I'll wait and go later if you don't want to go—if. Well." Mheth blew out an exasperated breath. "What I mean is, what is it you want to do now? Being as you're unexpectedly alive."

Jhinsei looked around the *Oni's Wake* galley. What did he want?

"How about this? I'll go with *you*, since this ride seems to be on offer to both of us . . . Also, I think," he looked at the rider with a slight lift of his brows, "we're both kind of responsible for—" He gestured.

The Tiyo paled, still staring at the rider, then dragged his attention back to Jhinsei and tried for his usual archness, "So you're saying I'm stuck with you?"

Jhinsei didn't rise to the tone, instead gave him a very serious, "Yes. Please?"

For the first time in their acquaintance, he saw Mheth blush. Then the Tiyo nodded.

In the following silence, their attention slid again to the rider.

Se was examining a kish-bei set, picking up each carved tile—fish, planets, stars, beasts and questor's sigils—turning it in hir fingers, clicking it back down. Sensing their attention, se looked up, skin flicking gold, then darkening again.

"What should we call you?" Mheth said.

The rider ran a finger over hir lips—Sara, the gesture echoed in Jhinsei's memory—eyes unblinking, considering.

"Any number of things might be appropriate," se said then, these first words a little husky, voice a deep, mellow timbre. Se examined hir hand, the glittering nails. "Lumin," se said, and Jhinsei couldn't tell if it was an answer to Mheth's question, or just a thought uttered aloud.

"Lumin?" Mheth's expression said that wasn't a good idea, but the rider nodded. Mheth continued to look as if he'd swallowed something sour; for some reason—it may have been the amount of beer he'd drunk—this struck Jhinsei funny.

Sobriance appeared then, saving Jhinsei from laughing out loud when it clearly wasn't appropriate. Drift, he was tired.

"All right," the captain said, rubbing a hand at the back of her neck. "The Thorough Order's taking custody of your brother and his men, Mheth. For now it remains an insystem concern with the Thorough Order mediating Ash complaints against Tiyo. Do you still want to accompany us to the Oversight office on Aggregate Prime?"

Mheth nodded. "Yes. I need to."

"Good then. Jhinsei," she turned to him. "Can we talk?"

The warm buzz of the beer evaporated as Jhinsei climbed to his feet and followed her to a room the size of a large closet off the spin deck. Though it was a closet with a view, currently of Ash's pale sky. By the clutter of kive cubes and the worn globe on the console, this was the captain's office.

She didn't sit, but leaned by the console, touched a small, abstract red sculpture by the globe, then folded her hands together.

"As I told you, we're working for a branch, a very obscure—" secret, she meant—"office, of Aggregate Control. Sinaiety activity was our mission of record, but it was largely because of the derelict and Termagenti's hauntings that we were sent originally. And when your name kept coming up, I . . ." She paused, oddly, then shook her head. "My superior wanted us to retrieve you." The captain, Jhinsei thought, watching her, was filled with some sorrow, haunted in her own way. He recognized it in her guarded eyes, her words and bearing.

"The possibility of a first contact so close to a strong talister presence with ties to a powerful trade axis—the Sinaiety here on Ash—is a possibility my superior finds alarming. Such a thing," she glanced briefly in the direction of the ship's galley, where the rider was, "could provide a dangerous flash point for the worst of talister factions. Then we got here and the investigations were complex, with Tiyo and Khat ready to arrest you as an alien contamination risk." She shook her head. "And now . . . well, it looks like . . . actually I don't know what it looks like. My superior will want me to bring you to her. But I want to know, what do you want?"

When he didn't answer, she said, "We're hopping to the Thorough Order center on-planet, then climbing out of the well. We'll stop at Termagenti if you want off there, or anything . . . it could get sticky, given the situation when you departed station, but . . . it's up to you. Otherwise, we're spinning directly for the deep." She shifted, dropped her gaze, and then brought it back to Jhinsei. "We could also drop you at any point here in the well." She shifted again, then stood and clasped her hands behind her, formal and stiff. "I'd like you to come. You're welcome aboard. If that's what you want." Her manner was diffident—which seemed to Jhinsei to be at odds with what he knew of her so far. It confused him.

His gaze went to the pale green of Ash sky visible out the view. He thought about station, about Essca; then these thoughts fell away.

He cleared his throat. "I don't want to go to station. Or stay on Ash. I'm going with Mheth. With you, for now."

Her face softened a moment. "Good, good." They regarded each other. She turned away first, clearing her throat and changing the subject. "One strange thing in all this is there's no sign of Tiyo Sarsone Tiyo anywhere. No one's able to contact him on-station or here in the well. He's disappeared."

Spin Deep

TUCKED IN A SLING, MHETH RODE OUT THE *ONI*'S CLIMB INTO THE Ash sky with Jhinsei and the rider swinging gently nearby.

He was seriously spooked by the rider. Hir resemblance to Sarsone was fluid, surfacing in the lift of a brow, the turn of hir gaze. Fluid but searingly clear and true when it came. Did se have Sarsone's memories, his madness? The glittering hair and nails, luminescing skin—these didn't faze Mheth; he'd seen things more bizarre in the wider Aggregate. Sexual characteristics beyond the common duality, also not particularly strange. But that the rider was, in some ways, his father... Would se try to stop Mheth from making report to Aggregate authorities of Tiyo mischiefs? Did se care? Hir eyes had flickered, expression canting to a familiar frown, when Captain Kohl told them Grath would be remanded to Thorough Order custody.

He thought then of his father's babblings of a new humanity, evolution. His father had, it seemed, achieved his vision. *Leviathan's bloody craw*, Mheth thought. He had.

Mheth considered his own plans: report to Aggregate Oversight and look up Kynan to make sure he was alive. Most likely Grath wouldn't go to prison, though he'd probably get Oversight on his back and deeply into Tiyo's affairs for a long time to come. Also some time in psych eval, no question. He'd hate Mheth; he might even be angry enough to hire some sort of revenge contract.

Mheth rolled his head in the sling, turning away from these thoughts. His gaze lit on Jhinsei, the Kiyr's newly white hair a gleam in the low lights, head nodding as he dozed, and there, at least, he found some comfort. Hope, even.

The Kiyr apparently thought they were responsible for the rider. They were, what, the rider's parents? That made Mheth parent to the child of his father's mad visions and death.

Other images, scrolling back like a flash kive in reverse—the sear of light as his father disappeared down to the tiniest particles of his being, Jhinsei lying in the needle humus, blood at his lips; and back, Grath's face and the arc of his pleasure over the pain he gave the Kiyr. From there a lifetime of memories roiled through Mheth, the most innocent ones, of childhood, rising to the fore to twist at his insides.

Grath deserved more retribution than he was probably going to get.

His skin prickled and he looked around into the rider's unsettling gaze. Se said, in that rough, musical voice, "If you don't like Lumin as a name, may I have the other half of yours, since you don't use it?"

Mheth blinked. "What—Ianne?"

Se nodded.

"Um. I'm sure there's a witty comment to be made here."

"It will come to you." Hir inflection was like Sarsone's.

Mheth opened and closed his mouth, then, "Apparently not," he said, "with quite the alacrity they used to."

The rider's strange lucent brows lowered, hir face serious. "He did, you know," se said. "Love you. Sarsone did. He fell into a kind of crack in himself, in pain," se drew a ragged line in the air, "and to escape it, he twisted himself so he could stop feeling the things that hurt. Love hurts."

Mheth stared at hir. He swallowed several times before he said, "Well, why not. As you say, I don't use it." And the people who did—who had called him Mhethianne—were no longer going to be part of his life. Mheth eyed the rider. Mostly.

He let his head fall back against the sling with a groan. "The universe is twisted."

Se nodded, eyes glinting. "Like a Jorian pretzel knot. A pepper-pear chocolate one."

Mheth studied the rider's expression. "You're hungry again, aren't you?"

Se nodded. "Starving."

Half-woken by their conversation, Jhinsei said, "Add an 's' and make it Iannes. That's a Megrantian name." Then the Kiyr rolled over in the sling and went back to sleep.

❋

A spike of sunlight falling down from a high dome intersected the public hall of the Thorough Order Arts Center, pending slowly across the green stone floor in a way that reminded Jhinsei of Revelation deck. He shivered slightly. The light measured a hand's length while he and the rider, with Dragon as chaperone, waited.

Captain Kohl had gone off with an elderly Thorough Order official, following the first party off the *Oni's Wake*, which consisted of Mheth, his brother and his brother's men, plus la Savre. Three obviaries whose arts had been taken in the martial categories had met them.

Jhinsei lagged behind on leaving the ship, unwilling to spend any time in Tiyo Grath's company.

As Sobriance left them, it was with an uneasy glance at the rider and a request to Jhinsei to keep hir close. She hadn't said anything more to him about the rider, other than to insist that both he and se come to the Thorough Order center, as their presence had been requested by Ramev.

He trailed the rider now, as se examined the art and Thorough Order ephemera displayed in column-and-arch coves ringing the hall. Se stopped by some holo-boxes in an underlit display case. A little curator plaque spoke, its voice pitched on an oscillation reaching only those standing in its sound cone.

Tincheian holo-boxes are an art dating from the first pre-Diaspora era; here we have reinterpretations of the medium created as renderings of patient dreams by mid-level obviaries in training during the early years of the Tincheian rapprochement . . .

The rider's skin luminesced briefly. Jhinsei glanced around, saw only Dragon watching them. Her expression was frank and curious, brows raised. She stood casually, slouching against a pillar in her maroon jump, but Jhinsei knew her cybered brain was feeding her information—though she stayed out of infofugue. The rider . . . *Iannes*, se had decided on as a name . . . leaned sideways against Jhinsei a moment. Se felt right there, comforting and necessary, very much like a child or a sibling—at least that was what Jhinsei thought, never before having had either.

He'd never been more intimate with another being, not even his team. Though that was part of the intimacy, se having shared the inside of his mind and body and having absorbed those remnants of Sara, Esker, Tomas, and Darshun. Along with the biomatter of one Tiyo Sarsone Tiyo and the material of hir own past self, Sarsone's suit made from the derelict ship. Plus all of the pigment in Jhinsei's hair.

These, apparently, were the bare minimum ingredients necessary to rebirth the remnant of a whole alien race in a new form.

Catching an impression of his self in one of the display cases, still unfamiliar, the white hair making his skin darker, it occurred to Jhinsei that after everything, the rider's newborn self—even ambiguously sexed and color-changeable—was a rather prosaic outcome.

Then Iannes grinned at him, a Sara grin, through and through, and that thought slid away.

None of them were all that prosaic.

No one, not one living thing in the universe. That knowledge the rider had left Jhinsei, a knowing down into the smallest matter of his bones.

Iannes turned then, and Dragon stood from her slouch; Jhinsei looked and saw someone crossing the expanse of green stone floor toward them: Ramev Evans, his red hair vivid in the light. His expression, when he reached them, had very little of the obviary in it. He clapped Jhinsei in a brief hard hug, and then set him back to survey him. His gaze went to the rider. A question, and then an answer he supplied himself, flickered in the obviary's gaze. He held out a hand; Iannes stared at it, eyes wide, then took it and gave it a shake.

"Hello Ramev," se said. "My name is Iannes."

The obviary's brows rose.

"You're going to have to go for a refresher course on obviary expression, or lack thereof," Jhinsei said.

They followed Ramev to a clinic room, airy and cozy at once, with a high ceiling and sesame-scented air through the semiperm from a small garden outside. More art, figures sculpted of fused glass in shades of gold, an arm's length tall and gnomic in attitude, gazed through the semiperm into the play of Palogenia's light. Iannes went immediately to the figures and ran curious fingers over them, then leaned toward the semiperm, breathing deeply. Hir skin luminesced just faintly.

"Amazing," Ramev said. He watched hir and then turned to Jhinsei, taking in the obvious and, Jhinsei was sure, not so obvious details. "Just." He shook his head. "Amazing."

Jhinsei began to feel uneasy. It should, perhaps, have dawned on him earlier: Iannes was an unprecedented scientific curiosity. An alien, a new breed of human, an anomaly of reproduction…a miracle…there was no end to the narratives and causes se could come to represent for various sects of humanity, not to mention the security threat some branches of Aggregate Oversight and Control were bound to find hir.

"What do you want, Ramev?" His voice betrayed his thoughts, for both Ramev and Iannes turned to him.

The obviary's brow knit, then he shook his head. "It's okay, Jhinsei. We—your captain, myself, others in the Order—thought it would be prudent to check you over and update your Aggregate profiles with warrant of well-being. Since you'll be traveling outsystem into the wider world."

Jhinsei took a moment, processing it. "That means…"

"Yes. Well. Having a Thorough Order warranted profile will help a little, in getting—Iannes—through custom checks, system gateways, well access points—but you'll still have to be careful. Stay out of the way of authorities and talister sects. And some factions of the Thorough Order, as well."

Jhinsei nodded, a little overwhelmed. Ramev's words posited a future, and future scenarios, to which he'd not given thought. Possibilities, desirable and otherwise, opened in his mind.

"Thank you," Iannes said in hir intimate, resonant voice, then jumped up on the exam table and stuck out hir tongue for examination.

When they were finished, Iannes issued a shiny new—but back-authenticated to appear old as se appeared to be—Aggregate profile kived and linked to hir chemical imprint, and Jhinsei's profile cleared of the Bromah Dictate, they found Mheth, Dragon, Sobriance, and la Savre waiting for them in an alcove of the green-floored hall.

Dragon, having finally succumbed to infofugue, had fingers to her temples. Antoine la Savre leaned against a column, arms folded. Captain Kohl scanned the hall continuously, then rolled her head from side to side, stretching neck muscles. She gave a brief, relieved nod as Jhinsei and the rider joined them.

Mheth, however, subdued and tense, barely raised his gaze. He ran one palm over an amazingly ugly, grey-hued biomech sculpture, the nubby material pushing and burbling back at his hand.

Jhinsei, the rider following, went to stand beside Mheth, offering what comfort there might be in that. The tight cant of the Tiyo's shoulders relaxed somewhat and when Iannes took his hand and held it something eased into Mheth's face, an expression that left him looking younger, lighter.

"Right then," Sobriance said, after a surveying glance over them all. "Let's ditch this dust sink."

Soon they were on the *Oni's Wake*, pressed into slings for the gees of well-climb. Ship chatter murmured around them, the back and forth of a crew at work.

Cydonie sounded well-integrated to Jhinsei, as if she'd already been part of the crew for many spins into the deep. He rolled his head against the pressure to watch Mheth, brooding in his sling.

"Mheth."

Slow shift, then the Tiyo gave a "hmmm?"

"Dragon has a huge collection of Djaina Xel adventure flash kives."

"Oh?" Something of the Mheth Jhinsei had first met surfaced in his expression, lazy and irredeemable. "How splendidly gauche of her."

"Yes. See if we can watch one later, yeah?"

Jhinsei found that he was gratified by the pleasure on the Tiyo's face as he said, "We'll watch them all."

Once they were well enroute out of Palogenia System, Cydonie came to find Jhinsei, where he sat at an unused post with a relay screen, viewing the cosmic deep as they spun through it.

Iannes had settled beside Mheth to talk, giving Jhinsei a Darshun-look that told him to scram. So Jhinsei had scrammed.

Now Cydonie joined him, perching on the console. She chewed her lip and Jhinsei made a guess as to what she wanted to say.

"Did Essca give you a message, or something?"

She shook her head. "Not really. Just. She regrets, that's all. My observation. What I mean is…she did care, that's all. Whatever… that was real, you should know that."

"I'm not sure that makes it better."

"No. But still." She reached over and took a piece of his hair between her fingers, tugged lightly. "Old man." Then she frowned, shifting, wondering, Jhinsei guessed, about the rider.

"You want to hear a story, Cyd?"

"A good one?"

"It's a little improbable. But, yeah, it's good." He watched the scatter and veils of light in the view screen. He could feel it, still, the touch of all that had passed through him, cosmic and intimate. An endless now of sweet, thundering continuum. The rider had whispered the most amazing joke in the universe through him, and though it nearly killed him, it left behind a silk of laughter, pure joy, lining his bones. It would probably fade, with time. Probably.

Maybe not.

Acknowledgments

This book had a long road. Big thank yous are due to early readers, Alyx Dellamonica, Ellen Van Hensbergen, and Jenn Volant. For helping to structure it into its final form, much gratitude to my late agent Linn Prentis and to my current agent Trodayne Northern for all his help under various hats. Thank you also to Darin Bradley for making the engine run more powerfully, and huge thanks to Mark Teppo at Resurrection House. The belief and support of all these people, and others, means more than I can say.

About the Author

Jessica Reisman's stories have appeared in numerous magazines and anthologies. Her story "Threads" won the South East Science Fiction Achievement award. A three-time Michener Fellow, she has been writing her own brand of literary science fiction and fantasy for many years.

Jessica has lived in Philadelphia, parts of Florida, California, and Maine, and been employed as a house painter, blueberry raker, art house film projectionist, glass artist's assistant, English tutor, teaching assistant, and editor, among other things. She dropped out of high school and now has a master's degree.

She makes her home in Austin, Texas, where well-groomed cats, family, and good friends grace her life with their company.

Find out more at storyrain.com.

CPSIA information can be obtained
at www.ICGtesting.com
Printed in the USA
LVOW03s0752230417
531849LV00002B/2/P

9 781630 230333